No Exit

More shouts and thumps sounded from outside. Someone was running toward the greenhouse.

Jace stood and looked around.

"We need to think of an excuse, a cover story. What are we supposed to tell them?" Melissa asked.

"A convincing reason for being here." He snapped a large pink bloom off a nearby plant.

"No kidding. Like what? I can't think of anything." She put her hands on her hips, exasperated that she was finally on board about how much danger they were in and now he was . . . *gardening*? "Jace, what are we going to do?"

He shoved the flower into her hair over her right ear. "This. We're going to do this." He yanked her to him and covered her mouth with his.

And just like that, the world around them faded away, leaving only the two of them. This kiss seared her from the inside out, breaking her down, molding her, changing her and reforging her into someone new, someone different, someone who would never, ever be the same again.

By Lena Diaz

EXIT Inc. series
NO EXIT
EXIT STRATEGY

Coming Soon
FINAL EXIT

Deadly Games series
TAKE THE KEY AND LOCK HER UP
ASHES, ASHES, THEY ALL FALL DEAD
SIMON SAYS DIE
HE KILLS ME, HE KILLS ME NOT

LENA DIAZ

NO EXIT

AN EXIT INC. THRILLER

AVONBOOKS

An Imprint of HarperCollinsPublishers

This is a work of fiction. Names, characters, places, and incidents are products of the author's imagination or are used fictitiously and are not to be construed as real. Any resemblance to actual events, locales, organizations, or persons, living or dead, is entirely coincidental.

AVON BOOKS
An Imprint of HarperCollins*Publishers*
195 Broadway
New York, New York 10007

First Avon Books mass market printing: February 2016

Avon Trademark Reg. U.S. Pat. Off. and in Other Countries, Marca Registrada, Hecho en U.S.A.
Avon, Avon Books, and the Avon logo are trademarks of HarperCollins Publishers.
HarperCollins® is a registered trademark of HarperCollins Publishers.

Printed in the U.S.A.

10 9 8 7 6 5 4 3 2 1

This one is for George, Sean, and Jennifer.
I love you.

NO
EXIT

Chapter One

Jace Atwell's Navy SEAL training hadn't included a course on how to be a successful stalker, but he was learning fast.

He tapped his brakes, allowing another car length to open up between him and the sleek silver Jaguar he was tailing. Following a woman on a nearly deserted two-lane road through the Colorado Rockies, without making her think he was purposely following her, was proving to be uniquely challenging.

Soon he would run out of road and out of daylight. They'd leave this snowy mountain and be back in civilization. Which meant other cars. And witnesses. He checked his watch. If Ramsey didn't show up soon, Jace would have to call it a night and figure out another approach tomorrow.

As if on cue, the roar of an engine announced the arrival of a white panel van, coming up fast behind him. *Finally.* It whipped around, but instead of weaving like a drunken driver per the plan and intimidating Melissa Cardenas into pulling over, it cut in front of the Jag, then braked, hard.

Damn it, Ramsey!

The Jaguar skidded sideways as its driver fought to avoid a collision. Jace wrestled his car to the shoulder on his right. But unlike his road-hugging classic Grand National, the sporty little Jaguar didn't stop. It must have hit a patch of black ice because it kept sliding toward the steep drop-off just past him.

Jace's stomach sank. *Let up on the gas. Steer into the skid!*

The car's two right wheels slipped over the edge of the road. Jace winced as the Jag slammed sideways into the ditch. Dirty snow and pine needles sprayed up in the air, and the windshield exploded in hundreds of tiny pieces.

Melissa punched at the air bag that had deployed, trying to move it out of her way, and Jace let out a relieved breath. He couldn't tell for sure that she was unhurt from his vantage point above her, twenty feet back. But at least she was conscious and moving around. He looked toward the van, expecting it to take off. But instead, it had stopped in the middle of the road, parallel to the wrecked car.

What are you doing, Ramsey? Get out of here.

If the goal had been to run the Jag off the road, Jace could have done that without Ramsey's help. But that wasn't the goal. The plan had been for Ramsey to force Melissa to stop on the shoulder. Then he'd take off, leaving Jace to play rescuer.

It seemed a rather ridiculous way to meet someone, but Melissa was rarely ever alone. A workaholic, she was usually with her father at his company. So, after months of surveillance and trying to figure out a way to get into EXIT Inc.'s inner circle, Jace's team had settled on this idea. If the mission was successful, he would use the "chance" meeting to garner Melissa's trust. Then he could build on the fledgling relationship over the course of a few days or weeks until he finagled a way to gain entrée into the company's top levels, preferably in a role that would give him access to the executive floor, where Cyprian's offices were located. But if Ramsey didn't back off, he'd ruin everything.

On days like today, Jace missed being a Navy SEAL, where he could count on his team to back each other up and stick to mission plans.

He popped open his driver's door. But he hesitated when the van's side door slammed back on its rails. Ramsey appeared in the opening, dressed in the disguise they'd agreed upon—all black, including his bulky coat, and a ski mask to conceal his features just in case Melissa glimpsed him through the van's windows. She'd met Ramsey before, when he'd worked for her father's company as a tour guide—or at least that's what *she'd* thought he was doing there. But Ramsey's hopping out of the van was definitely *not* part of the plan. And neither was his pointing a pistol down toward Melissa Cardenas.

WTF? Had Ramsey lost it? Had he decided that kidnapping Melissa would be the better way to get to their true target—her father? After weeks of arguing with his teammates, Jace had grudgingly agreed to use Melissa to get into the company she ran with her father. But kidnapping her and aiming a gun at her when she wasn't the one responsible for the deaths her father's clandestine activities had caused wasn't what he'd signed up for.

She frantically tugged at her seat belt, her wide eyes watching the gunman—which only ratcheted up Jace's guilt. A far-too-recent memory flashed through his mind.

A different place.

A different time.

A different woman.

Patricia Stanton's broken, battered body lying at the bottom of a crystal-clear pool, her sightless eyes staring up at him accusingly. Twenty feet away, the man who'd vowed to love her and cherish her until death did they part had also stared at Jace. But his eyes were gloating, the look on his face triumphant as the police handcuffed him and led him away. He'd won. Jace had lost. And his client had paid the ultimate price for his failure to keep her safe.

That wasn't going to happen again. Not today. Not on his watch. And it sure as hell wasn't going to happen because one of his men was taking his role as a bad guy far too seriously.

He jerked his gaze back to Ramsey, who was still standing in the road with his pistol, as if debating his next step. They might have started this morning as allies, working together to bring down a dangerous, corrupt antiterrorist organization pretending to be nothing more than a tour company. But the moment Ramsey had aimed a gun at a woman who might very well be innocent, he'd become Jace's enemy.

He popped open the glove box and grabbed his SIG Sauer 9 millimeter, a gun he hadn't even considered that he'd need today. Instead of getting out the driver's side, where he had no cover, he maneuvered his long legs over the gearshift in the middle console and slid out the passenger side. Ducking to keep the engine block between him and Ramsey, he scrambled to the front bumper. He fired two quick warning shots up in the air. Ramsey's dark ski mask swiveled toward him.

"Drop your weapon." Jace straightened, keeping his gun trained slightly to the left of Ramsey's body, hoping the other man would come to his senses and stop this madness.

Without lowering his gun, Ramsey looked back toward Melissa.

"Drop your weapon." This time Jace aimed his SIG dead center at the other man's chest.

Ramsey suddenly swung his pistol lightning fast toward him. Jace swore and dove beside his car. A deep-throated boom echoed through the trees. Metal pinged against the hood scoop, and a small hole opened up in the right fender.

Son of a bitch!

Another round plowed into the asphalt inches from where Jace had been standing. He glanced at Melissa in the ditch about twenty feet away. Her face was ghost white, and even from this distance, he could tell she was shaking. He crept toward the front bumper, staying low as he peered around his car back toward the center of the road.

Ramsey was gone. The van's side door slammed closed. Jace ran out onto the road just as the engine cranked to life. Seconds later, the tires squealed, and the van took off.

Jace debated shooting out the tires to give his associate a taste of what he'd just dished out to Melissa Cardenas. But no matter how pissed off Jace was, he didn't want to risk killing the man just because he'd made a stupid decision. He'd save his anger for later, when he confronted Ramsey over what had just happened. Instead, he fired several rounds harmlessly over the top of the vehicle into the pine trees in case Melissa was watching. The van raced around a curve and disappeared.

He uttered a few choice words about Ramsey's parentage and turned to check on Melissa. But the sound of another engine had him whirling around. A black limo was barreling down on him. He cursed and dove out of the way, the limo's wheels narrowly missing him as it screeched to a halt, rocking on its springs.

Jace groaned. He knew every line on that car, every shiny piece of chrome, even the small ding on the front passenger door. That limo was in EXIT's parking lot every day, the same parking lot where he'd spent countless hours watching Melissa coming and going. And he knew exactly why the driver had just tried to run him down—because the passenger in the back of that car wouldn't tolerate a man standing in the middle of the road with a gun when his daughter's car was in a ditch just a few feet away. That limo belonged to Melissa's father, the CEO of EXIT—Cyprian Cardenas.

Daddy dearest had just unwittingly come to his daughter's rescue—which meant Jace's plan to act as her white knight was nixed, pretty much guaranteeing this already-screwed-up mission would end in complete failure. Jace needed time with Melissa, alone, to gain her trust, to manipulate her into offering him the type of job that would give him the access he needed. Without that time, without that trust, he had no leverage.

And Cyprian's hypersuspicious nature, especially knowing that several of his enforcers had recently gone rogue, turning against their former employer, was already on high alert around strangers. Which doubly applied to someone like Jace—a former Navy SEAL who'd spent the past few years in the civilian sector as a bodyguard.

Yeah, he was pretty much screwed.

He did the only thing he could at this point: he stayed in character, determined to follow the fake scenario through and see if he could pull out a miracle. He jumped to his feet and positioned himself in front of the wrecked Jag as if to protect the driver from this newest threat—pretending that he didn't know that Cyprian and Melissa were related.

The rear doors on the limo flew open. Two ridiculously large, muscle-bound men in black suits got out, aiming equally large guns at him.

Ah, hell.

"Drop your weapon!" one of them yelled.

Jace weighed the odds. These guys were probably used to intimidating people with their size alone. They wouldn't expect him to put up any resistance. He could drop to the ground and probably shoot both of them before they fired a single round. No. Scratch that. He couldn't risk a firefight with a *maybe* innocent woman in the kill zone. He reluctantly pitched his SIG onto the road.

The men headed toward him while their boss stepped out of the car. And behind him, his two assistants got out, Sebastian and Tarek. Great. It was a highway reunion of everyone Jace had been investigating as part of figuring out how to manipulate his way into EXIT. This was bound to go well.

The assistants didn't bother to join the fray, choosing instead to remain by the car. Their boss pulled a black trench coat over his gray suit and surveyed the situation like a king overseeing his domain. His brow furrowed when he looked toward the Jaguar in the ditch.

"Wait, stop!" a feminine voice cried out.

Jace was stunned to see Melissa Cardenas standing on the edge of the highway. Her royal blue dress had a deliberate, sexy slit up one side. But the slit on her right shoulder wasn't a fashion statement. She'd torn it, probably while climbing out of her car and out of the ditch. Thankfully, there wasn't any blood or visible injuries. She seemed okay. Wavy, dark brown hair flowed out behind her as she hurried toward him, her heels clicking across the pavement.

Worried Cyprian's guards might hurt her in their zeal to defend their employer, who was now striding toward Melissa, Jace held out his hands to stop her. "Stay back."

One of the gunmen chose that moment to lunge at him, slamming a fist into the side of his jaw. The sucker punch whirled Jace around and knocked him to the ground.

Swearing like the sailor he used to be, Jace waggled his throbbing jaw. Luckily for the man who'd decked him, it wasn't broken.

"You get that one for free," he growled at his opponent. "The next one will cost you."

"Stop it." Melissa sounded furious. "Why did you hit him? He was protecting me."

The guard crouched over Jace and hauled back his fist to deliver another blow. Jace rocked back on his hips and delivered a brutal kick to the other man's knee. A crunching pop accompanied an agonized scream as the man dropped to the road, clutching his ruined leg.

Jace jumped to his feet and moved protectively in front of Melissa again to confront the second guard, who proceeded to shove a .357 Magnum in his face.

This was not going well.

"Enough." Unbelievably, the stubborn woman stepped around Jace again and stalked to her father, who'd stopped just short of the fray, watching the events with a dispassionate expression.

"Call off your thugs," she demanded. "That man was *protecting* me. A van ran me off the road, and the driver had a gun." She waved toward Jace. "He risked his life to scare the other guy away. He deserves our thanks, not a fist, or someone pointing a gun at him."

Cyprian's eyes widened as if only just then realizing how much danger his daughter had been in. He pulled her against him in a fierce hug.

The injured man groaned in agony, rolling around on the asphalt. Jace couldn't help being impressed with the clever epithets the man was hurling at him. He thought he knew every curse word imaginable. Now he had a few more to add to his arsenal.

"You heard Melissa." Cyprian set his daughter away from him, smiling at her reassuringly before letting her go. "Put your weapons away and wait at the limo with the others."

.357's mouth tightened with obvious disappointment. But he did as his boss ordered, aiming a warning glare at Jace before helping his partner hop-skip to the car.

The salt and pepper in Cyprian's hair marked him as past middle age. But his eyes were sharp and clear as they seemed to take in every detail around him— the Jag in the ditch, Jace's gun lying on the ground, the formerly pristine black coupe now sporting both an entrance and exit hole from the round that Ramsey had fired—although from this angle Cyprian probably couldn't see those bullet holes.

"You saved my daughter's life?"

Jace didn't respond to Cyprian's question. The man was used to people kowtowing to him and would expect it of someone trying to trick their way into EXIT. So, as if he didn't care what Cyprian thought—which, on many levels, he didn't—Jace took the opportunity to study Melissa up close for the first time in over two months of surveillance.

She was even more beautiful in person than through the lens of his long-range camera.

The Spanish influence from her father's side was evident in her dark brown eyes and nearly black hair. But her pale, silky-looking skin must have come from her mother. Her long legs were paired with curves that begged for a man's hand, his kiss. And Jace certainly wasn't immune to her appeal. But it was the deep intelligence staring back at him from her almond-shaped eyes that was sexy as hell and had him wishing, not for the first time, that she wasn't his enemy's daughter.

She shivered in the cold breeze that blew across the road, whipping her dress against her thighs.

By the time Cyprian thought to shrug out of his trench coat, Jace was already settling his own jacket around Melissa's shoulders.

"Thank you." She looked surprised but grateful as she snuggled into the jacket's warmth.

"Young man." Cyprian sounded annoyed. "I asked you a question."

He reluctantly dragged his gaze from the enchanting daughter to her far-from-enchanting father. "I don't know if I saved her or not. The van ran us *both* off the road. When he waved a pistol, I evened the odds. He decided not to stick around."

"Why did you have a weapon in the first place?"

Jace cocked a brow and motioned toward the limo. The injured man was inside, but his assistants were watching them, and .357 stood in the open doorway, looking like he couldn't wait for an excuse to charge at Jace. "I imagine I keep a gun in my car for the same reason that your men carry them. For protection. Not that it's any of your business."

The subtle tightening of the lines around Cyprian's mouth told Jace he didn't appreciate his lack of respect.

"You handled my men like a pro."

The accusation in the older man's voice was clear. He was just as wary as Jace's teammates had expected him to be, which was why they'd decided to approach him through his daughter—using Jace, who had no prior ties to EXIT. But Cyprian's suspicion-laced question was one that Jace was prepared for. And he didn't even have to lie.

"I spent most of my career as a Navy SEAL. But more recently, I was a bodyguard."

"Was?"

Patricia's lifeless, broken body wavered in his mind's eye, as it often did in his nightmares. He forced the image away. "My last mission didn't go as I'd hoped." He couldn't help wincing at that understatement. He'd quit his bodyguard job and had wallowed in his misery, and the bottle, for far too long. He might still be in that dark place if a mutual friend hadn't introduced him to Devlin Buchanan, who'd then introduced him to Mason Hunt. They'd recruited him into the Equalizers—a secret organization whose sole goal was to take down EXIT—and gave him hope again.

Joining them had been his salvation, another chance to prove he could be better than his one, horrible mistake and protect those who couldn't protect themselves. Or so he'd thought. Now, after Ramsey's foolishness, he wasn't as convinced that he'd made the right decision.

"Where did you say you're from?" Cyprian asked.

"I didn't. But I'm from Savannah, Georgia. Moved to Boulder a few months ago."

Something dark passed in the depths of Cyprian's eyes. Savannah didn't have pleasant memories for either of them, and Jace figured the older man was weighing the odds, making connections, perhaps wondering if Jace knew any former enforcers who'd been based out of Savannah—like Devlin. Cyprian hadn't survived this long in his line of work without being careful. But then again, neither had Jace.

"Who did you work for there?" Cyprian asked.

Melissa gave her father a reproachful look. "Stop badgering him. We haven't even introduced ourselves."

Taking her cue, Jace said, "I'm Jace Atwell. And in answer to your question, I was with Dawson's Personal Security Services. I was one of fifteen bodyguards working for the owner, Luke." He gestured toward Cyprian's car again. "Looks to me like you could use an upgrade in the bodyguard department. I could give you Luke's number."

Melissa put her hand on her father's shoulder as if to hold him back and frowned at Jace.

Cyprian surprised him with a rueful grin and

offered his hand. "You might have a point there. Cyprian Cardenas. Pleased to meet you."

Jace forced a polite smile and reluctantly shook Cyprian's hand. What he really wanted to do was retch as soon as he touched him—or put a bullet in Cyprian's brain to make the world a safer, better place. Men like Cardenas were the reason Jace had joined the Navy right out of college. They were why he'd later become a bodyguard, and why he'd recently joined the Equalizers.

Thanks to Devlin and Mason, the coleaders of the Equalizers, Jace knew all about EXIT and the infamous CEO before him. EXtreme International Tours described the Fortune 500 company's public mission. But it was far more appropriate to its true purpose, its clandestine side. EXIT Inc. was a front for a brutal organization of professional killers who were supposed to protect innocent people by taking out bad guys. But the abuses of power within the organization meant that all too often, EXIT's enforcers ended up killing the very people they were supposed to protect.

The Council that served as liaison between the company and the government had determined just last year that EXIT was manufacturing fake evidence to trick some of the enforcers into killing innocents while believing them to be criminals. And they'd put Cyprian on notice that the enforcement side of EXIT could easily be taken away from him if he didn't follow their rules. The Equalizers were therefore understandably sworn enemies of the man standing in front of Jace, the man who'd once been their boss. And they had no faith that Cyprian would abide by the Council's dictates.

"And this is my daughter, Melissa," Cyprian announced.

She smiled and held out her hand. This time, Jace didn't hesitate. Based on the reports that he'd read, and his own in-depth investigation, he was inclined to believe that she probably knew nothing about EXIT's secret charter and the double life her father led. He fervently hoped that was true. He couldn't imagine that the kind woman that he knew so well, on paper at least, would have anything to do with the evil that her father perpetuated.

His observations had also convinced him that she loved her father deeply. Which meant that when Jace and his teammates brought EXIT down and exposed Cyprian for what he was, she'd be hurt. And if Jace was able to manipulate her into offering him a job, thus getting him into EXIT's headquarters, Melissa would blame herself for what happened to her father.

For that reason, he'd argued against this mission. He'd spent hundreds of hours working up alternatives, trying to figure out a better way to infiltrate the top levels of the company that wouldn't take a ridiculous amount of time and had a chance of fooling Cyprian. But none of the other plans seemed viable. And the longer they waited, the more likely it was that innocent people were still being killed. So he'd finally caved.

The only stipulation he'd insisted on was that he would only "use" Melissa in her professional capacity as an officer of the company. He refused to try to develop a romantic relationship with her for the purpose of manipulating her. That was a personal line he would not cross, no matter how incredibly appealing she was.

He reluctantly let her hand go. "Miss Cardenas."

"You saved my life. You've earned the right to call me Melissa." She smiled again. "I'm the president of EXIT Incorporated. My father is the CEO. Dad, can you give him a business card? My purse is in my car."

Her father took a card from his suit jacket pocket and handed it to Jace. "We're both in your debt, Mr. Atwell. If there's ever anything that I can do for you, name it."

Jace studied the white card with elaborate gold letters and a green logo on top showing smiling tourists in a raft. "EXtreme International Tours, huh? I think I've heard of that. You take tourists white-water rafting up and down the Colorado River."

Cyprian's eyelids drooped as if he were insulted by Jace's simplistic description. "Quite a bit more than that actually. Although we're primarily headquartered here in Boulder, we have satellite locations all over the world, and a fairly new, secondary headquarters in Asheville, North Carolina. The trips we offer are unlike anything you'd ever experience from a traditional tour company. I'd be happy to give you a premium vacation package, on the house."

Jace shook his head. "Thanks, but I don't have much leisure time these days. Since leaving Savannah, I've been living off my savings, which is getting pretty slim. If I don't find a job soon, I'll be living on the street. Which is why I'm on my way to an interview right now. Or, I *was*." He checked his watch. "Not sure they'll still give me a chance since there's no way I can make it on time now. I assume you're going to call the police to file a report. But I'd rather not wait around. Can I give you my cell-phone number and have you explain to the cops why I had to leave? I'll head straight to the police station after my interview and answer any questions they have."

Cyprian's eyes narrowed. With suspicion? Or something else?

Melissa shot her father an odd look, then stepped forward, putting her soft, warm hand on Jace's forearm. "Mr. Atwell, you don't have to run off to an interview."

He frowned, not at all pleased at his body's overeager response to the simple act of her touching him through his shirtsleeve. Thankfully, she seemed oblivious to the way his pulse was crashing through his veins.

"I'm sure that in a corporation as large as ours, we have something that will fit your skills and experience," she continued. "Several of our guides are former military. And if you prefer an office job, we could arrange something along those lines as well."

Her offer genuinely surprised him. Somehow, in spite of the fiasco that Ramsey had made of this mission, Jace was still getting exactly what he'd set out to get—a way into EXIT Inc.

Operation Trojan Horse had begun.

AFTER PULLING THE white van to the shoulder and waiting several minutes to make sure Atwell didn't follow him, he'd shoved his ski mask in his pocket and continued down the mountain. A few miles later, he took the first exit ramp. A few hundred yards beyond that, he slowed and turned onto a gravel road.

The van bumped along until it reached the dead end beneath a bower of snow-covered pine trees.

He killed the engine, flipped the interior light on, then squeezed between the two captain's chairs and headed into the cargo area.

A low groan emanated from the man lying in a fetal position on the metal floor with his eyes closed. Surprise, surprise, Ramsey was still alive. The interrogation had been brutal, out of necessity. The former enforcer had held out far longer than *he* probably could have. Admirable, really. And as much blood as Ramsey had lost, he *should* have been dead. But since he wasn't, a decision had to be made. Let him live? Or finish it?

He inspected the zip ties around Ramsey's wrists and ankles to make sure they were still secure. Before trying to rouse his unconscious guest, he put the ski mask back on that he'd taken off before driving down the mountain. Might as well protect his identity until he made up his mind about Ramsey's fate. Before today, the two of them had never spoken to each other, so he wasn't worried about voice recognition. But if Ramsey had been watching EXIT for a while, there was definitely a chance of being recognized. It was better to be careful.

He poked him in the chest with the muzzle of his pistol. "Look at me."

Ramsey jerked, and his eyes fluttered open. He squinted as if to bring the world around him into focus. When he saw the gun, he sucked in a breath and arched back, trying to scoot away. But his movements were sluggish, and all he managed to do was plaster himself against the sliding side door.

"You did good, Ramsey. You didn't lie. It played out the way you said it would." He shrugged. "Except for the touches that I threw in."

Ramsey's mouth tightened. *"Whatdidyoudo?"* His words were slurred, running together.

Using the barrel of the gun, he shoved some of Ramsey's shoulder-length hair back to check the worst laceration on his scalp. Ramsey cursed and made a feeble attempt to move away.

"Easy. Just wanted to see how bad it is. Bad enough. Even if I don't finish you off, you probably won't make it. Especially not out in the cold. After losing so much blood."

The mumbled reply was too garbled to understand. But the anger in Ramsey's eyes wasn't.

He tapped the gun against his knee and considered his options. Killing for killing's sake had never been his thing. He did what needed to be done. But did this need to be done? If this rogue enforcer survived, would he, or his SEAL partner, interfere with *his* plan? Or would they help, simply by keeping Cyprian busy and off-balance? Ramsey's immediate fate hinged on the answer to those questions.

It had been a lucky break that he'd even noticed Ramsey earlier, performing surveillance from a car in EXIT's parking lot. He'd assumed, as the Council had, that the rogue enforcers from last year's debacle had backed off, gone underground to allow the Council to deal with Cyprian's mistakes. But that wasn't the case. At least, not with Ramsey.

Surprising Ramsey and forcing him to drive the van from EXIT to a secluded spot for the interrogation had worked out perfectly. A few hours later, Ramsey had revealed all the details about the planned fake assault on Melissa Cardenas, including the fact that it was a two-man operation involving a former Navy SEAL named Jace Atwell.

Taking Ramsey's place up on the mountain today had given him a chance to see Atwell up close, to put a face with the name. And since he knew what Ramsey and Atwell hadn't known—the exact time Cyprian had left EXIT—he was able to use that knowledge to his advantage. He'd known when Cyprian would come up that mountain. So he'd played up the assault ploy, taking it beyond what Ramsey and Atwell had planned.

Waving a gun at Melissa had been a brilliant move. Now Cyprian would be worried about whether this was random, or whether someone was trying to hurt his precious baby girl. That would make him vulnerable, distracted, and hopefully easier to manipulate than he'd been these past few weeks. He was so close to pushing Cyprian to the tipping point. Hopefully, this would send him right over the edge.

Of course, things could have gone better. He certainly hadn't expected Atwell to point a gun at him. But he didn't blame Ramsey for that even though Ramsey said no guns would be involved. Atwell struck him as an unpredictable sort of guy, a fast thinker on his feet. Kind of admirable, really.

Ramsey, the former enforcer, his comrade of sorts, had gone very still, a wary look on his face as he waited for his fate to be decided. Dead? Or Alive? Really, it could go either way.

He dug a hand into his pocket and pulled out a quarter. "Heads or tails. Live or die, Ramsey. Call it." He tossed the quarter into the air.

Chapter Two

In response to Cyprian's 911 call to report his daughter's encounter with a gunman, the Boulder Police Department had sent no less than four patrol cars and an ambulance. Jace couldn't believe the hoopla going on twenty feet away as BCP's men in blue fell all over themselves chatting it up with Cyprian and Melissa through the limo's open rear window. Either the Cardenases had a lot of friends in the department, or their wealth and social position were buying them special treatment. Jace was just jaded enough to assume the latter.

The whine of a winch had him looking at the flatbed tow truck pulling the wrecked Jag out of the ditch. At this rate, Melissa's car would get off the mountain before he did. He leaned back against his Buick, waiting for BCP's permission to leave.

The police had already interviewed him. They'd made sure every t was crossed and i was dotted in his concealed-handgun permit before allowing him to keep his SIG Sauer. And they weren't happy that he'd broken one of Cyprian's bodyguard's kneecaps, sending him to the emergency room. But with it being self-defense, and Melissa vouching for him, they couldn't do much about it. Standing here, waiting, was apparently Jace's punishment for causing them so much trouble. At least he had his jacket back, so he wasn't freezing. And the fact that it smelled faintly of Melissa's tantalizing perfume, reminding him of her curvy figure and smooth silky skin, was a bonus.

His attraction to her wasn't new. But it was certainly inconvenient, and an unwelcome by-product of the time he'd spent monitoring her. If what he felt for her was just desire, he could manage it, control it, tamp it down and . . . endure being around her for as long as it took to accomplish the mission. But it wasn't merely physical. He liked her for who she was even more than he desired her as a woman. And as hot as his blood ran whenever he saw her, that was saying something.

He admired her business acumen, her keen intelligence, how she treated her employees like equals, regardless of how far down they were on the corporate ladder. And he had an enormous amount of empathy for the tenuous position that she was in because of her father. Everything about her life was a lie.

And she didn't even know it.

Or at least, he didn't *think* she did. There was still that niggling doubt, that annoying voice in his head reminding him that, as smart as she was, if she wanted to hide her role in EXIT's clandestine side, she probably could.

Jace's current boss, of sorts—Mason Hunt—didn't trust Melissa at all, a fact that he'd grilled repeatedly into Jace, warning him to keep up his guard until they could be sure how much she knew. No matter how innocent she might seem, for now they had to assume she was dangerous and as much an enemy as her father.

One of the BCP officers straightened from his position by the limo's open window and motioned to Jace, then pointed down the road. Not wanting to give him a chance to change his mind, Jace slid behind the steering wheel and took off.

The sight of the bullet hole in the hood scoop sent a pang of loss jolting through him. This was his baby—his jet-black 1984 Buick Grand National—a car he'd painstakingly restored over the past six years with the help of his two older brothers and his now-deceased father. Working on the Buick had been his reward every time he'd survived another deployment. And it was the one thing that he could share with his family, with no need for any secrets between them.

They'd spent countless weekends toiling on this car, sharing beers, tall tales, and deep belly laughs. And when his father's lung cancer had him on an oxygen tank, struggling for every breath, Jace had settled him in a comfortable chair in the garage where he could order his sons around and still feel like he was contributing to their project. This was more than a car. It was a symbol, a reminder of the people he loved and why it was so important to make this world a better, safer place.

And now that cherished symbol had bullet holes in it.

Jace's hands tightened on the steering wheel. He fully intended to take the time and effort of fixing those holes out of Ramsey's hide. And while he was at it, he'd teach him about sticking to mission plans and *not* pointing guns at women.

But before dealing with his out-of-control partner, he had to give a long overdue situation report to the kid that Mason Hunt had left in charge of their headquarters while the rest of the Equalizers were out of town on other missions—the most recent addition to the team, Devlin Buchanan's baby brother, Austin.

Having never been to the Equalizer's headquarters, even though he knew where it was, Jace had yet to meet Austin in person. And he knew very little about him except that he'd recently gotten out of rehab. For what, Jace had no idea. What he did know was that every time he'd spoken to Austin on the phone, he came away with a sour taste in his mouth. The twentysomething-year-old kid had a prickly attitude that rubbed Jace every way but right.

He braced himself for another unpleasant conversation and set his phone in the console on speaker mode. "This is Jace, calling in the sitrep."

"It's about damn time," Austin's gravelly voice bit through the phone. "What'd you do, take a side trip down the Colorado River? You should have called an hour ago."

"Where's Ramsey?" Jace was determined not to rise to the bait.

"Wasting my time and making me wait, just like you. He hasn't bothered to report in."

Probably because he didn't like Austin any more than Jace did. Or maybe because he didn't want to admit he'd screwed up.

"I imagine Ramsey's reluctant to face us after his showboating. And he got way too serious with his role as bad guy, waving a gun around and shooting at me. He risked being recognized when he got out of the van, and now my classic muscle car looks like Swiss cheese."

"Hold it. What are you blathering about? Ramsey got out of the van? And shot at you?"

Blathering? Was this kid a jerk to everyone, or did he pull out the special treatment just for Jace? "That's what I said. It's only through luck and the grace of God that no one got hurt."

The sound of typing echoed through the phone. "Yadda, yadda. Whatever. Back it up. Tell me exactly what happened. And make it quick."

"Are you always a jackass, or is this a side effect of your stint in rehab?" So much for not letting the kid get to him.

"Bite me, Atwell. Tell me what I need to know."

Jace reined in his temper and answered Austin's questions. "In spite of Ramsey's escapades, everything worked out, even better than hoped. I'm supposed to report to EXIT Inc. tomorrow morning to see about a job. Looks like I'll be the inside mole for the next few days, or weeks, or however long it takes to bring EXIT down."

"Time-out, genius. Something isn't right. Ramsey's not the type to do what you said he did. He wouldn't go off half-cocked."

Jace sat up straighter, his irritation forgotten in lieu of the alarms that were starting to go off in his head. "I've only known him for a few months, so I can't predict his behavior. How long have *you* known him?"

"Long enough. Plus I've got detailed files on all of the Equalizers. And I'm telling you this doesn't fit his profile. Are you sure he's the guy you saw?"

A cold feeling of dread settled in the pit of Jace's stomach. He checked his mirrors and pulled to the shoulder of the road. Then he tried to picture Ramsey, superimposing him over the image of the gunman.

At first blush, they matched up: about six feet tall, muscular build, Caucasian—something he was certain of because the gunman hadn't worn gloves. And there was nothing remotely female about those hands or the person who owned them, so he discarded the possibility that the person underneath that ski mask could be a woman.

But had the gunman been standing up straight? Or had he hunched down against the cold? If so, he could be even taller than six feet, opening up more possibilities about his identity. But if the gunman wasn't Ramsey, who was he?

And where was Ramsey?

"You still there?" Concern leached into Austin's voice, lending it a sharper edge.

"The guy in the van wore a ski mask and a bulky black coat. I assumed he was Ramsey because I had no reason to suspect otherwise. But if you're right about the profile—"

"I am."

"If you're right," he repeated, "then let's assume the gunman was someone else and talk it through. There's no way another guy just happened to drive a white panel van up this mountain and decided to try to kill or kidnap Miss Cardenas at the same time that we were carrying out our mission. Whoever was in that van must have discovered what Ramsey was going to do and decided to take his place. Why, I have no idea. Have you tried calling him?"

"I waited to hear from one of you first, so I'd know the operation was complete. But as soon as you called, I sent him a text through my computer. He hasn't responded yet."

A tow truck chugged past Jace down the mountain road with Melissa's dented-up Jaguar sitting on its flatbed. Jace checked his side mirror. A caravan of police cars was coming down the mountain, with the Cardenas limo cocooned in the middle like a protected head of state.

He grabbed his phone from the console and held it to his left ear so anyone passing would realize he was on a call and wouldn't assume he had broken down on the side of the road. He didn't want the delay of any of them stopping to help.

"Have you tried tracking his phone through GPS?" Jace asked.

"Duh. That was the second thing I tried after pinging him. I got nothing."

The last of the cars headed down the road, its brake lights shining bright in the darkening gloom as a reminder that the sun would set soon. Every minute that passed without hearing from Ramsey made it that much more likely that something bad had happened to him.

"Okay. Keep trying his phone. Call Mason and let him know Ramsey's MIA. In the meantime, I'll check his house to make sure he's not there and retrace his steps."

Forty-five minutes later, Jace had checked everywhere he could think of and was back on the mountain, taking the same route that he believed Ramsey would have taken for their planned rendezvous. But he'd found nothing.

The sun had set. Temperatures were plummeting. If Ramsey was alive, and the gunman had left him outside in the elements, he wouldn't last long. They had to find him, fast. And there was only one other option he could think of that might give them the information they needed to locate him.

He called the Equalizer's home base again and headed down the mountain for the second time that day.

"You found him?" Austin's anxious voice carried through the phone.

"No. Do you have any contacts who can patch you into the city's traffic cameras? We might be able to track Ramsey's movements and see where he met up with ski-mask guy."

Austin snorted. "Oh sure. I'll ring up City Hall and ask them to search through hours of video to find the guy who was supposed to scare Miss Cardenas off the road instead of the guy who actually did. That'll go over well."

"What happened, Austin? Did you hear they were giving out asshole genes, and you jumped at the head of the line?"

"Actually, I was second in line. Right after you, *Ass*well."

Jace gritted his teeth and pulled around a slow-moving truck nursing its air brakes. "Maybe Mason or one of the others has a contact we can use. We'll brainstorm our options, figure something out. I'm coming in."

"What? No, no, no, *hell* no. Now that you've made contact with Cardenas, he'll want to keep an eye on you until he's convinced you're legit. He might already have someone tailing you to make sure you're not associated with any rogue enforcers. If you come to home base, you could compromise everything. You are *not* coming here."

"Austin," he bit out, "I was running special-ops missions while you were still figuring out how to get in some girl's panties at prom. I know what I'm doing. I know how to make sure no one is following me. And I sure as hell don't need your permission. I'll be there in twenty, and you'd damn well better let me in."

As HER FATHER's limousine turned out of her driveway and headed home, Melissa closed the double-glass front doors and slumped against the wall. She should have been worrying about the crazed gunman who'd forced her off the road tonight. Instead, she kept thinking about how hard it was pretending that everything between her and her father was okay. Because it wasn't, and it hadn't been for a very long time.

Wait. Shouldn't the alarm be beeping, warning her to punch in her code before it went off? She straightened and checked the panel. The status light was green. *Disarmed.*

"Miss Melissa?"

She whirled around, panic seizing her for the split second that it took to recognize the heavy Italian accent of her once-a-week housekeeper. She clutched her purse against her side and pressed a shaky hand to her throat.

The older woman and her adult son had just climbed the steps from the sunken living room into the open, two-story foyer.

"You startled me." Melissa gave a little laugh and

shoved her long hair out of her face. "Why are you here so late, Silvia? And Stefano, you don't see me enough at the office, so you decided to come visit me at home?"

She smiled to soften her words. Stefano's role as an EXIT tour guide meant he was usually gone for weeks or months at a time, trekking clients through the Rocky Mountains. But this was the off-season, so he was in the office a lot lately, planning for future trips.

"I never get tired of seeing you, Melissa." He winked, his spiky dyed-blond hair making her think of warm beaches and sand between her toes, something that would be highly welcome this time of year.

He leaned down and kissed her on both cheeks, a perfect gentleman. But he hadn't always been that way. Since his mother was her father's live-in maid, she and Stefano had grown up together. They'd shared everything from kindergarten to high school and had fought like true siblings. But even though she'd been guilty of just as many breaches of her father's strict code of behavior, Stefano usually bore the brunt of her father's wrath. That was why Stefano had moved out of the house the moment he'd turned eighteen. Thankfully, that was all behind them. He and her father got along much better as employer and employee than father figure and maid's son.

Silvia patted Melissa's shoulder. "I didn't mean to frighten you, *bebe*. I was worried when you didn't show up at your father's, so I called Stefano to wait here with me." Her forehead wrinkled as her dark eyes studied Melissa. "Is everything okay?"

She tucked her purse beneath her arm and took

the older lady's hands in hers. Just as Stefano had been like a brother, Silvia Conti had been like a substitute mother after Melissa's own mother and twin brothers had died when she was a little girl. But to this day, Silvia insisted on formalities, addressing her as *Miss* Melissa, or *bebe* only when she was worried or upset.

Melissa squeezed the other woman's hands. "There's nothing to fret over. I did have some, ah, car trouble, and Dad picked me up. By the time things were taken care of, it was already getting late, so we decided to skip our planned dinner. He drove me straight home."

Stefano put his arm around his mother's shoulders and pulled her against his side. "There. You see, *Madre*? I told you. Melissa's a big girl. Nothing to worry about." He tugged his reluctant mother toward the door and settled her coat around her shoulders before shrugging into his. "Come, Mama. Melissa doesn't seem like she's in the mood for company."

Melissa smiled gratefully but made no move to take off her own jacket that she'd retrieved from her Jag before it was towed. Silvia might see the rip in her dress, and she would worry.

Stefano urged his mother out the door. "Take care, Melissa."

She forced another smile and waited until they'd gone around the side of the house to the guest parking area before closing the door, shedding her jacket, and hanging it on the hall tree. Once Silvia's little Honda was on its way down the driveway, with Stefano's cherry-red BMW following close behind, Melissa flipped the dead bolt. She also settled the long iron bar in place over both doors, an extra lock her father had insisted upon when she'd bought the house but which she rarely used. Tonight, for once, she was grateful for her father's hypervigilance.

His smothering overprotectiveness was the main reason that she'd moved out of his estate after college and purchased this property in the White Hawk Ranch area thirty minutes away. One of their worst, ongoing arguments was over her refusal to hire a bodyguard. But she had some handguns hidden in her office and her bedroom on the unlikely chance that she'd ever need them. She also didn't want to feel like a prisoner, or pretentious because she had someone following her around all the time. And she'd never been paranoid enough to think someone was out to get her.

Until now.

After setting the alarm, she slipped out of her heels. She let them dangle from her fingertips and headed through the living room, then up the curving staircase to her bedroom at the end of the long, open-banister gallery.

Once she was ready for bed, she made a detour to the desk by the balcony doors and pulled open the top middle drawer. Two permanent markers lay inside: a black one and a red one. She took them both as well as the key that was hidden on the underside of the desk courtesy of a small magnet.

It wasn't that she didn't trust Silvia when she was here to clean. It's just that there were some things the sweet woman didn't need to know about, things Melissa wished *she* didn't know about.

The recessed TV cabinet on the wall at the foot of her bed beckoned her forward. She fit the key in the lock and pulled the doors open. In the middle was a large corkboard she'd had custom cut to fit the opening. It matched the corkboards she'd affixed to the back of each door.

There were dozens of photographs tacked to the boards. Colored lines connected them in a complex spiderweb reminiscent of police procedural shows. Except that the man whose picture was at the top middle, the man where all of the lines intersected, wasn't a stranger or an unknown subject.

He was her father.

She rolled the pens in her hands and studied the photographs and the words she'd written beneath them. Each piece of information was hard-won, from an overheard conversation, or a note her father didn't know she'd discovered, or a long, painful search on the Internet.

To the left and right of her father's portrait were photos of his previous assistants, along with security-badge pictures of his two current ones— Sebastian Smith and Tarek Vasile. She hadn't been able to find any better pictures of them since they didn't appear to have any social-networking accounts, at least not that she'd been able to find. That alone seemed odd. Everyone was on social media these days. But her wariness about them was heightened even more because of how secretive they acted and the way her skin crawled around them.

They'd been hired as a team, which was unusual. And when she'd asked her father why he'd hired two assistants, he'd claimed it was necessary because of the company's recent expansion into North Carolina. And they'd supposedly come highly recommended. But somehow he always managed to change the subject whenever she asked to see those recommendations. And there was nothing in their human resources files about previous jobs. She'd checked.

The assistant prior to "the twins," as she thought of them, had been killed in a home invasion. The one before that? Suicide. Either her father had remarkably bad luck in his choice of executive assistants, or something far more sinister was at work here.

Her stomach clenched as it often did when she looked at the names on these boards and considered the sheer number of people connected to her father who'd died young, violently, or suspiciously.

Including the man she'd been falling in love with. *Thomas Hightower.*

Bile rose in her throat, but she fought it down. It wasn't as if she believed her father had killed Thomas, or anyone else. The man who'd fought through his grief for the family he'd lost and forced himself to carry on for his one remaining child could never commit a sin as ugly and horrific as murder. She didn't believe that, *couldn't* believe that. But she couldn't ignore the evidence in front of her either. *Someone* was killing these people. And they were slowly and inexorably destroying everything and everyone that her father cared about.

She traced the lines between the names. Most of these people, thankfully, were still alive—at least as far as her research could confirm. Their names were written in black. Other names were written in red, either because they were dead or because she believed they were in danger. One specific subset of names she even put under the label "Enemies," because she'd heard enough to know that her father thought they were out to get him. Names like Devlin and Emily Buchanan, Ramsey Tate, Mason Hunt.

She knew Devlin and Ramsey and couldn't begin to understand why her father deemed them a threat. They'd both been excellent EXIT tour guides, extremely popular with clients for many years. And both had quit with no notice within a few months of each other. Shortly after that, she'd started hearing their names whispered in conversations between her father and his assistant at the time.

The other name listed with theirs, Mason, was a man she'd never met. It was only through overheard conversations a few months ago that she'd learned he even existed. Then, just as abruptly, he was never mentioned again. She could only pray that didn't mean he was dead.

When she'd asked her father if he knew why Ramsey and Devlin had quit, he'd claimed not to know. But that was a lie. She'd overheard Eddie, the head of EXIT's information-technology department, mention their names when speaking on the phone with her father last summer about an alleged outside hack into the computer system. But just as Melissa had been about to announce her presence and offer to help, she'd been frozen in the doorway by the rest of the conversation. It was bizarre and made no sense.

Eddie had talked about searching some "enforcers" database she'd never heard of to find out what real-estate holdings Mason had so they could find him. And although none of that made sense in terms of the company's day-to-day operations, what alarmed her the most was the menace and finality in Eddie's voice when he swore he'd get the information. The deadly promise in his tone had sent shivers of dread down her spine and had her quietly backing out of the room without revealing her presence. That very night she'd purchased the corkboards and had begun her quest for the truth.

When she'd seen her father next, she'd asked him whether he had any security concerns about their company or its data. She'd purposely been vague and tried to make it sound like she was just asking as part of her due diligence to keep the company operating smoothly. The fact that her father said nothing about his conversation with Eddie had spooked her almost as much as the earlier overheard conversation. Because, for the first time, she realized she couldn't trust him to tell her the truth.

She looked at the two pens in her hand: black for safe, red for danger. She pictured broad shoulders in a dark blue suit jacket over a fitted white shirt unbuttoned at the throat, minus a tie. Military-short dark hair framed a pair of smoky gray eyes that had looked at her with concern, protectiveness, and a hint of desire that had surprised her. But before she could dwell on the answering thrill that swept through her in reaction to that heated look, she'd seen her father's eyes narrow with suspicion. And something else . . . something dark and frightening. A look that had her thinking about these corkboards back home, with all the blood-red lines.

Did her father think the man had ulterior motives? That he was connected to the mysterious deaths? It certainly seemed far-fetched to Melissa that an extremely capable, former bodyguard and Navy SEAL just happened to be there in time to save her from a crazed gunman. Perhaps her father was right to wonder about him.

That was one of the reasons that she'd rushed to offer the stranger a job. She wanted time to figure out how he might fit into the pattern if he even did. But more importantly, she wanted to protect him. If he'd garnered her father's wary curiosity, if he fit into this web somehow, then he could be in danger from whoever was at the center of whatever was going on.

Which was why she was standing here now.

She tossed one of the pens onto a nearby decorative table, wondering why she'd even bothered to pick them *both* up when she'd known all along that she only needed the one. She stepped to the board and wrote a new name in the "Enemies" column: *Jace Atwell.*

She wrote it in red.

Chapter Three

Jace idled his car outside the wrought-iron fence in front of the rather unimpressive Equalizers' headquarters as the security gate rolled back. At least now he knew why everyone called it home base, emphasis on the "home" part. The men and women he now worked with had somehow managed to establish their base of operations in a mud-colored ranch house on the outskirts of a middle-class suburb in one of the few places in Boulder *without* a mountain view.

As soon as the gate was open wide enough for him to fit through, he hit the accelerator and zoomed up the driveway. He'd half expected Austin to make him wait, just to be obstinate. But as soon as he'd pulled up to the security camera, the gate had buzzed and began to move. Similarly, the garage door rose as he approached it. In spite of the kid's lousy attitude, at least he had the sense not to play games when every minute counted in their efforts to find Ramsey.

Once he pulled in beside a dark-colored van, the

garage door immediately reversed direction to close behind him.

Austin didn't greet him at the door that led into the house, but he'd left it unlocked. Jace hurried through an ordinary-looking laundry room, then stepped into an expansive family room that was anything *but* ordinary.

An *elevator* of all things, was to his immediate left, its thicker-than-normal steel doors standing open. A few feet from the couches and chairs were a dozen state-of-the-art computers and monitors covering a countertop that ran the length of the left wall. Rows of guns, magazines of ammunition, and Kevlar vests hung in glass-fronted cases above the computers.

But it was what sat in the middle of the room that made him pause: Austin Buchanan, in a wheelchair, his legs amputated below the knees, and raised burn scars peeking out from under the edge of the collar and cuffs of his long-sleeved shirt.

Ah hell. Every impatient word Jace had tossed at Austin had his face turning hot. He stepped forward, hand extended like a white flag of surrender. "Hey, man, I'm really sorry about how I spoke—"

Austin's lip curled in derision. "Don't bother. I hate it when people get a personality transplant the second they see this damn thing." He popped a wheelie and shot across the floor, stopping in front of one of the computers. "I've made zero progress in the traffic-cam department. You'd better have a backup plan."

Jace dropped his hand. He might as well get a picture of a donkey, paste it to his forehead, and start braying like the ass he'd become.

"Well?" Austin called out, the raspy quality of his

voice making sense now. His vocal cords had probably been damaged in the same fire that had given
him those burn scars and taken his legs. "You bul-
lied your way in here. You gonna gawk like a tourist
or help me find Ramsey?"

Jace hurried across the room, noting as he did so
that the floor and windows, even the walls, were
covered with bumpy sheets of gray metal. As he sat
beside Austin, he waved toward the wall in front
of them. "I imagine all this sheeting interferes with
cell-phone signals."

"That's kind of the point, genius. We use a landline in here, with encryption algorithms to scramble
the signal." He typed something into the screen in
front of him, then swiveled the monitor toward Jace,
revealing a map of Boulder with red lines and dots
marked on it.

"I noted the areas you already searched, and the
route Ramsey was supposed to have taken," Austin
said. "While I couldn't break into the traffic cams, I
did use a satellite street-view app to locate some key
cameras near Ram's house and the highway exits
the van might have passed when it went down the
mountain road." He tapped the screen. "If we can
get the video on these here, here, and here, we can
narrow our search grid."

Jace slid the keyboard in front of him. "Did you
reach Mason?"

"Left him a message. Everyone's pretty much in-
communicado right now, at least until they're out of
the danger zones on their current missions. I'm all
you've got. Deal with it."

"Then that'll have to be enough. Get me to the
main traffic screen, and I'll see what I can figure out."

Austin eyed him with open skepticism as he pressed a function key, bringing up the traffic monitoring system. "Somehow I don't see you as a computer hack."

"I'm something way better."

"What's that?"

"A Navy SEAL, with years of intelligence-gathering ops under my belt. Watch and learn." He punched up the log-in screen.

Austin rolled his eyes. "How sure are you that you can break in? Because if you can't, we need to brainstorm other ways to—"

"I'm in."

"What the . . ." He peered over Jace's shoulder and let out a low whistle. "How did you do that?"

Jace typed the necessary commands to locate the camera he wanted. Then he jumped the video to the time frame that he was most interested in—the window after the van left him and Melissa.

"Well," Austin prodded. "How did you hack in so fast?"

"Would you believe I used an algorithm I cooked up on the way over?"

He snorted. "Hell no."

Jace smiled and fast-forwarded to another section of the video. "As soon as I saw the main screen, I realized Boulder is using a modified version of an off-the-shelf package that I studied as part of my computer training. Since I already knew about a glitch that would let me in, I gave it a try, hoping the bug wasn't fixed in the latest release. It wasn't."

"In other words, you tried a log-on and password a programmer built into the system so he could backdoor in whenever he wanted."

"When you say it that way, it's not nearly as impressive."

"I wasn't impressed anyway."

"Yeah. You were."

He frowned but didn't argue the point. "Why aren't you looking at the cameras by Ramsey's house to figure out where he went this morning?"

Jace scanned another section of footage. "I'm making an educated guess."

"A *guess*?"

"I'm assuming ski-mask guy forced Ramsey to tell him about the rendezvous. And that he would have kept Ramsey with him in case the information didn't pan out, and he had to interrogate him again."

"What if you're wrong?"

"I very well could be. But I'm hoping that I'm right because it will save a lot of time."

And, possibly, Ramsey's life.

An image of the white van going down the mountain road popped onto the screen. Both of them leaned toward the monitor, trying to see inside the van.

"No one's in the passenger seat," Austin said. "And the driver's face is blocked by the sun visor."

Near the bottom of the mountain, the van slowed and turned onto a gravel road before disappearing from view.

"I know that road." Austin's jaw was tight with strain. "When we planned this mission, I used that same satellite app to scope out the surrounding area in case the mission went south, and one of you needed me to plot an escape route. That particular road is a dead end, isolated, no houses around it. And right behind it? The old city dump."

Jace shot him an alarmed glance, then noted the time on the video freeze-frame. When the vehicle came back into view, only six minutes had passed. There was only one reason he could think of for the driver to head down that road and return so quickly. He went there to dump Ramsey's body.

He shoved his seat back and stood. "Keep scanning through the videos. See if you can pick up Ramsey's movements earlier in the day in case I'm wrong about his being in that van."

JACE SHINED HIS powerful Maglite out the driver's window onto the tire tracks that he believed belonged to the van. Thankfully, it hadn't snowed again this evening, so the trail down the gravel road was fairly easy to follow. He kept well to the right side of the road so he wouldn't obliterate the tracks. Leaning halfway out the window, he watched for the telltale sign of a change in the tire impressions that would tell him when the van stopped, or if it pulled off into the woods at any point.

A snapping sound had him hitting the brakes and jerking the light toward the trees and winter-dead brush crowding in on either side of the car. He eased his right hand down to the pistol holstered on his belt and listened intently.

Snap. Crunch.

He grabbed his gun and aimed it out the window. A possum ambled out between two pine trees, its pinched white face and eyes reflecting like beacons in the flashlight beam. Jace let out a pent-up breath and shoved his gun back in the holster. He stomped the gas, sending the possum running back into the woods and the car moving forward.

Two minutes in, he reached the dead end Austin had told him about. But more importantly, he'd reached where the van had pulled to a stop. The gravel had shifted as the van braked, leaving a sliding impression that might as well have had a sign saying, "Bad guy stopped here."

"Austin," he said, knowing the phone in the console would pick up his voice, "looks like he stopped at the end of the road instead of just turning around. I'm getting out to see if I can find anything."

"I've got a bad feeling about this," Austin's voice rasped through the speaker.

"You and me both." This felt like a setup, an ambush waiting to happen. But it wasn't like he had anyone to call for backup. Keeping the line open, he shoved the phone into his jacket pocket so Austin would be able to hear him. Hopefully, Mason had gotten Austin's message by now and could get here in a hurry if the worst happened. Although, at this point, Jace wasn't sure what "the worst" would be. They already had a man down, or at least missing. And that was pretty much the worst-case scenario.

After pulling out his pistol and scanning the trees closest to the car, he made a run for the cover of the nearest pines, then aimed his flashlight back toward the road. No gunshots. No shadows moving toward his car. All clear. Or so he hoped.

He shined his flashlight toward the spot where the van had stopped. And then he saw it—a trail. Footprints, distorted from the gravel, making it impossible to gauge the shoe size. But definitely big, a heavy man—or a man carrying something heavy. Or some*one*. The prints led into the trees and disappeared where the snow thinned and gave way to rocky soil and pine needles sheltered by a thick bower of branches overhead.

He moved the light back and forth as he walked the grid, from rocky soil to light snow and back again.

"Jace?" Austin's voice crackled in his pocket. "What's going on?"

He bent his head so his mouth was closer to the phone. "I lost the trail. He definitely came this way, but . . ." He frowned and squinted in the dark, shining his light about three feet away. Something was there, an imprint. A shoeprint?

"Jace? Did something—"

"Hold on. Wait." He rushed forward and crouched down. Yes. That was definitely the impression of a heel, too crisp not to be recent. He frowned and pressed his fingers against a dark spot on a dried-up leaf then lifted his hand in the light. Blood, already turning tacky and brown.

Wind whistled through the trees, making an eerie, mournful sound. He aimed the light back at the road, then all around him, in a slow circle. But when he didn't see any movement, or hear anything more than the branches clacking together in the wind, he shined the light back on the blood drop. A foot in front of it was another, and another after that. He rushed forward, following the trail. Thirty feet in, the trail abruptly ended.

At Ramsey's body.

Jace cursed viciously and dropped to his knees to check for a pulse. But that was just a formality. Judging by the amount of blood on the side of Ramsey's head, he'd probably bled out long ago. And even if he hadn't, since he was only wearing jeans and one of his trademark NASCAR T-shirts, he'd probably succumbed to hypothermia within minutes of being dumped like garbage on the side of the road.

"What is it?" Austin demanded. "Damn it, Jace, what's going on?"

"I found him." He pressed two fingers against the side of Ramsey's neck.

Silence reigned on the other end, as if Austin was too afraid to ask the next obvious question.

"He's . . ." Jace frowned and pressed harder. Faint, but it was there. A pulse. He pressed his hands against Ramsey's chest. It barely moved, his breaths were shallow, but he was definitely breathing. "I'll be damned. He's still alive."

"Thank God," Austin whispered. He cleared his throat, as if embarrassed. "What happened to him?" he demanded, back in control. "Has he been shot? Is he—?"

"Give me a minute." He ran his hands down Ramsey's body, checking for injuries. "He has ligature marks on his wrists and ankles. Ski-mask guy must have cut off whatever he used to tie him up and took it with him so he didn't leave evidence. There's a deep laceration on his scalp, like maybe he was pistol-whipped. There are bruises down the side of his face and on his abdomen. But no gunshots. No knife wounds or obvious broken bones. He's unconscious. I'm guessing his head wound is our biggest worry. No telling how hard he was hit."

He took a quick look around, then put his gun and flashlight away to free his hands. He scooped Ramsey into his arms, grunting from the effort of lifting a man nearly as tall and brawny as he was. "I'm taking him to the hospital."

He draped him over his shoulder in a fireman's carry and shuffled back toward the road.

"I'm sending GPS coordinates to your phone," Austin said. "Devlin knows a lot of people around here, and several of them are doctors. I'll get one of them to meet you at his private office."

"Remember the part where I said Ramsey has a head wound? Unless your doctor has an MRI and a neurosurgeon in his pocket, I'm taking him to the trauma center at Boulder Community Hospital."

"No way. You can't go to BCH. Cardenas has feelers out all over the city for any former enforcers that pop up on the radar. Ramsey will be fish food there."

"Then you'd better figure out an alternative, fast." He reached the car and settled Ramsey into the front passenger seat.

From the swearing and loud computer keyboard clicking coming through the phone, Austin was obviously pissed. But at least he was trying to figure out another plan.

Jace wasn't waiting, though. He knew from experience how dangerous and unpredictable head wounds could be. He'd lost several good men in overseas ops because there wasn't sufficient expertise to handle those kinds of injuries. Nothing was going to keep him from making sure that Ramsey got the medical attention he needed, not when there was a perfectly good trauma center nearby.

He hopped into the driver's seat and peeled out, spitting gravel from underneath his tires as he raced toward the highway.

Chapter Four

Melissa clip-clopped down the long hallway toward her office, courtesy of a broken heel, as she tried to see around the book bag in her arms—thanks to an equally broken shoulder strap. She was also balancing a full and very hot cup of coffee that she desperately wanted to *drink* but was very much afraid she was about to *wear*.

This was karma for lying to her father earlier this morning when she'd turned down his offer of a ride to work. After giving him the lame excuse of needing to get there before him for a conference call in another time zone, she'd called a cab.

Big mistake.

The taxi had smelled like the drunk it had probably taken home a few hours earlier.

Her nerves were already frayed from last night's encounter with the gunman. Especially since her call to the police station when she woke up revealed that the detectives had no leads. Now, thinking about the true reason she'd needed to get here early, her temper was reaching a boiling point.

This is what you've forced me into, Father. Spying and

sneaking around to figure out what's going on. Why can't you just tell me the truth and stop the lies?

She caught a quick glimpse of Stefano as he zipped down an adjoining hallway about twenty feet ahead. She was about to call out to him for help when her always maddeningly chipper administrative assistant flitted past the same intersection just as quickly as Stefano, in spite of her advanced years.

Melissa changed her mind about calling for Stefano, knowing that Jolene would turn around to help, too. Dealing with the happy Pollyanna before getting a few dozen gulps of caffeine into her system might be dangerous for one or both of them.

Somehow, she managed to navigate the last leg of her journey into the reception area, then her office, without a disaster, and kicked the door closed behind her with a satisfying thud.

With her broken shoe clinging to life by the strap around her pinkie finger, she continued her desperate balancing act in the general direction of the massive cherrywood monster her father had gifted her with last Christmas. As with so many of his presents, she'd had to weigh her hatred of it against her love for her father. Unfortunately, love won, and she was stuck with the beast: the desk, not her father.

When she reached the behemoth, she ever so carefully set the coffee down, without spilling it. *Score!* She let out a huge sigh and relaxed her shoulders, surrendering her purse, her book bag, and her broken shoe to the plush carpet below.

Stretching her arms and flexing her hands and feet, she tried to straighten out everything she'd contorted earlier. Then she yanked off her stubbornly remaining shoe, let it drop to the floor beside its twin, and reached for the heavy book bag.

A tanned, masculine hand shot in front of her and plucked the bag off the floor as if it were weightless.

She whirled around, bringing up her fists in a boxing stance.

The man who'd saved her yesterday stood a few feet away, his eyes widening and his mouth crooking up in a ridiculously charming grin as he set the bag on top of her desk before holding his hands up in mock surrender.

"Morning." His sexy, deep baritone had her pulse racing much faster than she could blame on the fright that he'd just given her.

"Didn't mean to startle you," he said. "I was admiring the paintings on the back wall. The name's Jace Atwell, in case you forgot. I'm here like you asked, to discuss a possible job."

"I remember your name." She relaxed her fists, feeling foolish for overreacting. But, really, what was it with people sneaking up on her lately? "Give me a minute."

She grabbed her ruined shoes and padded across the carpet to the closet door beside the private bathroom to exchange them for another pair. Others might consider such luxuries an unnecessary extravagance. But at least she had clean clothes on hand for when her workload required all-nighters at the office. Or like this morning, when she broke a heel.

She joined him in front of the desk, standing back so she could meet his eyes without craning her neck at an uncomfortable angle. Yesterday, she'd noticed he was handsome. But she'd been so focused on the wreck, and the gunman, and trying to figure out why her father seemed suspicious of him that she hadn't allowed herself to take in all the details. Like the oh-so-masculine dark shadow on his jaw that even his fresh shave couldn't hide. And the way his tailored charcoal-gray suit, with a tie this time, hugged his broad shoulders.

He was certainly appealing. And his muscular build gave credence to his claim to be a bodyguard, and before that, a Navy SEAL. But she wasn't taking anything at face value. Not until she got some answers. Like why he'd been in her office when she wasn't.

In spite of his smile, there was obvious tension in the tiny lines crinkling at the corners of his eyes. He looked tired, drawn, as if he'd gotten very little sleep or was worried about something.

Like being caught snooping?

A quick look around confirmed that nothing seemed out of place. And she'd taken home anything confidential that she didn't want her father or his assistants to see, as she did every night, thus the ridiculously cumbersome, heavy book bag that had just gasped its last breath.

"Miss Cardenas?" He arched a brow in question, his smile fading.

"Melissa," she absently corrected him, before snagging the coffee cup and taking a much-needed shot of caffeine. Heck, with what she was planning this morning, maybe she should have laced her coffee with whiskey. She was already near her limit of what she could handle and now she had to deal with one more thing. Or, more accurately, one more *person*.

A look of concern entered his intriguing gray eyes. "Melissa? Are you okay?"

She realized he was holding his hand out toward her, and she hadn't taken it. She set the coffee down and shook his hand. The solid strength of those warm fingers wrapped around hers had her feeling uneasy. Jace Atwell would make an intimidating adversary. But his strength could also make him a useful ally. The trick was to figure out which category he fell into or whether she'd completely misjudged that incident on the road. Maybe Jace really was an innocent passerby who'd stopped to help her when she was in need and wasn't mixed up in whatever her father was mixed up in.

Bodyguard? Navy SEAL? With a gun in his car. Who happened by just when she had a crazy gunman after her? All coincidences?

She frowned. Maybe. It could also be a coincidence that a gun-toting madman chose to go after her not long after she'd become suspicious and started investigating her father and his associates. Yeah, those could all be coincidences. But she wasn't betting on it. Her instincts were screaming that the gunman and Jace were both involved, somehow, in whatever was going on at EXIT, and that Jace was one of the good guys. Or, at least, she hoped he was.

However, all that speculation was going to have to wait. The clock on the wall behind him was a glaring reminder that time was running out. Her father would be here in just a few minutes. If she wasn't upstairs before him, then getting here early and suffering through a smelly cab, broken shoe, and broken book bag would all have been for nothing. She forced a smile. "Sorry. It's been a bad morning, all around."

"The sun's not even up yet," he teased, "and you're already having a bad day?"

She frowned. Bad day? She wished all she was having was a bad *day*.

"If you want me to come back later—"

"Actually, I'm surprised to find you here so early, and in my office. Alone. Care to explain that?"

Her words came out sounding more accusing than she'd intended. But she didn't back down or apologize. If he was hiding something, she wanted to know about it. She was sick to death of the lies and secrets that swirled around her every day, and even more resentful that she'd been forced to resort to lies and secrets as well. She had her father to thank for that.

The tension lines around his eyes deepened. "Your assistant, Jolene, suggested I wait in here instead of the reception area—something about the chairs out there having been chosen for looks while the ones in here were chosen for comfort. She just stepped out and said she'd be right back. Is that a problem? Should I have told her no and waited in the reception area?"

Her shoulders relaxed, and she blew out a breath of irritation. Jolene. Of course. Always smiling, trusting Jolene who would probably offer to cut off the handcuffs of a fleeing felon and compliment him on his black-and-white-striped suit. How Jolene had attained blue-haired-lady status without becoming at least a little jaded was one of the mysteries of the universe.

Jace's jaw had tightened at her thinly veiled accusation, and that extra tension revealed a sexy dimple in his right cheek. Unbidden, memories of Thomas bombarded her. He'd had a dimple, too. She loved dimples. She also loved tall men, with narrow hips and broad shoulders. Men with deep, masculine voices that triggered all kinds of heating and softening inside her.

Men like Jace.

If he'd shown up in her life before the lying, *married* Thomas Hightower, before life and its many disappointments had destroyed her dreams of white knights and happy endings, she'd be flirting like a princess who'd just found her prince. But she already knew there was no such thing as a happy ending, at least not for her. And she had far more important things to worry about.

Like finding out the truth about whatever was going on at EXIT.

Jace gave her a curt nod and turned around, making her realize she'd been distracted once again while staring at him and hadn't answered his question about Jolene putting him in her office. The man probably thought she was the rudest person ever. Her always-proper father would be appalled at her lack of manners and its poor reflection on the Cardenas name.

"Coming here was a mistake," Jace called out over his shoulder as he headed toward the door. "You're obviously preoccupied. And I've ticked you off." He paused with his hand on the doorknob and looked back at her. "Let's just call this what it is—a waste of time—and be done with it. I'm sure I can find a job elsewhere."

"Jace, wait. *Please.*" She rushed across the carpet and put her hand on his forearm.

He gave her an irritated look. "I had a long, trying night with very little sleep. I have neither the patience nor the time for whatever you've got going on."

"We have that in common."

He frowned. "Which part?"

"All of it. Long night. Little sleep. No patience." She gave him an apologetic smile. "You're not catching me at my best. Not even close. I'll get right down to business. I want to hire you. Not just as a way of thanking you but because you seem like an extremely capable man. I think you'd be an asset here. We can always use another tour guide. Your background's excellent for that, for keeping our clients safe."

He shook his head. "No thanks. Coddling eccentric, inexperienced tourists through dangerous terrain where they have no business being isn't my thing. Instead of protecting them, I'd probably end up tossing them into a river just to shut them up."

She laughed, genuinely amused. "I'm guessing that kind of attitude doesn't get you too many repeat clients in the bodyguard business."

"The bodyguard business is about keeping people alive, not catering to silly whims that can get them killed." His voice was tight and deadly serious.

"I see." She smoothed one hand down her pencil skirt. "I take it you have an excellent track record then, in keeping those same clients alive?" Instead of his immediately saying yes, as she'd expected, his forearm stiffened beneath her hand. She dropped her hand and cleared her throat. "Is that a no then?"

His expression turned grim. "Every client who followed my instructions is alive today to talk about it."

Her breath caught. "Are you saying that not all of your clients . . . followed your instructions?"

A muscle began to tic in the side of his jaw. "All but one did. And that, Miss Cardenas, isn't something I'm going to discuss with you. Unless you want to hire me as a bodyguard, of course."

His quip was obviously meant to be sarcastic, but it suddenly dawned on her that it might be the perfect solution to her dilemma.

Last night, during the long ride home in her father's limo, he'd brought up their age-old argument about wanting her to hire protection, at least on the drive to and from work every day like he did. And she'd agreed to think about it. How could she not after what had happened? The only reason she hadn't immediately capitulated was because she knew all of *his* bodyguards and didn't like the idea of those particular men following her around. But Jace? He was completely different. Being easy on the eye was only part of it. He also was highly qualified to protect her. Assuming he was telling the truth about his background. And she certainly couldn't hold his one bad case against him, not if the client put themselves in danger against their bodyguard's advice.

"If you want to be a bodyguard," she said, "I'm in the market for one."

His brows lowered. "If that's a joke because of what I just said—"

She put her hand on his arm again. His muscles jumped beneath her fingers, but she didn't let go this time. She was too afraid he was ready to step out the door. "It's no joke. After last night, my father is pressing me harder than ever to hire someone to protect me. But I have no desire to have any of the men who work for him sniffing after me. You, on the other hand, would be perfect." Her face flushed hot as soon as the words left her mouth. "That, um, didn't come out the way I intended."

Amusement lit his eyes, and his muscles relaxed beneath her grip.

She cleared her throat. "What I meant to say was that I don't have a lot of faith in the company he uses. A former SEAL is a big step up in the security department. At least, that's my expectation. Will you consider it?"

He seemed to think about that for a moment, then nodded. "All right. As long as we can agree on terms."

"Terms? As in salary? Benefits?"

"As in you do what I tell you to do or I fire you as a client. I won't stand by while you do something foolish to put yourself in danger. And if you're not willing to follow my orders, you'll have to hire someone else."

She laughed, but when he didn't laugh, too, she sobered. "You're serious? You expect me to follow your orders? Even though I'm the employer and you would be my employee?"

He gave her a crisp nod. "That's the only way I'll agree to be your bodyguard."

The logical part of her brain told her that what he was saying made sense. But she was used to giving orders, not taking them. *Could* she take orders? She didn't know. All she was sure of was that the idea rankled.

Later. She'd have to deal with the details later. The clock on the far wall kept ticking, and time was running out.

"I'm sure we can agree on the particulars. Consider yourself hired, pursuant to a successful criminal-background check and verification of your previous employment. I'll need you to fill out forms in HR for that, and to get a security badge. I'll have Jolene set up an appointment with HR this morning."

"All right. Deal."

They shook hands. Then she led him into the reception area to wait—comfortable chairs or not— while she gave Jolene instructions both about HR and about not allowing anyone in her office when she wasn't there.

She checked her watch. Her father was probably already in his office next door. And in just a few minutes, he'd be heading to his next mysterious meeting on the top floor. A floor that was a construction zone and strictly off-limits for safety reasons while the contractor waited for the next round of permits to be approved. But that hadn't stopped her father from going up there last week when he didn't realize she was watching. And it hadn't stopped her from running up the stairs to spy on him, either.

By the time she'd quietly worked her way through the maze of equipment and half-built offices to find him and hide behind a cubicle wall to listen in, the meeting was half-over. And she could only make out a few words exchanged between her father and the stranger he was speaking to. But she'd heard enough to know this next meeting, the one in a few minutes, was important. And that some man from out of state, Marsh, would be there, some kind of Councilman. She didn't know what Council he was a part of, and what that might have to do with EXIT, but she was determined to find out.

After having to repeatedly reassure her assistant that she wasn't actually *angry* about her letting Jace into her office, Melissa finally turned back to Jace. "You're in good hands with Jolene. I'll check on you later."

He looked like he wanted to ask her something, but she couldn't wait. She rushed into the hallway, past her father's office, and headed for the stairs.

"MR. ATWELL?" JOLENE asked. "Do you want me to get you some coffee while I make your appointment? If you prefer, I can take you to the cafeteria on the first floor to wait. It should be open for breakfast by now."

Jace tore his gaze from Melissa's retreating figure. What was she up to? Why was she so nervous? And why had she raced toward the red door that was clearly a fire exit instead of taking the elevator?

"No, thank you," he assured the elderly assistant. "No need to go to any trouble on my account."

She smiled and waved to the chairs on the other side of the room as she picked up the phone. "Then have a seat. This won't take long."

He was about to give up his vantage point near the doorway when Cyprian Cardenas stepped out of the office one door down with one of his assistants—Sebastian. They headed down the hallway in the same direction that Melissa had gone but stopped at the elevator.

"Mr. Atwell? Is something wrong?" Jolene's voice called out.

The two men stepped into the elevator, and the door closed behind them. Jace stretched and leaned against the door frame, aiming a lazy smile toward Jolene, who was holding her hand over the phone.

"Not at all. I just prefer to stand. I've been sitting all morning."

She shrugged, then spoke into the phone.

He noted that the floor indicator above the elevator showed it had gone *up*, to the top floor instead of down. He'd gleaned enough during his surveillance to know that the upper floor was being completely renovated. And one of Mason's contacts in City Hall had verified the work was on hold, awaiting permits. So why had Cyprian and Sebastian gone up there?

He glanced past the elevator to the stairwell entry. *What are you up to, Melissa?*

"HR can see you now." Jolene rose from her chair, her cheery smile firmly in place. "I'll take you down there."

He held his hands up to stop her. "No need. I passed by the Human Resources Department when the security guard escorted me up here earlier. First floor, just past the lobby on the right. Thanks." He hurried out of the office before she could tell him to wait.

When he reached the elevator, he hesitated. Stepping through those doors onto the top floor without knowing the layout or whether anyone could see him when the doors opened didn't seem like a smart idea. Taking the stairs was a wiser choice. Was that why Melissa had taken them? Had she gone up or down? He'd bet his last bullet she'd gone up and that she was spying on her father right now. It would explain why she'd been more nervous than a long-tailed cat in a room full of rockers earlier. And the only reason she'd spy on her own father was if she was suspicious about something. Otherwise, she'd have taken the elevator with Cyprian and Sebastian.

He hurried into the stairwell. When he didn't see or hear anyone else, he quietly began making his way up to the next level.

He wasn't sure what to expect once he found Melissa. Devlin and Mason had told him different theories about her. Mason believed she had to know by now what had really happened to her former boyfriend, Thomas Hightower, and her father's role in his death. And since Melissa was still going to work every day and appeared to have a good relationship with her father, Mason was sure she'd gone over to the dark side and was just as corrupt as he was.

But Devlin thought the opposite, that she didn't know anything about enforcers, government-sanctioned missions, or what had really happened to the Hightower family. She had a solid reputation in the community as law-abiding, honest, kind. She saw the world in black-and-white, not shades of gray—exactly the kind of person who made the Council nervous. While the Council was supposed to be a force of "good" and keep Cyprian from abusing his power, they were also tasked with keeping the government's secrets from being exposed. If they suspected that Melissa knew their secrets, she'd be marked for execution.

Regardless of who her father was.

Jace didn't know which theory he believed. But he was sure about one thing. If she fell into Devlin's camp of thought, and she was caught spying on a meeting involving the secret side of EXIT, she was as good as dead.

The memory of Ramsey's bruised-and-bloody body flashed through his mind. Austin had worked magic last night. He'd arranged the confidential medical help that Ramsey needed, so they could keep him out of the hospital and out of harm's way. He was going to be okay. But it had been a close call for a while and a long night, especially since half of it had been spent on the phone arguing about the mission plan with both Mason and Devlin. All of them agreed the mysterious man who'd abducted Ramsey could be involved with EXIT, and the mission might be compromised. But Jace had told them that he'd invested too much time to quit now. He'd rather take the chance, keep his guard up, and see what happened.

The real reason was a bit more . . . personal. There was no way in hell he'd abandon a woman, knowing someone had tried to kidnap or kill her. He couldn't bear having another death on his conscience, especially not Melissa's. He might be a stranger to her, but he'd learned everything he could about her during his surveillance and felt like he'd known her for years. No, he couldn't leave her defenseless, especially not against a bastard who'd decided a man's fate with the toss of a coin.

He paused halfway up the stairs and automatically reached for his pistol. *Damn.* His gun was in his car. He hadn't wanted to risk blowing his cover as an out-of-work bodyguard there for an interview, just in case security had decided to run a metal-detector wand over him. A decision he sorely regretted now. Did he have time to go back for his gun? Did *Melissa* have time?

The sound of a door opening somewhere below had him pressing back against the wall. Footsteps rang on the metal stairs, and muted voices echoed against the walls. At least two men had entered the stairwell and were coming up fast. He had no way of knowing if they would stop on another floor or whether they were going all the way up. But he couldn't risk waiting around to find out. He was out of time. As quietly as possible, he raced up the remaining stairs.

Chapter Five

Cyprian sat ramrod straight in his chair in the half-constructed conference room facing the door, or where a door would be once construction was complete. At the far end of the table, Sebastian silently watched him, as he often did. But Cyprian ignored him as much as possible. Pretending he wasn't being followed and watched nearly every minute of the day was the only way to survive without going crazy. One way or the other, this torture had to stop. And bringing Adam Marsh here prior to the full Council meeting was the first real step toward making that happen.

The stakes were high: Cyprian's freedom to lead the clandestine side of EXIT without the Council's interference, and his daughter's life. Because he didn't believe for one second that last night's attack on Melissa could be unrelated to his role as head of EXIT's enforcement arm. He was convinced that someone on the Council, or connected to the Council, was responsible for what had happened. No one had ever dared to go after her before. The only thing that had changed was that Marsh and his team were monitoring him. He didn't buy that it was a coincidence. His daughter had just become a pawn in this deadly game. And that was something he would not tolerate.

The sound of the stairwell door slamming shut echoed from the outer room. A few moments later, two shadows separated from the maze of construction equipment and cubicle walls and headed toward the conference room. As a precaution, Cyprian slid his hand to the pistol concealed inside his suit jacket. But the shadows passed beneath a shaft of light from one of the few working fixtures, revealing them to be Marsh and Cyprian's other assistant, Tarek. He dropped his hand and stood.

Sebastian didn't bother to get up out of his chair. Cyprian noticed the slight in manners and arched a brow. Sebastian wisely rose to his feet.

Adam Marsh's tall, broad-shouldered form paused in the doorway. The man was about Cyprian's age, but his dark hair was still unmarred by gray, probably because he didn't work beneath the kind of pressures that Cyprian did. And yet, here Marsh was, judging him. That idea rankled even more now that he was seeing the man in person.

Distaste wrinkled the Council leader's brow as he surveyed the room, as if he were worried he might catch a disease. "Is there a reason that we couldn't meet downstairs?"

Forcing Marsh to conduct their meeting in this barely usable space when Cyprian had a luxurious, hidden office downstairs—an office no one on the tour side of EXIT knew about—was petty. He readily admitted it. But he wasn't about to cater to the Council leader's comfort when the man routinely treated him like a traitor at worst, an idiot at best. All because of a few mistakes that Cyprian's men had made last year, mistakes he'd been forced to cover up to salvage the company's mission. But that cover-up had fallen apart and cost him dearly.

Rogue enforcers, the *true* traitors, Devlin Buchanan and Mason Hunt, had somehow managed to inform the Council about their suspicions. They'd escaped without retribution, leaving Cyprian to weave an elaborate lie to conceal the worst of what had happened. But he couldn't hide all of it and hadn't managed to avoid punishment completely.

"My apologies." Cyprian shook Marsh's hand across the table. "There's a problem with the heat in my office. I believed you'd be more comfortable up here."

Marsh glanced around again before sitting down. "Comfortable might be a stretch. But at least the temperature's acceptable."

Cyprian smiled stiffly and sat across from him, while both of his assistants sat at the far end of the table.

Marsh pinned Cyprian with an openly hostile, dark-eyed gaze. "This is your gig. You *demanded* that I meet with you privately before the full Council meets. Well, I'm here. What did you want to discuss?"

Privately? He almost laughed at that. The only time he had a moment without Sebastian or Tarek dogging his every step was when he was home, and often not even then. A man could only tolerate so much. And he was well past his limit. He had to figure out a way to remove the roadblocks that were tying his hands, making him second-guess his every decision. It wasn't just his own sanity at stake, it was the safety of this nation. The Council needed to realize their crushing punishments were hurting far more than just Cyprian.

He carefully studied Marsh, watching his body language as he threw out his first volley. "You look well rested. I assume you flew in yesterday. Did you get a chance to enjoy any of Boulder's fine restaurants last night? The Flagstaff House is particularly good. I highly recommend the royal Ossetra caviar."

Marsh frowned. "Why would you care when I got here or where I ate?"

The confusion and impatience on Marsh's face, and in his tone, was disappointing. Cyprian had hoped to see wariness and suspicion when he mentioned "last night." That would have added weight to his suspicion that Marsh was behind the attack on Melissa. But now he'd have to look to the other Council members to find the true culprit.

He gave Marsh a bland smile. "Just making small talk."

"Don't bother. You and I will never be friends. We can skip the niceties."

Cyprian held on to his smile, just barely. "You don't like me very much, do you Marsh?"

"I don't like you even a little bit, *Cardenas*. If it were up to me alone, if I didn't have to act with the full support of the Council, you'd have been stripped of your leadership role in EXIT's enforcement arm months ago when your shenanigans came to light. I certainly wouldn't have given you the slap on the wrist that you received."

Cyprian clasped his hands into fists beneath the table. "A slap on the wrist? Hardly. And that's precisely what I want to talk to you about."

A dull noise sounded from the other room. Marsh immediately motioned toward Sebastian and Tarek, who drew their guns and rushed out of the conference room.

Cyprian frowned, annoyed that Marsh was giving *his* assistants orders. And far more annoyed that they were following them. It would be refreshing if they could pretend a bit more convincingly that they actually worked for him instead of the Council.

"This building is secure," Cyprian insisted. "That was probably the heating system kicking on."

"Perhaps. But I'm more thorough than you. I don't leave things to chance."

His snide remark had Cyprian bristling inside. But outside, he maintained a calm demeanor. He didn't take the bait.

Looking mildly disappointed, Marsh settled back in his chair. "Start talking."

MELISSA DREW A sharp breath and grabbed for the second box, just managing to catch it before it could fall to the floor like the first one had. She carefully set it back down on the small stack of boxes that she'd accidentally brushed against while pressing her ear to the wall of the cubicle. Not that it had done her any good. She'd completely misjudged the impact that the latest construction changes had made to the acoustics on this floor.

Every noise she made seemed to echo from one side of the building to the other. But the conversation between her father and the man named Marsh was effectively blocked by the thick glass the workers had constructed across the front of the conference room since the last time she'd been up here. Even the absence of a door didn't seem to matter. If she was going to hear anything worthwhile, she had to get closer.

She stepped to the cubicle opening and peered around the wall toward the conference room. Her father and his guest appeared to be having a heated exchange. Frustration curled inside her. What were they talking about? Maybe she could take the aisle behind this cubicle and edge up to the wall on the left side of the conference room, just out of sight, and hopefully close enough to hear.

Wait. Where were her father's assistants? They'd been in the conference room earlier. Now . . . their seats were empty. She peered into the gloom. Had they heard her knock over that box? Were they searching for her? She clutched the box in front of her in frustration. She couldn't let them see her. They'd report back to her father, and he'd be furious that she was eavesdropping on him. She crouched down, breathing out of her mouth to make as little noise as possible.

A thump sounded off to her left. She rushed around the wall and into the next aisle, or what would be an aisle once it was finished, and crouched behind a stack of wall partitions waiting to be installed.

Another thump. There, a shadow moved through the maze of equipment ten feet away. *Tarek*. He ducked into the cubicle she'd just left.

But not before she saw the gun in his hand.

Her mouth went dry. Why would one of her father's executive assistants carry a gun around EXIT? The pictures and names on the corkboards at home flashed through her mind, and her pulse started rushing in her ears. She'd never liked Tarek, had never trusted him. Did her father know that he carried a gun? More importantly, if Tarek discovered her, would he *use* that gun?

The conference room. Somehow she had to make it to the conference room without his seeing her. Her father would make him stand down. It would be humiliating to admit that she was spying. But keeping her secrets wasn't worth her life.

She tensed to make a run for it when she remembered Sebastian. The way he and Tarek shadowed each other, maybe he had a gun, too. *Where was he?*

A clear bell dinged in the quiet of the room. She leaned over and saw the elevator doors standing wide open. But from her angle, she couldn't see who was inside.

Tarek bolted toward the elevator. The doors slid shut seconds before he reached it. He cursed and repeatedly slammed the CALL button. But the elevator started down.

He rushed to the red door twenty feet away and ran into the stairwell. The sound of his footsteps clanging on the metal stairs faded as the door clicked shut behind him.

Melissa let out a shaky breath and debated her next move. Had Sebastian hopped onto the elevator, but Tarek didn't know it was him and went off in pursuit? Or was Sebastian looking for her with a gun? She couldn't cower here waiting for him to find her. She had to do something.

She stood. A hand clamped over her mouth, and she was jerked back against a man's iron-hard body. She twisted violently in his grasp, trying to free herself as he pulled her to the next aisle. He stopped, and held her so tight she could barely breathe.

"It's Jace," a whisper sounded in her ear. "Be still."

She froze at the sound of his deep voice. Jace was here. But why? He had no reason to be here. Unless he was in league with Sebastian and Tarek. Had she invited him to EXIT thinking to protect him, thinking to find out his connection to what was happening to her father, when all along he was one of the bad guys? Her blood rushed in her ears. *No, no, no.* She bucked against him, trying to break his hold.

"Damn it, Melissa. Stop fighting me," his harsh whisper sounded again.

He pulled her into the cubicle behind them. She tensed, her gaze flitting from surface to surface, as she looked for something she could use as a weapon. Her lungs burned, the adrenaline pumping through her body increasing her demand for oxygen far more than breathing through her nose would allow. Spots started to swirl in front of her eyes. She grabbed Jace's hand covering her mouth.

"I'm trying to help you," he whispered, sounding exasperated. "The first gunman fell for my elevator distraction. But there's one more in here. You have to trust me, Melissa. We have to be very quiet, so he doesn't find us."

Trust him? Was he lying? To get her to give up?

Footsteps echoed on the concrete floor, like death knells getting closer and closer. She stilled in Jace's arms. At this point, it was all she could do. Be quiet and pray that he wasn't working with her father's assistants and that he didn't announce their presence to whoever was coming toward them.

Please be a good guy, Jace.

He ducked down, pulling her with him behind an impossibly small box. Was it even big enough to conceal them? The footsteps stopped. The spots in front of Melissa's eyes swirled. The world began to grow dark. She sank against him.

The hand covering her mouth suddenly dropped away, allowing precious oxygen to rush in. Melissa drew a shallow breath, then another. The darkness faded. Good guy then. Right? Jace must have realized she was about to pass out and moved his hand. A bad guy wouldn't have cared if she passed out.

The muzzle of a gun came into view a few feet away as their pursuer stepped into the cubicle, almost directly beside their hiding place. Another step, and he'd see them.

"Sebastian, Tarek," a voice called out from the direction of the conference room. "Did you find anything?"

Melissa stared at the gun and the hand holding it. She clutched Jace's arm around her middle. As if to reassure her, he lightly squeezed her upper arm.

The gun disappeared. Footsteps sounded again as the man, presumably Sebastian, backed out of the cubicle.

"The elevator doors opened," he called out. Sebastian's voice. "Tarek went down the stairs to see who was inside." He continued his explanation as he headed toward whoever was talking to him. The man with her father? Marsh?

It didn't matter. All that mattered right now was that no one was pointing a gun at her. And that Jace had protected her. *Good guy then. Jace was a good guy. Thank God. And thank God for bodyguards.* She melted against him in relief.

"Don't relax just yet," he whispered. "We have to get out of here before he comes back. Come on."

He didn't wait for her to stand. He jumped up, tossed her on his shoulder and jogged down the aisle like a ghost, somehow making almost no noise.

She clutched his suit jacket, too stunned to do more than hold on. Offices, tools, stacks of boxes rushed by in a blur. He ducked down another aisle, maneuvered around several stacks of cubicle walls lying on their sides, jumped over some tools some-one had left beside a pile of two-by-fours. A moment later, he stopped and tugged her off his shoulder, holding her around the waist to steady her as he pushed open a door.

She blinked in surprise to see the stairwell in front of them. Jace grabbed her hand and pulled her onto the landing.

CYPRIAN WATCHED DISPASSIONATELY as Marsh re-turned to the conference room with Sebastian, hold-ing a pistol down by his thigh.

"What's going on?" Cyprian asked.

Sebastian holstered his gun and tugged his suit jacket over it. "Maybe nothing. Neither of us found anyone. But I haven't finished searching the entire floor yet."

"Where's Tarek?" Cyprian asked.

"We thought maybe someone had gone down in the elevator, so he went down the stairs to check it out."

Marsh shook his head. "You said this place was secure, Cyprian."

"It is. No one gets in or out of this building with-out being logged in unless they're escorted by me or one of my assistants, as you were, through the back entrance. And the electronic security there is impenetrable."

"Nothing's impenetrable. But if you have electronic logs of everyone coming and going, it shouldn't be hard to see who's in the building right now, to narrow down who might have been eavesdropping on our conversation."

"Eavesdropping?" Cyprian shook his head. "No one knew we were meeting up here."

"You sure about that?"

Bristling beneath Marsh's condescending attitude, Cyprian motioned to his assistant. "Have security perform a lockdown. Check the logs and verify where everyone is. There can't be more than three or four dozen employees here at this time of morning. Shouldn't take long to ensure that everyone is where they should be and not poking around up here."

"No," Marsh said, contradicting Cyprian's order. "Call Tarek. Have *him* do all of that while *you* finish searching this floor. Then hurry back so you can escort me out of this hellhole."

"Yes, sir." Sebastian pulled out his phone and his gun and headed through the doorway.

Once again, his men were following Marsh's orders. The day that Cyprian could fire Sebastian and Tarek without worrying about reprisals from the Council could not come soon enough.

He rose and faced Marsh. It took all of his concentration not to allow his contempt for the other man to show. But Marsh didn't give him the same courtesy.

"Are we done here?" Marsh asked.

"Not quite. We've discussed all of the steps that I've taken to ensure that what happened last year can't happen again. But you haven't told me when my probation will end."

"I don't know when it will end. That's something the entire Council has to agree upon."

Cyprian clenched his fists in frustration. "Then at least tell me whom you've appointed as the Watcher. It's unacceptable having some unknown person report every detail of my life, every single day, back to you. Tell me who he is, so I can have some peace knowing he's not watching me in my own home. Is it Sebastian? Tarek? Someone else?"

"First of all, I didn't appoint the Watcher. The Council did, as a whole. Second, if you knew his identity, you'd always be on your best behavior around him. Kind of ruins the whole point of a Watcher—to make sure you aren't sneaking around and breaking the conditions of your probation. Surely *even you* can understand that."

Cyprian jabbed his finger in the air, pointing at him. "I've proven myself a hundred times over since last year's incident. There's no justification for continuing this medieval torture."

Marsh's lips curled in derision. "Incident? Really? Mason Hunt. The Hightowers. And dozens, *dozens*, of others were impacted by your so-called incident. And you think a few months of probation are sufficient?" He shook his head. "If you'd told me over the phone that this was the *real* reason that you wanted to see me, I could have saved both of us some time. EXIT's enforcement arm is an essential tool for keeping this country safe. Having it run by someone who sleepwalks on the job and doesn't provide the rigorous leadership required of the position is a mistake of monumental proportions. You want your probation to be over? Petition the Council. We'll have a healthy debate at the meeting coming up. But don't expect me to argue for your side. Because when it comes to trusting you, my vote is no. It will *always* be no."

Marsh turned his back on him in dismissal, as if Cyprian weren't even there. Which was just as well. Because Cyprian was clenching his teeth together to keep from pouring out a stream of vitriol that would make Marsh's ears burn, words he knew he'd later regret because Marsh could use them against him in the Council meeting when he presented his appeal.

The hatred and fury coursing through Cyprian's veins, tensing every muscle, took enormous control to tamp down. But somehow he managed it. Barely a minute later, Sebastian appeared in the doorway.

"The floor is clear. And Tarek couldn't verify that anyone was in the elevator." He shrugged. "Could be a false alarm. But we initiated the lockdown. And Tarek's got the list from the security log. Thirty-three employees are in the building. He's accompanying a security guard to personally account for everyone's whereabouts."

"Excellent," Marsh said. "Now, if there truly was a security breach, if someone was up here, you'll know it. And that, Cyprian, is how you maintain order and ensure the sanctity of EXIT's enforcement arm—by facing problems head-on, without ignoring them until they become major . . . what did you call them? Incidents?" He motioned to Sebastian. "Get me out of here."

Cyprian stood unmoving as they left. His face

flushed hot, and he was certain he could feel his blood pressure spiking. No one, *no one*, had ever spoken to him like that before. Certainly not in front of employees. This situation was unbearable. It had to end.

As soon as he couldn't hear any footsteps, he tugged his suit jacket down, smoothed a wrinkle from the fabric, and headed to the elevator. When the doors closed, he punched a speed dial on his cell phone. The line clicked.

"Do it," he said.

MELISSA PULLED JACE into the first-floor main hall-way and stopped. "Look." She motioned toward the lobby, just visible through the opening at the far end. Two security guards stood by the front doors. One of them shook his head at a small group of employees on the outside.

"We're on lockdown." She kept her voice low. "They're not letting anyone in or out. Security must have figured out that something is going on. Maybe someone saw Tarek come downstairs with a gun. I have to warn them about Sebastian, too. And have them send a guard upstairs to check on my father." She started forward.

Jace grabbed her arm. "Hold it. You can't go out there, not without knowing where the gunmen are. It's too dangerous."

She frowned. "The security guards are right there. All we have to do is run to the lobby. We'll be safe."

"I'm not betting your life on that." His hold on her arm was like steel. He scanned the hallway, study-ing the doors and the signs over each one. He suddenly sucked in a breath as if he'd seen something and pulled her through one of the doorways into the cafeteria.

Without slowing down, he towed her past the food cases and buffet, past the cash registers, into the main dining area.

"What's going on?" she asked.

"We're about to have company." He shoved her into a chair and ran to the conveyor belt that diners used to dispose of their trash and leftover food. He grabbed two trays just before they could disappear into the trash chute and plopped them on the table in front of them.

"Tarek and a security guard are going to step into this cafeteria any minute," he whispered as he sat down across from her. "Until we know exactly what's going on, we need to play it cool. Don't mention anything about what happened upstairs. To anyone."

She frowned. "Is that one of your bodyguard orders?"

"It is. Trust me, Melissa. Don't say anything. Not yet." He glanced past her. "Pick up the fork. We've been here all morning, eating, while you interviewed me for a job. *Sell it.*" He grabbed the fork from his tray and laughed, his face shifting from intense concern to lighthearted like the flip of a switch. He began to describe where he used to work as if they really were conducting a job interview.

She looked at the fork on the tray in front of her, then back at him. Her eyes widened when she saw what he must have seen—Tarek and a security guard reflected in the mirrored wall behind Jace. The guard was carrying a pen and a piece of paper, and the two of them had stopped at the only other table with diners, on the other side of the room. The guard checked off something on the paper, like a schoolteacher taking roll.

"Pick up your fork," Jace insisted. "Now."

She grabbed the dirty fork, shuddering with revulsion as she played with the half-eaten food as if it were her own plate. Jace gave her a barely perceptible nod of approval.

"Miss Cardenas."

She started in surprise and looked over her shoulder. Tarek frowned at both of them. His gaze dipped to their plates. But it was the security guard beside him who'd spoken.

"Andre." Melissa smiled warmly. "How are you today? And Tarek." She couldn't hold on to her smile looking into his cold eyes, so she focused on the guard. "Is something wrong?"

"Sorry to trouble you, Miss Cardenas. We're tracking down a possible security issue. Nothing to worry about. Just checking on everyone in the building to make sure they're okay. Looks like you're finishing up breakfast. I hope it was good."

"Always. We have the best cooks in Boulder."

He nodded his agreement. "And the gentleman with you? I'm sorry, sir, but I don't remember meeting you."

Jace set his fork down and held out his hand. "Jace Atwell. Miss Cardenas is interviewing me for a job."

The guard shook Jace's hand and checked the piece of paper he was holding. "You must be the visitor another guard checked in this morning. He didn't record your name. I'll be sure to talk to him about that." He wrote Jace's name down, then drew a line through it. "That's everyone."

Tarek didn't move.

Melissa frowned. "Mr. Vasile, is there a problem? If you don't have enough work to keep you busy, I'm sure Jolene would love your assistance moving heavy boxes. She's been wanting to rearrange one of the file-storage rooms for quite a while." She arched a brow, selfishly enjoying the red flush that crept up from Tarek's collar. It was a tiny victory. And since he'd been after her with a gun earlier, she didn't feel the least bit guilty.

"Sorry to have bothered you, Miss Cardenas," he replied. "I'll check with your father to see what . . . tasks . . . he has for me."

"See that you do." She turned her back on him to face Jace again. But she half expected a knife to come slashing down to bury itself in her spine. "Mr. Atwell, I believe you were explaining about your most recent position."

"In Savannah."

"Right. With Dawson's security?"

"Yes." He rattled off details about his employer for a full minute before he stopped. "They're gone."

She dropped the fork in disgust. "Please explain to me why I just lied to a security guard who could have protected us, and why I didn't tell him that Tarek had a gun. How was that a good idea?"

"You really think that rent-a-cop could intimidate Tarek? Not a chance." His gaze flicked past her, and the renewed urgency in his expression had her stomach clenching with dread.

"Remember what I said about my one client who didn't follow my instructions," he whispered. "Do *not* say anything to your father about what happened upstairs."

"My father?" She blinked in surprise to see her father in the mirror. The couple at the table across the room had stopped him, probably to ask about the lockdown. And standing beside him were both of his assistants. The security guard was nowhere to be seen.

She stood in indecision, and Jace immediately joined her, placing his hand on the small of her back as if to reassure her—or more likely to remind her of his instructions. In spite of the doubts and questions that she had, in spite of those corkboards on her wall back home, it didn't seem right not to tell her father what had happened. But what if Tarek and Sebastian still had their guns with them?

They'd been in the conference room with her father. They wouldn't have left without his knowing about it. Was it even possible that he *didn't* know that they had guns? Wouldn't he have been the one to tell them to leave the conference room and perform that search?

Her father and his shadows started toward her.

"Don't tell him you were upstairs," Jace whispered urgently, just before her father stopped in front of them, with his assistants on either side.

He introduced himself to Jace again, and her father's gaze flicked down to their plates, as Tarek's had earlier. "You probably saw Sebastian Smith and Tarek Vasile last night, Mr. Atwell, by my car." Cyprian waved toward them. "They're my executive assistants."

The men shook hands, and Melissa was amazed at how calm and friendly Jace appeared. She needed to take lessons from him on how to *not* look flustered.

Cyprian smiled at Melissa. "I hope the lockdown

didn't alarm you. Everything appears to be in order. A false alarm."

"False alarm?"

He waved his hand in the air. "Someone thought they saw a stranger roaming the halls without an escort. The building has been searched. Everything is fine." He took her hand in his. "Tarek tells me you're interviewing Mr. Atwell. What position did you decide upon?"

She hesitated, feeling compelled to confide in him. Loyalty was so important to him. That had been drilled into her since she was little. How could she not tell him what she'd done? She opened her mouth to say something. Jace's fingers flexed against her back in warning.

Safe. Somehow, even though she barely knew this man, he made her feel safe. But when she thought about confessing to her father what she'd done, even once his assistants weren't around, all she could think about were those boards back home, and that feeling of safety evaporated.

And that scared her more than anything else.

She forced a smile. "Actually, Mr. Atwell won't be working for our company, specifically. He'll be working directly for me. I've decided to take your advice and hire a bodyguard."

His brows shot up. "Mr. Atwell? He's not even with a service. He hasn't been vetted. You can't have had time for a background check." He arched a brow at Jace. "No offense intended, of course."

"Of course," Jace said.

"We're going to take care of that background check right now," Melissa said. "Our next stop is Human Resources, to start the paperwork."

Her father glanced at her plate again before offering his arm. "Tarek can take him to HR for you. Did you forget about the planning committee meeting? It starts in ten minutes."

Damn. "I guess time got away from me."

Jace's jaw had just gone rigid. He looked like he didn't want to let her out of his sight any more than she wanted him to. And for the first time in her life, she was nervous about being alone with her own father.

Needing an anchor in this sea of uncertainty, she grabbed Jace's hand in an awkward hold that was more drowning victim grabbing a lifeline than an actual handshake. He squeezed her fingers and gave her a firm nod with a "you can do this" look in his eyes before letting go.

She swallowed hard. "See you later, Jace."

"Count on it," he promised.

Her father escorted her to the door while the others followed. "I thought you didn't like eggs." He held the door open.

She paused. "Eggs?"

"On your plate. There were eggs. I tried to get you to eat them when you were a toddler, and you'd always throw them on the floor in disgust. I gave up by the time you turned four."

She hesitated, then started forward again. "Tastes change. People change."

He gave her a curious look. "Yes, I suppose they do."

Chapter Six

By the time five o'clock rolled around, and Jace was grudgingly returned to Jolene's keeping, he was coiled tighter than one of the suspension springs in his Grand National. He couldn't sit still, in spite of the curious smiles that Jolene kept sending him. Instead, he paced the floor in front of Melissa's office door, waiting for her latest, and hopefully last, meeting to end.

He could only think of a handful of times in his life more frustrating than today had been. Considering all the missions he'd conducted, that was saying something.

Everyone seemed to have conspired to keep him from having more than a few stolen moments with Melissa. The only reason he hadn't forcibly barged into Cyprian's office and yanked her out of one of their endless meetings was because of the whispered assurances she'd given him whenever they managed to pass each other in the halls. She swore everything was okay.

But that didn't stop him from worrying. Especially since Tarek had made it his sacred duty to act as Jace's personal shadow. He monopolized Jace's time, keeping him holed up in security most of the day with the flimsy excuse that his Navy SEAL background made him an excellent candidate to review EXIT Inc.'s security procedures for potential flaws.

When Melissa's office door finally opened, an older woman with glasses hanging from a gold chain around her neck stepped outside.

"Thank you so much," Melissa told her. "I appreciate that you put a rush on this." She thumped the manila folder in her hand.

The woman beamed at Melissa, nodded at Jace, and headed into the hallway.

"Ready?" Jace asked.

"Ready for what?"

"To go home. Your home."

At her blank look, he blew out an impatient breath. Either she'd developed excellent acting skills since this morning or her daily routine had numbed her perception of danger. She'd probably convinced herself that everything was okay, that they'd both overreacted. Maybe she'd even told herself that her father's assistants wouldn't really have hurt her if they'd discovered her hiding upstairs, that they were just concerned about her father's safety, like his bodyguards who escorted him between home and work every day. In other words, she was in denial.

He rested his arms on the door frame above her. "You did hire me as your bodyguard. Remember? Where you go, I go."

"Oh . . . right." She frowned. "I seem to recall that we needed to talk terms first."

He leaned down close to make sure Jolene couldn't hear him. "If you think after this morning's little jaunt upstairs that you're leaving here alone, unprotected, then you're dreaming with your eyes open. Not gonna happen."

She thumped his chest with the folder. "If we're going to work together—"

"We are."

Her frown deepened. "*If* we're going to work together, then you'd better stop the caveman stuff right now. I don't like being bossed around."

"Then you aren't going to like me at all. Because that's one of my terms. You follow my orders."

The folder crinkled in her grip. "I suppose you want some outrageously high salary, too."

He crossed his arms and threw out a ridiculous amount, just to see her reaction.

She gasped. "Are you serious? That's, that's . . ."

"Outrageous?"

She sputtered, then looked past him. Her mouth tightened. "Deal. I'll get my purse."

He turned around. Sebastian stood just inside the reception area, not even bothering to pretend that he wasn't watching them. And although Jolene might not have noticed the slight bulge of the pistol on Sebastian's hip beneath his suit jacket, Jace did.

He narrowed his eyes in warning. As soon as he sensed Melissa's presence at his elbow, he reached for the book bag he knew she'd be carrying. Without taking his gaze off his adversary, he hefted the bag under one arm and grabbed Melissa's hand.

He tugged her to the doorway and would have bulldozed through Sebastian if the man hadn't stepped aside at the last possible second.

A few minutes later, they were in Jace's car on the long drive to Melissa's house. He expected her to bombard him with questions, but other than telling him her address, so he could key it into the GPS when they'd first gotten into the car, she didn't say anything. She nervously tapped her nails on her thigh and kept looking in her side mirror as if she expected to see a fast car zooming up behind them at any moment.

Once they were on the highway, Jace pressed Melissa's hand to stop the tapping before it drove him insane. "No one's following us. You can relax."

"How can you be sure?"

"Been doing this awhile."

She yanked on her shoulder belt, loosening it, and turned to face him. "The fact that no one's following us speaks volumes. I don't know whether to thank you or fire you."

"Fire me? What the hell for?"

"I've been thinking all day about what happened this morning, and—"

"That's what I was afraid of." He steered around a pothole, and she braced her arm against the dash.

"You're afraid that I was thinking?" The irritation in her voice made him want to smile, but he didn't dare.

"I figured you were way too calm when I went to your office to get you. You talked yourself into thinking this morning's gun chase wasn't a big deal, didn't you? Let me guess. You've decided maybe it makes sense that Sebastian and Tarek would go search the floor because they'd heard something. And that they wouldn't have hurt you if they'd found you. You're thinking I made a crisis out of something that never should have been one. Am I getting warm?"

"Maybe." She crossed her arms.

He checked the mirrors, then passed some slow-moving cars before settling back in the right lane. He preferred that lane, so he was closer to the exits if he had to pull off fast. "Do you have an executive assistant?" he asked, already knowing the answer.

"No."

"But your father has two."

"Yeah. Well, he's the CEO."

He decided not to argue that one. He didn't have a clue what a CEO did versus a president. "Okay, how about your administrative assistant, Jolene?"

"What about her?"

"Does she carry a gun to work?"

"Of course not."

"But it doesn't bother you that your father's assistants do?"

She straightened in her seat and started tapping her thigh again. "I didn't say that. But my father is big on security. His armed guards pick him up at the house every morning and drive him home every night. Maybe he's gotten some threats that he hasn't told me about, so he hired those two as additional armed security on top of being assistants. I don't know."

"Hm."

She flopped around in her seat again. "Instead of discussing my father, let's talk about you. Why were you on the top floor?"

Knowing the best way to hide something was to stay as close to the truth as possible, he said, "From my vantage point in your reception area I saw you go into the stairwell. A few moments later, your father and Sebastian headed up in an elevator."

And this was where the lies began. "Sebastian's suit jacket flipped open as he turned around, and I saw his gun. Without knowing whether you'd gone upstairs or down, I decided to go up, just to make sure that you weren't in danger."

"Hm," she said, echoing his earlier disbelief.

"If you think I'm lying," he said, taking a chance, "then why do *you* think I went upstairs?"

"I'm thinking," she said.

"Uh-oh."

She lightly punched his shoulder. "Knock it off."

He grinned and took the exit that the GPS unit told him to take, the exit that he already knew from his earlier surveillance would lead them toward the White Hawk Ranch area where she lived.

"Okay, answer this," she said. "Why did you warn me in the cafeteria, repeatedly, not to tell anyone that I was upstairs? In particular, you seemed concerned about my telling my father. Why?"

He shrugged. "I'm new to EXIT. I don't know your father's assistants, or even your father. But their having secret meetings on a floor under construction, and at least one of them having a gun, rings all kinds of alarms for me. Your safety is my top priority, so I preferred that you not say anything until we could sort all of this out later. In private. Like we're doing now."

"Hm." This time she didn't sound so skeptical. She sounded like she might believe him.

He slowed and made another turn. There was far less traffic here than there'd been on the highway. Gas stations and convenience stores dropped away, gradually replaced with spacious homes and expansive lawns that would probably be bursting with color come spring but that were muddy brown with patches of snow right now.

"What about you?" he asked. "Why did you sneak upstairs to listen in on Cyprian's meeting?"

She didn't reply and instead looked out her window as if the scenery had suddenly become enthralling.

A few minutes later, Melissa dug the remote control out of her purse to open her garage. Jace pulled in and killed the engine. The door closed behind them and he waited for her to say something. When she didn't, he leaned across her and grabbed his pistol from the glove box.

She put a hand on his forearm, stopping him. "What are you doing?"

"Taking my gun inside the house. Although, I suppose if there are any bad guys waiting for us, I can try to karate chop them instead. But sometimes a gun is the easier way to go."

Her lips twitched. "Good point." She dropped her hand, seemingly unconcerned about the gun after that. He'd half expected her to recoil when she saw the SIG Sauer. A lot of his clients were afraid of guns, perhaps because it was a symbol of their own mortality and a reminder that they were in danger. But she'd simply seemed curious about why he felt he needed one right now. Go figure.

Since he wasn't wearing his holster, he shoved the pistol into his waistband.

"You should give me your cell-phone number, I guess, for after you check everything out and leave," she said, grabbing her phone out of her purse. "I'll call you in the morning when I know what time I want you to pick me up and take me to work."

"I thought I made myself clear back at your office. Where you go, I go. I'm not leaving."

Her brows shot up. "You want to stay here? At my house?"

"You have a problem with that?"

She shook her head. "Actually, no. I'm kind of relieved. I wasn't looking forward to being alone after the day I just had. Thank you."

He nodded and popped the driver's side door open. "I'll grab my go bag from the trunk."

"Go bag?" She opened the passenger door.

"A week's worth of clothes, ammo, my gun holster. I always keep a bag around in case I have to hit the road unexpectedly. Saves time."

"Be prepared, right? Isn't that the SEAL motto?"

"I think that's the Boy Scouts."

Her face flushed. "Oh. Do the SEALs have a motto?"

"The Only Easy Day Was Yesterday."

She winced. "No offense, but I hope that motto is a big, fat lie. I really need tomorrow to be better than today."

He didn't tell her what he already knew. Odds were that this was all going to get a whole lot worse before it got better.

"Wait for me," he said. "Just a precaution. I need to make sure the house is secure."

"I've got an alarm. If there was a problem, the company would have called me."

"Only if they *knew* there was a problem. Alarms might slow a professional down, but they won't stop him." He left her with that sobering thought and retrieved his duffel bag from the trunk, strapping it over his shoulder like a backpack to leave his hands free. Melissa joined him at the door, her purse on her shoulder and the heavy book bag cradled in her arms.

"Leave the bag," he said. "I'll come back for it after I clear the house."

She shook her head. "I'm not helpless. I can carry it."

It wasn't worth arguing about, so he let it drop. "I go in first. Don't come in until I tell you to."

"But I'll have to turn off the alarm. Assuming it's still on." She gave him a brave smile, but he could see the worry and tension in her face.

Unable to resist the temptation, he smoothed her hair back from her face. "It's going to be okay."

Her eyes widened the moment he touched her. But she didn't pull away. Instead, her breathing hitched. Just a little. Just enough to let him know she wasn't unaffected by him—any more than he was by her.

Damn. He shouldn't have touched her. Now all he wanted to do was touch her again. *Focus, Atwell.* "Does anyone else have a key or know the security code?"

Her breath fluttered out of her on a soft sigh. "My, ah, father." She cleared her throat. "My father has a key, and the code. And Silvia Conti does, too. She's his live-in housekeeper. But she comes here once a week to help out."

He drew his pistol. "Where's the alarm panel?"

"This door leads into the mudroom. Another door to the left goes into the kitchen, which runs along the front of the house. The panel is on your immediate left."

"Is the kitchen a separate room or open?"

"Open. Basically the foyer, kitchen, and sunken

living room are all one big room. There are short hallways on the right and left that lead to the dining room, my home office, and a bathroom. Everything else is upstairs."

"Give me the upstairs layout."

A few minutes later, armed with all the information that he needed, he held the pistol out in front of him, trigger finger on the frame. "Unlock the door and step back."

"Wait. Do you have another pistol in your car, or your go bag? I can cover you."

"You're serious?"

"I would never joke about firearms. I've got two of my own inside. If you want backup, in case someone is waiting on the other side of that door, I'm your girl."

He did have an extra gun in his bag. But he wasn't about to give it to her. Although he was much more inclined to trust her after meeting her in person, he still wasn't going to put his life in her hands without knowing exactly where her loyalties lay. If she knew he was an Equalizer, sworn to destroy EXIT— and her father, if necessary—she might turn on him. And he'd rather that she wasn't holding a pistol when she did.

"I've got this. Where do you keep your weapons? Are they locked up so an intruder can't get to them?"

"Both have trigger locks."

He noticed she hadn't told him where the guns were. Maybe she didn't trust him either. One of his priorities before he went to bed tonight would be to confiscate her guns if he could find them. "Let's go."

She unlocked the door and jumped out of the way. Jace rushed inside, sweeping his pistol back and forth, then up toward the balcony that over-looked the living room. The warning beep of the panel behind him was reassuring. But he took a few more seconds to scan the balcony and hallways.

"Clear," he called out.

"Is that SEAL-speak for I can come in?" Melissa's voice sounded from the garage.

He smiled. "Yes. You can come in."

The tap of her heels on the marble floor an-nounced her arrival. He kept the parts of the house that were in shadow in his gun sights while she turned off the alarm and flicked on the lights.

"Go ahead and set it again," he advised. "Minus the motion detectors."

"Already did. We're locked up tight."

"We'll see about that. Take me on a tour, so I can check all the doors and windows. But stay behind me."

The tour ended upstairs in her bedroom at the end of the gallery. Jace looked out the back curtains while Melissa set her purse and book bag on top of the four-poster bed.

"I don't like this balcony," he said.

"I do. It has a gorgeous view of the Indian Peaks."

He shoved his gun in his waistband. "That's not what I meant."

"I know what you meant. You're worried some-one could climb up into my room. But I'm sure you noticed the steel bar over the doors. And the glass is reinforced, supposedly bulletproof. My father is paranoid and insisted I replace the glass in all of the doors and windows when I bought the place."

"I can see your father being worried about your safety after last night's encounter with ski-mask guy. But why do you suppose he was worried before that?"

"I always assumed it was because of what happened to my mom and my brothers. They were killed when I was a little girl. He never remarried, and I'm all he has. He worries all the time that something could happen to me. I think he's afraid he'll end up alone."

"I'm sorry for your loss." And he was. He already knew her background, of course. But since she was talking, opening up, he didn't want to do anything to discourage her. Especially if she told him anything useful for his mission that he hadn't already discovered. "How old were you? When they died?"

She ran her fingers across the carvings on one of the wood posters. "Five I think. My brothers were six years older than me, twins. We were on a family vacation in Europe that summer, staying at a villa in Paris. Since Mom was usually home taking care of me back in the States, and my brothers were in school, she didn't get as much time with them as she'd like. She thought it would be fun to take them on a two-day trip to Florence, just her and the boys, for some mother-son bonding."

The corner of her eyes tightened with remembered grief. "The day they were supposed to return, a previously unheard-of extremist terrorist group—Serpentine—hijacked their plane, demanding some of their comrades be freed from prison. Back then, smuggling a bomb on board in checked luggage was much easier than it is now. The Italian government refused to give in to their demands. The terrorists weren't bluffing." She shivered. "Everyone perished. They say it was instantaneous, that my mom and brothers felt nothing. I don't know if that's true, but I'd like to think it is."

Jace pushed away from the balcony doors. The sadness in Melissa's eyes gave him the crazy urge to take her in his arms and comfort her. But all the reasons that he should keep his distance kept him from reaching out.

He checked his watch. Six thirty. Lunch—an extremely uncomfortable half hour spent in the cafeteria with Tarek—had been a long time ago. "I make a mean grilled cheese. I could whip up some sandwiches for both of us."

Her lips curved in a reluctant smile. "As tempting as it is to be twelve again and eat a cheese sandwich, I don't have much of an appetite. I'll probably read some financial reports for a while before going to bed. Make yourself at home, though. There's a TV in the living room. Remote's in the drawer in the coffee table. When you're ready to call it a night, there are four guest rooms on this floor, and they're always made up and ready to use. Silvia's fanatical about keeping every inch of the house clean and having fresh sheets on all the beds even though they're rarely used."

"If you change your mind, let me know. I could throw in a Pop-Tart for dessert."

Her smile finally reached her eyes. "Be still my heart. Maybe some other time."

He strode past her to the door.

"How long were you a Navy SEAL?" she called out, stopping him.

He paused and looked over his shoulder. "Six years. Why?"

She anchored an arm around one of the footboard posters. "The last meeting I had today was with HR, to get your security and background report. What you just said matches that report. The write-up also stated that you served with distinction, that you saved many lives, including the lives of men in your unit at great risk to yourself. Your last commanding officer's final evaluation called you honorable, brave, loyal, and above all else . . ." She swallowed hard. "Trustworthy."

He slowly turned around. "My evaluations wouldn't be shared in a background check."

She smiled sadly. "Yes, well, my apologies for that. My father pushed for more information. He has an uncanny ability to convince people to answer his questions." Her smile turned bitter. "One of my deepest regrets is that I've turned a blind eye for so long and haven't made *him* answer enough questions."

He cocked his head. "Are you ready to tell me why you snuck upstairs today? What you hoped to learn by listening to your father's secret meeting? Or what you even think the meeting was about?"

She started to say something, then seemed to think better of it and shook her head. "No. Not yet. I need to . . . think."

As soon as the door closed behind Jace, Melissa ran into the bathroom and threw up. She retched until she was sore, and there was nothing left. When her stomach finally settled down, she brushed her teeth, washed her face with a cool, wet cloth, and faced the woman in the mirror: the woman who was considering something that both sickened and terrified her.

Betraying her father.

DO IT.

That *order*, barked at him over the phone this

morning, had him fisting his hand around the hilt of the jagged-edged knife as he stood in the middle of the dusty room that time—and the enforcers—had forgotten long ago.

A broken, ladder-back chair with a shredded twine seat blocked his path. Like this rotting, dying place, it had succumbed years ago to the ravages of humidity, mildew, and rat feces.

He kicked it out of the way with the toe of his boot and peered out the broken window at the little ghost town. The nondescript car he'd chosen for tonight's work crouched like a forlorn child in the moonlit, weed-choked gravel out front, gravel that hadn't been driven on for at least a decade until a few months ago, when he and Cyprian had first begun to use this place for their meetings.

Do it.

Cyprian had said those words like the dictator that he was, expecting his command to be carried out quickly, efficiently, without question. As always. And he *would* obey that command. But not because Cyprian wanted him to. He'd carry out the order because it suited *his* purposes. Because, after all, it's what he'd been manipulating Cyprian into for months, with every meeting they had in this place.

How apropos that Cyprian would choose to conduct their planning sessions here. Even the *name* of the fake town, Enforcement Alley, was a tribute to his bloated ego. Though to be fair, this copycat training facility really was better than its FBI counterpart, Hogan's Alley. Or at least, it *had* been in its heyday.

But Enforcement Alley had proven to be too dangerous, the maze of forgotten mines with their rotting supports and lost caches of explosives beneath the surface making the ground too unstable, unpredictable, deadly. Whole cars had been swallowed and buildings heavily damaged when sinkholes opened up without warning.

Even the rocky cliffs that surrounded the town were unstable, crumbling at the worst possible times, sending several enforcers to their deaths during training missions. Ten men had paid the ultimate price for Cyprian's arrogance before he'd reluctantly agreed to shut the place down and create a new, safer facility miles away from Boulder, its existence just as closely guarded as this one's had been.

But even this many years later, the attributes that had made this one-street town with its Spaghetti-Western storefronts and wooden boardwalks so ideal remained. It was isolated, deserted, difficult to find unless you knew about it, and untouched by technology—*almost*. Even cell phones wouldn't work out here except in a few, select spots, like this old jailhouse. But most of the rest of Enforcement Alley had high concentrations of minerals in the soil that interfered with signals, and most electronic equipment, making it secure from electronic surveillance. All of that combined to make it the perfect spot for meetings.

Or anything else that went on behind these walls. *Do it.*

Yes, he would. But the word "it" had so many connotations, so much wiggle room, so much . . . freedom for interpretation. And this time, there'd be no toss of a coin to decide the result. The result had been decided the moment that Cyprian had given him that terse command. Or, rather, what he was about to do had been decided a long time ago. It was only the timing that had been decided this morning.

He carefully folded the letter with Cyprian's signature on the bottom and set it aside. Then he turned around. The man lay in the corner, naked, asleep thanks to the drug whose dosage had been carefully calculated to ensure it would be out of his system long before authorities found him. Because he couldn't die yet. Not until after *she* did or the setup wouldn't work.

Her yellow dress was decorated with little blue flowers. Her face was smooth and pale except for a smattering of orange freckles across her cheeks. Thick, burnished red curls hung past her full breasts to her narrow waist, teasing the zip ties around her wrists. Her moss-green eyes stared at him above the gag across her mouth, filled with desperation and terror.

It was a shame to kill her. She was quite pretty. And she'd been nice to him in the moments before she'd realized he was a threat. But it couldn't be helped. He had his instructions. And sometimes progress required a few sacrifices along the way, unfortunate collateral damage.

"It will be over soon. I'll make it quick, and as painless as possible," he promised her.

A gurgled sob sounded from behind her gag.

He glanced at the second man, also gagged but fully dressed, bound to a chair on the other side of the room, studying him with hate-filled, resentful eyes. His time would come as well, but not today. Not until his usefulness was over.

After pulling out his cell phone and checking the screen, he smiled, pleased that the old jail still had reliable reception. It was time for the Watcher to check in. He crossed to the man in the chair and pulled out his gun.

Chapter Seven

Melissa paused at the top of the stairs and smoothed her hands down the jeans she so rarely wore. But since she'd decided not to go into the office today, dressing comfortably seemed the thing to do. Her only pair of jeans had seen better days. The hem was ragged and tended to shed threads. But they helped her distance herself from her usual persona as the president of EXIT. Because she needed that distance today, more than any other time, just to survive the next few minutes.

Not going into the office was a calculated risk. Her father would certainly wonder why she wasn't there and might not believe the lame excuse she'd given Jolene when she'd called her a few minutes ago. But it was a risk Melissa was willing to take if not working this one day could get her closer to the truth.

Morning light poured in through the back wall of windows, revealing the golden tones of Jace's skin as he perched on the couch, watching the local news. No jeans for him. He was freshly shaved and painfully handsome in navy-blue dress pants and a crisp white dress shirt unbuttoned at the throat, no tie. His suit jacket was draped over the arm of the couch, and beside it, on the floor, sat his duffel.

When she stepped off the bottom step, music signaled a breaking news bulletin. A live shot showed a reporter standing in the parking lot of a motel at the edge of town, with flakes of snow drifting down onto his perfectly styled hair. Behind him, yellow crime-scene tape cordoned off a section of the parking lot. The camera zoomed in on the open trunk of a blue Cadillac where a coroner's assistant was shaking out a white sheet, then quickly jerked away when a policeman yelled something at the reporter and ran to block the shot.

But not before Melissa saw what the camera had seen.

A young woman, obviously dead, in a yellow dress almost the exact same shade of the crime-scene tape, with her long red hair tangled around her face. Melissa shivered and rubbed her hands up and down her arms.

The TV switched off. Jace pitched the remote onto the couch and stood, watching her with an unreadable expression. Melissa noticed the gun holstered on his hip. Guns didn't scare her. They were a symbol of strength. And safety. It was the people behind the guns who scared her. And right now, she was about to bet everything on the man behind that particular gun. She was pinning everything on her instincts and her belief that the words in his background report were true. Honorable, brave, loyal, trustworthy.

The trustworthy part was the one that was giving her fits and had kept her up so late last night. Because she was convinced he was lying to her, about that incident with the van, about why he'd suddenly shown up in her life, probably about why he'd gone upstairs yesterday at EXIT. But sometimes it took a lie to do the right thing. Like the lies she'd been telling her father.

She had to lie, to protect herself, to protect others. And she believed, she hoped, that Jace wanted that as well. So she was rolling the dice, placing her trust in him, betting that he wanted what she wanted—to do the right thing.

Even if it was the most painful thing she'd ever done.

"Good morning." Her rarely used sneakers squeaked on the floor as she crossed to him. "Did you sleep well?"

"No. Neither did you."

She self-consciously smoothed her hair, wondering if she looked as tired as she felt. "Why do you say that?"

"I heard you pacing in your room most of the night." He shrugged. "Light sleeper, especially during a mission. I wasn't trying to listen."

"Mission. Seems like an odd choice of words."

Something flickered in the depths of his eyes. "Assignment, mission, job . . . it's all semantics."

Maybe. Maybe not. She smoothed her hands down her jeans again, then clenched them at her sides to keep from advertising her nervousness. She drew a deep breath and fired her first shot. "I want to know who you really are."

He arched a brow. "You ran a background check. Jace Atwell isn't a stage name."

"I want details, *real* details."

He shoved his hands in his pockets and rocked back on his heels. "Let's see. I'm single, never married. Love kids, want a handful of my own someday. My mom and two brothers live in Savannah, where I've lived my whole life until I moved here. I love cats. Dogs are okay, but cats have attitude. I respect that. And my favorite color? Black."

"Don't patronize me."

"You said you wanted details. I gave you details."

"That's not what I . . ." She clenched her hands at her sides. "Things aren't adding up. I want to know how you knew that I needed help upstairs at EXIT yesterday."

His brow wrinkled in confusion. "Didn't I answer this already?"

"You gave me *an* answer. But I don't believe it was the right answer."

His eyes narrowed, but he didn't say anything.

"Did you know my father before you met him on that mountain road?"

"Never met him before. And, again, answered this already. What's going on, Melissa?"

They faced each other with a mixture of truth and lies between them. But what was the truth? And what was a lie?

She rubbed her hands up and down her arms, unable to dispel the chill that had settled inside her from the first moment that she'd begun to suspect something was terribly wrong at EXIT and hadn't left her since. "Your background report didn't tell me why you decided to move to Colorado. It certainly wasn't for a job that you already had lined up since you were interviewing for one when I met you."

"I needed a change of scenery."

"You just said that you lived in Georgia all your life. Something significant had to happen to make you move."

His jaw tightened. "I moved here to get away from the daily reminders of my biggest failure."

"The client you lost?"

He nodded curtly.

"You said you would tell me about that . . . if I hired you." She searched his eyes, waiting, hoping.

Level with me, Jace. Trust me, so I can trust you.

He let out a ragged breath. "It was my last mission as a bodyguard. I protected a woman for three months from her abusive boyfriend. There were a few incidents in the beginning, when he tried a few tricks to get around me. But he quickly learned I wasn't letting him anywhere near her. Things settled into a routine."

He paused, the barely suppressed anger and self-recrimination in his voice too raw to be faked.

"I should have known something was up," he continued. "She was acting happy, as if she'd suddenly gotten over her boyfriend when she'd been struggling with missing him the whole time. She was stuck in the cycle of abuse, blaming herself for what had happened instead of placing the blame where it belonged—on her abuser. She'd been seeing a therapist, and had struggled with depression. But those last few days . . ." He shook his head.

"She'd been sneaking notes to him through a friend who had no idea of the kind of danger she was inviting. He wrote telling her he loved her and that he was sorry, that he'd never meant to hurt her. When she didn't come downstairs one morning, I went up to check on her. She wasn't there. She'd snuck out of the house to meet him." His jaw worked, his skin turning pale. "They found her body—"

"Oh, no," Melissa whispered.

"They found her body," he continued, obviously struggling to finish his story, "at the bottom of the pool behind her boyfriend's house. She'd been raped, beaten, drowned. And *that's* why I quit. That's why I had to get out of Savannah, to escape those memories, my biggest failure."

She lifted her hand toward him but thought better of it and dropped it to her side. "I'm sorry. I didn't mean to cause you pain. And I'm sorry to keep pressing this, but it's important. I need to know why Colorado, why Boulder specifically."

He shrugged. "There wasn't anything specific about it. I put most of my belongings in storage, packed the bare essentials in my car, and took off for Seattle."

"Seattle? As in Washington state?"

He nodded. "I wanted to get as far from Savannah as I could. But after two long days of driving, I decided there wasn't much point in going any farther. The memories I was trying to escape had come along with me. Continuing on wouldn't have made a difference. So I rented an apartment for a few months until I could decide what I wanted to do long-term. I'm still not sure that I've decided. But I could have picked a far less beautiful place to land."

She looked past him toward the snowcapped mountains framed in the windows along the back wall. It wasn't hard to believe his story when she agreed with his sentiment. Colorado was home. She couldn't imagine living anywhere else. But Boulder wasn't exactly a stop off a major highway. People came here because they wanted to, not because they were passing by on the way to somewhere else and happened to pull off an exit ramp. That part of his story didn't ring true.

"So you thought Colorado was a nice place to stop. I can see that. But Boulder isn't exactly easy to get to."

He gave her a wry smile. "No. It's not. I did the tourist thing at first, trying to keep my mind off . . . what I'd left behind. Drove around the state, visiting the major cities and seeing what Colorado had to offer. But once I saw this place"—he waved toward the back windows with the gorgeous mountain view—"I lost the desire to leave."

She nodded. His story was certainly plausible. And the edge of pain in his voice, his eyes, reassured her that he was telling the truth about one thing, the client that he'd lost. He was opening up to her, and she regretted dredging up such a tragic memory.

"I'm sorry, for what happened to your client. But it sounds like it wasn't your fault. I hope you can stop blaming yourself someday."

His jaw worked, but he didn't say anything.

This time she didn't try to stop herself from touching him. She flattened her palms against his chest. "I have complete faith in your abilities as a bodyguard. Your client, the one who died, that's on her. Not you."

His eyes closed briefly. Then he closed his hands on top of hers, lightly squeezing before letting her go. "Thank you." His voice was quiet, barely above a whisper.

She reluctantly dropped her hands. Touching him, however briefly, was an unexpected pleasure.

But it was also distracting, and she needed to focus. There was too much riding on this conversation for her to allow physical attraction to interfere with what was important.

"I'm confident that you can protect mè, or rather, *help* protect me. I do know how to handle a gun. I'm not helpless. But what worries me is whether I can adequately protect *you*."

He laughed, but when she didn't laugh, too, he sobered. "You're serious."

"I am. When you rescued me from the driver of the van, then met my father a few minutes later, I saw something in the way he looked at you that . . . concerned me. I think he saw you as a threat."

He didn't say anything. Because he *was* a threat? Guilt rode her hard, as it had last night. If Jace was dangerous to her father, she should stop. Right now. She shouldn't share her fears, the things she'd learned, the things she suspected.

But how could she live with herself if she didn't? If more people died because she stayed silent? She wanted to protect her father, but she also had to do the right thing. The trick was to try to find a way to do both.

"I need to show you something, Jace. But before I do, I need you to promise that you'll keep an open mind. Or at least try, until I explain everything. Can you do that?"

"I'll listen to what you have to say. That's all I can promise."

"Then I suppose that will have to be enough."

JACE WAITED BY the back windows for Melissa to return. After her mysterious interrogation of him, she'd gone upstairs, saying she'd be right back. He wasn't sure what he'd expected, but seeing her lugging some kind of rectangular board covered in a sheet wasn't it. He rushed to the bottom of the stairs and reached for her burden, but she pulled it away.

"I've got it, thanks." Her knuckles whitened as she tightened her grip. "It's not heavy. Just cumbersome." She stepped to the couch, lifted the board onto the seat cushion, then hesitated. "You mentioned I was up late last night pacing. You were right. I was thinking and debating my next steps. And I convinced myself that I would only show you this, that I would only involve you, if I felt at peace with your answers to my questions this morning. Well, I'm *not* completely at peace with your answers. I'm convinced you have a hidden agenda for being here with me. I think that you *do* know my father, from before the attack by the gunman. And I believe that my father might be the real reason that you came to Colorado."

"Melissa—"

"No, please. The time for lies is over. My point is that it doesn't matter whether I believed your answers this morning. Because whether you realize it or not, you're a part of this"—she thumped her hand on the sheet—"and your life is in danger. So I don't have a choice. I have to tell you everything that I know. I have to make sure that you take the risk to yourself seriously and take the necessary precautions."

"I told you, I can take care of my—"

"Let me finish, please."

He crossed his arms.

"There's another reason that I decided to show

you these boards. As pathetic as it sounds, I'm desperate. Probably not a surprise after what happened on that mountain, and yesterday at EXIT. Everything is crashing down around me, and I need someone to help me navigate through it, to help me decide what to do—someone independent of my father, someone who won't be influenced by him. I'm hoping that this 'someone' is the former Navy SEAL standing in front of me. And I'm betting both my life, and my father's life, that this man is as honorable, brave, loyal, and trustworthy as his former CO thought he was."

Her faith in him was making him uncomfortable. She made him sound like a saint. And he was far from that. "You're not making sense, Melissa."

"Close your eyes, please."

"No way in hell."

She sighed. "I don't suppose it matters anyway." She whipped the sheet off.

And what was underneath changed *everything*.

Chapter Eight

Anger burned through Jace, and he gave silent thanks that he'd searched the house last night and found the two handguns Melissa had hidden in her office. Because what he was looking at now didn't seem like the markings of an innocent woman, or a woman he should have trusted enough to have closed his eyes and slept in the same house with last night.

He stared at the pictures, the names, the red lines linking them all together. In the middle, beneath a picture of Cyprian Cardenas, beneath the label "Enemies," were pictures and the names "Mason Hunt" and "Devlin Buchanan." And beneath those was another name. *His.*

"What the hell is this, Melissa? Half the people on these boards are marked as 'dead.' And why is my name listed under 'Enemies'?"

"I was hoping you could tell me. I created these boards based on information that I've picked up, without my father's knowledge. Why does he think you're his enemy?"

"He told you that? He thinks I'm his enemy?"

"No. His reaction when he first saw you told me that."

As she explained how she'd begun to suspect that something was going on at EXIT several months ago because of a conversation that she'd overheard between her father and an IT guy, Jace's anger changed to alarm.

The more he listened, the more worried he became. Not about Melissa's culpability. He no longer believed she could be in league with her father. Because Cyprian would never condone her even having this kind of information, let alone her *sharing* it. What made him nervous was realizing how much digging and eavesdropping she'd done at EXIT. All it would have taken was one little slip, and she'd have gotten herself killed, as she very nearly had yesterday.

When she pointed to another name on the board and explained the story behind it, his disgust for her father increased tenfold. How could a man be so selfish that his actions had forced his daughter to choose between loving her father and following her conscience?

Cyprian had put her in the position of feeling that she had to confess to a relative stranger in order to save that stranger's life and the lives of others. The misery those actions caused her shone in her eyes, sounded in every word, appeared in every gesture that damned her father and killed her a little more inside.

He hated Cyprian for that.

When she finished her explanation, her throat sounded raw. "Am I wrong to think that none of this is a surprise to you?"

There was no point in denying it now. She obviously wasn't buying that he was just a bodyguard. His cover was blown. The mission was over.

"You're not wrong."

She let out a ragged breath. "And you . . . rescuing me up on the mountain. That was a lie, too, wasn't it?"

The hurt in her voice sent a stab of guilt straight to his gut.

"The man in the ski mask," she continued, "the man who ran me off the road and waved a gun at me . . . he was, what? A friend of yours? You risked my life to play hero, to make me grateful? To what end?"

"It didn't happen the way it was planned. No one was supposed to point a gun at you. My . . . friend . . . was supposed to drive recklessly, forcing you to pull over. Then he'd head down the road, leaving me to check on you. You were never supposed to be in any danger."

"And what was the point of this fake friendship that you wanted to cultivate?" She waved at the boards. "What's *your* role in all of this?"

She deserved the truth. But he couldn't tell her the truth. He couldn't compromise the Equalizers. Only Devlin and Mason could authorize the sharing of information about them. And Jace doubted that Mason could ever trust Melissa Cardenas, the daughter of his mortal enemy, the man who'd almost killed Mason and his wife.

Jace was pretty damn surprised that he trusted her himself, at least as much as he could trust anyone. But he wasn't a fool. If she ever had to choose between saving her father or saving him, he wasn't going to place any bets that he'd end up on the top side of six feet under.

"What's your role in this?" She asked again, searching his face, tension pulling her skin so tight across her cheekbones that she looked fragile, like she might fall apart at any moment.

Damn, he hated this mission, hated that he'd ever agreed to involve Melissa in any way. He'd never wanted her to get hurt, but he'd plowed ahead anyway, consequences be damned. In some ways, he was treating her no better than her father was. And he hated himself for that.

"It's obvious that you know about at least some of the people listed on those boards," she said, continuing to push, refusing to give up even though she wasn't getting the answers she sought. She was tenacious, and maybe not as fragile as he'd assumed.

He faced the boards, carefully weighing his response and whether it could compromise his teammates in any way. Finally, he said, "You're right. I do."

Excitement lit her eyes. "And you knew my father, or at least you knew *about* him, before meeting him on that road? The truth this time. *Please.*"

The truth. "I knew about him long before we met. Yes."

"So, I was a pawn? To get to him?"

"Yes."

Her mouth flattened, and anger flashed in her dark brown eyes. "You, Jace Atwell, are an ass."

"You'll get no argument here."

Her brows crinkled, her anger fading as quickly as it had appeared. "But you won't tell me your plan? What you hope, or hoped, to accomplish?"

When he didn't answer, she thumped her finger

against his chest. "At least tell me my father's role in all of this. Tell me he's caught up in something that isn't his fault." She searched his eyes.

The pain and desperation stamped in her expression, laced in her tone, had him longing to pull her into his arms to try to soothe the hurt. But he knew she wouldn't welcome his touch. Whatever attraction they might feel for each other didn't matter now. If it ever had.

"Jace. Damn it, you owe me an explanation. Tell me he's not responsible for the deaths of all of these people." She waved at the boards.

Unable to deny her any longer, he gave her the answer she thought she wanted, but not the answer he knew she needed. "I wish I could tell you that he's innocent. But I can't."

He braced himself for tears. The pain was there in her eyes, in the stark angles of her face. He expected her to shatter in front of him.

But she didn't.

She straightened her shoulders and crossed to the back wall of windows looking out at the snow-topped mountains.

Operation Trojan Horse was obviously over, and a complete failure. The only reason Jace didn't leave right then was because he felt duty-bound to make sure she'd be okay. She did need a bodyguard. That hadn't changed. And it was imperative that he convince her to hire someone else before he left. So he waited for her to compose herself.

A few minutes later, she turned around and crossed to him with sure strides. Gone was the pale, fragile-looking woman who'd begged him to tell her that her father wasn't the monster Jace knew him to be. And in her place was the confident, determined executive who commanded a multimillion-dollar-a-year corporation. And she looked like she was ready to go into battle.

"Who are you working for?" she demanded.

He took a wary step back, but she moved forward, allowing him no retreat.

"Who are you working for?" she repeated.

"What makes you think I'm working for anyone?"

"Ski-mask guy. You said a friend was supposed to have pulled that stunt with you. Is it just you and this friend working together? Or are there others?"

Had he really thought that he needed to stick around to convince her to hire a bodyguard? Hell, the woman standing up to him now could be one of Cyprian's enforcers.

"Are you working with the police? Undercover? Is that why you didn't call them yesterday? Are you trying to get evidence against my father? To send him to prison?"

He very nearly laughed at that suggestion. Cyprian would never see the inside of a courthouse. The Council would never allow that.

"Answer me." She crossed her arms like a mini-warrior, glaring up at him. Damn, she was beautiful. And her show of courage made him want to smile. But he ruthlessly tamped down that urge, knowing she wouldn't appreciate it.

"No. I'm not working with the police. My turn. What are you going to do now that you know your father is guilty of causing the deaths of these people?"

Her brows rose. "I don't know that he's guilty. I have your word on that. But I don't *know* that."

He frowned. "Then what was the point of showing me the boards, of telling me about your research?"

"I showed them to you because I want you to help me stop whatever's going on."

"But not if it means going after your father."

"I didn't say that."

"Yeah, you pretty much did. Even after everything you've seen, everything you know, you're in denial. You can't see past your loyalty and your love for your father to see the truth. That leaves us with no middle ground. We're on opposite sides." He grabbed his jacket and go bag and strode toward the steps. "I'll call a bodyguard service to send someone out here to take my place."

She caught up to him as he headed into the kitchen. She jumped in front of the door that led into the mudroom and garage, holding her hands out as if she actually thought she could stop him.

"Wait," she said, frustration heavy in her voice. "We're *not* on opposite sides. We both want to stop whatever is going on, don't we?"

He gave her a curt nod.

"Okay. But without proof, I have to cling to the hope that what I know about my father, about the man who raised me, hasn't changed. Inside, he's a good man, with a good heart. There has to be some kind of . . . of conspiracy here. Maybe someone is blackmailing him or manipulating him. Maybe that's what that meeting was about yesterday. I don't know. But I can't do anything about this situation without knowing the facts."

He shook his head in exasperation. "There is no conspiracy. Your father is the head of the snake.

Nothing happens that he doesn't know about or arrange. Whether you choose to believe it or not, every person on those cork boards who has died—and others that you don't even know about—has died or is in danger because of *him*. He might not have killed anyone by his own hand. But he's responsible just the same."

The blood drained from her face. "There are more? Others have died?"

He gave her a curt nod.

She shook her head back and forth. "None of this makes sense. My father is a businessman. He works hard, long hours. He's always at the office. He's got a successful tour company. He's not the evil person you're making him out to be."

He braced his hands on the wall on either side of her, caging her in. "Right. So you snuck upstairs yesterday because you didn't want to miss a legitimate company meeting?"

Anger flashed in her eyes. "I'm not an idiot, Jace. I knew the man he was meeting has nothing to do with the running of EXIT. That's why I wanted to listen in, to gather more evidence, so I can put the pieces together. *So I can stop this.* But I'm not ready to throw my father under the proverbial bus and let him take the fall for whoever is orchestrating everything. I want facts. And it's taking too damn long to get them on my own. Why can't we work together, regardless of our individual opinions about my father's character? We both want the truth."

He laughed harshly. "You definitely don't want the truth."

"You're wrong. I do want the truth. I want to know what's really going on."

He flexed his fingers against the wall beside her. "The truth? Okay, the truth. Your father runs a side of EXIT Inc. that you've never seen, a completely different organization that uses the tour service as a front. While you handle the day-to-day operations of the EXIT Inc. known to the public, your father oversees his own personal team of *assassins*. Professional, trained killers at his beck and call."

Her eyes widened. "No. No, you're making that up. That's absurd."

He wished she was right, but when former enforcers, Devlin and Mason, had recruited his help, they'd shown him proof of Cyprian's deeds. They'd shared pictures, reports, secret documents—with Cyprian's signature on them—culled from EXIT's own computers during an earlier security hack into the system. They'd even had both of their wives— Emily and Sabrina—talk to Jace over the phone, telling him their personal stories about how Cyprian had sent enforcers to kill them, even though they were innocent.

Perhaps the most damning evidence was something he'd found out just two nights ago, when he was watching over Ramsey while the doctors were working on him. Austin had been on the phone, asking for updates, and was convinced that Cyprian had to be behind Ramsey's getting hurt. When Jace had asked Austin why he was so convinced, Austin told him that he was in a wheelchair, and had nearly been burned to death, because of Cyprian and his men. And here Cyprian's daughter stood, accusing Jace of making everything up about her father.

"Why would I make it up? Oh, the assassins— your father calls them enforcers—didn't know they were hurting innocent people at the time. And there are plenty of missions that don't involve killing anyone. Plus, enforcers certainly weren't hurting innocent people in the beginning. But things changed. Instead of being assigned to take out terrorists and other bad guys, their orders were lies, fabrications, making the innocent look guilty. Cyprian, and his assistant at the time, sold the enforcers' services to the highest bidder. And to cover it up, Cyprian gave orders to kill the very men who'd sworn their loyalty to him."

She shook her head, her long dark hair flying out around her. "No, that's ridiculous. And horrible. Stop lying."

"Everything I just said is the stone-cold truth. The people who work for your father, these enforcers, are supposed to enforce the law, *preemptively*. Meaning, they take out bad guys before they act, before they kill others. Or at least, that's what they were supposed to do originally. But all of that has changed. It's out of control, and innocent people are paying the price with their lives. That's why the Council appointed a Watcher, to keep an eye on him."

Her eyes widened. "Council? Watcher?"

He blew out a breath. He hadn't meant to tell her about the Council or the Watcher. But he supposed now that he'd mentioned them, there wasn't any reason not to tell her the rest—as long as he kept the Equalizers out of it.

"A Council of six men and women is the liaison between the government and EXIT, so the government can distance itself from what happens. Very few enforcers even know about the Council. But a select group did, and involved the Council last year to rein in your father's excesses. The Council agreed that something had to be done. They put Cyprian on some kind of probation and appointed a Watcher, whose identity only the Council knows, to secretly watch your father and report regularly to the Council."

He waved his hand impatiently. "All of that is irrelevant. The point is that the Council's actions haven't gone far enough. What they should have done is dismantle the enforcement side of EXIT completely. No matter who heads up the clandestine side of the company, the lure of absolute power vested in one person is too great, too dangerous. The killing has to stop. Your father has to be stopped. EXIT has to be destroyed."

Her mouth fell open. "You really believe everything you're telling me, don't you?"

He snorted. "Hell, Melissa. I not only believe it, I know it."

"Then prove it. *Show* me."

If he did, he'd be skirting too close to the truth, that Cyprian's enemies were united against him as the Equalizers. That they were growing stronger every day and poised to make a difference. But he couldn't go there, couldn't tell her about that. Not without betraying his friends. And not without risking their lives, risking that Cyprian might go after them before they were ready, and able, to withstand such an attack.

"I can't do that," he said.

"Why not? Because you *have* no proof?"

"This argument is pointless. We're done here."

He lifted her out of his way and headed into the garage. She cursed behind him as the security panel started beeping, forcing her to shut off the alarm while he got into his car.

The garage door was only half-raised when the Buick's passenger door opened and Melissa hopped inside, shoving her arms in a jacket she must have grabbed on her way through the mudroom.

Damn it. He should have locked the door. "Get out. We're not discussing this anymore."

"Just because you're ready to end the conversation doesn't mean that I am. Your goal on that mountain was to get me to trust you, and hire you at EXIT, so you could snoop around, right?"

"Well, it sure as hell wasn't because I admired your father and wanted to work with him."

"Stow the sarcasm, Atwell. I'm being an adult here. Join me."

He gunned the engine. "Get. Out."

"You wanted a way to get into EXIT," she snapped. "I can help with that. As far as my father knows, nothing has changed. You're still my bodyguard. We can use that to get you back inside, to do whatever snooping you want."

He searched her eyes. "You really mean that."

"I'm not cracking jokes here. Yes, I mean it."

"Why would you help me get into EXIT?"

She threw her hands up in obvious frustration. "I already told you. I want the facts. Not conjecture. Even before I came downstairs this morning, I called Jolene and told her we weren't going in to the office. I had her reschedule my meetings. She thinks I'm taking you around to the tour outposts to give you a better understanding of what we do, so you can weigh the dangers, figure out how to keep me safe no matter where I have to go. No one except me knows that you aren't what you seem. I want to be your partner in this investigation. I want to help you."

He shook his head. "That doesn't make any sense, not after everything we just said to each other."

She clenched her fists in her lap. "I have to stop you from destroying my father."

He leaned across her and popped open the passenger door. "And that, Melissa, is why you're getting out of this car. We're on opposite sides of this war. That makes us enemies, not allies."

"That's where you're wrong." She slammed the door shut and pressed her hand against his chest.

He swore and backed away, or tried to, but his shoulders were too broad to allow much room to maneuver. He lifted her hand off his chest. "Get out," he repeated.

She twisted in her seat to face him. "No. I didn't ask for this *war*, as you call it, or to be dragged into the middle of it. But that's exactly what my father, and you, have done—dragged *me* into the middle. And now that I'm here, I'm not going anywhere. I deserve a chance to prove that he's not the man that you think he is. I deserve a chance to . . . to . . ."

"To what?"

"To *save* him."

He groaned and let his head fall back against the headrest.

She relentlessly continued her assault. "If EXIT the tour company is really a front for some . . . assassin side of EXIT, and innocent people are dying, then someone else is involved, pulling the strings. I know my father has his faults. And I can't ignore that it looks like he's probably done some bad things. But I also know he wouldn't hurt innocent people if there was any way he could stop it. Someone else has to be behind that. If we work together, we can find the real person responsible."

He stared at the roof of the car above him. "And what if the person who's responsible for everything *is* your father?"

"I'll . . . I'll cross that bridge when we come to it."

He lifted his head. "What exactly are you offering?"

"I want us to work together, as a team, to make sure that no one else dies. If you think about it, the only thing we disagree about is the identity of the person who caused or ordered those people's deaths. We both want the same thing. Justice."

"Justice." He laughed bitterly. "Do you think we're going to gather evidence, send it to the police, and they'll make an arrest? Is that the justice that you think is going to happen?"

She swallowed hard. "Isn't that what *should* happen?"

"Ideally, yes. But EXIT is a clandestine organization, a powerful company that could destroy the reputations and careers of a lot of powerful people within the government if its secrets are revealed. There won't be any arrests. EXIT's allies, and its enemies, would never allow that to happen."

Her mouth dropped open again. "What are you saying? That once you find the person responsible, you're going to . . ." She curled her fingers around the edge of her seat. "You're going to . . . kill him?"

"If I just wanted to *kill* him, I could have done that already. My goal is to figure out how to shut down the entire organization—including your father. If stopping him means that I have to kill him, then yes, that's what I'll do. Without hesitation. Without regret."

The look of horror on her face, an instant before she turned away, had him despising himself all over again. His angry words had spewed out like venom. When had he become such an unfeeling jerk?

She smoothed her hands across the denim over her thighs and cleared her throat, twice. "I need to show you something." Her voice was so quiet that he had to lean toward her to hear her.

"I need you to understand the type of man that I see when I look at my father. Please. Give me two hours. That's all I ask. Two hours, and an open mind."

He sighed heavily. "Melissa, there's no point. Whatever you want to show me doesn't matter. It won't change anything."

She pinned him with an accusing glare, her eyes glittering with unshed tears. "The man you hate so damn much is my father, Jace. *My father.* He's the only family I have left, the only person in the world who loves me. All I'm asking is for two hours of your precious time. Surely a life, any life, is worth two hours before you condemn someone."

He winced, unable to deny the wisdom of her words, unable to deny *her*. "All right. Two hours." He shifted into reverse. "Where are we going?"

She let out a ragged breath and settled back in her seat. "To the cemetery."

Chapter Nine

Granite and marble headstones in gray, black, and pink marched in somber rows across the winter-dead grass. As Jace weaved his way through the graves behind Melissa, he couldn't help thinking there was nothing sadder and more depressing than touring a graveyard when everything around it looked just as dead as its inhabitants.

The trees had dropped their leaves long ago and looked like lifeless, arthritic sentinels keeping watch over the souls interred here. And what few flowers had been placed against the headstones had succumbed to the frost and were now curled and drooped over the edges of their marble vases.

But the tombstones didn't hold his attention for long. It was the thick trees behind the iron perimeter fencing that had the hairs sticking up on the back of his neck. Because if he were the man in the ski mask and wanted to kill Melissa, those trees would be the perfect vantage point for a rifle. One squeeze of the trigger, and the gunman could melt into the trees, knowing the fence would give him the head start he needed to get away.

Thinking like a SEAL, or in this case a bodyguard, was second nature. And it was still his job, as far as he was concerned, regardless of what happened at the end of the two-hour reprieve he'd given Melissa.

After scanning the trees and bushes for a potential assailant, he looked back at the graves they were passing. He couldn't help noticing that the tombstones were getting smaller and smaller. Many of them had little white lambs etched into them, or statues of angels with their wings spread protectively and marble tears running down their sad, cold faces.

His heart stuttered when he realized this section of the cemetery was essentially a baby graveyard. He stopped and read the poem on the stone at his feet, noting the heart-wrenchingly short life span carved into the black granite. He scanned the entire area, shocked at the sheer volume of little markers, all segregated from the rest of the cemetery. Why? Why weren't they mixed in with the larger graves of the adults who'd once loved them?

"They're orphans, mainly." Melissa's soft voice broke the quiet as if reading his mind.

"I don't understand." His voice sounded gritty. He forced a cough to clear it.

She waved her hands toward the dozens of little tombstones. "These are the forgotten and abandoned children that no one claimed. Or babies of families with no money to bury them. Children who were never adopted and spent their short lives in foster care, with no loved ones of their own to lay them to rest in a family plot. The state springs for a tiny bit of land for each of them, but little else. The coarsest coffin. No headstone or vase, just foot markers to show where each grave ends."

"But there are headstones on all of these graves, expensive ones from the looks of them. Statues, poems carved into granite. These don't look like they've been abandoned or forgotten. They're just . . . alone."

She pressed her hand against his chest, right over his heart, making him suck in a breath in surprise. Even through his jacket, he swore he could feel the heat of her fingers, burning him. He should have stepped back. But her hand felt too damn good for him to dredge up the will to move. And after their heated arguments earlier, he craved the softer emotions between them, if nothing else than to make him feel better about the hurt that he'd caused her. And *would* cause her.

"My father was at a charity dinner years ago when someone spoke about losing a loved one and burying them in this cemetery. They were shocked to see a forlorn section back here with overgrown weeds and barely anything to mark each little grave. My father couldn't bear the idea of children being forgotten like that. He immediately established a trust to rehabilitate this part of the graveyard. That trust continues to this day, ensuring that each child buried here will always be treated with respect, and love, and given the best that humanity can offer as their final resting place. Does that sound like an evil man to you? Someone capable of killing innocents?"

He reluctantly peeled her hand from his chest and took the step back that he should have taken earlier. He'd seen the true evidence of Cyprian's character. He'd read the names of the people who'd died in the reports from Mason and Devlin. He'd listened to his fellow Equalizers' firsthand accounts about what Cyprian and his men had done to them. And he'd met Austin Buchanan, seen the scars, seen the wheelchair that he was sentenced to use for the rest of his life, all because of Cyprian.

He waved his hand to encompass the small tombstones surrounding them. "Your father sounds to me like a man with a lot of money who thought of a great way to generate goodwill toward his company and get a hefty charitable tax write-off along with it."

Her hand curled around the wings of an angel statue. "You're a cynical man, Jace."

"I'm a realist."

"Then let me show you something else that's real."

She headed toward another section of the cemetery. The rows between the graves gradually widened. The size of the tombstones grew larger. The occasional mausoleum dotted the landscape, often surrounded by ornate, black wrought-iron fences with arched, decorative gates. This was the wealthy section of the graveyard. The dead here might not have been able to take their riches with them when they died, but they'd purchased a fine piece of land for their final resting place.

Melissa opened one of the gates and led Jace inside a whitewashed-stone building with CARDENAS carved over the entrance.

Even though he already knew that Melissa had lost her mother and twin brothers when she was a little girl, it was still a shock to step into a mausoleum and be faced with three marble squares on the wall with the names of her dead family members.

Pictures of them were sealed in glass and affixed

to the marble squares. Knowing that his future actions might destroy what was left of this family had him feeling guilty all over again, like an intruder. Being here felt . . . wrong.

"I can wait outside if you want to spend some time in here alone."

"No. I want you here. I want you to see. Turn around."

Dreading whatever he was about to see, he turned. Pictures and cards, scores of them, filled every available inch of wall space, many of them overlapping. There were birthday cards, anniversary cards, Christmas cards, Easter cards . . . every holiday, every special occasion was represented. Many were faded, yellow, brittle with age. But he could read the flowing script inside some of the newer ones. And they all bore the same signature—Cyprian Cardenas.

Melissa rested her right hand on his jacket sleeve as she studied the wall. He doubted she was even aware that she was touching him. Her need to touch, to connect with what was around her, seemed instinctive, a part of who she was. As if she needed an anchor when the world around her was in turmoil. And he hated that her every touch seemed to reach a little deeper inside him. He needed to stay objective, to guard himself against caring for her.

"It's been over twenty years," she said, her voice solemn. "Twenty years since they died. And in that time, my father has never once missed a holiday, a birthday, an anniversary. Even if he's in the middle of an important trip, he always comes back to leave them a card, a note, some kind of memento: because he loves my mother and brothers, his wife and sons.

He'll never let their memories die. You can't tell me that a man who loves this deeply could be the monster behind all those deaths on my boards."

It amazed Jace that two people could look at the same thing and have completely different interpretations. Where Melissa saw a devoted husband and father with a caring heart, Jace saw a man obsessed and unable to move on with his life. He saw the kind of fanaticism that helped explain why Cyprian was so driven to keep the secret part of EXIT going even after so many things had gone wrong and so many innocent lives had been lost. This mausoleum wasn't his tribute to his family, EXIT was. EXIT was their legacy, Cyprian's way of fighting back, of getting revenge for the losses *he'd* suffered.

He probably justified every death of an innocent as necessary collateral damage, an unfortunate price of making the world safer for others so no one else would suffer the way he still did. If anything, seeing this wall made Jace even more wary of what Cyprian Cardenas might be capable of. And it made him wonder, if his daughter ever came between him and his tribute to his dead wife and sons, if she ever threatened EXIT in any way, what would Cyprian do? Would he remain the loving father she believed him to be? Or would he turn on her, like a rabid dog turning on its owner?

"What about *your* birthdays?" he asked.

She frowned. "What do you mean?"

"Does your father drop everything he's doing to come see you every year on your birthday like he does for the dead?"

Her eyes flashed. "Dad and I run a company together. I wouldn't want him to stop important business in another state, or on the other side of the world, just to come back for my birthday. But if I did want him to, he would."

Listening to her justify that her father cared less about his living daughter than he did about the family he'd lost over twenty years ago sickened him. But what bothered him more was that Melissa didn't even seem to realize that she was being slighted. Damn it, she deserved better. And she needed to understand that Cyprian was *not* the man she believed him to be.

"If he's such a good man, if you really think he's innocent and that he would never hurt anyone, then why are you hiding those boards? Why not march into your father's office and put them on his desk? Why not demand that he explain all the connections between the living and the dead? And why they all point back to him?"

Her eyes widened.

Jace grabbed her upper arms. "You can't, can you? Because you're afraid. You're afraid that if you show him those boards, you'll see the truth in his eyes. And then you won't be able to deny what's in front of you anymore."

"Let me go," she demanded.

He released her, fully expecting her to break down, or slap him—which he deserved, or maybe even stalk out of the mausoleum. Instead, as she had several times already, she surprised him. An eerie calm settled over her, and she held out her hand.

"There's one more thing that I have to show you."

He hesitated. "Melissa. I don't think—"

"Just one more thing. Then I'm done."

He looked at the walls of photographs and cards,

not sure how much more *he* could take of Melissa's ill-placed faith in her father, a man who deserved no such faith. "Okay. Just one more thing."

He put his hand in hers, and she pulled him with her through the entryway. She led him up and down the rows to another section of the cemetery. And then he saw them—a grouping of three graves set slightly apart from the others, all with the same last name etched into the granite. His mouth went dry. *No. Keep going.*

She slowed. Then stopped. Right in front of the first marker. And slowly traced her fingers across the name.

Thomas Hightower.

She looked up at him. And the truth was in her eyes.

He grabbed for his pistol, then froze. Too late. The derringer in her hand was small, but just as lethal as his SIG Sauer nine millimeter. She must have had it with her all along, probably in her jeans pocket when she'd come downstairs with the boards. Mason Hunt had been right about her. She knew what had happened to the Hightower family, and she couldn't be trusted. Jace slowly raised his hands and laughed bitterly. "I should have known that when you told me you only had two guns, you were lying. After I found those two in your office last night, I should have kept searching."

"You wouldn't have found this one. It was under my pillow."

"Like any good Cardenas."

Anger flashed in her eyes again. "Like any woman who lives alone in a remote area. I keep it for protection."

"And you need protection from me?"

"At the moment, yes. Back up." She motioned with the derringer.

He moved a few feet away from her.

"A couple more," she said. "I don't want you lunging at me before I'm finished."

"Finished with what?" He stepped back two more feet.

"With my story. I still have twenty minutes."

He scanned the graveyard, the stands of trees, the mausoleums down the hill. Her heavy sigh drew his attention back to her.

"There isn't anyone else here," she snapped. "I didn't bring a team of assassins with me." Her lips curled with bitterness. "You know, like any good Cardenas would."

"Melissa—"

"Toss your gun."

Stupid. He'd been so stupid. He never should have let his guard down around her. He dropped his hand by his holster.

She steadied the derringer dead center at his chest. "Slowly."

Very carefully, he pulled the SIG out, then threw it a few yards away. "Now what?"

"Now, you listen."

She gestured toward the Hightower tombstones. "Thomas died first. His parents died several months later. I never met them." She fisted her free hand at her side. "I'm not sure if I loved Thomas or not. I could have loved him. Eventually. I certainly fell for him, hard. We dated for several months. And then he was killed, in a mugging, downtown."

"He was killed by an enforcer, with orders from your father. No point in sugarcoating it."

Her gaze snapped to his. "You may be right. I don't know. But I'd never heard of enforcers until you told me about them."

"You expect me to believe that? While you're pointing a gun at me?"

"I expect you to listen."

He gave her a curt nod, and watched, and waited for his chance. For that moment when she'd be distracted, and he could get the gun away from her—hopefully without getting either of them killed.

"It was only after Thomas's death that I found out that he'd played me for a fool," she continued. "He was married."

Jace let her talk. It didn't matter. None of this was news. Mason had already told him everything about the Hightowers, because Sabrina Hightower was Mason's wife.

"My father never met Thomas. I'd mentioned him, of course. And I'd hoped to get them together one day, but their schedules never worked out. Of course, now I know it's because Thomas was using a fake last name and didn't want my father to find out. He was using me. I was just a . . . a fling to him."

The fingers of her free hand made swirling motions on her jeans, plucking at the loose threads and letting them fall. But the derringer in her other hand never wavered. "The Hightowers are a prominent family in Colorado. The grandfather made a fortune in mining. So when his grandson was killed, the story went viral. That's how I found out the truth—I saw Thomas's picture on the news, along with his true last name."

Her eyes looked haunted as she swallowed. "I was devastated, both by his death and his deception.

But I couldn't just ignore what we'd had together. Whether I meant anything to him or not, he'd meant something to me. I had to . . . I needed . . . closure. I went to the funeral they held in that open field where they hold all of the services here, at the other end of the graveyard, behind you."

She waved, but he didn't dare turn around to see what she was talking about.

"I stood far back, so I wouldn't intrude," she continued. "But Thomas's sister still noticed me. I think she was . . . curious . . . and tried to find out who I was. I took off, never saw her again. But that wasn't the end of it. I remembered later that I'd heard the Hightower name before, *before Thomas was killed*, when I didn't even know that he was lying about his last name."

He frowned. Mason hadn't told him this part. "Where had you heard it?" he asked softly.

"At EXIT. It was really late, and I was in the parking lot heading to my car. I heard voices, two men talking beside a truck a few aisles over. I wasn't trying to listen, but I heard Thomas's name—the fake name that he'd given me—and I froze. They mentioned my father, and the name Hightower. It didn't make any sense that night, and I felt guilty eavesdropping, so I quietly hurried to my car. A few days later, Thomas was dead, and I saw his picture on the news and realized that Hightower was his real last name. And I remembered the conversation in the parking lot."

"Did you ask your father about it?"

"I did. He was angry that a man I'd been dating was killed. And he was shocked on my behalf that Thomas had lied about who he was, about being married. He claimed not to have any idea who might have been in the parking lot and why they were there. I believed him because I *wanted* to believe him, because I *needed* to believe him. But months later, I heard him on the phone with our IT guy. And I knew . . . I knew something wasn't right." A tear spilled down her cheek, and she impatiently wiped it away. "That's the day I started those boards."

He braced himself against her tears, against feeling sorry for her. She didn't deserve his sympathy, not when she was aiming a gun at him. "What's the point of all of this?"

"I'm a good person, Jace. I follow the rules. I pay my taxes. I obey the law."

"Except for the one that says not to point guns at people?"

She frowned. "I've never hurt anyone. Ever. I'm a good person. Even if my father isn't."

"On that we agree."

"Damn it." Her knuckles whitened around the grip of the derringer. "I'm trying to make a point here."

"What *is* the point? Why did you really bring me here?"

"I brought you to the cemetery because I thought . . . I hoped . . . that I could show you those little tombstones and make you see a side of my father that most people don't know about. I wanted you to know how deeply he has loved, and lost. I wanted you to feel some compassion."

He took a step toward her.

She shook her head violently. "No. Let me finish. I could see in the mausoleum that nothing was getting through. You're never going to have empathy for my father. But I thought, maybe, if I bared my soul, if I told you everything that I knew, that you might have empathy for *me*."

She waved toward the tombstones beside her. "I've lost everything. My mother, my brothers . . . Thomas. And even if my father isn't the person that I thought he was, that I wish he could be, I can't bear to lose him, too. If you ever hold my father's fate in your hands, and you can't show mercy for *his* sake, please, *please*, show mercy for *mine*."

He clenched his jaw. "In other words, you're trying to manipulate me. You want me to feel sorry for you, and because I feel sorry for you, you want me not to hurt your father."

"Yes." Her voice was bleak, bitter. Honest. She slowly turned the gun around, offering it to him.

He lunged forward and grabbed it. But when he hefted the derringer, he realized it was light. Too light. When he saw why, he stared at her, stunned. "It's not loaded."

"Of course not. I would never point a loaded gun at you."

"Ah, hell. Now why'd you have to say that?" He cursed himself for a fool and pulled her to him, crushing her against his chest. She let out a soft cry and tightened her arms around his waist. As she soaked his jacket with her tears, he brushed his hands through her soft, silky hair, whispering nonsensical words of comfort. And it dawned on him, that in spite of everything, he trusted her. *And she trusted him.*

Which wasn't necessarily a good thing.

He'd made a vow, sworn his allegiance to his band of brothers. He'd promised to keep their secrets, to keep their very *existence* a secret. And he was honor-bound to keep trying to find a way to bring Cyprian and his empire down.

But where was the honor in destroying EXIT if an innocent woman was destroyed in the process?

The whole reason that the Equalizers were going after EXIT was because it had strayed from its original charter of protecting innocents. How were the Equalizers, how was *he*, any better than Cyprian Cardenas if they were willing to sacrifice Melissa to achieve their goals?

He had to talk to Mason. He had to make him see that what they were doing was just as wrong as what EXIT was doing. Somehow, he had to convince the Equalizers to trust the daughter of their enemy.

Chapter Ten

"What the hell were you thinking?" Mason Hunt swore through the phone.

Jace winced and shifted his stance on the sidewalk. When Mason had picked up on the first ring, Jace had been relieved, hoping that meant Mason was back in town now, and they could work as a team. But that wasn't looking very likely at the moment, at least not the team part. Mason was royally pissed.

At Melissa's questioning look from inside the café, he smiled reassuringly. She smiled back and took another sip of her broccoli cheddar soup.

"I was thinking that my cover with Melissa was blown, and I had two choices: give up, or devise a new plan, another way to get into EXIT. I found another way."

"The hell you did." Mason swore again. "Look. I know she's beautiful—"

"That's not why I agreed to work with her."

"I'm sure you don't *think* that's the reason, but can you absolutely swear it wasn't a factor? If she weren't so sexy, are you certain that you wouldn't have told her no?"

He'd like to think he wasn't that shallow, that he'd still have agreed to help a woman in need in spite of her looks. But, of course, he *couldn't* swear to it. Which was Mason's point.

"Arguing over this isn't going to change anything," Jace said. "What's done is done."

"She's probably using you, to see if you're working with anyone else. You know that, right? How much have you told her about us?"

Jace gritted his teeth. "Not one damn thing. I wouldn't tell her about the Equalizers without your approval. She doesn't even know our team exists. She thinks I'm calling an old Navy buddy to see if he can help us out. Look, I just want to arrange a meeting. Let me bring her in to meet you. I can blindfold her and make sure she can't tell anyone where home base is. Just because the original plan failed doesn't mean the mission is over. The goal remains the same—to make sure that no more innocent people die at the hands of EXIT's corrupt leadership. If we all work together, we can still accomplish that goal, in a different way."

"*Your* goal. Not *our* goal. Not anymore."

Jace grew still. "What are you saying?"

"I'm saying that we almost lost a man. Yes, Ramsey's already up and around, joking and pretending he's not in pain, as if his injuries weren't serious. But you and I both know he would have died if it weren't for you. You saved my best friend's life. And you'll always have my gratitude for that. But that gratitude doesn't extend to putting the rest of the team in danger unnecessarily."

"The team won't be in danger. I told you that I'd blindfold her. It's just a meeting, Mason."

"A meeting where you reveal to a *Cardenas* that the enforcers that Cyprian thinks have gone dormant, given up their fight, are actually actively recruiting. If he finds out that we've organized into a counteragency, and that we're ramping up for an all-out war to bring him down, he'll throw everything he has at us. We're not ready for that. He could decimate us before we even have a chance. So, no, it's not *just* a meeting. Don't worry about your mission anymore. It's officially canceled. You're out of the Equalizers."

"Mason, you're overreacting. There's no reason to—" The line clicked. The call went dead. Jace kept his face carefully blank in spite of the urge to shout. He didn't want to alarm Melissa. Which, of course, lent weight to Mason's belief that his attraction to her could be clouding his judgment.

He'd hoped the Equalizers would agree to meet with her and decide for themselves whether her stated desire to stop EXIT's abuses was legit. And then, if they agreed she could be trusted, he'd know that he hadn't completely lost his ability to judge someone's character. Then maybe they could work as a team, including Melissa, to get this job done.

But there was no chance of that now. As far as Mason was concerned, Jace no longer existed. Because Mason didn't trust him. That stung. Jace had never, not once, been disloyal to a teammate—be they a Navy SEAL, bodyguard, or an Equalizer— and he never would. But he couldn't turn his back on someone in need either. And Melissa definitely needed his help.

Tarek and Sebastian had acted suspicious of *him* yesterday. And they'd also acted suspicious of *her*, especially Tarek. That innocent comment her father had thrown out about not realizing she liked eggs had Tarek suddenly watching Melissa with extreme interest. Had he mentioned his concerns to Cyprian? Was her father suspicious of her, too? And there was still the driver of that van to worry about. What was his connection to Melissa? Would he try to go after her again?

With all of those concerns, and all of those players in the mix, he was completely on his own. No backup. No teammates to help him. No sounding board for any decisions. He blew out a breath in disgust. Hell, this wasn't the first time he'd been in enemy territory with no one to rely on but himself. He'd make this work. He had to. Or Melissa would pay the price.

He put his phone away and headed into the diner.

Her welcoming smile faded as he sat across from her. "I have a feeling that call didn't go as planned."

"Not exactly." He took a sip from his water glass and scanned the café. It was only eleven in the morning, too late for breakfast, too early for lunch for most diners. Aside from a couple of teenagers who'd obviously ditched school and were whispering in the first booth, he and Melissa were the only patrons. Which was why he'd chosen this place for their meal.

He shoved his half-eaten burger and fries away since they were mostly cold now anyway and rested his forearms on the table. "We're on our own."

She nodded, not looking surprised. "Is it because of me? Your friend doesn't trust me?"

"He's . . . cautious. Don't worry. I've got a Plan B. I'd originally hoped to use a job at EXIT to sneak into the computer room. I'd directly access EXIT's mainframe to get around any firewalls and security algorithms. But I can't do that now, not after the way Tarek and Sebastian were acting yesterday. They'd never let me out of their sight."

"What kind of information do you want?"

"Personnel files from the enforcement arm of the company, files that won't be kept on any human resources database. We need to establish all the players, get logistical information, mission details. The more we know, the better prepared we'll be to come up with a plan to dismantle the company from the inside out."

"Can't I get that for you? No one would question my going into the computer room."

He shook his head. "No way. Your father's assistants are just as suspicious of you as they are of me. We can't risk it, even if you could figure out how to get past the tour layer into the enforcement layer. It's too dangerous."

"Then what can we do? What's Plan B?"

"Your father."

"Okay. So, what, you want me to sneak into his office while he's in a meeting? See if he has any of these files that you want?" She smoothed her jeans. "I'll have to go home and change first. He'd throw a fit if he saw me at the office in denim."

"You're not going to EXIT."

She paused with her diet soda halfway to her lips. "I'm not?"

"Your father is from a different generation. He's

old-school, pretechnological age. I'm betting that he keeps physical backups of key files, paper copies. And I'm also betting that he wouldn't store them with the tour company's backups. He'd keep them somewhere else, completely separate, somewhere he has absolute control. A place where he'd never expect anyone to look for the files, so he won't have the types of security they have at EXIT."

She frowned. "And where would this amazing place be that my security-paranoid father wouldn't keep as secure as EXIT?"

"His house. Should be easy to get in because you probably have a key and his alarm code. Just like he has yours. But there aren't any security guards, or nosey executive assistants around."

She shook her head. "No, no, no. Working together to find the truth is one thing, but snooping through my father's home is unnecessary and disrespectful. Not happening."

"Are you going to tell me that in all the time that you've been working on those boards, you've never once searched a medicine cabinet in his house, or thumbed through a file on his desk?"

Her cheeks flushed. "That's different. I didn't bring someone with me, someone who's his enemy."

"Have you already changed your mind about finding the truth?"

"Of course not. I just think there has to be a better way. I'm happy to take you to the office. But I'm not taking you to my father's home. That's his sanctuary. It would be a terrible violation of his privacy. It would be the ultimate betrayal, disloyal."

He tossed his napkin on the table. "Then I guess

we're done. I'll take you back home, we'll say our good-byes, and call it a day. I'll get that bodyguard company I mentioned to send someone over."

She grabbed his arm, her dark brows an angry slash. "Knock off the threats and bullying tactics. Okay, I'll do it. But I don't like it. When do you want to go?"

Jace knew an awful lot about Melissa and her family, including the people who worked for them: the housekeeper she shared with her father, Cyprian's cook, his chauffeur. He knew their schedules, and already knew that right now would be the perfect window of time to go to the house. But since she'd be furious if she knew that he knew all of that, he played dumb on the details.

"What time does Cyprian get home?"

"Six thirty or seven most days."

"Where's his house?"

"Twenty minutes outside of Boulder, on the opposite side of town from my house."

He glanced at his watch. "If we leave now, we can be in and out long before he gets there."

"You want to go *now*? Right this minute?"

"Are you finished eating?"

"Yes."

"Then why wait?"

"Fine. But we'll have to think of an excuse for going over there when he's not home. Silvia will be there, of course. Richard arrives around four, I think. Before you ask, Richard Kellar is my father's chef, has been for years. He doesn't live at the mansion anymore. He has his own house and a catering business downtown. But since my father fronted him the money for his business, and refuses to let Richard pay him back, Richard still cooks him dinner every night before he goes to the restaurant. Dinner's always in the refrigerator, ready to be re-heated when my father gets home."

Jace tapped his fingers on the table, thinking it through. "Do you ever go to your father's house when he isn't there?"

"Rarely, like if I need to get something out of the attic. I've got a lot of old files up there, archives from EXIT from before I bought my house."

"Where does your father keep *his* files?"

"I assume in his home office. It's on the first floor. It's always locked. And, no, I don't have a key and have never been in there without him."

"Locks aren't a problem for me. Getting into his office without the housekeeper seeing us is the con-cern. But we'll figure that out once we arrive."

She didn't look happy about his plan. In fact, she looked downright miserable. But she was going along with it anyway, and she'd agreed quickly with little convincing. That surprised him and had him feeling uneasy. Trust could only go so far, especially when family ties were involved. He would do well to keep Mason's warnings in mind, just in case Me-lissa's guilt over essentially betraying her father won out over her desire to right the wrongs he'd done.

She signaled the waitress to bring their check, then frowned. "I just realized I ran out of the house so fast earlier that I didn't get a chance to grab my purse. I don't have any credit cards with me."

"We're not paying with credit. That leaves an electronic trail. Cash only, from here on out."

"Why would an electronic trail matter? We're just having lunch."

"You also told your admin that we were visiting EXIT outposts today. Are any of them near this diner?"

She slowly shook her head. "No. No, they aren't. But neither is my father's house. I'm sure he'll find out about our being there, eventually, even if Silvia or Richard don't tell him. For one thing, I'll have to shut off the alarm to get inside. He'll know the alarm was turned off."

"I agree. But since you've been there before to get files out of the attic, that's the excuse we can use this time, too. We *don't* have an excuse for being at this diner, which just happens to be the first decent restaurant on our way into town from the cemetery. We don't want anyone knowing any of our movements if we can keep them secret. It gives us more options if we need to make up cover stories later." He tossed a couple of twenties onto the table. "Time to see if you have any burglary skills."

MELISSA STOOD UNDER the massive portico that could probably hold back the pelting rain of a hurricane, if Colorado had hurricanes, and fit her key into the lock. Guilt gnawed at her for abusing her father's trust, but no more so than the guilt she'd feel if he'd done everything Jace believed he'd done—or if, God help her, he really was involved somehow in Thomas's death—and she did nothing to stop him or bring him to justice.

She pushed the eight-foot-tall front door open, one without any glass in it because her father believed all doors should be solid enough to stop heavy artillery.

Stepping into the two-story circular foyer, she

disabled the alarm and looked around. "Silvia? It's Melissa." She tugged off her coat and laid it on one of the benches against the wall. No answer. She turned to tell Jace that Silvia was probably cleaning another section of the house. But he hadn't followed her inside. He was leaning into the back passenger side of his car, apparently getting something out of the duffel bag he'd thrown in the backseat earlier.

"Jace?"

He straightened and shoved something into his pocket. "Right behind you." He strode across the brick pavers and jogged up the steps.

"What were you doing?" she asked.

He tossed his jacket onto the bench with hers. "I was, oh, hello." He smiled and looked past her.

She turned around.

Silvia stood in the middle of the foyer, a duster in her hand, her eyes wide with surprise. "Miss Melissa? Something is wrong?"

Leaving Jace to close the door, she hurried to the housekeeper. "No, no. Sorry. Did we frighten you? I'm sorry if we did."

Silvia patted her hand. "It is my turn to be startled, no? You come to visit me?"

Guilt had her face flushing warm. She kissed the older woman's cheek. "I should definitely do that more often than I do. I'll come see you sometime soon. But not today. I'm here on business. I need to look through some of my old client files that have been archived off the computer. If I can target some discount programs at clients who gave us great reviews but never booked second trips, we might be able to create a bump in our summer tour reservations." She waved toward Jace. "This is Jace Atwell.

He works with me now. He's going to help carry anything heavy."

He took Silvia's hand in his and pressed a kiss against her knuckles. "You must be the infamous Silvia Conti. Mel speaks very highly of you."

Melissa blinked. *Mel?*

Silvia's eyes widened before a smile lifted the wrinkles around her mouth. Melissa wasn't sure, because of Silvia's olive complexion, but she just might have blushed.

"Mr. Jace." She waggled her finger at him. "I am too old for this flirting nonsense. Save it for the younger ladies."

He clicked his heels together and bowed, actually bowed.

"My apologies, madam." He drew Melissa's arm into the crook of his elbow and winked. "I'll be sure to ply my wares elsewhere in the future."

Melissa's mouth fell open. *Who was this man?*

Silvia put her hands on her hips, the duster's bright pink feathers providing a startling contrast to her drab brown uniform. "You need my help?"

"No," Melissa said.

"Yes," Jace said.

What was he doing? Having Silvia shadow them would make it pretty much impossible to sneak into her father's office.

He let Melissa's hand go and gestured to encompass the foyer. "This is quite an impressive home. How many square feet? Seven thousand?"

"Eight thousand two hundred forty-two," Silvia answered. "You want the grand tour?"

Jace's eyes lit with interest. "Miss Conti, I would be delighted, although due to our schedule, perhaps

I could have the mini-tour, just some of the main rooms downstairs. Would you mind? I wouldn't want you to go to any trouble."

Melissa lifted her hands in question behind Silvia's back.

He ignored her and headed off toward the left side of the house, with Silvia prattling on about crown molding and Prussian carpets. Melissa didn't know what she was supposed to do. Follow them? Try to break into her father's study and snoop around? They'd never talked about taking a tour.

Jace stuck his head around the living room archway. "You coming, Mel?"

What was with him calling her Mel all of a sudden, a nickname she'd always hated growing up? Funny how she didn't hate it when he said it. It actually sounded kind of . . . sweet.

"Mel?" he repeated.

What was she supposed to say? "Um, yes?"

He nodded approvingly.

She hurried to catch up and fell in step beside him as Silvia led them from the drawing room into the formal dining room at the front of the house. When Silvia turned to point at one of the paintings on the wall and recite its history, Melissa tugged on Jace's sleeve to get him to lean down.

"What are you doing?" she whispered.

In answer, he reached into his pocket and pulled out a handful of dime-sized metallic circles that were flat on one side with tiny suction cups on the other side.

"What are those?" she whispered.

He bent closer to her ear but Silvia suddenly turned around. Jace closed his fingers over whatever he was holding and pressed a kiss against the side of Melissa's neck.

She jerked in response, too shocked to even try to hide her surprise. And too surprised by the way her entire body flushed with heat from that tiny little touch to do more than stare at him with wide eyes.

Silvia shook her duster at them. "Not in my house, young mister and miss. Respect. You must respect Mr. Cyprian's home."

Since Melissa's nerve endings were still firing sparks all over her body, she didn't even try to respond to her housekeeper's chiding.

"Sorry, had to distract her," Jace whispered before straightening. And then he was rounding the dining-room table, his hand trailing underneath the carved top as he apologized to Silvia for his behavior. Somehow he managed to steer the conversation into a discussion about the silver tea service on the sideboard, and a moment later, to another one of the paintings, which he ran his hands around as if enthralled.

When they paused in the doorway to the kitchen, Jace turned. "Mel? Are you joining our little tour?"

"Used to live here, remember? For over twenty years?"

"Good point." He waved toward the table as if he were the host. "We'll be back in a few."

She pulled out one of the chairs and sank down onto the upholstered seat. What had just happened? Her neck throbbed where Jace's hot mouth had branded her skin. That one, incredibly brief touch was like a shock wave pulsing through her body, leaving her tingling and . . . confused.

There was no denying that she found Jace attractive. But until this moment, it had been tempered by the craziness going on around them: the fear, the doubts, the worries about their safety. She'd just never really stopped to think about him in that way.

But suddenly that was the only thing she *could* think of.

She let out a deep sigh and closed her eyes, feeling like a traitor for responding to him the way she had. She shouldn't be thinking about this. But since when did hormones or passion follow the dictates of logic? She sat there for several minutes, keeping her eyes closed, selfishly shying away from the real reason she was there and clinging to the pleasurable memory of that unexpected touch from Jace.

"Melissa?"

She slowly opened her eyes and stared into a pair of stormy gray ones, just inches from hers. Jace was back already? Just how long had she sat there day-dreaming? He was kneeling in front of her chair, his brow furrowed with concern. As if he genuinely cared about her.

A wave of aching loneliness crashed over her. Concern. Wouldn't it be nice if he really did care? She'd felt so isolated, so alone for so long, with no one to share her burdens. It would be so wonderful to feel connected again, wanted . . . cherished. Even if it was just for a moment.

"Is something wrong?" he asked. "Silvia's off cleaning. We can—"

She traced her fingers against his lips.

His eyes flew open wide. "What are you—?"

"I'm so tired of being worried, Jace. I'm tired of second-guessing everything and everyone around me. For just a moment, I'd like it all to go away, to just . . . let go . . . and feel. Do you think you could pretend that you want me, that you care about me, for just one tiny little moment?"

He hesitated, his surprise obvious as he stared at her, as if he were trying to figure out how to turn her request down without being too cruel.

She groaned and dropped her head in her hands, her face flushing with embarrassment. Thank God she hadn't been stupid enough to actually say the words she'd wanted to say. *Kiss me.* "Sorry. Forget it. I shouldn't have asked."

He gently but firmly forced her hands down and cupped her face. "Mel?"

Her breath caught in her throat at the hunger in his eyes. "Yes?"

"I don't have to pretend." He pressed his lips to hers.

Her eyes fluttered closed. Drowning. She was drowning in pleasure. Sweet heavens, this man knew how to kiss. He was torturing her with pleasure, taking her places she didn't even know that she could go with only a kiss. And then he swept his tongue inside and took her to a new plane of existence. She whimpered and dug her fingers into his shoulders, clinging to him, drinking him in. He made a sexy noise deep in his throat and deepened the kiss even more, turning it from sweet to wild to inferno with one wicked sweep of his tongue.

Billy, Michael, Jonah. Thomas.

The memories of her other kisses, in high school, college, and later, flashed through her mind and went up in flames. Forgotten ashes on the hearth two seconds after he parted her lips and stroked her tongue with his. There wasn't a cell in her body that didn't burn for him, yearn for him, clamor for the molten heat of his touch.

Her belly tightened almost painfully, and her breasts grew heavy, hot, readying for . . . *more*. She wanted more. But all too soon the kiss changed, from volcano to a roaring fire, to smoldering heat, then, finally, to a whisper soft caress. It was as if he knew she'd be lost, cast adrift at the absence of his touch if he ended the kiss too soon. So he brought her out of her passionate haze gradually, until he was pressing soft, butterfly kisses against her lips, the corner of her mouth, the column of her throat.

And then he was gone.

But his hands remained, framing her face, anchoring her into the mortal realm instead of the fantasy world where he'd taken her moments ago.

Her eyes fluttered open, and the naked hunger on his face, just inches from hers, had her body mourning for what could never be. There were too many obstacles between them.

"Wow," she breathed.

"Ditto," he whispered.

Gradually the room around her came into focus, surprising her. She'd completely forgotten where they were. And just like that, the beautiful feelings he'd fanned inside her became memories she was forced to tuck away, to take out at some future time when she was alone, and lonely, remembering the magic and wishing for what could never be.

Seeing him on his knees on the dining-room floor sent an entirely new kind of urgency coursing through her. She glanced past him, then looked behind her, before pushing herself upright in the chair and forcing herself to let go of his shoulders.

"Where's Silvia?" she asked.

"After our tour, I convinced her that I could find the dining room on my own. She went off to clean something-or-other."

"We need to get out of here before she decides to check on us." She scooted her chair back and stood. "What do we do now?"

"Not what I want to do, unfortunately," he mumbled beneath his breath as he climbed to his feet. "Come on. Let's go find those files."

He herded her through the living room and into the foyer.

"It's over there," she whispered, motioning toward the door to the right of the stairs.

The barely perceptible shake of his head had her dropping her hand.

"She's already checking on us." His voice was so low she barely heard him. But she shifted their direction toward the main staircase.

They climbed the stairs to the top landing, discussing tours and the fictitious marketing campaign she was supposedly planning. After turning right, they walked down a long corridor, stopping in front of the door at the end.

"This is it." She pulled the door open and flipped on the light inside. A narrow, steep set of stairs greeted them. "What now?" she whispered.

His hand moved to her neck, his thumb tracing across her skin in a gentle caress. He leaned in toward her. "Don't turn around. She followed us. We'll have to keep up the pretense."

He waved his hand for her to precede him up to the attic.

Chapter Eleven

Melissa plopped down on one of the larger boxes and dumped her newest collection of folders on top of another box she was using as a table. She flipped through the first folder, trying to focus on the pages inside instead of the man standing a few feet away, peering out the attic window at the backyard. Because if she thought about Jace, if she thought about what had happened downstairs between them, it just . . . cluttered up everything inside her, confused her.

"Do you think you could pretend that you want me, that you care about me, for just one tiny little moment?"

"I don't have to pretend."

What had he meant when he'd said that? That he didn't have to pretend that he wanted her? Or that he cared about her? Or both? And how could he have given her that scorching kiss that curled her toes inside her sneakers, then act as if nothing life-changing had happened between them? The world had stopped, or tilted, or something. Had that only happened for her?

How humiliating. Somehow, she had to put that

disastrous kiss behind her and pretend it hadn't happened. That it hadn't *mattered*. That it hadn't . . . changed her, awakened her from the cold, bitter shell where she'd existed since Thomas's betrayal. She'd gotten used to being numb, to locking all of those feelings away. Not feeling, wanting, or caring was comfortable, easy. No one could hurt her there.

Damn you for making me feel again, Jace. For making me care.

The pages crumpled in her hand. Great. Now she was destroying important company documents. Documents that really did have useful marketing information on them. She smoothed the papers out and studied them more closely. Yes, this was the kind of data that could give her an advantage in the marketplace. She tossed the folder into the box on the floor and grabbed another folder.

Jace turned away from the window and crossed to her. "That box is already two-thirds full. Don't you think you have more than enough to convince Silvia of our cover story for being here?"

"Maybe," she said, absently. "Huh. I remember these clients. They had a terrific time, gave us glowing reviews. Swore they'd be back the next year. But I'm 99 percent sure they never booked a second tour. I wonder why?"

"I think you might be taking this fake marketing idea too seriously."

"Who says it's fake? Repeat business is the lifeblood of any corporation. If I can use this sampling of clients to try new strategies, I might be able to increase our market share."

Jace motioned toward the window. "Looks like Silvia's taking advantage of the milder temps today."

She leaned over to see out the window. Silvia was wearing a light jacket over her brown uniform, crunching through the melting snow on what would be a manicured, pristine lawn when winter released its hold, and the gardeners worked their magic.

"She's probably going to the greenhouse to cut some fresh flowers." She turned back to her folder. "There's also a stream about a hundred yards back with a bench and a view of the mountains. Maybe she's taking a break and wants to dip her toes in the water, if it isn't iced over. Although, even if it isn't, it's still got to be close to freezing. She's likely to get frostbite. So maybe that's not where she's going." She flipped another page, fascinated by the potential in front of her.

Jace gently tugged the folder out of her hand and grinned. "Earth to Mel. Silvia's out of the house. This is our chance to get inside your father's study. You know, the whole reason we came here in the first place?"

"Oh. I guess I got . . . distracted." Her face flooded with heat, and she started straightening the folders.

"You think?" he teased, laughter heavy in his voice. "We'll take all of these so you can look at them as much as you want later." He tossed the entire stack into the open box. "Come on. We may only have a few minutes before she returns, and I want us to be inside that office by then." He tugged her behind him out of the attic.

When they made it down both flights of stairs without a Silvia-sighting, they hurried to the double doors that guarded her father's domain. Jace set the box down and crouched in front of the keyhole.

"I'll keep an eye out for Silvia." Melissa turned her

back on him, listening intently for the distant sound of a door or footsteps across the polished-marble floors. "How long do you think it will take you to—?"

"You coming or not?" his teasing voice called out.

She whirled around. Jace was standing inside the office, the box of folders sitting on the floor in one of the eight-by-eight-foot rectangular patterns of inlaid wood.

"Huh. That was fast." She stepped into the room, and he locked the doors behind her. "How did you get the door open so quickly?" She kept her voice low, so the sound wouldn't carry. "How did you get it open at all?"

He held up a long, thin piece of metal no larger than a bobby pin. But before she could examine it closely, he slid it into his hair over the top of his right ear. It immediately disappeared.

Her mouth dropped open. "Do you always carry lock-picking tools? In your hair?"

"Always. And that's not all I carry with me."

Was he teasing this time? She wasn't sure. "Okay, I'll bite. What else do you carry?" Her gaze slid down his chest to his hips and back up. "And where do you hide it?"

He grinned. "A gentleman never tells. Come on. Help me search this place. Quietly. We don't want to alert Silvia when she gets back in the house. And make sure that you move only one thing at a time. Put it back exactly the way you found it before moving something else."

It wasn't very comforting that he seemed to be an expert on performing illicit searches. Then again, if he carried lock picks—and other items—all the time, what did she expect?

He weaved his way around the couch and two recliners that formed a conversation group on the left side of the room and went straight to the floor-to-ceiling bookcases.

Melissa chose to start with her father's desk, which dominated the other side of the room in front of a wall of windows. If she took sensitive files home, that's where she'd put them. So it made sense that her father would, too.

She sat in the huge leather chair and feathered her fingers across the smooth, glassy surface of the massive cherrywood desk. It was completely devoid of papers or anything that might mar its beauty, except for an old-fashioned desk phone. But even that was stylish and classic, with cherrywood accents built in. Even the buttons were wood. Expensive, tasteful objects and furnishings were always her father's preference when it came to decorating.

When she opened the top, middle drawer and saw five boxes of fine-quality pens side by side in a neat row, she couldn't help but smile. Only the best. And always in ridiculous quantities. She supposed it was because his parents had grown up during the Great Depression, painfully poor, in a shack that was practically falling down around them. He tended to overcompensate now, buying only the finest, durable goods, and far more than he'd ever need.

Since there was nothing else in the drawer, she closed it and opened the first of three much deeper drawers on the right side of the desk. This one contained folders, but the contents of each one pertained to the tour company. The second drawer down was more of the same, except that the folders were hanging instead of stacked. But again, none of the information would help them.

"Finding anything?" Jace whispered from across the room. He was already halfway through searching the bookcases, and she'd barely gotten through three drawers.

"Nothing so far."

"No laptop anywhere?"

She frowned. "Actually, no. And knowing how my father likes to have backups of everything, I'd expect at least one laptop in addition to the one he takes back and forth to work every day."

"Keep searching." He turned back to the shelves.

The bottom drawer didn't contain a laptop, or folders, or boxes of office supplies. It was completely empty. She closed it and slowly opened each drawer again.

"Something bothering you?"

She started in surprise to see Jace standing beside her.

"Could you please not sneak up on me like that?" she whispered.

"Sorry." He motioned toward the desk. "What is it about those drawers that has you frowning?"

"The bottom one. It's empty. It's a big drawer. It could hold a lot of supplies, but it's empty, while the other drawers are completely full. I suppose it could be so he puts his briefcase inside it each night. That would make sense. I suppose."

"Or it could be empty for another reason altogether." He knelt on the floor and ran his hands along the sides of the drawer. Then he angled his left arm so he could rub the underside of the wood above it. "Ah-ha."

"You found something?"

"Maybe." He sat back on his haunches and looked under the desk. Then he looked at the floor underneath and around it. His eyes lit with excitement. "I think we may have found where your father keeps his confidential files."

She studied the floor beneath the desk. "I don't see anything."

"Not there." He pointed to the rectangular pattern to the right of the desk. "There. See anything different in that section of the floor?"

"No."

He stood and held out his hand. "Come on."

She put her hand in his, and even though she was prepared this time for the heat that flared inside her at his touch, it still amazed her how something as simple as holding this man's hand was like running a blowtorch over every cell in her body. She just wished she wasn't the only one who felt that way. Numb, cold, and lonely was way better than being the only one on fire. And way less embarrassing.

"Do you see it?" He pointed to the eight-by-eight pattern. "The way the sunlight plays along the edges of the rectangle, where the border meets the other rectangles?"

She focused on the floor, trying to see what he saw. She stepped back, letting the sunlight from the windows behind the desk flood across the rectangular patterns. And that's when she saw it—an imperfection, a slight indentation along the edges of two sides of the rectangle that she wouldn't have noticed except for the light slanting through the windows.

"The two longest sides are dented."

"Yes. They are. I think it's a trapdoor."

She blinked. "Seriously? A trapdoor?"

"Seriously. Step back and let me see if I can get it to open."

She eagerly moved back by the couch, not wanting to fall if a trapdoor suddenly swung down.

After rolling the desk chair out of his way, he dropped to his knees behind the desk. He reached underneath the bottom drawer again. A slight clicking noise sounded, but nothing else happened. He tried again. Another click, but again, nothing.

Melissa shook her head. No matter how hard she tried to see it, she couldn't picture her father getting down on the floor like Jace to press a button. He was always proper, obsessed with manners, and looked his best at all times. Which meant he wouldn't risk getting his pants dirty kneeling on a floor, no matter how clean that floor might be.

She hurried to the desk. "I have an idea."

He clicked the button again, but when nothing happened, he climbed to his feet. "Be my guest."

"Out of the way."

He cocked a brow but moved back by the windows. Melissa rolled the chair up to the desk and sat down. She scooted it closer, trying to picture her father's long legs and how close he might sit, adjusting her position.

"What are you doing?"

"Trying to think like my father would. He definitely wouldn't kneel on the floor to open a trapdoor. He would sit in the chair. It's more dignified."

"Dignified?"

"If you knew my father as well as I do, you'd understand that dignified describes him perfectly."

"I believe you. And that's good thinking. But how

would he reach the button if he's sitting down? I have long arms, but I couldn't do that."

"Are you sure that button is the mechanism that operates the trapdoor?"

"I don't see any other purpose for it. However, it's possible it's a return device, rather than the initiating switch. Systematic, not manual or meant to be pressed by human hands."

"In English?"

He grinned. "He might use one mechanism to open the door from up in this room, and a different one for operating it from wherever the trapdoor leads. The button under the drawer might depress remotely from below, and *only* works if triggered from below. Essentially, it's a decoy. That would certainly explain why nothing happened when I pressed it."

"Okay. Not sure I get it, but I'll go with it. He wouldn't leave a drawer open if he doesn't need to press that button. So we're looking for another button somewhere else." She slid the drawer closed and tapped her hands on the desk. Her gaze slid to the only item within her reach with the drawers closed: the phone, and it was *covered* with buttons. "Could the phone operate the door?"

He strode to the desk and studied the buttons, then flashed her another grin. "You'd make a good spy, Mel." He pressed the red button first, then two of the numbers. Nothing happened, but he didn't seem worried. He pressed the red button again, and the same two numbers, in reverse order. This time a click sounded, followed by a low, barely perceptible hum.

He jumped out of the way as the rectangle with

the indentations dropped down about two inches. Then it slid back underneath the rectangle beside it, leaving a large hole in the floor. Lights flickered on below, revealing a set of carpeted stairs.

"Holy cow," Melissa exclaimed.

He pressed his finger to his lips, then motioned toward the double doors.

In her excitement, she'd forgotten about Silvia. "How did you know which numbers to press?" she whispered.

"The red one seemed obvious. But the other two numbers were the most worn."

"So, basically, you guessed."

He smiled. "You'd be surprised how often my guesses pay off."

Jace pulled her chair back. "I'll grab our box. If we find anything worthwhile down there, we can throw it in with the other folders."

She warily eyed the opening in the floor. "You mentioned a return mechanism. That implies that the trapdoor might close after we go down."

"Probably. But I'm sure we'll figure out how to open it again."

"On a scale of one to ten, how sure are you?"

He shrugged. "Seven?"

"That doesn't exactly inspire confidence."

He smiled and retrieved the box from beside the double doors and a decorative table covered with picture frames and waited by the trapdoor. "Ready to explore?"

"No, but I will anyway." She joined him on the top step. A desk and chair were visible below, with bookshelves behind them that were bursting with binders. They might very well have found the secret files that Jace had hoped to find by coming here. "I have to admit that when you suggested the floor might be a trapdoor, I was skeptical. And I'd hoped to find another explanation for those indentations."

"Why?"

She smoothed her hands down the front of her jeans. "Because only people with secrets have trapdoors and hidden offices."

He put an arm around her shoulder. "This will all work out. You're a strong woman. Whatever happens, you'll face it, you'll see it through. You'll be okay." He dropped his arm and headed down the stairs, carrying the box.

She drew a shaky breath as she stood at the precipice and looked down. Jace thought she was strong. Was she? She'd certainly worked long and hard to make it through a difficult course load in college. And she'd been helping steer an incredibly successful company for several years now. But succeeding in the academic world, succeeding in business, required a completely different set of strengths than what she was facing now. And she already knew that she might not want to discover whatever was at the bottom of these stairs. Because if it was anything like what was on her boards back home, the truth was a very scary thing and could change her world forever.

Jace came into view again, looking up at her. "You coming?"

She blew out a shaky breath and nodded. No point in avoiding the truth any longer. Whatever the future held, she would have to face it. And, somehow, she'd have to find the strength to deal with it and do what had to be done. She started down the stairs.

She'd just cleared the opening when a low hum sounded. She turned around. As Jace had anticipated, the trapdoor automatically began to slide over the opening. When the floor clicked into place, and the humming stopped, she rubbed her hands up and down her arms, unable to dispel a feeling of impending doom.

Jace smiled up at her sympathetically, as if he could sense how nervous she was. He set the box of folders on the desk and leaned toward the wall of bookcases behind it, examining one of the hundreds of binders crammed together on the shelves.

Melissa started down the stairs again. But the frayed hem of her jeans caught on a piece of baseboard beside one of the steps, and she lost her balance. She cartwheeled her arms and let out a gasp of alarm. She just managed to grab the banister before she would have hurtled down onto the concrete floor.

Jace whirled around, his brow furrowed in concern. "You okay?"

She shoved her hair back from her face. "No thanks to whoever built these stairs, but yes, I'm fine." She noted how narrow the spacing was between each stair. "The contractor didn't follow building-code regulations, I guarantee that."

"You know all about building codes I suppose?"

"As a matter of fact, I do. I had a ton of renovation work done on my house after I bought it. And I researched everything they did to make sure it met safety standards."

"I wouldn't expect anything less." He pulled one of the binders out and thumbed through it.

She narrowed her eyes. "Are you making fun of me?"

"Nope. Just stating a fact. You're a savvy businesswoman. I wouldn't expect you to blindly accept the word of a contractor without checking behind him." He flipped another page.

"Her."

"Sorry?" He looked up.

"You said checking behind 'him.' How very sexist of you. My contractor was a woman."

His lips twitched. "Touché. And you're absolutely right. I shouldn't have made that assumption. My apologies."

She waved her hands. "Forget it. I'm sorry. That was rude of me." She pointed at the ceiling above them. "I'm just spooked about the door. I hope you're right that we'll be able to figure out how to open it from down here."

"We'll find our way out. No worries." He set the binder down and made a circuit of the room, which was a large rectangle about thirty feet by twenty feet.

Melissa paused on the last step. As with everything associated with her father, this surprisingly large room was clean and orderly. The office portion consisted of the desk, a chair, bookshelves, and filing cabinets along the right side of the room. No laptop though, which was disappointing. They might have been able to find something useful there. The remainder of the space was filled with dozens of neatly stacked boxes in straight rows. And each box had a label. She vaguely wondered if her father had ever lost anything in his life, as organized as he was. Probably not.

"Looks like my father's been storing paperwork down here ever since he created the company."

Jace thumped one of the boxes. "Unfortunately for us, it might be the wrong company. Everything I'm seeing is for the tour side of the business."

"Are you sure? I can't imagine his going to the expense and trouble of creating a room like this just to store regular paperwork. And the attic still has plenty of room. I know he stores paperwork up there, too. I saw the labels earlier."

"Then maybe the labels on these boxes are decoys. I'll open a few and see."

"I'll help." She stepped off the last stair onto the concrete floor.

The lights went out, plunging them into darkness.

CYPRIAN STOOD AT the window in his daughter's office at EXIT Inc., looking down at the parking lot. Normally, he'd see her Jaguar parked below. But, of course, the Jag was still in the body shop getting dents pounded out of it and being repainted.

He pressed his fingers against the windowsill. Whoever had forced her off the road was proving to be an elusive foe. All of his usual contacts had yet to figure out who was responsible. But he wouldn't give up. He would find the man who'd frightened and almost hurt her. And justice would be swift.

He turned around. The desk he'd bought her sat in its usual place, of course. Full of papers, folders, office supplies. But even though the surface was far more cluttered than he would have liked, it was still neat, tidy, organized. Everything had a place and everything was in its place. She was a lot like him in that regard. She was a lot like him in a lot of ways.

Like coming to work every weekday, no matter what.

Neither of them took vacation days. They worked leisure time into their business trips. If they were sick, they suffered through it. And holidays? Sometimes they'd work those, too, when the rest of the company was off with their families celebrating. It all depended on what needed to be done at the time. Fortune 500 companies didn't run themselves. And yet, here it was, midday, and her office was still empty.

"Mr. Cardenas?" Jolene stood in the doorway. "Is there something that I can do for you, sir?"

"Yes. You can tell me where my daughter is. I've been in meetings all morning, and apparently, she never came to work. Sebastian tells me she might have called you?"

"Oh, yes, sir. She did. She's working off-site today."

"Off-site?"

"With that new employee, I mean bodyguard, Jace Atwell. They're touring the outposts. She said he wants to get his bearings with the company and what all we do. Something about planning his security detail around her day-to-day operations."

He smoothed his suit jacket. "Since when do her day-to-day operations include going to outposts?"

"Sir?"

"Never mind." He crossed the room and stopped in front of her. "I need to speak to Melissa. And she's not answering her cell phone. I'd appreciate it if you could find out which outpost she's at right now and ask them to have her call me."

She stepped out of his way. "Of course, sir. Right away, sir."

He gave her a curt smile and headed into his own office. A few minutes later, the desk phone rang. He grabbed it without looking at the caller ID. "Melissa?"

"No, sir. It is Silvia."

He frowned and leaned back in his chair. "Is something wrong?"

"I don't know. Miss Melissa, she came here earlier with Mr. Jace."

He stiffened and sat up straight. "Melissa's at my house? With Jace Atwell?"

"*Sí*. But I can't find them."

"What do you mean, you can't find them?" A sound had him glancing up to see Sebastian standing just inside the doorway. Watching him. As usual. And behind him, Tarek's retreating back as he headed into the hallway. "Silvia?"

"Yes, sir. They went to the attic to get some old files. But when I brought up a snack tray they were gone. I look through the house, nothing. But the black car, Mr. Jace's car, is still out front."

He stood and jerked his suit jacket into place. "Thank you for calling. I'm sure they're fine, probably out touring the property, and they forgot to let you know. But I'll come home and check, just to be sure."

"Thank you, Mr. Cyprian."

He hung up the phone and headed around his desk.

"What's going on?" Sebastian asked.

"I'm going home for a late lunch."

Sebastian arched a brow. "You don't mind if I go with you, do you?"

Hell, yes, he minded. But until he finished dealing with this Council situation, he had little choice. Without a word, he headed out the door, with Sebastian following behind.

Chapter Twelve

J ace stood at the bottom of the steps with his gun out, aiming it up in the direction of the stairs even though he couldn't see them in the pitch-black room. Behind him, Melissa waited in silence, her hands curled into the top of his belt. But after a full minute passed without hearing any sounds or the trapdoor sliding open, Jace shoved his gun into his holster and used the flashlight app on his smart phone.

He aimed the light at the ceiling, casting a small halo around the two of them. "Having the lights switch off must have been some kind of security feature in case someone who has no business being here found their way down here."

"Like us?" She pulled her hands from his belt and stepped beside him.

She sounded dangerously close to insisting they give up their search before it had even begun, so he didn't respond to her remark. "If we split up, we might find a light switch faster. Does your phone have a flashlight app?"

"Yes. But it won't help."

"Dead battery?"

"My phone's in my purse. At home."

"Well, I can see why that might make it difficult to use. Come on. We'll figure this out together. I can't imagine that your father would work in the dark down here. There has to be a light switch."

After searching the desk area again, which seemed the logical spot for a light switch, Jace pulled her toward the left side of the room. But when she looked back toward the desk, without the phone flashlight pointing that way anymore, a green speck of light caught her attention.

"Wait, I see something." She pulled her hand from Jace's and felt her way down the one part of the wall not covered by bookcases, right above the desk.

His light swung toward her.

"No, turn your phone away. I can't see it in the light."

He aimed the phone at the ceiling instead. "See what?"

"A tiny green circle, glowing, like an LED light." She bumped into the desk. There. About a foot up. She ran her hands up to the circle, covering it with her fingers. It was small, but she could definitely feel the outline of a button. She pushed it, and the fluorescent lights overhead flooded the room with light. She grinned triumphantly. "Found it."

Jace was already putting his phone away. "You did indeed." He joined her at the desk and felt the button. "It blends right into the wall. I never would have seen it. Good catch." He checked his watch. "We've already been gone from the attic longer than

I'd hoped. Let's keep an eye out for the door mechanism while we're searching the files. We don't want to be gone so long that Silvia goes looking for us."

A FEW MINUTES later, Jace stood in the middle of the room, scanning everything around him. What was he missing? Something wasn't right.

Neither of them had found a way to trigger the trapdoor, or even any useful files. The desk, bookshelves, and filing cabinets contained only official tour-company documents—probably decoys in case anyone ever managed to find this room. That certainly fit Cyprian's personality and went along with having the lights switch off. But assuming that his true purpose in building this room was to store files from the enforcement side of the company, where would he hide them? And where would he put that damn trapdoor mechanism?

The answer to those questions probably rested with the person who knew Cyprian a lot better than he did.

"Mel, we're going about this all wrong."

They met each other in front of the desk.

"What do you mean?" she asked.

"You figured out how to open the trapdoor upstairs because you put yourself in your father's shoes and did what he would do. That's what you need to do here. Talk it through. You're Cyprian. What's the most logical area to put a mechanism to open the door? And how would you hide documents down here? Or something important enough to warrant building this space?"

"The boxes. There are so many. It makes sense that he'd . . . that I . . . would hide critical documents in at least some of them. Or maybe in the bottom, beneath tour documents."

"Maybe. Probably. But that wouldn't make it easy for quick retrieval if he wanted to come down here and work for a short amount of time, like on a lunch break. Think like him. Be him. What would you do down here? How would you trigger the door?"

She put her hands on her hips and studied the desk, with its wall of bookshelves behind it. "I'm my father. I like things simple, easy. And I'm not a fan of technology even though I have to use it. At work, I have a Rolodex on my desk. The only reason I have a smart phone and know how to use it is because my daughter forced me into the current century a few years ago. But whenever feasible, I use an old-fashioned landline phone instead."

He nodded. "That's it. So what would you do, given those parameters?"

She glanced around the room. "The only good work space is this desk. And I want to be comfortable. I wouldn't stand to look through any files. I'd definitely use the desk, and this chair." She pulled out the chair and sat down, scooting it in just like she had upstairs.

"Economy of movement," she said. "And no more technological gadgets than absolutely necessary." She glanced up at Jace. "There's no phone. And nothing remotely electronic except for one thing."

A slow smile tilted his lips. "The green button."

"Yes, but that turned on the lights."

"Yes, it did. When you pressed it the first time. You said he likes simplicity." He cocked a brow. "Let's find out what happens if you press it again."

She shrugged. "Here goes nothing." She pressed the button.

A faint hum sounded, but not from above. The bookshelves split in the middle and slid back into the wall like pocket doors, revealing another layer of shelves behind them. Those shelves moved forward into place, and the humming stopped.

She shook her head, her eyes wide with wonder. "I'd like to go on record that I'm jealous that my father never showed me this. It's way too cool to keep to himself."

"I'll agree on one thing. It's certainly cool. I'll bet that if we press the button again, the shelves will switch back, and the trapdoor will open. But let's wait before we try it. We may have hit the mother lode, and I want to see if there are any key files that we can use."

The shelves contained row after row of half-inch-thick binders with names and dates on them. Jace moved around the desk, walking down the length of the bookcases, reading the spines. Most of the names and dates meant nothing to him. But since Mason had told him the names of the Council members—information that he and Devlin knew from their recent dealings with the Council after the Hightower debacle—he was mostly on the lookout for binders with those names on them. If he could find files showing that the Council leader—Adam Marsh—or anyone else on the Council knew of and had approved the loss of innocent lives, acceptable collateral damage of civilians, he could use that as leverage to get a "good" Council member to turn. Eventually, the whole Council might follow, a domino effect, until the foundation between the government and EXIT collapsed.

Or if that failed, he could use the information to approach current enforcers. As they learned about the corruption at EXIT, more and more would agree to fight against their employer instead of for him.

He pulled out several promising-looking binders and shoved them into the box of folders they'd taken from the attic. "We can't take very many, or they might be noticed," he warned, since she had a sizable stack on the desk in front of her as well. "They might be noticed anyway, as meticulous as your father seems to be. But hopefully not before it really matters. I recommend that you choose three or four and put the rest back."

She looked a little pale as she held up one of the binders. "This probably trumps anything you found. And it explains why my father hired two assistants instead of just one."

He paged through it, then let out a slow whistle. "A full background on Sebastian and Tarek. Looks like they're badass enforcers. Marsh probably assigned them to shadow your father as part of his probation."

She shot him a strange look. "Marsh?"

"Adam Marsh. The head of the Council. Why?"

"I've heard that name before. I've seen him, too, from a distance. That's the man who met with my father on the top floor of EXIT."

His stomach dropped. But he kept his expression carefully blank so he wouldn't alarm her. He didn't have to ask if Marsh had seen her. Because if he had, she'd already be dead. The realization that she'd come so close to being executed by EXIT's top brass scared the hell out of him.

She flipped through another binder, as if the news about Marsh wasn't a big deal. "He's the one who appointed this Watcher guy that you mentioned back at my house, right?"

"I imagine so, with the consensus of the Council." Devlin Buchanan used to be *"The* Enforcer," Cyprian's main guy, who executed enforcers who went rogue, enforcers who were deemed a threat to the nation's security. Because of that role, he was privy to a lot of insider information about EXIT that most enforcers weren't—including details about the Council. And he'd passed that information to Jace. That gave Jace a considerable advantage to offset the fact that he'd never personally been an enforcer. He knew a hell of a lot about how EXIT operated. But the more Jace knew, the more he was worried about what could happen to Melissa.

"Do you think Sebastian or Tarek could be the Watcher?" she asked.

"I'm sure they report on Cyprian's activities at work. But it's doubtful they're watching him all the time or that either of them is the official Watcher. The idea of a Watcher is someone you never see, or if you do, you wouldn't suspect that they're the person assigned to keep tabs on you. The Watcher is keeping an eye on your father at all times, either through remote surveillance or by being part of his inner circle without your father even realizing it. Or both."

After putting the binder in with the folders, he noticed an odd emblem on the spine of another binder. "This looks strange. A snake coiled around a dagger."

Melissa blinked at him and stared at the binder. "Oh my God."

"What is it?"

She pressed her hand against her throat. "Open it. I need to see what's inside." She abandoned the pages she'd been looking at and stepped beside him.

He frowned but pulled the binder out and opened it on the desktop. When he saw the word printed at the top of the first page, he drew a sharp breath. *Serpentine.* The terrorist group that had killed Melissa's mother and brothers. He shot another look at her, but she didn't notice. She was too busy reading.

Together, he and Melissa skimmed the first few pages, then flipped through the rest of the folder. It was surprisingly thin for what he imagined was supposed to be an in-depth investigation into the terrorist organization.

"From the dates on these pages," he said, "it looks like your father has spent years trying to find out more about the organization that blew up your mother's plane. But other than this one unconfirmed airport-witness account of a man with a tattoo of a serpent around a dagger on his arm who might or might not have spoken to the terrorists before they boarded the plane, there's not much here."

She flipped a few more pages. "The last note is dated less than a year ago. He's still searching for information on the hijacking, after all these years. I can't believe it."

Jace put his hand on her shoulder. "Maybe that's his way of coping with the loss."

She closed the binder. "That and leaving cards in a mausoleum, right?"

Her voice sounded bitter, which surprised him.

She'd been so intent on protecting her father earlier and had defended him back at the cemetery. Why the change all of a sudden?

As he shelved the Serpentine binder, Melissa took a few binders she'd had on the desk and shoved them into the box, spines turned away from him.

"Did you find something else interesting?" he asked.

She shrugged. "Nothing special. Notes about missions and enforcers, like you've said all along. I figure I'll read them later to get a better understanding of what you've been trying to tell me." She picked up the other binders she'd taken and started reshelving them.

Jace studied her posture. He'd watched her for months. He knew her smiles, her frowns, her mannerisms. He knew that her back went ramrod straight when she was angry, that she gestured a lot when she talked, that running her hands across the textures around her was second nature, something she didn't seem to realize she was doing. And he knew that when she was upset, she avoided eye contact, got very quiet, and went into what he thought of as her OCD mode—straightening everything around her as if her life depended on things being neat and orderly.

And she was definitely in OCD mode right now.

She'd finished reshelving the binders. Now she was straightening the ones already on the bookshelves, making them perfectly flush with the edges of the shelves. And this meticulous attention to detail had started the moment she'd put that last set of binders in with their folders from the attic.

He reached for the box.

She whirled around, grabbing the binder he'd just taken out, but not before he saw what was written on the spine.

HIGHTOWER.

She hugged the binder against her stomach, her face pale, her eyes wild.

And his heart ached for her. "Mel—"

"Don't." She held out her hand to stop him. "Don't tell me I'm better off not knowing. It's killing me to even suspect him. But I need to know. I've seen enough in the last five minutes of browsing these files to realize you've been right, that I've been living in a bubble, and that I've been naïve and stupid to think that my father isn't far more involved than I'd hoped. Well, my eyes are wide open now. I have to know the truth. And you're not going to take that away from me."

"You're not naïve, and you sure as hell aren't stupid. You're a daughter who loves her father. But Mel, I know the truth. And I promise you, knowing isn't going to make you feel enlightened or better in any way. Please, put it back. You don't want to read it."

"You know? Then will you tell me what really happened?"

He hesitated.

"I didn't think so." Her mouth tightened into a hard line, and she shoved the binder into the box. As she closed the flaps, she stared at him with a mutinous look, as if daring him to stop her.

He backed off for now. Later, once they got out of here, he'd try to reason with her again. Or hide that damn binder before she could read it. But not now.

"I think we should get out of here, don't you?" he said.

She blinked, apparently surprised he was giving in so easily. "Yes, okay." She poised her finger over the tiny green light. "Ready?"

"Ready."

She pressed the button. Just as they'd hoped, the low hum started again, and the shelves shifted and moved, restoring them to their original position.

"Now press it again."

The door above them began to slide open.

His gaze jerked to hers. "Did you press it?" he whispered.

She shook her head. "Not yet."

Footsteps sounded on the floor above them. The trapdoor clicked into place.

Ah hell. Jace swiped the box off the desk and grabbed Melissa's hand. They raced across the room and crouched behind a row of boxes in the far corner just as a pair of shiny men's dress shoes stepped down onto the top stair.

Chapter Thirteen

Trapped.

Melissa crouched behind some boxes beside Jace, waiting to see who was coming down the stairs.

Before she'd skimmed through files about enforcer missions, and read notes in her father's own handwriting about his involvement in those missions, she would have been worried, maybe even a *little* scared, about his finding her and Jace down here. But now, she had no desire to test the strength of their father-daughter bond if he was the one coming down those steps.

Jace peered through a crack between two boxes, his gun clutched in his right hand. Melissa watched the stairs through another crack, wishing she had a gun, too. Not that it would have mattered if that was her father—because she didn't think she could ever shoot him, not even in self-defense, if it came to that.

Before the man descending the stairs came into full view, she knew it wasn't her father. He would never wear an off-the-rack suit. But when she saw

the man's face, she clenched her teeth together so
hard they hurt.

Sebastian.

Beside her, Jace tensed, every muscle in his body
coiled, ready to spring. Without taking his eyes off
the assistant, he held a finger to his lips, warning
her to be quiet. The warning wasn't necessary. She'd
been hunted by Sebastian once already. She certainly wasn't going to make any noise that would
tell him where they were hiding.

"Sebastian." Her father's voice called out from
above. "What are you doing in my private office
without me?" Another pair of shoes appeared at the
top of the stairs. Her father was coming down.

"I told you to wait for me in my office *above*
ground. I didn't give you permission to come down
here." Her father's tone left no question about his
current mood toward his assistant. He was furious.

"You were busy talking to your housekeeper, so
I made an executive decision. I've never been down
here before and wanted to check out your little sanctuary." He waved toward the first stack of boxes
near the stairs. "What's the point of all this? Looks
like the same crap you have at EXIT."

"How did you know how to open the door?"

Sebastian laughed, not at all intimidated by
Cyprian's anger. "You're not the most original
person when it comes to technology. I punched
the same code into your desk phone here that you
use to open your hidden office at EXIT. You really
should vary your routine. You've become predict-
able. Maybe I'll join your little dinner party tonight
and tell the Council that you've grown careless."

"Get out. And mind your words, or you'll find

yourself on the next plane back to whatever gutter you call home. Council or no Council, I refuse to put up with poor manners and insubordination."

Sebastian laughed. "You wouldn't fire me. You can't fire me. Only the Council can do that."

Rapid-fire angry words said too low for her to make out sent a shiver of dread up Melissa's spine. Suddenly, a small pistol was in her father's hand, pointing directly at Sebastian's chest, just a few steps down from him. Melissa must have reached for Jace's hand, because his fingers closed around hers, and he gently squeezed as if to reassure her.

She started to shake.

Jace bent down next to her ear. "Keep it together," he whispered.

She nodded to let him know she was okay even though she really wasn't. The man she'd loved, adored, all her life, the man who'd been her rock, her world since losing her mother at such a young age, had just pulled a gun on another man *because that man was being rude.* And from the pale cast of Sebastian's face, she knew that he believed her father was entirely capable of pulling the trigger. No, she was *not* okay.

She watched with relief when her father slid his pistol into his suit-jacket pocket and waved for Sebastian to precede him. Without a word, his assistant climbed the stairs and disappeared through the hole in the ceiling. Her father started to follow him, then stopped. He bent down and ran his hands over the carpet, then looked down into the basement. After slowly scanning the room, his gaze settled near the area where she and Jace were hiding.

Had he seen them? Heard them?

"Are you coming? Sir?" Sebastian sounded contrite for a change instead of sarcastic or condescending. "I assume you'll want a full search of the property for your daughter. I can call Tarek. He should be back from his errand soon."

Cyprian straightened. "You will call no one until I check the house myself and decide the next course of action." He headed up the stairs. Footsteps sounded above, and a moment later, the panel slid shut, and the lights went out.

Melissa sagged against the boxes and slid to the floor. The light from Jace's phone lit up their little corner of the basement as he holstered his gun and crouched in front of her.

"You okay?" he whispered.

"I don't . . . I just . . . I need a minute," she whispered in an equally quiet voice. Seeing her father with that gun, hearing him threaten Sebastian . . . it was just suddenly too much.

Jace sighed but didn't say anything else. Melissa dropped her head in her hands as the sounds of shoes echoed again on the floor above them. A door opened and closed, then everything went silent.

"I wish I could give you more time, Mel," Jace whispered. "But they're searching the house for us. We have to get out of here in case they come back. We have to get out of here *now*."

The urgency in his voice cut through the grief and fear that were sucking her into a dark void. "My father would have shot him, wouldn't he? If Sebastian hadn't backed down? And he would have hurt me, hurt us, if he knew we were here?"

"*Sebastian* would have hurt us, without hesitation. I know your father cares for you, and he might have tried to stop him. But if he thought we'd seen his secret files . . ." He shrugged. "Maybe not. Either way, I'm not willing to bet your life on speculation. Are you?"

"No. And I'm not willing to bet yours either. Let's get out of here."

She started to get up, but stopped when Jace gently pushed her hair back from her face and smiled.

"You're an amazing woman. You know that?"

She blinked in surprise. "Why do you say that?"

"Because no matter what life tosses at you, you don't let it keep you down. You're also a hell of a lot more brave than half the men I know. We're going to be okay. *You're* going to be okay. All right?"

She drew a shaky breath and nodded. "All right."

He smiled again and pulled her to her feet, then tugged her with him to the desk, using his phone app to light their way. A few quick presses of the button behind the desk, and the trapdoor above them slid open.

"Thank God." Melissa started up the stairs.

"Hold up."

She looked back, surprised to see Jace in the corner where they'd hidden moments ago. He turned with their box of folders and binders in his arms. "Wait, Mel. I go out first," he whispered, reminding her of the need to be quiet. They thought her father and Sebastian had left the office, but even if they had, they could be close by, or the doors to the foyer could be open.

He jogged to the stairs, adjusted the box under his left arm, and pulled out his gun before heading up the rest of the way into the office. She followed behind and hurried to her father's desk to press the buttons on the phone to close the trapdoor while Jace set the box down beneath one of the windows.

The panel in the floor slid into place and Jace jogged to the closed double doors. After listening against the wood for about half a minute, he turned around, his expression grim. He strode across the room to the bank of windows and looked out.

"They're in the foyer?" she whispered.

"Someone is. I heard fabric on fabric, like someone shifting in their chair or standing outside the door. We'll have to go out a window."

She helped him unlock the window and shove it open. As he lowered the screen and dropped it to the ground, she leaned in close. "Our coats are in the foyer. We can't just sneak out the window and run to your car and leave. They'll know we were up to something if we disappear without an explanation."

"Yeah. I'm working on that. Come on."

"Well at least I can be thankful that I'm not wearing a skirt." She lifted a leg to climb over the windowsill.

"I wouldn't have minded the skirt. And a stiff breeze." He winked and lifted her the rest of the way through the opening. Then he was gone, and a second later he was handing her the box. She set it on the ground and grabbed the screen. It couldn't have been more than thirty seconds from the moment he'd opened the window to when they were both out, and the screen was back in place.

A cold breeze swirled her hair around her shoulders and had her rubbing her hands up and down her arms. It was cold, but it wasn't snowing. That was something to be thankful for she supposed.

"Where's that greenhouse you told me about earlier?" he whispered, seemingly unaffected by the cold. He lifted the box again and managed to hold it against his side with just one arm while he scanned the yard and the acreage that surrounded them.

"Over there, just past that stand of oaks."

He looked around again. "All right. Don't stop until you reach the greenhouse. *Go.*" He put his hand on her back, giving her a gentle push. But it was the raw tension in his voice that galvanized her into action—that, and the fact that he had his pistol out again.

The short sprint across the dead-looking lawn seemed more like a marathon. But maybe that's because it took years off her life in terms of worry. They raced around the first thick oaks and didn't stop until they were at the door. A shout sounded from behind them somewhere. She sucked in a breath and looked back, but the trees blocked her view.

"They must have seen us," she whispered.

"Count on it. And I'll bet they saw the box, too, so I can't just hide it like I was going to do. That would make them suspicious."

"Like they aren't suspicious already?" She glanced past him, expecting to see Sebastian at any moment, pointing his gun.

"We would have heard them shouting earlier if they'd seen us running from the house. They probably just caught a glimpse of us whipping around the first tree and don't know what direction we came from."

He yanked open the door and pulled her inside. Crouching down, he quickly shuffled the binders from her father's office to the bottom of the box and placed the folders from the attic on top.

"I don't see why it matters what direction we came from," she said, as he shoved the box to the side. "Only guilty people run. Isn't that what they say in those courtroom TV shows?"

More shouts and thumps sounded from outside. Someone was running toward the greenhouse.

Jace stood and looked around.

"We need to think of an excuse, a cover story. What are we supposed to tell them?" Melissa asked.

"A convincing reason for being here." He snapped a large pink bloom off a nearby plant.

"No kidding. Like what? I can't think of anything." She put her hands on her hips, exasperated that she was finally on board about how much danger they were in and now he was . . . *gardening*? "Jace, what are we going to do?"

He shoved the flower into her hair over her right ear. "This. We're going to do this." He yanked her to him and covered her mouth with his.

And just like that, the world around them faded away, leaving only the two of them. Their first kiss had been a surprise, all about discovery, awakening feelings inside her that she hadn't felt in a long time, if ever. But this . . . this was consuming, ravenous, wild. This kiss seared her from the inside out, breaking her down, molding her, changing her and reforging her into someone new, someone different, someone who would never, ever be the same again.

And she didn't want to be.

She embraced the change, drinking it in, tangling her tongue with his. He made a ragged groan deep in his throat and put his hand beneath her bottom, lifting her in his arms to bring her closer. Every wish, every desire, every longing she'd ever had focused into a raw, aching need at the very center of her. She lifted her legs and wrapped them around his waist.

"What do you think you're doing, Melissa Ann Cardenas?"

Her father's voice broke over her like a bucket of ice water. Her eyes flew open, and she yanked back, blinking in shock to see him standing three feet away, holding the coats they'd left in the foyer, his face beet red. Beside him, Sebastian coughed as if hiding a laugh.

Jace turned with her in his arms and set her on her feet. Then, as if suddenly realizing how livid her father was, he shoved her protectively behind his back. "Mr. Cardenas, I—"

Her father slammed his fist against the side of Jace's jaw, knocking him to the ground.

"Daddy! What did you do?" She dropped to her knees and bent over Jace so her father couldn't hit him again. She glared at her father over her shoulder. "I'm not a little girl anymore. I'm a grown woman. You had no reason to hit him."

He pointed at Jace. "I have every reason. He's on my property mauling you like a randy—"

"Dad! Stop it! You're embarrassing me."

"You're embarrassing yourself with this undignified behavior."

"Oh, good grief," she said.

Jace gently forced her back and sat up. "I'm okay, sweetheart. No worries."

She lifted a hand to his jaw.

He winced and jerked away.

"We need to put some ice on that," she said.

"I'm. Fine." He sounded irritated now.

"It's not broken is it?"

He rolled his eyes. "No. It's not broken. But I've about had it with the sucker punches around here. Next time I'm throwing the first punch." He aimed an aggravated look at her father, then grinned. "You've got a good right hook there, sir. I'll give you that."

Cyprian swore.

Melissa's mouth dropped open, and she stared at her father in shock. In all her years, she'd never, not once, heard him swear. He'd been incredibly strict, especially about what he called "bad" words. She could remember more than a few times as a teenager when he'd washed her mouth out with soap.

Sebastian dropped a handful of files back into the box near the door. Melissa's stomach clenched. She'd totally forgotten about her father's assistant, and the box.

"Nothing in there but old client files from tours," he announced. "I'll meet you back at the house." He yanked the door open and headed outside.

Melissa silently mouthed "thank you" to Jace, grateful that he'd thought to bury the binders at the bottom of the box. If he hadn't, or if Sebastian had been more thorough and had looked at everything in the box, they'd have been in trouble.

He gave her a barely perceptible nod and rose to his feet, pulling her with him.

"Mr. Atwell, consider yourself fired from EXIT Incorporated," her father said. "Don't bother coming into work tomorrow."

"He doesn't work for the company, Dad. He works for me. You can't—"

"I can. I did. Get yourself a new bodyguard, young lady. I'll see you at the office in the morning, once I'm calm enough to discuss this disgraceful episode. And for the love of God, take that ridiculous flower out of your hair and change out of that . . . that . . . denim. Put something decent on."

He threw open the door, then frowned at the coats still in his arms. He tossed them at Jace and headed back toward the house in long, angry strides.

Melissa pulled the hibiscus blossom out of her hair. She couldn't believe her father was furious about her wearing jeans and kissing a man. He'd been so furious about her lack of decorum that he hadn't even asked her why she was at his house. The whole situation suddenly struck her as hilarious. She let out a laugh, then another, and then she was laughing so hard, tears started running down her face.

Jace stared at her like she'd lost her mind. For some reason, that just made her laugh even harder. But then, like the flip of a switch, her laughter turned to tears. All the fear, the revelations, the shock of reading those files, and feeling trapped, was too much. She covered her face with her hands.

Dropping their coats to the ground, he scooped her up and hugged her to his chest. He carried her to one of the benches deeper inside the greenhouse and sat down with her in his lap. The silly words he whispered were probably supposed to be soothing. And from the way he was awkwardly patting her back, he'd probably never comforted someone like this before. Which had her thinking how incredibly nice and sweet he was to try. And that just made her cry even harder.

The emotional storm was a big one, but over

almost as quickly as it had begun. Her face flushed hot over her loss of control. She wasn't a crier. Had never been a crier. And she hated that Jace was the one she'd cried in front of when she'd finally broken down. She wiped her eyes and pushed against his chest. "I'm okay now. You can put me down."

"I'd rather not."

She thought he was teasing. But the look on his face was anything but amused. His arms tightened around her.

"You're driving me crazy, Mel. You know that don't you?" He gently swept her hair back from her face. It was incredible how that one, sweet gesture that seemed to be becoming a habit made her flush hot all over.

"I'm . . . driving you crazy?" she whispered, still tingling from his touch.

He nodded. "I'm completely off-balance around you. Normally, I can read people. I know what to expect, how they tick. But I can't . . . I don't." His jaw tightened. "I don't want you to be miserable. I don't want to hurt you. I want you to be safe. And happy, damn it. I want you to be happy."

She blinked. "You want me to be happy?"

He gave her a curt nod. "No more crying."

"Jace?"

"What?" he snapped, looking so adorably bemused and irritated that she wanted to kiss him.

"You know that I can't control whether I cry or not, right?"

He mumbled something under his breath.

She cupped the side of his face. "Thank you for worrying about me, and for trying to comfort me. I know that was difficult for you."

"Damn right it was."

Her mouth twitched, but she didn't dare smile. "I'll try very hard not to cry again."

"See that you don't." He set her on her feet. "Let's get out of here before Sebastian's evil twin shows up and decides to look through our box of files."

"You don't have to tell me twice." She retrieved their coats and handed him his while she shrugged into hers. "Wait a minute. Evil twin. They *are* almost always together. It's rare that I ever see Sebastian without Tarek. Doesn't it seem odd?"

"Sebastian mentioned an errand when we were in the basement office."

"I wonder what constitutes an errand in the world of evil twins."

"That's not something I want to find out. And it's just one more reason to get out of here as fast as we can." He picked up the box, and they went straight to his car out front, not wanting to chance another encounter with her father or either of his assistants.

It wasn't until they were on the highway, miles from her father's house, that Melissa was finally able to relax back in her seat. She blew out a deep breath and forced herself to release her death grip on the armrest.

"You okay?" Jace asked.

"I will be. Thanks to you." She rolled her head to look at him. "You think fast on your feet. Burying those binders beneath the files saved us when Sebastian looked through the box. And I never would have thought to use a kiss as a way to throw both of them off. My father must have assumed that I was giving you a tour of the property, and we were so overcome with passion that we ran into the greenhouse for privacy." She laughed. "I've never seen him so shocked. Thank you for kissing me to save my life."

He stared through the windshield. "My pleasure."

"Saving me? Or kissing me," she teased.

His mouth curved into a sensual smile. "Both."

She smiled, too. But all too soon, reality seeped in like a slow-moving fog, floating through her mind, blanking out some memories while revealing others.

"You're too quiet," he said. "What's bothering you?"

"You think you know me so well?"

"Starting to. What's wrong?"

She tapped the armrest and looked out the window. They were driving toward town. She didn't know where he was going, and for the moment, she didn't really care.

"Mel?"

"That's what's bothering me. The whole 'Mel' thing. And the kissing thing."

"You didn't like it when I kissed you?"

"You're kidding, right? You're like . . . the world's best kisser ever. Of course I liked it."

He grinned. "Then what's the problem?"

She straightened, tugging on her seat-belt harness to loosen it so she could face him. "The problem is that I lose my mind when you touch me. And before you take that in the arrogant vein that it was *not* intended, my point is that you kissed me in the dining room to distract Silvia. You didn't want her to see whatever it was that you had in your hand. And because my hormones take my IQ points on a holiday every time you touch me, I didn't remember that until just now. What did you have in your hand in the dining room?"

His expression turned wary.

"Jace? What did you have in your hand?"

He glanced in the rearview mirror, then the side mirrors, a habit he did faithfully at least once a minute.

"Bugs," he finally said.

She jerked up her feet and looked around. "Where? What did you see? A spider?"

He shot her an amused look. "You're afraid of spiders. Good to know if I ever have to torture information out of you. But that's not what I was talking about. In the dining room, I was holding bugs. Not the kind with six legs. Voice-activated listening devices. I planted them under the dining-room table, on a painting, and in other rooms in the house when Silvia took me on the tour."

She put her feet down and straightened, her face flushing hot with embarrassment over her freak-out. She really did hate spiders. But what she hated more was that Jace had just told her he'd planted listening devices in her father's home, a terrible intrusion into her father's privacy—*and that it didn't bother her one bit*.

Her allegiance to her father was fast becoming her last concern. Her *primary* concern was in staying alive and in keeping Jace alive. What exactly did that say about her as a daughter?

"I guess that was good foresight," she said. "Sebastian mentioned a Council meeting tonight. We'll be able to hear what's going on."

"You aren't angry that I bugged your father's house?"

"No. I'm angry at my father that we *need* to bug his house to find out the truth. Where are we going? Back to my home?"

"Not yet. I'm on E, so we'll have to stop for gas.

Then we'll head to my place. I want to go through those files we got from the basement. And . . . some other files at my apartment. I hadn't planned on showing them to you, but they'll help us prepare for tonight. Maybe we can get a better bead on everyone who will be at that meeting. And maybe we can come up with theories about the Watcher and ski-mask guy."

He was hiding something. She could see the tension around his eyes. "Jace?"

"Hm?"

"What aren't you telling me? You got a funny look on your face the moment you mentioned files at your apartment. What's in those files? The ones that you never intended to show me?"

His mouth tightened, and he checked the rear-view mirror before answering. "They're surveillance files. From the past two months."

"Surveillance?"

He nodded.

"You performed surveillance on someone? For two months?"

"Yes," he bit out, looking even more uncomfortable.

She narrowed her eyes. "On who?"

"I think you mean whom."

"Jace."

He blew out a deep sigh. "You. I performed surveillance on *you*."

Chapter Fourteen

Jace parked by the gas pump closest to the building and scanned the street before cutting the engine. He was about to get out of the car when Melissa reached for her door handle.

He grabbed her arm. "What are you doing?"

Her face flushed a light pink. "I need to go to the ladies' room." Her voice was tight and clipped, and she hadn't looked him in the eye since he'd admitted that he'd been essentially stalking her for months. Not that he blamed her for being upset. But he couldn't let her annoyance with him compromise her safety.

"Wait in the car until I pump the gas. Then I'll escort you inside."

She gave him a sour look. "That hardly seems necessary."

"It is."

She uttered a few choice words, probably to make sure he knew she was still pissed at him. Then she settled back in her seat and closed her eyes, dismissing him. He leaned across her. She popped an eye open and arched a brow.

"Just locking you in."

She shut her eyes again.

He grinned. He'd just discovered that Melissa had a temper. Which only had him wanting to kiss her again and make those angry lips soften beneath his. When he realized he was actually considering doing exactly that, he made himself get out of the car.

What was it about her that fascinated him so much? Then again, what was it about her that *didn't* fascinate him? He had to get a handle on this . . . obsession . . . and quit letting himself get distracted. Like he'd been in the greenhouse. He'd started that kiss to throw Cyprian and Sebastian off, to make them believe what their eyes told them instead of thinking things through. Because if they'd thought about it, they'd have realized a bodyguard wouldn't last long in that profession if he was kissing his clients instead of guarding them. And then they would have known the kiss was a ruse.

Or at least it had started out that way.

He hadn't even realized that Cyprian and Sebastian had entered the greenhouse until Cyprian spoke. And that scared the hell out of him. He had to get his focus back. But damned if he knew how to do it. He was well past fooling himself into thinking he didn't care about Melissa, that his protectiveness of her was just the job. He didn't want to label how he felt, but it was a hell of a lot more than concern.

And here he was, distracted again.

He shook his head in disgust and swiped a prepaid credit card from one of his untraceable aliases to turn the pump on. After setting the nozzle on autofill, he pulled out his phone. Mason Hunt might have decided he couldn't trust him anymore, but Jace had made a vow to the Equalizers, one that he intended to keep—to help them bring down EXIT. He couldn't let an opportunity like tonight's Council meeting go by without giving Mason and the others a heads-up that the full Council was in town. But calls to Mason, Devlin, the Equalizer home base, and even Ramsey, all yielded the same thing—a computer-generated voice saying the numbers were no longer in service.

How could you have so little faith in me, Mason?

A few minutes later, while he waited outside the restroom for Melissa, he watched the closed captions scroll across a TV hanging from the ceiling. A news bulletin gave an update on the woman found dead in the trunk of a Cadillac yesterday at a local motel. Her alleged killer had been found dead of a self-inflicted gunshot wound inside one of the rooms. The coroner said his time of death was shortly after the woman's. The two were from out of town. And police were investigating their deaths as a murder-suicide, possibly a love triangle since the woman was married, but not to the man at the motel. The deceaseds' names flashed across the bottom of the screen.

What the hell? Jace straightened and automatically dropped his right hand by his holster, hidden beneath his suit jacket.

"What's wrong?" Melissa had just come out of the bathroom. She looked up at the TV. "They found that poor woman's killer?"

"Don't count on it." He grabbed her hand and pulled her toward the door.

When they were in the car, she gripped the steering wheel, preventing him from driving off. "You knew the man that they said killed that woman?"

"I didn't know either of them, not personally. But I know who they were."

"Who?"

"Council members. And I don't buy that the Councilman killed that Councilwoman." He pushed her hand off the steering wheel and peeled out of the gas station.

"What's going on Jace?"

He shook his head. "All I'm sure of is that those two Council members were some of the good guys. They have . . . they *had* . . . a lot of influence on the rest of the Council. Maybe there's an important vote tonight, and someone was afraid of which way those two would vote. Or how they might sway others to vote. I don't know."

"Someone set them up."

"Probably." He tapped the steering wheel, his jaw working. "Everything that's happening seems to center around the Council, be it Marsh's going to that secret meeting at EXIT or these latest deaths. I need to find somewhere safe to put you while I go to your father's house and listen in on that Council meeting tonight."

"Somewhere safe to *put* me?"

The anger in her voice surprised him. "There's nothing wrong with your hunkering down where you'll be safe."

"Is that what you think of me, Jace? I thought you said I was brave, earlier. Was that a lie to keep me from breaking down? You think that I'm a helpless woman who can't contribute to her own protection? Damn it, Jace. You're in danger, other people are in danger, because of this clandestine organization that this Council, and my father, put together. Well, he's my responsibility just as much as anyone else's, more actually. Because EXIT is my company, too. I should have known what was going on."

She waved her hand impatiently. "Water under the bridge and all that. Sitting around, waiting for someone else to take care of everything is in the past. I'm moving forward, doing whatever I can to stop this. And you can either work with me or get out of my way."

He didn't know whether to be impressed or incensed at her little speech. She certainly wasn't a coward. He'd give her that. But keeping her with him didn't seem like such a good idea, either. Maybe he should—

"Jace?"

"Yes?"

"Whatever you're thinking right now, you can just stop. You're not getting rid of me. We're a team. Period."

He frowned again.

"And Jace?"

"*What?*"

"When we get to your apartment, I want my derringer back."

He couldn't help it. This time he smiled.

TERMINATE J.A. IMMEDIATELY.

Instructions didn't come much clearer than that. He shoved his phone into his pocket, *again*, and checked the clock on his dash, *again*. When he'd first received that text, he'd been just down the street from Atwell's apartment building. So he'd grabbed what he needed and hurried over here. But Atwell's car wasn't parked out front, so he'd been forced to sit in his car in the parking lot across the street in a neighboring apartment complex to wait. That was almost two hours ago. Where the hell was he?

As if on cue, the distinctive black Buick Grand National turned the corner at the end of the street. He adjusted his ball cap and sunglasses and slid lower in his seat until the Buick parked right in front of building number three.

He could just make out the bullet hole in the right side, the hole he'd put there. Had he known how tenacious Atwell would be, he might have stuck around and ended everything right then. But that wasn't the plan at the time.

Atwell hopped out of his car, scanning the bushes and vehicles near him before heading toward his apartment. No, wait. He was stopping at the passenger side of his car. Someone was getting out.

Melissa Cardenas.

He slammed his fist on the steering wheel. No, no, no. He'd assumed she'd be at her house. Why had Atwell brought her here? His orders were to kill Atwell, not Melissa.

The front door to the apartment closed behind the two of them, and he was left simmering in his car. He grabbed the phone and was about to punch SPEED DIAL, but stopped. He already knew what he'd be told—don't kill her. Find another way to eliminate Atwell. But Atwell was a freaking Navy SEAL. And those weren't easy to kill.

Of course, *he* was just as badass as Atwell. That would mean even odds, more or less, if they faced off against each other. But he didn't want even odds. He wanted the advantage. Which was why he'd chosen this particular method of eliminating his opponent.

He picked up the small charge, no bigger than a quarter, and rolled it in his palm. This was quick, easy, clean. It would look like an accident. Nothing to point back to him. And even better, no risk to him like there would be if he went toe to toe with the other man. But if Atwell and Melissa were together, and he did this, *both* of them would die.

What to do? What to do?

Too bad he didn't have a coin to toss.

MELISSA EYED THE stacks of binders that Jace was unloading onto his kitchen table. While she wanted to read the information inside them, she wasn't keen on spending the next few hours reading them. Not when she was keyed up and nervous about the upcoming Council meeting. It would be hard to concentrate. She might miss something important.

"I'll grab the other files I mentioned earlier," Jace said as he finished stacking the binders on the kitchen table. "I've got to print some of them out, so it'll be a few minutes."

"No worries. I'll sort everything and get started."

He hesitated.

She put her hand on his arm. "Don't worry. I'm not going to read the Hightower information yet. I don't want the distraction while I sort through all of the facts to help us prepare for tonight's surveillance. I'll save that for later."

"I wish you wouldn't read it at all."

"What makes you so sure of what's in that binder? How do you even know about the Hightowers?"

"I told you. I performed surveillance—"

"For two months. On *me*. The Hightowers died long before that. Who told you about them?" She put her hands on her hips.

His expression flattened out, all hints of emotion gone, as if he was trying to put on a poker face. Which only made her more suspicious. What was he hiding?

She moved in front of him, so he couldn't escape down the hall. "You sure know an awful lot about enforcers and Councils and Watchers to have never been an enforcer yourself. Or did I miss that part in your background check?"

He stepped around her.

She angled herself in front of him again and braced her hands on the hallway walls. "I've told you everything that I know about EXIT, about the mysterious deaths, even about the man I once thought I was falling in love with. I bared my soul to you, shared my pain. But other than telling me about the client that you lost, you haven't shared anything. You're still keeping secrets. How did you find out about the enforcement side of EXIT?"

He shook his head as if he thought she was silly. "It's called research. Like you, I saw discrepancies, things that bothered me. And I dug in and looked for connections."

"Really? You saw discrepancies . . . half a country away? In Georgia?"

He sighed and stared at a spot over her head.

"Oh, I bet I know," she said, sarcasm dripping from every syllable. "You picked up an EXIT brochure in a travel agent's office. The ones they make to recruit enforcers. Right under the section about the 401(k) plan and dental insurance."

His mouth twitched. Amusement lit his eyes.

She inhaled sharply. "Are you laughing at me? Do you think this is funny?"

He shrugged. "Maybe a little."

She clenched her fists. "You . . . you . . . oh!"

He'd grabbed her around the waist and set her out of his way as if she were no more substantial than a doll. "I'll get those files now." He escaped down the hall into the apartment's only bedroom, shutting the door behind him with a loud click.

"Coward," she yelled. She blew out a breath in frustration and debated going after him. But it wasn't like she could force him to talk to her. Mumbling a string of curses that would have earned her a gallon of soap if her father had heard her, she trudged back toward the eat-in kitchen and plopped down at the table.

But she immediately jumped back up. If she was going to make any notes about the contents of these binders, she'd need pen and paper. The kitchen seemed the obvious choice for that, but after a quick search, she realized that Jace might be the only person on the planet without a junk drawer.

The apartment was painfully small, and incredibly sparse, with nothing on the walls. She couldn't have lived here more than five minutes without hanging up some pictures or paintings, let alone several months as Jace had. He definitely didn't appear to be settling in for the long haul. Which had her wondering where he planned to go when this was over. Back to Savannah? That was his hometown, assuming anything she knew about him was the truth. Was that where he wanted to live, or had he decided to make Boulder his home?

It didn't matter. It *shouldn't* matter, not to her anyway. After all, they barely knew each other, even if the opposite felt true. She couldn't remember feeling this comfortable, this fast, with anyone else. Ever. But the whole situation was impossible. No matter how much they both wanted to save lives and stop the killing, there would always be one thing to keep them apart.

Her father.

Thankfully, their relationship was purely one of physical attraction at this point. He'd only kissed her twice—two incredible, mind-blowing kisses—but they'd both been to distract someone from their trail, playacting as a way to keep their mission intact. She would do well to remember that and not allow her heart to become entangled, especially when she knew Jace was playing a role, lying to her, and that his heart wasn't even in the game.

She just wished that didn't bother her so much.

He chose that moment to come out of the bedroom. He had an armload of files, and when he plopped them on the table she saw that he'd thought to include a couple of legal pads and pens.

She was about to thank him when he held up his hand to stop her.

"I'm not discussing anything with you except these files and our plan for listening in on tonight's Council meeting."

"Suits me." Because, really, what did it matter? It wasn't like she needed to learn everything about him. Why worry about his past if they didn't have a future?

He gave her a curious look. "Did something happen while I was in the bedroom?"

"Nope." She checked her watch. "When does this dinner party start? I don't remember Sebastian mentioning a time."

"He didn't. I figure as long as we're there by five, even if it's an early dinner, we'll be in position with plenty of time to spare."

"I agree. No respectable dinner party starts before six, and most start later."

"Five it is. Let's look at these first." He plopped a file folder in front of her.

She flipped it open, surprised to see headshots of men and women, with names typed beneath them. "What is this? Wait, I know some of these people. They work at EXIT."

"It's from the surveillance I performed. I wanted to catalog as many employees of EXIT as I could, or regular visitors. Since we want to figure out the Watcher's identity, I thought maybe you could look these over and tell me if any of them are usually out of town but have been back for several months. Their return might have made sense, but looking at it in terms of someone being chosen by the Council to keep an eye on your father, maybe you can look at them with fresh eyes."

"Makes sense." She pointed at a dark-haired man with a mustache on the first page, halfway down. "I can tell you right off that he fits your description— Ethan Garcia. He's a tour guide, and he's always, for years, worked tours out of the country as his main gig. But late last fall, he requested to work out of the Boulder office, said he needed a break from all that travel. We didn't really need him locally, not during our off-season, but he's been a loyal employee for years, so I gave him an office and put him to work planning future tours. He's there every day."

Jace snapped a picture of Garcia's headshot with his phone. "All right. Anyone else?"

She pointed out two more candidates for the Watcher role, with similar stories to Garcia's, then closed the folder. "That's it. Not sure how helpful that was."

He shrugged. "You never know. Let's go through these binders now."

Two hours later, they'd gone through every binder, except the Hightower one, and all of the surveillance files that Jace had—noticeably minus a file specifically on *her*. She assumed he didn't want her to get upset if she saw what all *he'd* seen in those two months. And he was right. She'd rather not know. But in spite of all of their hard work reading the reports, throwing out theories, brainstorming, they were no closer to figuring out anything that seemed remotely helpful. They certainly hadn't found whatever Jace was hoping to find, judging by how disgusted he looked. And they weren't any closer to knowing the identity of either ski-mask guy or the Watcher.

Melissa rubbed her shoulders, which were starting to ache and bunch up from leaning over the table for so long. "I don't think I'm cut out for this investigation stuff. I'd much rather pore over financial reports all day long than spend even five more minutes doing this."

Jace scrubbed his face with his hands. "I was sure there'd be something useful in those files on the Council. If something doesn't shake loose tonight, we might need to plan another trip to your father's hidden office."

"No way. Forget it. That place creeped me out, and we almost got caught. I'm not going back in that dungeon."

"Now, Mel. It wasn't that bad."

She crossed her arms.

He held up his hands in mock surrender. "Okay, okay. We'll discuss it later. I'll grab what we'll need for tonight's little operation."

"There's nothing else to discuss. I'm not going back inside that hidden office, ever," she called to him.

He held a hand up in the air. "Yeah, yeah. Whatever." He went into the bedroom.

Impossible. The man was absolutely impossible. She plopped down in a chair and stared at the stacks of binders, sorted into piles, and the legal pads with all of their notes.

Then, as if drawn by an invisible force, her gaze went to the one binder they hadn't reviewed. The one that said Hightower on the spine.

She glanced down the hall, then back at the binder. She'd promised she'd look at it later. That she'd focus on planning tonight's surveillance. Well the plan was in place. And it was definitely later. She drummed her nails on the table.

She wanted to know the truth. And Jace had certainly proven that he wasn't the one she could count on to tell her that. So, what, exactly, was she waiting for?

She grabbed the binder and pulled it toward her.

JACE SET THE duffel bag on the bed and double-checked everything. Receivers for the listening devices. Extra ammo. Binoculars. A first-aid kit an ER would be jealous of because, hey, always be prepared. He smiled at that, remembering Melissa quoting the Boy Scout motto. He tossed in a few bottles of water and some energy bars, zipped the bag closed, and headed to the kitchen. As soon as he saw Melissa, he knew he'd made a mistake. He should have taken that damn Hightower binder and hidden it. Or better yet, destroyed it.

Her eyes were red, and the binder lay closed on the table in front of her. But she wasn't crying, at least, not anymore. She looked composed and at peace.

Crouching beside her chair, he set the bag on the floor and took her hands in his. "Are you all right?"

"My father ordered the murder of a man I was dating. And that started a domino effect, resulting in the deaths of both of his parents. Are you sure you want to ask me if I'm all right?"

He winced. "Yeah. Poor choice of words. I guess what I meant is can I do anything to help?"

"Yes. You can stop treating me like I'm fragile. I'm strong. I'll get through this. If you think about it, I've had months to prepare. It's not like I didn't wonder every time I added a picture to my boards, every time I drew a red line. I just . . . I really, really hoped you were wrong about everything." She pushed his hands down and stood. "If we're going to make it to my father's by five, we should probably go."

She headed to the door. Jace swung the duffel over his shoulder and grabbed her before she could open it.

"Hold it."

Her brows drew together. "What?"

He wanted to erase the haunted look in her eyes,

the barely concealed pain that had tension lines at the corners of her mouth and drew her skin taut across her cheekbones. He didn't want her to be afraid, or hurt, or to have the realization that her father—the one person in the world she should be able to trust and rely on—was the one person who was responsible for all of her pain. But he could do none of that. So instead, he decided to do the only thing he *could* do. He would tease her and try to make her smile, and maybe, just maybe, he could take away the hurt for a little while.

"You forgot one thing," he said, affecting a serious look.

"I did?" She looked back toward the table. "What did I forget?"

"It's customary to send a warrior off to battle with a kiss."

She looked back at him, her brows arching up in surprise and confusion. "You're a warrior now? Going into battle?"

He nodded.

"But I'm going with you. I'm not sending you off to fight for me."

"Okay. Well, in that case. Maybe I should kiss you instead." He pulled her into his arms and kissed her—thoroughly, completely, until she was moaning in his arms. Or that might have been him. He wasn't sure. He just knew if he didn't stop right this second, he was going to drag her down the hallway and make love to her for the rest of the night, and the world be damned.

He broke the kiss, forcing himself to let her go and step back.

She blinked up at him, her eyes unfocused, glazed.

Damn. Now he just wanted to kiss her again. He reached for her.

She backed up, holding out her hands. "No, stop. I mean . . ." She shook her head. "Holy cow. Wow. But, we can't . . . we have to . . ." She drew a shaky breath. "We have to go."

He grinned. "Holy cow? Is that good or bad?"

"Good. Oh, it's good. Definitely good." She smoothed her jeans. "Aren't you forgetting something?"

Now it was his turn to glance around the room. "I don't think so. Everything we need's in the duffel."

"Including my derringer?" She held out her hand.

The determined look on her face told him it would be pointless to argue, even if he'd wanted to, which he didn't. It made sense for her to have a gun, so she could protect herself if something happened to him. He just hadn't thought of it earlier because, well, he'd never protected someone before who was determined to help with their own protection.

He gave her the gun, and ammo to go with it this time.

After loading it, she shoved the derringer in her jeans pocket. The gun was so small he wouldn't have known it was there if he hadn't seen her put it there. But small or not, it was a deadly weapon.

She reached for the doorknob.

"Let me make sure it's clear first." He gently pushed her back and cracked the door, scanning everything around them. "All right. Let's go."

Chapter Fifteen

Melissa clutched the armrest as Jace steered around another sharp curve. They were on the same twisty road she'd been on when the van had forced her into the ditch, a road she usually tried to avoid. There were so many curves and desolate sections where only narrow shoulders and low guardrails stood between a careless driver and a deadly plunge off the side of the mountain. And it was particularly dangerous during the winter, like now.

Her fear of driving on this road and her desire to avoid it had directly influenced where she'd bought her house in relation to her work. And it was the sole reason that she only went to her father's house about once a month to have dinner with him. Unfortunately, the only other way to get to her father's would be to go around the mountain. She and Jace didn't have time for that if they wanted to get into position well before the time when they were guessing that the Council meeting would begin.

"Melissa," Jace said. "Smile and look at me."

She turned and frowned. "Why?"

"That's not a smile."

"This road is scary. It's snowing. And we're going to be freezing our derrieres off soon, hiding in the woods by my father's house. What do I have to smile about?"

His mouth quirked up. "You've got me there. If you can't manage a smile, just promise me something. No matter what I say, keep looking at me. It's important. Can you do that?"

"You're making me nervous."

"Promise me."

"Okay, okay. I promise. What's going on?"

He checked the mirrors. "Someone's following us."

The instinct to turn around and look behind them was almost impossible to fight, but she resisted the urge, only because he'd warned her. She pasted a smile on her face. "I'm guessing it's not some random tourist taking the scenic route?"

"I don't think so. He's been following us since we left town, pulled behind us from a side street about the time we hit the city limits."

"He?"

"If I'm not mistaken, it's your father's chef, Richard Keller."

She laughed. "Richard? Trust me, he's not following us. Not on purpose anyway. He's probably running late and in a hurry to get to my father's house. I can't imagine Dad having a dinner party without his favorite chef. Wait, how do you know what kind of car he drives? Or what he looks like? Oh, wait, never mind. Because you performed surveillance on me. I really wish you hadn't brought that up." She shook her head. "Then again, I guess I'm the one who did."

"Let me know if you actually want me to join in on this conversation we're having."

"What? Oh, sorry. Why do you think Richard is following us? Assuming that it *is* Richard."

"Because when I slow down, he doesn't try to pass me. He's had plenty of opportunities, especially back on the straightaway before we began climbing into the mountain. He's just keeping pace."

She rolled her eyes. "He's a very careful driver, ridiculously so. That's why he doesn't pass us. Pull over."

"Hell no. He could slam the bumper and send us crashing into a guardrail. I'm not willing to test whether it will hold."

"Richard isn't one of the bad guys. I doubt he even knows that this is your car or even who you are. Trust me. Pull over."

"I've got a better idea. Tighten your seat belt."

"Jace—"

"Now."

She frowned at him and tightened her seat belt. "If you kill us, I swear I'll come back and haunt you."

"Won't that be hard to do if I'm dead, too?"

"I'll find a way. I'll make your eternity a living hell. So don't get us killed."

"Well, gee. I was totally going to try to kill us before, but now that I've been warned, I'll be more careful."

"Jace?"

"Yes, Mel?"

"No one likes a smart-ass."

He grinned. "*You* do. I know because when I kissed you in the greenhouse, you made sexy little noises in the back of your throat. And then you wrapped your legs around my smart ass and rubbed your—"

"Jace!"

He laughed and steered through the next curve onto another straight section of road before checking the mirrors again. "Here we go." He stomped the accelerator.

Melissa let out a yelp as the car rocketed down the straightaway. She bit her lip to keep from crying out again, and had to close her eyes when he skidded around the next curve. A few more slips and slides, and he barreled down another straight section of the highway.

"Hold on," he yelled over the roar of the engine.

"If I hold on any tighter, I'll shred your armrest."

"Well don't do that. Do you know how hard it is to find parts for this car?"

She hurled a few inventive curses at him and held on as tightly as she could as he skidded around another curve. His grin had her glaring at him. "Please tell me you are not enjoying this!"

"I'm not enjoying this."

"Liar."

He laughed again, then suddenly slowed, throwing her against her seat belt.

"Sorry," he called out. "Here we go."

"Here we go . . . where?"

He jerked the steering wheel, making a hard right into one of the few picnic areas this little mountain road boasted. He slammed the brakes, skidded in a 180-degree turn, and jerked the car to a stop, facing back toward the highway under the shelter of some trees. He immediately killed the engine and relaxed back in his seat as if they hadn't just run the Daytona 500 through a twisty, winding mountain road in the dead of winter. In the snow. And she was pretty sure there had been some ice.

A bird had the audacity to chirp somewhere outside her window.

Melissa gulped in huge lungfuls of air as she tried to calm her racing heart.

Fifty yards away, almost hidden by some scraggly bushes and evergreen pines, was the opening to the park and a view of the highway they'd just left.

A few seconds later, Richard's sleek, deep green BMW drove past. And shortly after that, an old black Mercedes drove by.

"Doesn't anyone drive American anymore?" Jace grumbled.

"Excuse me?"

"Nothing." He started the engine. "You were probably right. Richard would have given chase if he was purposely following us. But at least we blew the cobwebs out of the cylinders. If we get in a real chase later on, we should be good to go." He patted the dash.

She narrowed her eyes. "If you ever drive like that again with me in the car, I swear I'll put another bullet hole in your paint job."

He winced. "Duly noted." He pulled back onto the highway toward her father's.

She frowned at the light snow falling onto the windshield. "I hope you thought to pack a water-resistant blanket in the duffel bag, or we're going to be miserable at my—"

Bam!

The car rocked wildly and spun around, tires screeching.

Melissa screamed and braced herself against the dash.

The car kept spinning, round and round, out of control. Jace fought the wheel, pumping the brakes. Melissa watched in horror as they veered toward a guardrail, and beyond that, empty space.

"The cliff! Oh my God! Jace!"

He swore and punched the gas. Then he jerked the steering wheel, sending them straight toward the railing.

"What are you doing?" she screamed.

"Hold on." He wrestled the wheel. "Shit, shit, shit." He stomped the accelerator and jerked the steering wheel the other way.

Whump! The car slammed sideways against the railing. Metal squeaked and bent. The car shuddered and rocked crazily.

We're going over. Oh, God. We're going over! She squeezed her eyes shut, unable to suppress a whimper.

A groaning noise sounded. Tires spun. The engine roared, and she was thrown back against the seat. She covered her face with her hands.

The car shuddered again, and everything went still. And silent.

"Melissa?"

Her breaths were coming so fast, she felt dizzy.

"Mel?" Warm hands gently smoothed her hair back from her face. "Honey? It's okay. We're okay."

She peeked between her fingers. Jace was leaning over the console, his face inches from hers. She looked around. They were sitting on the shoulder of the road. Parked. As if nothing had happened. She very slowly lowered her hands.

"We're . . . we're not dead?" she whispered.

He shook his head. "No. But it was close there for a few seconds. We had a blowout and hit some ice."

"A blowout?" She looked out the passenger window. The guardrail about fifty feet back was twisted at a crazy angle, one section completely missing. "Oh my God. Oh my God."

He put his hand beneath her chin and forced her to look at him. "We're okay. That's all that matters."

She threw her hands around his neck. "We almost died."

He hugged her tight and ran his hand up and down her back in a soothing motion. "But we didn't. We're okay. Everything's okay."

She clung to him until she quit shaking. Then she forced herself to let go and sit back. She pressed her hand to her chest. "My heart's still racing. I don't think I've ever been more scared in my life."

"You and me both." He smiled and kissed her softly. "Better?"

She nodded. "Better."

"Let's see what kind of damage we're dealing with. Come on. It's safer if you're not in the car when I jack it up to change the tire."

The flat was on the front passenger side. When Jace got the spare and the jack out and headed around the car to change the tire, he froze.

Melissa winced on his behalf. She'd already seen what he was just now seeing. The whole side of his car was dented in, from front to back. And the paint had been scraped down to the metal. "I'm so sorry about your car."

He feathered his fingers over the worst of the damage. "It's not just a car. It's the last project I ever did with my dad. We searched for months through junkyards until we found this door. It took years to complete the restoration."

"Last project? Your dad, he's . . . gone?"

"Lung cancer." He shook his head in disgust and went to work on the flat.

"I'm so sorry." She smoothed the hood, which thankfully didn't look damaged all that much . . . except for the bullet hole it was sporting from earlier.

He didn't answer. He frowned as he inspected the hole in the tire.

She sighed and settled in for a wait. But it seemed like only a minute or two had passed before he'd put the spare on and they were driving down the road again. He'd been incredibly fast. If he ever got tired of being a bodyguard, maybe he could make a living as an auto mechanic. Or a pit-crew member for a professional racecar driver.

Once they were safely off the mountain, the tension drained out of her shoulders. A few minutes later, they'd pulled to a stop beneath some trees a few hundred yards from her father's house, off the road hidden from view.

When he cut the engine, she let out a sigh of relief and laughed. "I guess your Navy SEAL motto was right after all, huh? *The Only Easy Day Was Yesterday*? Who'd have thought after everything else that we'd almost get done in by a stupid accident?"

He pulled something out of his jacket pocket and tossed it in her lap.

She frowned and picked it up. It was a tiny piece of charred, twisted metal with a little wire hanging from it. "What's this?"

"A remote-control detonated charge. That's what

I found sticking out of the hole in the tire when I changed the flat. The blowout wasn't an accident. Someone just tried to kill us."

CYPRIAN RAN HIS finger along the back of one of the dining-room chairs, checking for dust. But as usual, everything was pristine. His dear Silvia was most efficient. He wished he could instill that kind of work ethic in all of his employees—not that Silvia was just an employee.

She chose that moment to enter the dining room through the opposite archway, a glove on her right hand as she checked the cleanliness of the buffet and straightened a painting that was slightly off-center.

"Silvia, dear, everything is perfect. As always. Thank you."

She smiled the smile that she reserved for him, a smile that had warmed him in and out of bed for many years. She was a passionate, caring woman, and he didn't know what he would have done without her help in raising little Melissa after the death of his cherished Isabella and their sons, Marco and Marcelo. And in spite of her hellion son, Stefano, she'd managed to help him ensure that Melissa got the attention she needed in order to grow up well-adjusted, and feeling loved, after losing her mother and brothers.

But Silvia could never replace his beloved, and both of them knew it. He'd done his best to make that up to her, giving her all the money she could possibly need, if not his love. And even though she could have bought any house she wanted and hired her own maid, she'd vowed to stay with him as long as he needed her. Because above all else, she was loyal, as loyal as his own Isabella had been.

It was selfish to bind her to him when he could never give her his name, or the lost pieces of his heart, but he also couldn't imagine ever not needing her. So she stayed. She was the only person who could keep his oppressive loneliness at bay and help him fight the constant battle against depression.

There were many days when it was a struggle just to get out of bed. And it was only because of Silvia, and the carrot of seeing his beautiful daughter at the office, that he was able to get up. It wasn't the life he would have chosen. But it was the best he could hope for after having his heart ripped out by a terrorist's bomb.

She stopped a proper distance in front of him, always formal and maintaining decorum whenever they were outside of the bedchamber. It was one of the things that he appreciated most about her. Politeness, manners, and proper behavior were appallingly lacking in today's generation.

"Mr. Cyprian, Richard arrived a few moments ago as requested for your dinner party. He said the meal will be ready in precisely one hour."

"Excellent. Thank you, Silvia. You may retire to your suite for the evening. My guests prefer to maintain their privacy, and they'll be arriving around seven. You understand."

Her smile slipped a little, but she obediently nodded and headed out of the dining room toward the back of the house. With her gone, and Richard relegated to his domain, the kitchen, he'd have the house to himself—and the Council, of course, once they arrived.

Sebastian, his constant shadow, had left long ago, at his insistence. There was only so much of his assistant's smirks that he could stand in one day. And he'd be damned if he tolerated him in his home any longer than necessary. But Tarek hadn't proven to be quite so amenable. He claimed that Adam Marsh had requested his presence at the meeting. Cyprian didn't know why Marsh would do that, but he'd certainly make that the first point of discussion. For now, he'd ordered Tarek to take himself off somewhere and stay out of his sight.

He headed through the house and into his office. As always, he paused before the family portrait on the wall to the right of the double doors. A much younger version of himself, sitting at the same cherrywood desk that remained in this office today, stared back at him with eyes that were still full of life and happiness, untouched by the traumatic loss that would happen just a few weeks after this portrait was hung.

Standing behind him, her hand upon his shoulder, was Isabella. Her long dark hair hung in perfect waves down her demure blouse, buttoned to the throat as it should be. And standing on either side of the chair were Marco and Marcelo. Little Melissa cuddled a baby doll at her mother's feet.

He smiled at the memory and ran his fingers across his wife's cheek, his sons' hair. Then he moved to the small table set against the wall decorated with various knickknacks his wife had picked out when they'd built the house. He knew every surface of those dust collectors because he was the one who kept this room clean, not Silvia. She was forbidden to enter here.

A five-by-seven photograph taken just a few years ago beckoned him. He picked it up and stared down at his daughter. She was smiling into the camera. They both were. *Had she known back then?* Wouldn't he have seen it in her eyes? Hiding the horrors that his duties often required was the first thing he thought of every morning and the last thing he thought of before he closed his eyes at night. Because Isabella wouldn't have wanted her daughter to be touched in any way by his quest to save others from the heartache he'd had to endure. Isabella would have wanted him to do whatever he could to keep Melissa sheltered and happy. And even though his ongoing quest to find and eradicate any traces of the Serpentine terrorist group had so far failed, he thought he'd succeeded in keeping Melissa ignorant of his activities.

Until today.

His gaze settled on his desk by the windows. He'd been avoiding this for hours, but couldn't put it off any longer, not with the Council on their way. There were decisions to be made.

After setting the picture frame down, he slowly crossed the room. He sat in his chair and rolled it up to the desk, then picked up what he'd set on top of the cherrywood surface hours ago—a small piece of blue thread.

He'd picked it up from the stairs in his private office as he'd followed Sebastian. And although it had puzzled him at the time, he hadn't figured out its significance until he'd seen his daughter in that disgusting embrace with Atwell.

And saw the torn and ragged cuffs of her blue jeans.

IT WASN'T AN ACCIDENT.

Those words kept running through Melissa's mind, chilling her far more than the frigid wind blowing through the trees. She wrapped her arms around her waist, huddling against the cold while Jace finished setting up their equipment.

She still couldn't believe that someone had tried to kill them. The danger to her, and now to Jace, had never felt completely real until now. And what terrified her more than anything else was not knowing who was trying to kill them. Or why. How could they protect themselves when they didn't know who their enemies were?

Was it the Council? Sebastian? Tarek? This Watcher fellow? She'd voiced those same questions to Jace, and he'd added another name. Cyprian. She'd shook her head at that suggestion and hadn't said a word since. Regardless of what else her father might have done, she refused to consider that he could want her dead. It made no sense. He had no reason to kill her. He loved her.

And so, here she and Jace were, together and yet worlds apart, sitting beneath the tarp Jace had rigged over the branches above them to keep out most of the snow. He'd used some kind of thermal insulated blanket on the ground to help block out the cold, but nothing could completely stop the face-tingling chill of winter once the sun went down.

They might have been freezing, but at least the equipment was working. The phone-sized receiver in Jace's hands brought the conversations in the dining room in loud and clear, so clear that he had to turn the sound down when a Council member sitting close to one of the bugs spoke.

The meal passed like any other. There was a brief
mention early on that two of the members might be
late, but nothing else was said about them. Did the
Council not know that the two members had been
killed? And what was the purpose of the meeting?

Melissa was about to suggest she and Jace pack
it up and leave when a ringing sound, like someone tapping a wineglass with a piece of flatware,
brought conversation to a halt.

"Now that dinner is concluded," a man's voice
said, "our host, Cyprian, has expressed his desire to
petition the Council to end his probation. However, I
think it's far more appropriate to discuss something
else first: the fact that two of our Council members
were murdered yesterday. By Cyprian."

If Jace could have saved Melissa this pain, if somehow he could have taken it on himself, he would
have. But it was too late. All he could do now was sit
beside her and wait for the revelations to stop. And
then, if she'd let him, he'd try to help her pick up the
pieces of her life.

"You lured them to the motel room with this
letter," Marsh's voice proclaimed. "You set up an alleged meeting. Your signature is on the bottom."

"It was supposed to be a *real* meeting," Cyprian
insisted. "It wasn't a ruse. Since I haven't been able to
sway your opinion about my probation, I approached
them to help plead my case at *this* meeting."

"The Watcher saw you go into the hotel room,"
Marsh continued. "When you left, the Councilman
and Councilwoman were dead. And he found your
letter."

"As I said, I went there to talk. What would I gain by killing them? I needed them here to help my petition."

"Perhaps they told you they would vote against you, so you killed them."

"This is ridiculous. I didn't kill them."

The meeting continued, with Marsh arguing against Cyprian, and Cyprian proclaiming his innocence. And then Marsh made a motion to remove Cyprian as head of the enforcement arm of EXIT.

Jace closely watched Melissa. Her face was pale, her eyes downcast. Did she realize what was at stake? That if the Council voted to remove her father, they meant it in the most serious possible interpretation of the word? Removal was a death sentence. Cyprian knew too much. If he could no longer be trusted at the helm, he could no longer be trusted with EXIT's secrets. He'd never live to see another sunrise.

When the debate was over, and the votes were counted, Melissa blinked and finally looked at Jace.

Her father had been given a reprieve. Two days to prove that he didn't kill the Council members. If he couldn't prove his innocence in that time, he would be removed as head of the enforcement arm.

The meeting ended, and the sounds gradually faded as the members took their leave. It was a long time before she finally spoke.

"What happened to innocent until proven guilty?" Her voice was scratchy and raw. "How is someone supposed to prove innocence?"

"EXIT operates by its own set of rules."

She shivered and wrapped her arms around her

middle. "They said they'd remove him. Do you know what that means? Is it a code word for . . . something else?"

He hesitated.

"Just tell me, Jace. No sugarcoating."

"Okay. Yes. I believe it's code for . . . something else."

She gave him a jerky nod and drew a deep breath. "What do we do now?"

"We go home. Sleep on it. Take a fresh look tomorrow to decide what our next steps should be."

"What about my father? We have to help him."

He shoved himself to his feet and started packing up the equipment.

"Jace, please. He's my father. I can't ignore what I just heard. This Council is going to kill him if we don't do something."

He zipped the duffel closed. "That's between your father and the Council."

The flash of hurt in her eyes sent a stab of guilt through him. But what did she expect? She'd read the Hightower binder. She knew what her father had done, what he was capable of. How could she expect Jace to want to protect a monster like that?

He settled the strap over his shoulder, so the duffel was on his back, and held his hand out to her. "Ready?"

Shoving his hand away, she leaped to her feet and started to pass him on her way to the car.

"Don't." He grabbed her arm. "Don't let your anger rule your head. Just because you're pissed at me doesn't mean you should go stomping off by yourself. We go together."

She gave him a stony look but didn't try to pass him again.

They were almost to the car when a man suddenly stepped out from behind a tree twenty feet in front of them, holding a pistol.

Tarek.

Chapter Sixteen

S omeone was going to die.

    Melissa crossed the familiar brick pavers of the long circular driveway in front of her father's mansion, drawing inexorably closer to what had once been *her* home, too.

Someone was going to die.

Unless she could do something to stop it.

Behind her, Jace was so close that she could feel his heat at her back, even through her coat. She could also sense the tension radiating off him, feel it in the stiffness of his gait every time he brushed against her, hear it in the sureness of his steps, as if every movement was planned, as if he was only waiting for the perfect opportunity. Then he would strike.

And someone would die.

"When we're almost to the door," his whisper sounded behind her, "dive down and to the right, then run like hell. Circle back through the woods to my car."

"Jace, please—"

"Stop talking," Tarek called out from behind them.

He was closer than before, but not so close that Jace could knock the gun out of his hand. Tarek had made Jace toss his gun, so he didn't have one. She still had her derringer, only because Tarek hadn't even considered that she'd have a gun. But what good did that do? There was no way she could win a gunfight with someone like Tarek, especially when he already had his gun out.

So what was Jace going to do? He would sacrifice himself, she *knew* it, to give her the head start that he thought she needed. Because that was the kind of honorable, brave man that he was.

"Get your derringer ready," he whispered. "Put it where I can grab it."

She swallowed hard and did what he asked, even as she debated whether to let him try whatever he was thinking about trying. They were going to the house. Her father would protect them once they were inside. He'd make Tarek stand down. There was no reason for Jace to try anything. It was too dangerous.

He believed her father was evil, that he would kill them both once Tarek revealed that they'd listened to the Council meeting. Jace would probably assume that her father would use that to sway the Council, to make them see that he wanted to protect them. Maybe he thought he could use their deaths to bargain for his life. That's what Jace would think. Could he be right? She didn't know. But no matter what, she couldn't let him do what she thought he was planning to do—trade his life for hers.

"Jace, don't—"

"I'll take your gun in a few seconds. When I tell you to, dive down, to the *right*. I'll cover you."

Cover her? Tarek already had his gun out. How could Jace possibly cover her without getting shot himself while using his body as a shield?

They reached the portico. Twenty feet to the door.

What could she do? *Think. Think!* How could she stop this?

Fifteen. The sound of Jace's breathing changed, as if he were tensing up, getting ready to make his move. *To sacrifice himself.*

Ten feet.

He edged closer to her and slid her gun out of her pocket.

Nine.

Closer, closer.

"Now, Mel," he whispered harshly.

He gave her a little shove. She whirled around, just as he did. His gun came up. Tarek's did, too. She dove, not to the right, but at Jace. A gunshot rang out, and the two of them fell to the ground. She slammed down on top of his chest, clutching at his shoulders, looking into his beautiful gray eyes, wide with shock.

She blinked in surprise, then lifted her head and looked past him. Tarek lay unmoving on the bricks, blood pooling beneath his head. "You got him," she said. "I can't believe you got him."

"And I can't believe you got yourself shot. Damn it to hell, Melissa. What were you thinking?"

"Shot?" She looked down and saw the blood spattered on her shirt, seeping from her shoulder. White-hot agony seemed to suddenly spread everywhere at once, arching her backward. "Jace?"

He swore savagely, scooping her up in his arms. "Don't you dare die on me, Mel. Don't you dare." He clasped her against his chest and ran. She squeezed her eyes shut, sucking in a breath as each step sent a jolt of pain through her.

When they reached the door, he gave the doorknob a savage kick. The wood frame splintered, and the door sagged open. So much for her father's impenetrable security. She laughed, then sucked in another breath at the fresh wave of pain.

"What are you doing here? What happened?" Her father. "*Melissa*?" His voice cracked.

"Out of the way," Jace growled. He carried her through the house. More jarring pain. But not as bad as before. Was she going numb? Was she . . . dying? She swallowed and clutched Jace's shirt.

He looked down at her, the corners of his eyes crinkling with tension. "I've got you, Mel."

"Put her here. I'll grab a pillow from the couch. What happened?" her father demanded.

"Don't bother with the fake surprise," Jace snarled. "Your minion, Tarek, shot her. Presumably on your orders. He's dead, by the way."

Her father stiffened. "I don't know what you're talking about. I didn't tell Tarek to . . . I didn't even know you were on my property."

"Well, now you do. And if you try pulling a gun on me while I'm checking on your daughter, I swear to God I'll kill you."

"Jace," Melissa whispered through the pain. "Don't."

"Save your strength, Mel. Don't try to talk." He lowered her onto something hard. The desk? A pillow was shoved beneath her head. The muted sound of a zipper, then tugging, lifting. Her coat was gone. And then Jace's strong, warm hands pressed against her skin, running up beneath her shirt, down her belly, searching, probing, gently lifting. She sighed and closed her eyes, enjoying the feel of his hands far more than seemed appropriate given the circumstances. The pain wasn't even that bad anymore.

"Mel? Can you hear me, sweetheart?"

Sweetheart? Jace calling her sweetheart was the kind of heaven she'd take any day.

He shook her, and she opened her eyes, blinking until he came into focus.

"Jace? Where am I?"

"On the desk, in your father's office. I need to stop the bleeding. This is going to hurt." He pressed down on her upper left shoulder.

She gasped and let out a ragged moan at the searing pain.

Jace looked past her. "Call 911."

"No." Her father's voice.

Jace snarled. "She's your daughter, man. She needs medical attention."

"Yes. She's my daughter. And I love her dearly. But there are things in play here that you don't understand."

Oh, Daddy. What are you doing?

"Spare me the lies and cover-ups," Jace snapped. "I'll save us both some time. I know all about EXIT, the Council, and the enforcers. And so does your daughter."

Cyprian sighed deeply. "I suspected as much. Well. That does save us time. I assume you're working with them, the rogue enforcers who turned on me? You've been working with them all along?"

"I work alone."

"Now who's lying, Mr. Atwell?"

"Are you going to make that 911 call, or do I have to move my hands and risk her bleeding out to make the call myself?" Jace bit out.

The pressure of his hands on her arm made it throb. She blinked against the pain, trying to focus on what they were saying.

"If we call for help," Cyprian said, "we're signing her death warrant, if you haven't already. You and I will be tied up with police interviews, and she'll be alone in the hospital, vulnerable. I won't be able to protect her. The Watcher—I'm assuming you know about that, too—may have already told Marsh that you killed Tarek. That makes you their enemy, and by association, since you're obviously together, Melissa as well. They won't waste time with an investigation to find out what she knows or doesn't know. And as you just confirmed, she *does* know what's going on. So an investigation wouldn't help anyway. Regardless, if either of us makes that call, she dies."

Melissa's heart sank at her father's words. Was he right? Would calling for help put her in more danger? Or was he just concerned about his own safety, about trying to explain why Tarek had been pointing a gun at them and why he was at the house? Had she ever really known this man? She blinked against the tears that burned at the backs of her eyes, threatening to spill down her cheeks.

Jace cursed beneath his breath. Since he didn't go for the phone, he must have agreed with her father's assessment of the danger. "Get my first-aid kit from my car. It's a couple of hundred yards due south of here in the woods. And get me some towels to stop the bleeding."

"I have a first-aid kit. I'll have Silvia—"

"No. Get mine. It's got everything I need for a field dressing, including anesthesia. And trust me, she'll want anesthesia."

Her father whirled around and left the room.

Melissa grabbed Jace's hand.

He bent over her, looking more angry than concerned. "What were you thinking, jumping in front of me? You could have been killed."

"I was trying to save you."

"Bodyguard. Hello? It's *my* job to save *you*." He leaned in closer. "Don't you *ever* do something like that again."

"If you're making threats, does that mean I'm going to live?"

He glanced toward the closed double doors before answering. "If you don't, it will be the first time I've ever lost anyone to a flesh wound." He lifted his hand. "Looks like the bleeding's almost stopped."

"Flesh wound?" She lifted her head. "There's blood all over my shirt. Are you sure the bullet went all the way through?"

"Don't sound so disappointed. You still get bragging rights when you're old and gray and comparing scars in the old-folks home. The bullet barely touched you. A graze through the upper part of your arm, close to your shoulder but missing anything vital. You're going to be fine."

"So asking my father to call 911 was, what, a ploy? To make him feel guilty?"

"He damn well deserved it." He smoothed her hair back from her face. "I swear to God, Mel, you scared the hell out of me."

She swallowed against the lump in her throat.

"My father would not approve of all of this foul language," she teased.

"Frankly my dear, I don't give a fucking damn."

She laughed, then sucked in a breath. "Just a graze, huh? For all of this pain you'd think I'd at least earned a stitch or two to brag to my nursing-home friends. After all, it isn't every day that I leap in front of a bullet."

He cupped her face. "I could have lost you." He kissed her, his lips achingly gentle, and sweet, and so full of angst and concern that those tears threatened to spill again.

"You wouldn't have lost me," she whispered. "You're too strong and tough to let me die from a puny gunshot wound."

He gave her a curt nod. "Damn straight I wouldn't."

One of the doors swung open and her father hurried inside with his arms full of thick, white towels and carrying what looked like a small suitcase.

"Jace," she whispered, "I think we need to tell him I'm going to be okay."

"He hasn't suffered enough yet."

"*Jace*," she warned.

"It's about time, Cyprian," he called out, giving her an I-dare-you-to-say-otherwise look. "You're lucky she hasn't bled out by now."

She rolled her eyes.

Her father dropped his armload of towels and the first-aid kit onto the desk and leaned over her, his face as white as the snow falling outside the window. "Melissa, are you going to . . ."

"Die?" Jace callously asked, as he pressed one of the towels over her arm.

She sucked in a sharp breath and glared at him.

He eased the pressure. "Mel, you don't have to be so brave. You can close your eyes. I won't think anything less of you if you faint. I know you're strong."

"Oh for Pete's sake, I'm not going to—"

"No, no, no," he assured her, smoothing her hair back again. "Of course you aren't going to die." He clucked his tongue. "I shouldn't have said that in front of you."

Her father's eyes widened.

"Jace," she warned. "If you don't stop—"

"Get me a needle and thread," Jace barked. "Quickly, so I can sew her up before she loses more blood than she can afford."

It didn't seem possible, but her father turned even more pale. "You're going to stitch her wound? Do you have any medical training?"

"Isn't it a little late to be asking that? Get the needle and thread. Hurry."

Her father ran out of the room again.

Melissa pinned Jace with an accusing look. "Can I assume that monster-of-a-first-aid-kit is yours?"

"Yep."

"It looks big enough to conceal a small child. And you don't have needle and thread?"

"Hm." He made a show of digging through it. "Oh, look. Needle and thread. My bad." At her aggravated look, he said, "What? I'm just making sure the lesson soaks in."

"I think you've tortured him enough."

His eyes flashed with anger, and all signs of teasing disappeared. "No. He hasn't suffered *nearly* enough. And he has a lot to answer for. Did you forget that someone tried to send us hurtling over a cliff on the way here? How do we know Cyprian isn't the one behind that?"

"Someone tried to kill my daughter?" Cyprian's choked voice sounded from the doorway.

Jace looked over his shoulder. "The banged-up side of my car didn't give that away?"

"Richard didn't mention the car when I sent him to get the kit." His gaze dipped to Jace's hand. "It appears that you already have what you need for the stitches."

"Oops."

Melissa tugged Jace's free hand and pressed a soft kiss against his knuckles before letting go. "Please. Stop it."

He gave her a defiant look, but he didn't tease her father again while he cleaned her arm with an antiseptic.

"What happened?" Cyprian asked, directing his question to Melissa. "Someone tried to run you off the road?"

She gave him a quick version of their brush with death, including that someone had planted a small charge to make their tire blow out.

"I swear to you that I knew nothing about this," he said, clutching her hand.

"What about Thomas?" she asked softly. "Did you know nothing about that?"

His eyes widened, and the truth was there for her to see. She tugged her hand out of his and turned her head away from him. "Jace, are you about done?"

"Just finished." He smoothed a piece of tape into place on her arm and wiped his hands on a towel.

"Can I get up now?" she asked, avoiding her father's eyes.

"You've lost a lot of blood. You might feel weak or nauseated. Maybe you should stay here," Jace said.

"Yeah, well. The desk is kind of hard. Just saying."

Before she realized what he was going to do, he'd lifted her in his arms and was halfway across the room.

"I thought she needed stitches?" her father called out from behind them.

"False alarm." Jace carefully set her on one of the two recliners and propped her up with pillows. "Comfortable?"

She moved her arm, trying to ease the ache. "I'm fine."

He didn't look like he believed her. He snagged a bottle of water and some pills from his bottomless first-aid kit and made her drink them down. "Those should kick in fairly soon."

"Thanks."

Jace sat in the chair beside hers and swiveled to face her father, who'd followed them over and was sitting on the couch watching them.

"All right, Cyprian," Jace said. "This is where you get to prove what kind of a father you really are. Someone is trying to kill your daughter. If you give a damn about her, you're going to help me figure out who they are. And you won't stall or lie. Because if you're right, and the Watcher knows we're here, and that Tarek has been killed, he's already told the Council. And even though the Council is supposed to be a voice of reason for your little fiefdom, I'm not trusting anyone with Melissa's life."

"You think someone's after her because they tried to run your car off the road. Are you sure they weren't after you? And didn't know she was in the car?" her father accused.

The hatred that flared in her father's eyes had Melissa straightening in her chair. Jace must have caught the same look because he narrowed his eyes and swore.

"Who'd you send to kill *me* then?" he demanded.

"Jace, I don't think he—"

"Stefano. And I can assure you, he won't make a mistake like this again."

Melissa's mouth dropped open. "Wait. You're saying you ordered Stefano to kill Jace?"

He nodded. "But he wasn't supposed to hurt you. I'll take care of Stefano."

"What? No, no. You won't. You can't just *take care* of someone. Not the way you're implying. I don't understand. How did Stefano get involved in all of this?"

"I'm guessing he's an enforcer," Jace said.

Her father nodded in confirmation.

Melissa gasped. "Oh no." She looked toward the double doors. "Does Silvia know?"

"That her son works for me instead of you? No. Stefano and I agreed to protect her by not telling her from the beginning. She knows nothing about any of this. And that's the way it shall remain. I don't want her hurt."

The emotion in his voice had Melissa staring at him in shock. "You're in love with her."

"No. I'm in love with your mother. But I care about Silvia. I must protect her."

"Too bad you didn't care enough about your own daughter to protect her, too," Jace gritted out.

Her father turned his brooding gaze on Melissa.

"I've lived my entire life protecting you. And how do you repay me? You break into my office, into my private files. I can only assume you were snooping around this evening as well, or Tarek wouldn't have gone after you."

Not the speech full of regret and apologies that she would have expected, begging her forgiveness for all the lies and terrible things he'd done. Instead, he sounded almost . . . accusing.

"How did you know we broke into your office?" Jace asked.

"A little blue thread. I found it on the stairs. And after seeing Melissa in jeans, I knew who'd left that thread."

"When I stumbled on the stairs," she said. "The hem must have snagged."

"I'd have known anyway. My office window was unlocked, apparently from when the two of you escaped through it this afternoon. I never leave it unlocked. Once I was over my disgust at your behavior in the greenhouse, I put it all together. But I suspected much earlier than that."

"What do you mean?" Jace asked.

"For the past few months, my daughter has been acting very curious and has been asking a lot of questions. Then I found that blue thread. Knowing *your* background, Mr. Atwell, and having been suspicious of you from the start, I assumed the worst might have happened, that the rogue enforcers who've plagued me had used my very own flesh and blood to betray me."

"Betray you?" Melissa clutched the arm of her chair. "I was trying to find the truth! You had Thomas *killed*."

"Which I regret, but only because it obviously disturbs you. And because it was the catalyst for everything else that has happened." He pointed his finger at her. "That man used you, lied to you. I couldn't allow that to go unpunished."

She pressed a hand to her throat. "Disturbs me? Unpunished? He had an affair. And yes, he lied to me. But he didn't deserve to die for that. You talk about killing like it's nothing."

"This is why I had to protect you all these years," he accused. "Because you were too young to understand, to suffer like I did when those terrorist bastards took Isabella, Marco, and Marcello. You don't live with the pain that I do. You have no understanding of the importance of my work, of keeping this country and its people safe from the kind of loss that I've endured. To keep others from suffering that same loss. You're too soft, too weak, too judgmental to appreciate the sacrifices that I've made."

He thought her weak? Too judgmental? Because she didn't want him to *kill* people? In all her nightmares, she never could have imagined this conversation, or her father sitting there so calmly, so composed, without a trace of guilt over anything he'd done.

Without taking his eyes off her father, Jace moved his hand on top of hers. She turned her hand palm up, entwining their fingers, grateful for the strength and support he offered her with that one small action.

"Is that why you sent that letter to those two Council members? The ones found dead at that motel?" Jace asked. "So you could set them up, to kill them, so they wouldn't vote against you in the meeting? Just like Marsh said? All so you could run your precious company because you're so enlightened and the rest of us aren't?"

"So you *were* listening in on the meeting. How?"

"It doesn't matter."

He shrugged. "I suppose not. But you're wrong. Marsh is wrong. I sent that letter to schedule a meeting, nothing more. I was set up."

"By whom?" Jace asked. "Who did you give the letter to?"

"The same man I told to terminate you."

Jace's jaw tightened. "Stefano."

Melissa rubbed her hand across her forehead, soothing the ache that even the pills Jace had given her weren't touching. "I can't believe you're saying this like it's nothing. You told Stefano to kill Jace. And, what, now you're saying you weren't going to kill the Council members, and that Stefano killed them and tried to frame you? Is that your claim?"

"It's the truth."

Melissa pressed a hand to her throat. "This can't be happening."

The hard mask of indifference on her father's face cracked, and she caught a glimpse of the loving, caring man she'd always thought him to be.

"You have to understand, Melissa. I had to protect my legacy, preserve the company your mother and I began, for her memory, and your brothers, and for you. That's why I'm trying to get the Council to drop my probation, to stop stifling me so I can run everything the way it needs to be run."

"Is that what Jace was doing? Stifling you? So you sent Stefano after him and almost killed me, too?" When he didn't answer, she said, "Is Stefano the man in the ski mask, too? Did you send him to scare me, to wave a gun at me and force me off the road, because you knew I was investigating EXIT?"

His brow furrowed. "I assumed the man in the ski mask was someone working with Mr. Atwell."

"Well he wasn't."

"Maybe ski-mask guy is the Watcher," Jace interjected. "What's the Watcher's real name?"

"I have no idea. The Council appointed him, but his identity is protected."

"Could he be Sebastian? Or Tarek?" Jace asked.

"They certainly watch me as much as they can," he said, his voice sounding bitter. "But I'm able to shake them when I need to. No, the Watcher is someone else."

Melissa didn't say what seemed obvious to her, that Stefano was probably the Watcher, that he might be taking orders from the Council and manipulating her father at the same time. She couldn't say it. Because if she did, her father might try to kill him. He might try anyway because Stefano had almost killed her when he'd gone after Jace.

How had everything gotten so horrible and so royally screwed up?

She closed her eyes, tears flowing down her cheeks. She brushed them away, hating that she was showing such weakness again. Crying had never been her thing, and here she was, crying for the second time in one day.

Jace stood and slung his duffel bag over his shoulder. "We're done here. I want my car brought around. And I want my gun."

"It's in your car. And your car is already parked out front, with the keys inside."

Jace carefully drew Melissa to her feet. He swiped her jacket from a nearby chair and helped her into it before shrugging into his own. When he bent down to pick her up, she stepped back.

"I'm fine. I'll walk."

He didn't look happy with that, but he let her pass. He kept his hand on the small of her back as they crossed the room and made their way to the front door.

"Melissa?" her father called out from behind them.

Jace yanked the door open and scanned outside as Melissa looked over her shoulder at her father.

"I should have protected you better. I'll find out who was in that van. And I'll figure something out with the Council. I'll find a way to keep you safe."

She shook her head. "No, Dad. I don't want you doing *anything* on my behalf. I know what happens when you *protect* someone." With her heart breaking inside her chest, she stepped out the door and didn't look back.

CYPRIAN STOOD FOR a long time at the front windows in the foyer, looking out at his property, the architectural outdoor lighting casting a soft yellow glow far beyond where the tree-lined driveway disappeared down a hill. This home had been Isabella's dream. It was an anniversary gift to her. And just a few short years later, she was dead. Along with the sons he'd hoped to pass his empire to.

He pressed his hand against the cold, dark glass, as if he could reach into space and somehow bring his family back to him. His dream had died that day. But he'd done his duty, raising the daughter Isabella had doted upon. And little by little, Melissa had worked her way into his heart, becoming nearly as important to him as his sons had once been. The more he praised her accomplishments in school, the harder she tried—earning the highest marks, winning the attention of only the best and brightest colleges. Her quick wit, intelligence, and business savvy had delighted him and sparked a new dream—one that saw her eventually taking his place at the helm of the enforcer side of EXIT as well as the tour company.

But Melissa had proven to be too soft-hearted, too firm in her convictions, unwilling to bend or see his vision. Every time he'd considered revealing the truth about EXIT to her, something would happen to convince him it would never work, that she could never see the world the way he did. And he'd finally accepted that if she ever found out the truth, then his dreams, all of them, would be over.

"Mr. Cyprian? It is late for you to be up. Is something wrong?"

Silvia. He'd been worried that she might have heard the gunshot earlier, but then he'd remembered she always wore earplugs to bed. A habit born out of necessity from when they slept together, because he tended to snore, and she couldn't sleep otherwise.

"Nothing is wrong. Go to my room, darling. I'll be there momentarily."

She shuffled down the hall to use the back stairs to his master bedroom. It certainly wasn't necessary, not with the house empty. She could have used the main staircase. But she wasn't nosey, never asked about his business or whether anyone else was around. It was her habit to always *assume* the possibility that someone *might* be around, a lesson learned because of their one failure: the day her then-teenaged son had come into the house unexpectedly and caught them sharing a passionate embrace in the foyer.

After that, Stefano had been impossible to deal with. He was angry that his mother wasn't good enough to marry and only good enough to *screw*, as he'd coarsely put it. Stefano hadn't understood their relationship. He'd rebelled. But once he'd reached adulthood, he'd matured. And they'd come to an understanding.

Little by little, Stefano had proven himself as a tour guide. And later, as an enforcer. When Stefano had seen how arrogant and disobedient Sebastian and Tarek had acted, he'd approached Cyprian, offering to help in any way—the implication being that he'd risk the wrath of the Council by eliminating the two assistants if that was what Cyprian required. He'd proven his loyalty by making that offer, and Cyprian had believed he could trust him completely after that.

Apparently, he'd been wrong. Horribly so. Stefano had played him for a fool. He'd encouraged Cyprian for months to meet with some of the more amenable members of the Council, to convince them to rebel against Marsh and end the probation. He'd even gotten Cyprian to pen a letter, but Cyprian had waited on sending it. He'd wanted to try one more time to convince Marsh first, without going behind his back. But after that disastrous meeting at EXIT, where Marsh had nixed any hopes that he'd support ending the Council's punishment, he'd told Stefano to do it, to send the letter to the Council members, to set up a meeting.

But Stefano had really been setting up Cyprian to take the fall. All these years, Stefano must have been burning up with hatred for him because of his mother. And he'd patiently waited until the right opening came along to destroy him. He very likely was the Watcher. He'd probably eavesdropped on Cyprian's discussions with the Council and heard they were going to appoint a Watcher. And then maybe Stefano had volunteered for the position so he'd know what all was going on. So he'd be sure that no one was watching *him* as he set Cyprian up.

Clever. Stefano had been far too clever. And Cyprian had never even suspected that he'd been used. Stefano must have laughed when he'd been ordered to kill Atwell. He must have seen the opportunity to kill Melissa at the same time as the ultimate way to hurt Cyprian.

Ordinarily, that alone would have gotten Stefano a death sentence. But Melissa had turned against Cyprian, too. She'd betrayed his trust and was associating with his enemies. Instead of worrying about her, and what she'd done, and what he should do about it—he should be focused on figuring out how to get around the Council's forty-eight-hour deadline to prove his innocence.

If he brought them the man responsible for the murder of the two Council members—Stefano—they wouldn't believe him. Stefano was presumably their Watcher, after all. He was the only person who made sense as the Watcher. They obviously, foolishly, trusted him. So where did that leave Cyprian? What options did he have? How could he salvage everything?

An hour passed as he stared out the windows,

immersed in his thoughts, considering all of the possibilities. And when he finally headed into his office, he knew exactly what he had to do.

He sat behind his desk, with Atwell's forgotten first-aid kit sitting on top. Apparently the man had been in such a hurry to get Melissa away from her own father that he hadn't thought to take it. Cyprian shook his head, then noted the stains around the kit. The desk's cherrywood finish was ruined from the peroxide and blood that had dripped onto it while Jace had cared for Melissa's injury. He frowned and made a mental note to have someone come out as soon as possible to refinish the surface. Thankfully, the phone wasn't soiled as well. He picked it up and made the first of two calls.

The line clicked. "Marsh."

"It's Cyprian. I'm afraid there's been a terrible accident involving Tarek. I need to see you right away."

He was proud of himself for keeping his poise during the distasteful conversation. Marsh was his usual arrogant self. But he'd taken the bait. So listening to his condescending comments was bearable.

He keyed another number in.

"Yes?"

"Stefano, did you take care of my last instruction?"

"Uh, yeah. Yes, yes, sir. Atwell's dead. Like you wanted."

He smiled. He could well imagine Stefano's panic and anger when he'd searched along the mountain road to confirm that the car had gone over the railing, only to discover that it hadn't. He was probably going frantic trying to figure out where Atwell was so he could finish him off before Cyprian found out he was still alive—and so he could play his ultimate card, the revenge Stefano had wanted all along—to punish him by telling him his daughter was dead.

"Excellent. Good work. There's another task I'd like your help with. But we'll need to discuss this in person. Yes, the usual place. No, not right now. I have something else to take care of first. Tomorrow will be soon enough."

Chapter Seventeen

"Barely hurts anymore." Melissa shifted in the passenger seat of Jace's worse-for-wear car and raised her left arm to demonstrate that she felt fine, in spite of the dull ache that still throbbed where the bullet had grazed her. She forced a smile, hoping her little white lie was convincing. Because insisting she was okay every five minutes when he asked her, again, was really getting irritating.

Jace shot her a suspicious look. "The words coming out of your mouth are in direct opposition to how pale you are. I should take you to the hospital and get you some prescription painkillers."

"No, you shouldn't. Neither of us wants to have to explain my injury. I imagine emergency-room doctors can recognize a bullet wound a mile off even if it's only a *paltry* flesh wound."

He winced. "Did I really call it paltry?"

"You really did."

"Sorry. I really am. I never should have taken you with me tonight."

"If you hadn't, if my father hadn't admitted right

in front of me the things he's done, I'd still be doubting you and trying to argue that you're wrong, even after reading all those files. I guess it's just human nature to hope your father isn't, well, that he hasn't done all those things. It hurts like hell knowing you were right. But at least my eyes are open now."

He squeezed her hand.

She looked out the window, but there weren't many lights in this lightly populated area. Mostly all she saw were the white lines in the middle of the two-lane highway. "Where are we going? We've been driving for over an hour, and nothing around here looks familiar. I don't think we've passed another car in the last five minutes."

"I didn't want to chance driving through the mountains again, just in case Stefano, or anyone else, was waiting up there for us. I took the long way around."

"Around to where? Where are we going?"

"Right here." He slowed and turned into the parking lot of a dilapidated two-story foam-green motel that was off by itself and looked like it had maybe twenty rooms, total. Peeling green-and-white railings framed the second-floor outside hallway. And there were only three cars in the lot, parked at the far end.

"Be still my heart. You sure know how to spoil a girl."

He parked in one of the empty spots at the opposite end from the other cars. "We can't risk going to my apartment or your house, not with your father knowing that we know about EXIT. And I don't have enough cash with me right now to spring for something nicer."

She put her hand on his. "I was only teasing. I can rough it like anyone else. My only concern is that I don't have a go bag like you. I've got nothing to wear."

A slow smile spread across his face. "Doesn't sound like a problem to me."

She slapped his forearm and laughed.

He hurried around to her side to help her out of the car. But she pushed the door open and stood before he reached her.

He frowned with disapproval.

She put her hands on her hips. "Jace, in spite of the mountain of gauze you strapped to my arm, I know I've essentially got the equivalent of a skinned knee. So how about stop treating me like an invalid who can't do anything for herself?"

He opened his mouth as if to argue.

She jabbed her finger against his chest. "Don't you dare ask me if I feel okay or argue with me that my arm is worse than I'm saying. I'm through talking about it. I assume we're here to get a room for the night. So let's get one."

His sigh could have toppled a tree, but he escorted her to the manager's office without another word.

Less than a minute later, Mr. and Mrs. John Smith were booked into room eight. The manager didn't even blink at the made-up names, and barely looked up from the basketball game he was watching on TV to give them a room key.

The door to their bottom floor *bungalow* was so grimy that Melissa wasn't sure if it was supposed to be gray or had once been white. "I sure hope the inside is cleaner than the outside."

Jace dropped his go bag beside them and fit the

key into the lock. "That just proves the main difference between you and me. You're an optimist."

"And you're a pessimist?"

"I'm a realist."

She rolled her eyes as he pushed the door open.

Something whipped past her from above and made a zapping noise. Jace stiffened and fell to the ground, writhing in pain. Melissa looked up in horror to see a man dressed in black with most of his face covered by a dark cloth, hanging down from the railing on the second story, holding the other end of a Taser.

"Jace!" She lunged for the coiled wires pulsing electricity through his body. Someone grabbed her from behind. She opened her mouth to scream, and a rag was stuffed inside. The man who'd gagged her slapped a piece of duct tape across her mouth.

She drew back her fist and slammed it into the side of his jaw.

Laughter sounded from the balcony above. Her captor cursed and grabbed her. She twisted and kicked, trying to get away, but he held her arms like a vise. Had her father sent someone after them? How? How could anyone have followed them? Jace had done everything right, checked his mirrors, turned down side roads. They'd never seen any lights behind them.

The zapping noise stopped. Jace lay on the ground in front of the door, his chest heaving, his teeth drawn back in a snarl. He shoved himself to his feet. *Bzzzt.* The Taser sent another charge through him. He fell to the ground again, his body bowed up against the concrete.

"Stop it! Stop it!" Melissa tried to yell, but it came out a muffled sob against the gag.

A dark-colored van zoomed up beside them. Its brakes screeched, and before it had even stopped, the side door slid back on its rails. A man with a bandana tied over the bottom half of his face and a baseball cap covering his hair hopped out.

No, no, no. *Stefano.* It had to be. He'd kill them for sure this time. She desperately strained against the man holding her. Her hurt arm throbbed in protest, but all she could think of was getting to Jace. She couldn't bear it if he died because of her. She cursed against the gag in her mouth and tried to turn around and rake her captor's eyes with her nails.

The man she assumed must be Stefano yanked a hypodermic needle out of his pocket and flipped off the plastic cap. She bucked like a wild horse, knowing that if he stuck her, she and Jace would both be as good as dead.

"Damn it, hold her still."

"I'm trying. She's stronger than she looks."

The voices were unfamiliar. Not Stefano then. The men shoved her against the building. Tears of anger pricked her eyes as the needle bit into her neck. Her body went limp. She fell into a dark void.

JACE STRUGGLED THROUGH layers of darkness, trying to open his heavy eyelids.

"He's coming around. But *she* should have been alert by now. I told you not to dose her too heavily. How much did you give her?"

That voice sounded familiar. Was the man talking about Melissa? He remembered lying there, writhing in pain, helpless to stop them as one of them shoved a needle into her neck. Why couldn't he open his eyes? Had he and Melissa both been drugged?

"I found this in his car. Might explain why she's so groggy."

A clacking noise, like maracas. *Or maybe . . . someone tossing a bottle of pills?*

"Painkillers. You're probably right. Use the smelling salts."

A moan sounded from somewhere nearby, then a startled yelp.

Was that Mel? *Damn it. Open your eyes, Atwell.* He shook his head, trying to clear the fog in his brain.

"Whoa, whoa, whoa. Hold on there, Miss Cardenas. Careful, or you'll start bleeding again. Settle down."

Bleeding again? What the hell? Jace's eyes flew open. He blinked at the light, trying to focus. Standing directly in front of him was Mason Hunt. To Mason's right were Devlin and Ramsey, who was wearing his usual NASCAR-themed T-shirt and bearing some purple-and-black bruises on his face but who otherwise seemed okay. Austin took up a position in the corner, looking bored as he balanced his wheelchair on two wheels.

Jace cursed at Mason, but there wasn't much point with a gag in his mouth and tape over that. He tried to get up, but his arms and legs were roped to the chair he was sitting in. He scanned the room, searching for Melissa. Relief flashed through him when he saw her, sitting about ten feet away on his right, apparently unharmed.

Like him, she was restrained, but only by a pair of handcuffs on one wrist. And she was sitting in a plush recliner, with her injured arm propped on a pillow. She wasn't gagged, either. But those small allowances for her comfort didn't mean that she wasn't in trouble. It all depended on why Mason had brought them here, wherever "here" was.

Based on the lack of windows, the concrete-block walls, and concrete floors, they were probably in a basement, albeit a warm, comfortable one. Couches and recliners were scattered around the room, and enough cots lined the walls to accommodate a small army: or a handful of former enforcers calling themselves Equalizers. And judging by the unique gray-mesh texture covering the walls, the ceiling, and even the floor, Jace was 99 percent sure he knew exactly where they were: the Equalizer's home base. But in the floor below the one he'd been in last time. That explained the elevator.

He glared his displeasure at his former associates, putting special emphasis on silently communicating his loathing to the man he figured was the ringleader in all of this—Mason Hunt.

Mason seemed unimpressed with his glares and crossed in front of Melissa, with Devlin and Ramsey following and standing off to his side. "Miss Cardenas, do you know who I am?"

She looked over at Jace as if asking whether she should say anything. But he had no way of telling her what to say, and he wasn't sure what to tell her even if he could. He thought that he'd known these men, that he could trust them. But they'd turned their backs on him when he needed them. So now he had no way of being sure what their agenda was, or what they planned to do. All he could offer her was a shrug.

"Miss Cardenas?" Mason prodded.

She pinned him with a haughty stare. "Based on your voice, I'd say that you're the jerk who stuck me with a needle back at the motel. As for the rest of you . . ." Her brows raised as she looked them over. "The men standing by you are Ramsey Tate and Devlin Buchanan." She nodded in greeting and they shifted uncomfortably, as if embarrassed at their current role.

"Ramsey and Devlin used to work for me," she continued. "They were tour guides for EXIT. And then they disappeared last year. I'm glad to see you're both okay, gentlemen. A little notice would have been nice. Or a call so that I knew you were even alive. But then again, I gather you were never really tour guides were you? You probably worked for my father the entire time, as assassins."

Mason cleared his throat, regaining her attention. "What about me? I'm sure Jace told you who I am." He waved toward Austin who was still in the corner. "And him, too."

"No. Jace didn't tell me about any of you." She motioned toward the far wall, where the corkboards from her house were propped up. "But you obviously broke into my home. And since you're associating with Devlin and Ramsey, I assume your name is under the heading 'Enemies' like theirs are. Therefore, either you're Mason Hunt, or the gentleman in the wheelchair is. I really couldn't say. I'd apologize for that, but it wouldn't be sincere. So I won't bother."

The disdain in her voice had Jace smiling against his gag. He took a quick inventory of their surroundings while everyone else was preoccupied watching Melissa and Mason. From his vantage point, he didn't see any exits. But based on the pistols the other men had strapped to their belts, even if he wasn't tied up, trying to fight his way to freedom might not be the wisest course of action. When he spotted the Taser holstered on Ramsey's thigh, he swore against the gag in his mouth.

Mason crouched in front of Melissa. "You expect me to believe that you put those boards together without Jace's help?"

She rolled her eyes.

Undaunted, he said, "Obviously, someone has told you about the enforcement side of EXIT or you wouldn't have said anything to Ramsey and Devlin about their being assassins. Was it your father? Or Jace?" He waited, but she still didn't respond. "You expect me to believe that you really don't know my name, or the name of the man in the corner?" He waved toward Austin. "You can quit these games. It's obvious that Jace has shared information about our group with you."

She shook her head as if he were a simpleton without the intellect to grasp what was right in front of him. "There's no 'obvious' about it, Mister whatever-your-name-is. I'm not in league with my father. And Jace hasn't said anything about any of you to me. Although, as I recall, he did try to call an old Navy friend to help us a few days ago. But his friend turned him down. Looking back, and based on what *you* just said, what's *obvious* is that he probably called one of *you* for help. And since no one *has* helped us, I can tell you with absolutely no reservations that I don't give a damn what you believe about me or Jace. Because you aren't the kind of man who stands behind a friend in need. Instead, you abandon him. Which tells me everything I need to know about your appalling lack of character."

Mason's brows shot up.

Jace chuckled against his gag. If he could have raised his hands, he would have applauded.

"We didn't abandon him, ma'am," Mason insisted.

"Really? Because from where I sit, you not only abandoned him, you've completely turned against him. Whatever 'honor' you might have had when you started this little band of merry men is long gone. You're no better than my father and that Council of his. What I want to know is why you bothered to show up now? If you've come to help us"—she rattled her handcuff—"you have an odd way of showing it. And you can also forget it. Jace and I have survived this long on our own. We'll continue to do just fine without your interference." She stared at a spot over Mason's head, effectively dismissing him as if he were a speck of lint she'd brushed off her jacket and had already forgotten.

Mason slowly straightened and scratched the stubble on his chin. He looked a bit dazed, as if he didn't know what to do next. Devlin, who was now leaning against the far wall, shook his head as if he thought Mason was losing it. Ramsey appeared to be struggling not to smile. And Austin didn't even bother to hide his amusement. He laughed, then dropped the front wheels of his chair to the floor and wheeled over beside Melissa, turning around to face the others as if the two of them were the best of friends.

"Any idiot can see that she's telling the truth,"

Austin said. "And those corkboards just confirm what Jace already told you on the phone. Plus, if he was trying to conceal anything, he wouldn't have tried to call us so many times." He looked at Jace. "My computer-genius brother back in Savannah remotely rigged the phones to make it seem like the numbers had been disconnected, but they logged every time you tried to reach us."

Jace gave him a curt nod to let him know he appreciated Austin's support and his show of solidarity with Melissa.

Pushing off the wall, Devlin strode up beside Mason again. "Enough. Austin's right. Anyone can see that Miss Cardenas isn't lying. And with all hell breaking loose over the past few days, seems to me that these two are in the perfect position to shed some light on that, if we give them a chance. And with two Council members down, we don't have time to waste on a useless debate."

Devlin waved toward Melissa. "Based on that bullet hole she's sporting, it's clear she's not in EXIT's good graces. And she fought like hell to help Jace at the motel. The clock is ticking. We need to get all of this sorted out fast before more innocent people die. And that, my friend, is the reason we started this *merry band of brothers* in the first place."

"She's our enemy's daughter," Mason reminded him.

"And I used to be the biggest, badass enforcer out there, the one tasked with eliminating rogue enforcers—like you. And yet you trust me now."

Mason's jaw tightened.

Devlin motioned to Austin. "Take the cuffs off her." He stepped past Mason, stopped in front of

Jace's chair, and yanked off the duct tape over his mouth.

Jace spit out the rag and thanked Devlin as he went to work on his bindings. Melissa's surprise was obvious when Austin unlocked her handcuff. She rubbed her wrist, a flash of fear and vulnerability crossing her face before she composed herself again. She shot a questioning look at Jace, and he realized how terrified she must have been on the inside all this time, perhaps thinking they were both about to die. And yet, she'd shown none of that turmoil while Mason questioned her. Instead, she'd shown only courage and defiance.

Damn, he was proud of her.

"Are you okay?" he asked. Devlin had freed his legs but was still working on the ropes around his arms, so Jace couldn't go to her yet even though it was killing him not to.

"Other than being confused, and really ticked off, I'm fine. The pain pill has finally kicked in." She reached for Austin's hand. "Thank you for taking the handcuff off."

"Any time, especially if good ole' *Mace* here doesn't want me to."

Mason shot him a sour look.

"How did you find us at that motel?" Jace asked.

"GPS," Devlin said. "Ramsey stuck a locator under your bumper the first time you two met, just in case something like this happened, and we needed to find you."

"Normally, I'd be fuming over that," Jace said. "But in this case, I'm grateful. What made you decide to come looking for us after turning me away when I called?"

"We found out about the murdered Council members and cut our missions short to join up with Mason, who'd already come back to check on Ramsey. We started following up, trying to figure out what was going on. When we checked your apartment, we saw the files you'd gathered and realized you were still on the case even though Mason told you to drop it."

"I made a vow," Jace said.

Devlin nodded. "I know. I think that's when the tide turned, when we realized you were still trying to bring EXIT down. Mason might seem hard, indifferent. Mainly, he's just careful, and takes his job as coleader very seriously. He doesn't want to put anyone at risk unless absolutely necessary. But those files had him wondering if maybe he'd judged you wrong."

"Huh. Could have fooled me."

Mason, who was standing a few feet from Devlin with his arms crossed, rolled his eyes but didn't look at Jace.

"Yeah, well. We decided to break into Miss Cardenas's house." Devlin winced. "Those boards pretty much changed Mason's opinion again, back the other way. He thought you were both colluding against us and that you'd told her about the Equalizers."

"I didn't—"

"I know. It all worked out."

"Are you hungry?" Austin asked Melissa. "We have beer and pizza."

"I don't think—" she started to say.

"No," Mason snapped. "She's not hungry."

"Actually, a beer sounds really good," she said,

taking obvious relish in goading the man who'd been grilling her with questions earlier.

"You got it. I'll be back downstairs in a few minutes with all the goodies." Austin whirled his chair around and rolled out of the room.

Mason threw his hands up. "I've lost control."

"You never had it." Ramsey chuckled behind him.

"This is ridiculous," Mason said. "We can't treat them like allies without interrogating them and figuring out whether we can trust them."

Devlin gave Mason an exasperated look as he cut the last of Jace's bindings. "You need to catch up with the rest of us. How long are you going to hold a grudge? You thought Jace betrayed us, that he broke his vow. You were wrong. And based on the way he's been glaring daggers at you, I suggest you be extremely polite to Miss Cardenas from here on out. Maybe you should take the elevator up with Austin and help him get the pizza to give Jace some time to cool off."

Mason stood with his legs braced apart, narrowing his eyes as if he dared Jace to approach him.

"Suit yourself," Devlin said. "And, hey, Ramsey?"

"Yeah, man?"

"In case you haven't noticed, Jace has been eyeing that Taser of yours. You'd better watch your back, or you'll be the next one to take a five-second ride on that thing."

Ramsey's startled gaze shot to Jace.

Jace slowly smiled and rose to his feet.

"I, uh, think I'll help Austin." Ramsey hurried out of the room.

Chapter Eighteen

Melissa sat on a folding chair in the basement of these men's headquarters, mostly a group of former enforcers who'd turned rogue against EXIT and now called themselves Equalizers. She half expected them to whip out capes like a bunch of superheroes.

She sat beside Jace and the others at the makeshift table—a piece of plywood thrown over some boxes—while they ate pepperoni pizza and nursed ice-cold bottles of beer. It was nice not to be handcuffed anymore, and to be treated as a guest instead of a prisoner. But after an initial discussion about how this house had been retrofitted to make it into a base of operations, the conversations had splintered off into groups that did *not* include her. Even Jace was ignoring her.

She could only make out a few words here and there of his conversation. He had his back to her as he spoke to the man beside him, a man she automatically liked because he'd ordered her cuffs removed—Devlin Buchanan. Across from her, Mason and Ramsey were in an equally intense, hushed conversation.

The only person not ignoring her was Austin, and he was mostly occupied scarfing down pizza and staring at her as if he were trying to figure something out. He chased the last bite of his second slice, or maybe his third, with a deep swig of beer, then pitched his paper plate onto the table in her direction. "Hey, Mel, toss another slice on there, will ya?"

Jace looked over his shoulder, arching a brow at Austin. "Mel?"

"I don't mind," she assured him. At least someone was talking to her. She was beginning to feel like the invisible woman. She plopped a piece of pizza on the plate before sliding it back to Austin. "Mel sounds a lot friendlier than being called Miss Cardenas all night. Or my personal favorite, our enemy's daughter."

She aimed that remark in Mason's direction. He paused midsentence and frowned. Perhaps she wasn't as invisible as she'd thought. But he obviously wasn't ready to cross to the dark side to be friendly with her. Without responding to her jab, or even looking at her, he started up his discussion with Ramsey again.

Beside her, she heard Jace say, "Council." And a moment later "Cyprian." She fisted one hand on the table, the other in her lap.

"You're an only child aren't you?" Austin shoved his plate aside, apparently deciding he didn't want that last slice after all. He waved toward the others. "I can tell you aren't used to this. I'm the youngest of five, and this happened all the time growing up. Hell, it still does. I was usually odd man out. Sucks, doesn't it?"

She smiled. "Yeah. It kind of does. And since my

brothers died when I was too young to really remember them, I guess you could say I *am* an only child."

He winced. "Sorry about that."

"Don't be. You didn't know. Five, huh? I can't imagine. What was that like?"

"Noise and chaos." He shrugged. "But you get used to it. And you get used to being alone even when surrounded by others. If you know what I mean."

She shot an aggravated glance at Jace's back. "I'm beginning to."

"Here, this is how you get their attention." Austin jabbed his elbow into Mason's ribs. Mason jerked around, looking like he wanted to slug him, but he hesitated.

Austin winked at Melissa. "One of the few benefits of being in this thing." He thumped his wheelchair. "I can do pretty much what I want without fear of retribution because of the guilt factor."

"No guilt here," Mason argued. "A pipsqueak like you just isn't enough of a challenge."

Austin shoved him, hard.

Mason shoved back, equally hard.

Melissa half rose from her seat, thinking to intervene, when both of them laughed and called each other crude words. Men. She relaxed back onto her chair.

Jace turned around and clapped his hands, gaining everyone's attention. "I think we've had our sidebars long enough. We've pretty much got our plan of attack set."

"Plan of attack?" Melissa didn't like how ominous that sounded.

Jace glanced at Devlin, then Mason. "Full disclosure?"

Devlin sat forward beside Jace with his arms crossed on the table and immediately nodded. Everyone else waited for Mason. He stared at Melissa from the other side of the table for a long moment before giving an obviously reluctant nod.

"I have a feeling I'm not going to like this," Melissa muttered.

"You already know the Council consists of six members," Mason told her. "The leader, Adam Marsh, was at your father's house tonight, along with three others. You also know the other two were killed. A few hours after the Council meeting, the remaining four members disappeared."

"Disappeared?" Her stomach dropped, and she was glad she hadn't eaten much pizza. "You think someone killed them?"

"It's possible. Or they might have been abducted," Mason said.

"Why would someone do that?"

"I don't know."

She glanced around the table, her stomach dropping at the looks of sympathy in most of their eyes, and the lack of it in Mason's. "You think my father is behind whatever happened."

No one said anything. The answer was obvious.

She squeezed her eyes shut. Jace's warm hand pressed against her back, his thumb rubbing slow, soothing circles, and somehow calming her. Instead of engaging in an argument with Mason, she pressed her lips together and leaned into Jace's side, grateful to have an anchor in the stormy sea that her life had become.

"We need to keep an open mind," Jace reminded them. "Cyprian was with Melissa and me for much of the night. It would have been difficult for him to arrange the Council members' disappearance."

Devlin shook his head. "I know you're trying to be fair. But all signs point to Cyprian. He could have easily arranged everything well before tonight's meeting, or even right after you two left. We have to assume he could be the one pulling the strings, especially since he has the most to gain. Without the Council, he'll have free rein to do as he pleases. And he won't have to worry about this so-called Watcher the Council assigned to keep an eye on him. Cyprian's power will be absolute. Things just got a whole lot more dangerous around here."

"Maybe the Watcher is the one with everything to gain," Jace suggested. "Melissa and I think he might be Stefano Conti, an enforcer whose mother works for Cyprian as a live-in housekeeper."

"We'll have to check him out," Devlin said. "We've been investigating several enforcers who are stationed here locally. We'll keep looking into them as well."

"I don't understand," Melissa said. "The Council works for the government to oversee my father, right?"

Devlin nodded.

"Then, if something happens to them, the government would just create a new Council, wouldn't they?"

"Not necessarily, or at least, not right away. The Council is autonomous. EXIT isn't like any other alphabet agency. EXIT's true nature and association with the government is a closely guarded secret to protect the government if EXIT is ever exposed. Although there are people sprinkled in the various agencies who know bits and pieces, we don't think there are many who know the whole picture. Mainly it's just the Council members who know, and, of course, the few people who've spent thousands of hours putting it all together." He waved at the others. "Us."

"What he's saying," Jace said, "is that if the Council is destroyed, we think there will be barely a ripple among the few contacts in the government who know about EXIT's true purpose. To them, their communiqués and requests for funding or collaboration would still come across the same, secret channels. They'd have no reason to suspect anything had substantially changed at EXIT. It would mostly be transparent. Which means, whoever is behind this current scheme stands to gain everything. And if they succeed, no one will remain to stop them. All of the power over life and death that EXIT maintains will be concentrated in one person, with no safeguards to keep them from wielding the company as the ultimate weapon. And that would make EXIT ten times more dangerous than it is today."

She shivered as a chill of foreboding swept through her. "Even from what little I've learned about the power in the enforcement side, if you're right about this, it sounds terrifying."

Murmurs of agreement sounded from around the table.

"I agree," Jace said. "Which is why we can't afford to make any assumptions. While it seems that Cyprian might be behind the disappearance of the remaining Council members, we have to consider that he might not be. It could be Stefano, acting on his own. Or even one of the Council members attempting his own takeover."

He looked at the men around the table. "And don't forget the Watcher. I believe he's probably Stefano. But he might be someone else. Either way, we can't be sure of his motives and what his role is in all of this. We have no idea how he fits into the grand plan. Maybe without the Council to guide him, he'll go back to being an enforcer. Or maybe he's working with whoever kidnapped the remaining Council members. We really have no idea what we're up against."

"And on that cheerful note," Austin said, pushing his wheelchair away from the table, "I'm going to brush my teeth and get ready for lights out. We've got a long day ahead of us tomorrow." He zipped through the room like a rocket, surprising Melissa with how fast he could maneuver even though the floor was covered in a bumpy, steel-mesh material.

"He's right," Devlin said, keeping his voice low. "Except for the 'we' part. I promised him he could help, by driving us around in his van and keeping watch. But I only did that to get him to quit asking. I don't want my brother coming with us. He's just a few weeks out of rehab, and he's not a former enforcer or former Navy SEAL. It's too damn dangerous to involve him. When we leave in the morning, everyone needs to be stealthy about it. I don't want Austin to know we're gone until it's too late for him to try to tag along."

Everyone nodded as they stood and gathered their trash to throw it out.

"That doesn't seem fair," Melissa said to Jace, as

they moved away from the table. "I'm sure Austin could help in some capacity. And he wants to. Shouldn't that be his choice?"

"I'm sure he could, too. But he's Devlin's brother. That's between the two of them."

She wasn't sure she agreed, but she didn't argue. "What are the plans? What is everyone going to do in the morning?"

"Devlin, Mason, and Ramsey will follow up on some leads about where the Council members might have been taken."

"When did you hear about these leads?"

"While you were eating, I suppose."

"Oh, I remember," she grumbled. "That was when everyone was ignoring me and huddled together whispering."

"Now, Mel. We weren't completely ignoring you."

"Uh-huh. And what are *we* doing tomorrow?"

"*We* are going to stay here and dig into Stefano's background to see if his identity as the Watcher holds up. If it doesn't, we'll look deeper into those other people you already noted that you'd seen regularly at the office in the past few months who might not have been there on a regular basis before then. Those are our most likely candidates to be the Watcher."

"But we already discussed them."

"We'll discuss them again. And try to get more information about them."

"Doesn't sound exciting."

"Exciting, no. Important, yes. We have to figure out who all the players are and what's at stake. And I also want you to be safe. That's my number one priority."

When he looked at her with such concern, how could she complain? "Okay. I guess there could be worse assignments. Although I don't look forward to dealing with Austin's disappointment when he realizes the others left without him."

A metallic scraping noise had her glancing around. Alarm shot through her as she realized the men were setting up cots throughout the room. "Um, Jace? Where am I sleeping tonight?"

He grinned. "What, you don't relish the idea of bunking out on a cot in a basement with a bunch of men you barely know?"

"It's not at the top of my bucket list, no."

Austin rolled back into the room, waving at her and wheeling over to his brother.

She counted the cots that had been set up. "Only five? There are six of us. And I'm pretty sure those are too narrow for two people."

"That's one of the things I like about you. That steel trap mind of yours," he teased. He crossed to the cot nearest to them and picked it up, tucking the blanket and pillow beneath his arm. "You and I are sleeping upstairs."

He put his other hand on her back and led her toward the elevator.

"You and me?" she whispered, her body flushing hot at the idea of spending the night with him. Maybe the cot wasn't too narrow after all.

"Of course. You don't think I'd let you sleep with all of these guys do you?" he whispered back, punctuating his comment with a wink.

She swatted his arm and stepped inside past the already open doors, which was one of the "smart" features Devlin had bragged about at dinner when he'd talked about the retrofitting they'd done to this house. Whichever floor the elevator was at, the doors would stay open by default: definitely a convenience instead of someone having to push the button and wait for the doors to slide open. Why hadn't anyone else ever thought of that when designing elevators?

As soon as Jace pushed the button for the ground floor, the thick, heavy, steel doors zipped shut—instant safe room, according to Devlin's bragging at dinner. And it had all been designed with Austin in mind.

But Austin obviously hadn't appreciated that particular conversation at dinner. His caustic comment about people treating him like a child because he was in a damn wheelchair had ceased all conversation until Ramsey awkwardly turned it to a totally unrelated discussion about NASCAR racing.

Melissa's heart had ached for the embarrassment and anger on Austin's face. He obviously thought his brother was being overprotective. And since Devlin planned to leave Austin here tomorrow rather than take him on the mission with the others, she couldn't help but agree.

When the doors opened on the ground floor, everything was pitch-black except for the lights inside the elevator and some blinking LED lights in the room announcing the presence of electronic equipment.

"Don't worry," Jace said, as if sensing her nervousness. "The security in this place rivals some of the best military installations that I've ever seen. It's not impenetrable, but we'll have advance warning if someone comes onto the property. And by the time they figure out how to break inside, we could be long gone. I've also got my gun again. But even without it, I promise you no one is going to get to you without going through me. And I'm not an easy kill."

She shivered. "Don't talk like that. I don't want anything to happen to you."

He squeezed her hand, causing all kinds of warm feelings to rush through her, sweeping away her fear. Well, almost.

"What about *my* gun? Did you get that back, too?"

"Sorry. No."

Her shoulders slumped.

"Come on, little warrior. I'll show you to your suite."

She blew out a shaky breath, hating that he'd let her hand go. And fervently wishing she didn't light up like a match every time the man touched her, no matter how innocently. Touch? Who was she kidding? Just looking into his eyes or hearing the deep, sexy timbre of his voice had her melting inside.

She cleared her throat. "Suite, huh. I'll believe that when I see it." There, she didn't sound like she was getting all soft inside just thinking about him. She hoped.

He flipped a switch on the wall beside the elevator, turning on the lights. "Maybe not a suite, but a lot more comfortable than a cot."

"But you're carrying a cot."

"The cot is for me." He took her hand and pulled her with him through a large room full of computers on one side and collections of guns in glass cases above them. She swallowed hard at the reminder of the danger they all faced and followed Jace down the hallway on their left.

They passed a bathroom and two bedrooms that were bursting with boxes and equipment before he led her into what must have been the master bedroom when the house was built. But now, even though it had a king-sized bed along the left wall, the right side was filled with more boxes like the ones in the rooms they'd passed.

She took a quick tour of the bedroom and stepped into the surprisingly large and clean master bathroom, which was stocked with fresh towels and toiletries. Seeing the soaps and shampoos almost had her whimpering with gratitude. This was like staying at the Ritz compared to that ratty motel they'd *almost* stayed in.

She stepped back into the bedroom to see Jace with his arms crossed, leaning back against the wall. The cot he'd brought with them in the elevator was sitting in the hallway, visible through the open doorway.

"Got everything you need?" he asked.

I need you. "Yes, thank you. I'll, ah, have to rinse out my clothes for tomorrow, I guess. Maybe we can stop by my house and grab a few outfits when we leave here."

He was shaking his head "no" before she'd finished. "Not happening. Too dangerous. But Devlin's wife, Emily Buchanan, is going to drop off a go bag for you in the morning. She'll make sure you have everything you need."

"Shouldn't I talk to her first, tell her my sizes?"

His gaze leisurely traced a path down her chest, to her hips, then . . . lower, before reversing with a slow thoroughness that sparked every nerve ending and made her belly clench with desire.

His lips curved in a sexy grin that had her fingers curling into her palms. "That won't be necessary. I have a good . . . feel . . . for that sort of thing. I gave the information to Devlin to relay to his wife when we were eating downstairs."

Her pulse was hammering so hard, she was amazed that he couldn't hear it. "You mean while I was eating, and you were ignoring me."

He slowly shook his head and crossed the room toward her. Good grief the man was *hawt*. Every cell in her body was on fire just watching him come closer. If he touched her, she just might burst into flames.

Stopping so close that she could smell the masculine mixture of soap and the subtle fragrance of his aftershave, he tilted her chin up to look at him.

Yep. Flames. She was burning. And it felt *so good*.

"How's your arm?" His gaze dropped to her lips.

Yes! Kiss me. "M . . . my arm?" She remembered those lips, how they'd felt on hers. Magic. His kisses were pure, exquisite, magic. When he'd given her that life-altering first kiss in the dining room, she knew she'd never experience anything that incredible again. Until he'd kissed her in the greenhouse. That kiss had propelled her into a whole other universe of pleasure and desire. A third kiss . . . if she could be so lucky . . . just might kill her.

And she'd die happy.

"Mel?"

"Um hm." She licked her lips.

His Adam's apple bobbed in his throat. "Your

injury? Does it hurt?" His voice was tight, as if it was taking a Herculean effort to form coherent words.

"O . . . only a little," she whispered, lifting her hands to his chest, smoothing her fingers across the delicious, hard muscles so achingly close. She wanted that shirt off him. Desperately.

He closed his eyes as if in pain and gently but firmly lifted her hands off his chest as he stepped back. "Okay. Sorry. That should have been my first concern after dinner, getting you some more pain pills. I left them downstairs." He swallowed again. "I'll go and—"

"No, don't go. I'm fine." Had she whined? She cleared her throat. "Really. No need to go to any trouble. Don't leave." *Please.*

He shook his head. "You're in pain. I'll get the pills."

He headed toward the door. *No, no, no!* If he left her now, she just might die, for real. But she would *not* die happy. The desire she'd read in his eyes, in his voice, equaled hers. And there was no way she was going to let him walk out that door and risk something happening that might delay him coming back—like him convincing himself she was in too much pain for them to spend some *quality* time to-gether. Or that jerk, Mason, involving him in some long, drawn-out impromptu strategy meeting. If this was going to happen, she had to stop him from stepping into that hall.

She frantically grabbed the edges of her blouse and yanked it up over her head, careless of where it landed. He was almost to the door. She reached around behind her, ignoring the twinge of pain in her arm as she unhooked her bra and dropped it at her feet. "Jace!"

Her shout had him whirling around, his hand reaching for his gun.

He stumbled to a startled halt, his jaw dropping open.

Chapter Nineteen

Two seconds. That's how long it took Jace to stalk across the room like a conquering warrior and crush Melissa in his embrace. In those two, agonizingly long seconds, seeing the raw hunger transform his face into a feral predator, seeing the way his body shook with need, everything inside her had softened, melted, readied itself for him.

And that third kiss? It was everything she'd hoped it would be, and, oh sweet merciful heavens, so much more.

He consumed her, drawing her into his very soul, worshipping her with his mouth, his tongue, his hands as they framed her face and he wrung every ounce of pleasure from her. And then he went in for another kiss, lifting her, turning with her in his arms, pressing her against the wall.

Yes, yes, this. This was what she'd always wanted, the way she'd always known, hoped, prayed that a man could want a woman. Not the lukewarm, sloppy kisses from high school. Not the half-drunken fumbling in the backseat of a car from college. But the full onslaught, firing on all pistons, going for it with the everything-he-had way that a man could love a woman. As if nothing else in the world mattered, nothing else existed except the two of them. And for now, nothing did.

She didn't remember taking off the rest of her clothes. She didn't remember him taking off his. But she definitely remembered the first moment his hot, naked skin met hers. She whimpered with pleasure at the hard, heavy feel of his wiry-haired chest crushing her breasts as he pulled her legs around his hips. They didn't make it to the bed. They only made it to the wall.

With one hand beneath her bottom to support her, he fit himself to her entrance then stopped, groaning deep in his throat, his forehead pressed against hers, his eyes tightly shut.

"We can't," he rasped. "I don't have protection for you." His words sounded wrung from him as if he were on a medieval torture wrack being pulled apart.

"Don't you dare stop. I swear I'm healthy. You?"

"That won't stop you from getting pregnant."

Why did the idea of having Jace's child make her hotter than before? Good grief, she adored this man. And she wanted him so much she wouldn't have cared if she were protected or not. But he needed to know not to worry.

"It's okay," she gasped, unable to stop from squeezing her legs, desperate to pull him inside her. "I'm on the pill, to regulate my cycle. It doesn't matter. Just, please, don't stop." She squeezed her legs again.

With a shuddering groan, he covered her mouth with his. And then he surged forward, filling her, spreading her, setting her on fire all over again. If he hadn't been kissing her, she'd have screamed her pleasure for the world to hear—or a handful of Equalizers in the basement. As it was, her cries became moans, and his answering groans had her digging her fingers into his shoulders and meeting each thrust with an answering arch of her hips in a rhythm as old as time.

Just when she was about to go over the edge, he broke their kiss and pulled out of her completely.

"Jace," she whimpered.

"Slow down, sweetheart. I want to make this good for you." He turned with her and carried her to the bed.

"Trust me, it's *good*. No need to go to any extra trouble. Just finish what you started."

He laughed and laid her far too gently back on the bed. She wanted him rough and hard and fast like he'd been, but suddenly he was gone. She propped herself up on her elbows to see where he'd gone, wincing at the sharp pain that zinged through her hurt arm. But then she saw his gorgeous, tight, beautiful rear as he strode in his naked glory toward the door, and she promptly forgot how to breathe.

Wow.

With the door shut, and locked, he shut the light off. She was about to complain that she really preferred to see every yummy inch of him when the bed creaked beneath his weight. And before she could utter her complaint about the light, he kissed her—

There.

She dug her heels into the mattress and arched off the bed as fireworks went off behind her closed eyelids. "Holy cow!"

He laughed again, his hot breath washing over her thighs. And then he focused all of his considerable talents on the very center of her, kissing her, loving her, stroking her until she cried from the beauty of his lovemaking, begging him to let her touch him the way he was touching her.

The mattress shifted, and the angle of his kisses and his incredible, wonderful, roving hands, changed. And in the dark, she found him, and began loving him the way he was loving her. She'd never, not once, done this before, shared at the same time in the same way that he was sharing with her. Had never wanted to, and yet, nothing had ever felt so right. Giving and taking, stroking and being stroked, tasting . . . and being tasted. The sensations were so incredible, so over the top, she knew she couldn't last much longer. And from the way he was shaking, obviously holding himself back, she knew he was just as close.

"Jace," she whispered.

He stroked her with his tongue, making her arch off the mattress again. One last, hot kiss against her hip and he was turning and moving up her body, planting kisses as he went . . . on her belly, his mouth lightly sucking her skin. Then underneath each breast as his hands stroked, cupped, molded.

"You're killing me," she gasped, as he sucked one of her nipples into his mouth.

He swirled his tongue around her, then kissed her before letting go. "No, sweetheart. I'm showing you how to *live*."

And he was right. Because she'd never felt so alive before.

He pulled back, his hands skimming down her

sides to her hips. Then he was lifting her, fitting himself to her, angling them both for the deepest penetration. And then he surged inside.

She climaxed instantly, her cries of joy smothered by his mouth suddenly covering hers. He broke the kiss and drew her to his chest as he sat back, still buried deep inside her. His powerful thighs supported her bottom and he wrapped his arms around her back, surging upward with deep, powerful strokes.

Clutching his shoulders, she drew up her knees, rocking against him, taking him impossibly deep. He shuddered and reached down between them, stroking her in an entirely different way, bringing her up to the same fevered pitch as before and keeping her there, hovering on the edge, until she was whimpering, begging him to end it.

"So beautiful," she cried as she rode each thrust. "So beautiful."

"Yes, you are," he growled next to her ear. "And I want to make this perfect for you."

"It is," she gasped. "It already is. So close. I'm so, so close."

And then he lifted her again, but instead of sending her over the edge, instead of filling her one last time to end the exquisite, wonderful torture, he turned her around. She marveled at his strength in holding her, and then he was surrounding her with his heat, her bottom against his groin, her back pressed to his chest, his arms holding her secure beneath her breasts.

"Jace? I don't know what to—" She sucked in a breath as he surged up inside her again, the angle so perfect, the pressure so intense that she could have sworn fireworks really did explode behind her eyelids this time. Never in her life had she imagined it could be like this. Every pulse, every push, every pull was amplified a hundred times over until she was biting her fist to keep from sobbing out his name.

It was so beautiful that hot tears splashed onto her hands, onto his hands. He drew her tighter against him, riding her hard, his hand sliding down her belly to her center, cherishing her, drawing her pleasure out to the breaking point. And then he whispered the most erotic suggestions in her ear, telling her what he would do to her next time. And the wicked things he whispered had her melting all around him, clamping down on his hand, on *him*, in a near frenzy of desire.

One last, deep stroke, and he was pulsing inside her, his entire body stiffening. One wicked, swirling movement of his clever fingers against her core, and she went over the edge with him, convulsing and drinking in every shudder of his powerful body deep inside her until they both fell exhausted and wonderfully sated to the mattress.

She'd barely recovered from the most intense lovemaking session she could have ever imagined before he was making demands of her body again, and taking her to new levels of sensation she hadn't thought possible. Afterward, they showered together, and he ever-so-carefully tended her arm, using disinfectant and bandages he found in the bathroom. And insisting she take some of the over-the-counter meds that were also in a bathroom drawer, to stop the throbbing that had started in her arm from their vigorous lovemaking.

And then he'd carried her back to bed and gently laid her down. Spooning himself behind her, Jace wrapped his arm around her waist and tucked his body around hers protectively, forming a warm, loving cocoon of safety. She'd fallen asleep with his lips against her neck and a smile on her face.

The next time she awakened, it was early morning. Since heavy, steel shutters blocked the light from the window, she only knew it was morning by the sounds drifting up from the basement below: deep voices, laughter at some joke, metal scraping the concrete floor, probably the cots being moved. The Equalizers were getting up, getting ready to begin their missions.

She should have immediately woken Jace, so they could get dressed and start their own mission of logging onto the computer and searching for the information that could be the key to finding the Councilmen. But he was sleeping so soundly, worn-out from lavishing her with such attention during the night, that she chose not to disturb him while she brushed her teeth and tamed her hair.

She would have gotten dressed, too, but since Emily Buchanan was going to drop off some fresh, clean clothes for her, she didn't want to put on her old, dirty ones. So, instead, she sat on the bed beside Jace, wrapped in one of the bath towels, and debated whether or not to wake him.

His face looked so handsome and youthful in the soft glow from the bathroom light. And even now she could feel desire curling through her just by looking at him and breathing in his scent. But it wasn't desire that had her feeling confused as she studied him. It was the fierce protectiveness that swept through her, making her nails bite into her palms at the thought that this warm, strong, noble man might have to face any of EXIT's enforcers. It was fear that had her shaking as she clasped her hands against the urge to grab him and hold on to him and never let him go. She wanted him, yes. So much that it was almost painful. But it wasn't just physical desire that pained her. It was so much more, this powerful wanting, because it came from a place completely unexpected.

Her heart.

She pressed her hands against her chest, her breath leaving her in a surprised rush. How? How did this happen, and how did it happen so fast? When had her physical desire become something . . . more? And how was she supposed to survive knowing she'd foolishly managed to lose her heart to the one man who could completely destroy her?

It wasn't fair. She'd thought she was safe. She'd thought desire was *all* that she felt for him. But somewhere along the way, it had changed.

She covered her face with her hands. What was she going to do? This was a disaster. She couldn't . . . no, she *wouldn't* put a name to these feelings. Whatever she felt for Jace was impossible. Because it had happened too fast to trust. And there was no way they could ever plan a future together even if he felt the same way toward her.

They might have the same goal—to save innocent lives. And that might mean destroying the company she'd worked so hard and long to build and grow. But she could never stand by while Jace, or anyone else, destroyed the man who'd raised her, the man who'd loved her no matter what, the man who'd spent his whole life trying to keep her safe and happy. Regardless of what her father had done, of who he had become, she *still* loved him. And, somehow, she had to protect him, even if that meant going against her newfound friends—the Equalizers—and the man she was falling in love with. Somehow, she had to find a way to bring her father to true justice, the kind meted out in a court of law, not by some well-intentioned vigilantes. She had to find a way to stop him but also to save his life. But to do that, she knew she'd probably have to trick or betray Jace. And that was killing her inside.

Warm strong hands tugged hers down from her face. Jace's gray eyes were filled with such concern that she wanted to weep.

"What's wrong?" His thumb gently stroked her cheek.

She forced a smile. "Nothing. Everything is fine." She shoved up off the mattress, grasping her towel tightly around her. "I, ah, got ready, but I'm waiting for that go bag you promised me, the one Emily is supposed to bring."

His frown told her that he didn't buy that everything was fine, but in his thoughtful, wonderful way, he gave her the space she needed and didn't pry. Which only made this new wound in her heart hurt all the more.

He scrubbed the stubble on his jaw and stood. "I don't hear anything downstairs." He grabbed his phone from where he'd left it on top of a box last night and checked the time. "I should have been down there an hour ago. The others have probably already left."

"Sorry," she said, and meant it. "I should have woken you when I got up."

He leaned down and pressed an achingly sweet kiss against her lips. "Don't apologize. I'm a grown man. I'm responsible for waking myself up. I should have set the alarm." He grabbed his go bag off the floor. "Be back in a few."

She plopped down on the bed as the bathroom door closed. Handsome, smart, brave . . . add thoughtful to the list. And nice. So damn nice. A lot of men she'd known would have been angry with her for not waking them. Instead, Jace was matter-of-fact about it being his own responsibility to get up on time. How sensible and mature of him. Which only made her ache for him even more.

Flaws. He had to have a flaw or two, right? No one was this perfect.

Yes, he had a flaw. A huge one. It was the same fatal flaw that she had: their diametrically opposed views about justice, about her father.

And that was an impossible flaw to overcome.

JACE HURRIED THROUGH his morning routine, then stuffed his toothbrush and shaver into his go bag. As he yanked his dress pants on and tucked his shirt in, he berated himself for sleeping so late. Normally, he could set his internal clock and wake up without an alarm—courtesy of his Navy SEAL training—but last night . . . he shook his head, unable to stop a grin as he threaded his belt through his pants loops. Last night had worn him out. In the most amazing, wonderful way.

He'd known he was falling for Melissa Cardenas long before he actually met her in person. And he'd tried to steel himself against her, knowing that his work for the Equalizers meant there was nowhere to go with those feelings. But the inevitable was happening. He wasn't just falling anymore. He was free-falling without a parachute.

And he wouldn't have stopped the fall even if he could.

Knowing her father's role in EXIT had seemed like an insurmountable obstacle in the beginning. But not anymore. Melissa knew what Cyprian had done. Well, not everything, but enough to understand that he had to be stopped. They were on the same team now. And they would face the future together.

He yanked his boots on and brushed the lint off his carefully folded suit jacket before shrugging into it.

A light knock sounded on the bedroom door, from out in the hall. Jace grabbed his holster and gun from the counter and hurried into the bedroom just as Melissa was reaching for the doorknob.

"Hold it." He snapped the holster onto his belt and drew his pistol.

She blinked at the gun and backed away. "Okay, but impenetrable fortress and all that. And it's just Emily with my clothes." She waved toward the towel covering her as if to remind him that she was nearly naked.

He tried not to think about the luscious body beneath that towel. Her safety was what mattered. He pointed the gun down at the floor. "Who is it?" He motioned for her to get behind him.

"Emily, Devlin's wife," a feminine voice answered. "I brought Miss Cardenas some clothes."

"How did you get inside the house?" Jace asked.

"Austin let me in."

"Jace," Melissa whispered. "Isn't this a little ridiculous?"

"Austin? Are you out there?"

A pause, then, "I'm here. Open the door." Another pause. "I don't have all day."

Jace smiled and shoved his gun into his holster. "Now that sounds like the Austin I know." He opened the door and froze.

Tarek's surviving evil twin, Sebastian, stood in the hallway pointing a .357 Magnum at a woman whom Jace presumed was Emily Buchanan. He'd only ever talked to her over the phone and had never met her in person. She stood with her right wrist handcuffed to Austin's wheelchair. Austin's left hand was cuffed to the same bar, effectively rendering him helpless: a fact that was highlighted by the combination of embarrassment and fury turning his face red.

His glare was no less heated than the one Emily was aiming at Sebastian. Both of them looked like they would have tackled him, in spite of the handcuffs, if it weren't for the gun pointed at her head. But it wasn't the .357 that Sebastian held that had Jace going cold inside.

It was the Remington 870 shotgun in Sebastian's other hand, the one aimed at Jace and Melissa.

If it had been a pistol pointed his way, Jace might have taken his chances and lunged at Sebastian to try to knock the gun out of his grasp. But one shot from that Remington would pepper the room in a deadly spray of pellets. If by some miracle none of them hit Melissa from that first blast, a second shot would.

Jace slowly raised his hands.

Chapter Twenty

When Jace raised his hands in the air, Melissa's stomach dropped as if she'd just stepped off a cliff. What was going on? She couldn't see past him into the hallway.

"Don't move," a gruff voice ordered.

Melissa leaned to the side. She wasn't sure what she'd expected to see, but it wasn't Sebastian Smith pointing a wicked-looking shotgun at Jace and pointing an equally terrifying handgun down the hall, where Austin and Emily must be.

The blood drained from her face, leaving her cold. She had to do something. She clutched the towel and glanced around the room, looking for something, anything, to use to defend them. But other than the gun holstered at Jace's hip, there was nothing but boxes shoved up against the wall. Why hadn't she insisted he give her a gun last night? The Equalizers had plenty to spare.

"Miss Cardenas," Sebastian ordered. "I need you to very slowly take Mr. Atwell's gun and slide it across the floor to me."

"Jace?" She refused to follow Sebastian's orders. But she'd follow Jace's.

"He's not the one telling you what to do here." Sebastian's knuckles whitened around the shotgun. "The gun, Miss Cardenas."

"Go ahead," Jace reassured her. "Do what he says."

Sebastian didn't look happy that she was following Jace's instructions, so she quickly stepped forward to placate him. After securing the edge of her towel so it wouldn't fall down, she reached for Jace's gun, swallowing hard as she slid her fingers around the handle. She hated to give away their only weapon.

"It's all right. We'll be all right." Jace's voice was calm, sure, his eyes devoid of fear, which gave her the strength she needed to follow through.

"Put it on the floor and slide it to me," Sebastian ordered.

She set the gun down, but quickly realized she couldn't do what he'd asked. "The floor isn't smooth. It's covered by metal grating. I can't slide the gun across it."

He frowned but didn't look down. He kept glancing between Jace and the two in the hallway. Sweat beaded on his forehead, telling Melissa he was just as nervous as she was. And that maybe he was beginning to realize he hadn't thought this scenario through well enough. A nervous man holding two guns couldn't be a good combination.

"What if I just unload it?" she asked, trying to reassure him the way Jace had reassured her.

Sebastian hesitated, then gave her a curt nod. "Hurry up. He's waiting." His jaw tightened, like he'd just realized he'd said too much.

She glanced up at Jace again. He gave her a subtle shrug. He didn't know who Sebastian was referring to any more than she did.

She released the magazine and pulled it out.

"Empty the rounds, too," Sebastian ordered.

She ejected all of the ammo and stood with an overflowing hand of rounds, clutched against the front of her towel.

"Toss everything under the bed," Sebastian ordered.

She hesitated again. She *really* didn't want to throw away their only gun and ammunition. It seemed like suicide.

"My instructions are to bring *you* back with me, Miss Cardenas. If I have to shoot Mr. Atwell to convince you to do what I say, I will."

She immediately pitched everything under the bed. "There. Now what?"

The sweat was running freely down the sides of Sebastian's face now. He glanced from her to Jace, then down the hall. He had to realize if he made her and Jace step into the hall, they'd pass within a few feet of him. Which meant he'd have to lower the shotgun. Was he worried that Jace would overpower him and take the handgun?

"Hey, whatever your name is," Austin called out. "I don't like a guy with guns to be so nervous. Let me make this easy for you. It's not like I can go anywhere fast in this chair, especially with Emily attached to it and the wire mesh on the floor. You had to see the steel shutters on all the windows and exterior doors when you came in. So you know the only way out of this place is through the garage. And that's on the other side of the house. Do you really think Emily and I could make it that far before you could catch us?"

Sebastian swallowed hard but kept most of his focus on Jace and Melissa. "What are you suggesting?"

"Let Emily and me clear out of the hallway. We'll go into the family room and wait for you there. That way you can back down the hall, directing Jace and Melissa without worrying about our being in the way."

He shook his head. "No way. I saw those cases of guns in that room. You're trying to trick me."

Austin laughed harshly. "Look at me, man. What do you think I'm going to do? Magically grow legs, climb on the computer countertop, oh, and get the keys—you did see the locks on those cases right?—and then open them up, undo the clasps holding one of the guns, find some ammo to go with whichever one I manage to get, and—"

"Enough," Sebastian yelled. "Enough. I get it. You're a cripple. But Mrs. Buchanan isn't."

"Yeah dude, but she's handcuffed to this chair. Even if she dumped me on the floor, how's she going to climb that countertop to get a gun? This heavy-duty chair alone weighs over seventy-five pounds. Do you seriously think she can lift that and do everything else I just said to get to a weapon?"

Sebastian chewed his bottom lip, considering what Austin had said. Melissa could sense Jace close behind her. He'd inched forward every time Sebastian looked down the hall at Austin.

"Okay, okay," Sebastian said. "Go. Clear the hallway, but stay in my line of sight. Don't disappear around the corner, or I'll come after you. And I promise I *will* shoot if you try anything. Both of you. No tricks."

"No shooting. No tricks. It's all cool. Come on, Em. Help me wheel this thing down this bumpy hallway. I hate that metal grating. It's not like it can stop a bullet or anything. It's useless. Dev should have ripped it off the floor when he bought this place."

"You know how he is. He doesn't think about details like that," Emily replied, and soon the dull sound of the wheels bumping across the grating echoed down the hall.

Melissa frowned. What was Austin up to? She'd seen him zip across the same type of floor downstairs last night with no problem. And she'd also seen him pop wheelies on that chair. It couldn't weigh more than thirty pounds, if that.

"Stop," Sebastian ordered, glancing down the hall. "Stay right where you are."

"Whatever you say. It's all good," Austin called out.

Sebastian backed farther out into the hall, still pointing the shotgun toward her and Jace and the handgun toward Austin and Emily.

"Step out of the room and follow me. Slowly," he ordered.

Jace immediately moved in front of Melissa and stepped into the hall.

Sebastian's eyes widened like an owl's. "No, no. Stop right there. Miss Cardenas goes first. You follow behind."

"Not going to happen." Jace held up a hand toward Melissa, stopping her in the doorway but never taking his eyes off Sebastian.

"Then I'll shoot you," Sebastian promised.

"Not without risking hitting Melissa. And who-ever sent you doesn't want her hurt, do they? Who sent you? Her father? Why are you following his orders? Didn't you hear that he'd killed two of the Council members? And your buddy, Tarek?"

Sebastian's Adam's apple bobbed in his throat, and his eyes took on a wild look. "That's bullshit. I haven't heard any of that."

Jace shrugged. "You weren't at the Council meeting last night with Tarek. You missed Marsh an-nouncing the murders of two Council members and pinning it on Cyprian. There was a bloodbath. Cyprian killed Tarek, and everyone scattered for the hills."

"You're lying."

"Yeah. Okay. Suit yourself. Find out the hard way when Cyprian kills you, too."

Sebastian looked like he was bordering on ter-rified. He must have known about the Council meeting and that Tarek had been there, which gave validity to what Jace had said. But he didn't seem to know if any of the rest of it was true.

And from what Sebastian had said and responded to, it seemed obvious that Cyprian was probably the one who'd sent him after her. Why would he do that after the way things had been left between them? And how had Sebastian even known where to find her?

"Just shut up," Sebastian finally said. "I'm the one giving orders here. Step back into the room and send Miss Cardenas down the hallway. Do it now."

"Hey, what's taking y'all so long?" Austin called out. "Anyone hungry? I love cold pizza for breakfast. Come on, Emily. Let's go to the kitchen and get some leftover pizza for everybody."

Sebastian jerked around. "No, wait!" He cursed and ran down the hallway.

Jace shoved Melissa back into the room. "Stay here." He slammed the door in her face.

She blinked in surprise, listening to his footsteps as he chased, unarmed, after a man with two guns. A dull rumble sounded. Was that the elevator? A shout, cursing. *Bam! Bam! Bam!* Gunshots echoed from the living room.

No! Oh, no. Please, God. Let Jace be okay. She had to help him. But what could she do? She needed a gun. *Jace's gun.* She dropped to her knees and scrambled under the bed, searching for it. There, against the wall by the headboard.

She grabbed it and frantically gathered some of the ammo she'd dropped to the floor. She felt around until she found the magazine she needed to load the gun. She'd loaded five rounds into it and was about to load a few more, not sure how many she might need, when footsteps sounded down the hall.

Sebastian? Was he coming for her now?

She dropped the rest of the rounds and slammed the magazine into position. Whirling around on her knees, she aimed toward the door just as it flew open.

Her mind registered that it was Jace a split second before her finger jerked on the trigger. He dove to the floor, and she let out a cry of dismay. She immediately dropped the gun and scrambled over to him.

"Jace! Oh, no. Jace, are you okay?" She reached for him and he rolled over, holding his shoulder, staring at her like he thought she'd lost her mind.

Her hands shook as she ran them over him. "Did I shoot you? Oh my God."

He sat up, shaking his head. "My shoulder's just bruised from hitting the floor." Impossibly, he laughed. "I guess you paid me back for not having an extra gun for you."

"I'm so sorry," she said, feeling miserable. "I'm normally much more responsible with firearms. I was just so damned scared."

He shoved himself to his feet and pulled her up with him. "It's all right."

She put her arms around his waist and pressed her head against his chest. "Thank goodness you're okay. I'm so sorry. So, so sorry."

He hugged her tight, then pushed her back to look at her. "Everyone's okay. You, Emily, Austin, me. That's what matters."

She shuddered with relief.

He shoved his gun in his holster. A second gun was already in his waistband. He must have gotten it from one of the cases on the living-room wall.

"Come on. I'll grab a fresh magazine instead of trying to find my ammo scattered all over the floor. Let's go ask Sebastian where he was supposed to take you after kidnapping you."

She pressed a hand against his chest, stopping him. "He's alive? I heard shots."

"He's alive. But if he doesn't tell me what I want to know," he said, his expression grim, "he'll soon wish he weren't."

Running footsteps sounded in the hallway again. Jace shoved Melissa away from the doorway and pulled out one of the guns.

"Don't shoot," a woman's voice yelled. "It's Emily."

He immediately lowered his gun. A second later, Emily caught herself against the door frame, slightly out of breath from running through the house. She, too, had a gun shoved into her waistband.

"What's wrong, Emily?"

"I only took my eyes off him for a second. I swear."

He moved protectively in front of Melissa. "What happened? Did he escape?"

"No, no. He didn't escape. Sebastian is dead."

JACE TRIED TO convince Melissa to stay in the master bedroom once she got dressed, courtesy of the go bag Emily had brought. He didn't want her seeing Sebastian. But Melissa didn't want him trying to shelter her, so he reluctantly gave in.

Once in the family room, he encouraged Melissa to stay back by the wall while he joined Emily in the center of the room by Sebastian's body. But the stubborn set of Mel's jaw told him no amount of arguing was going to make her sit idly by while the rest of them worked the mission and tried to figure out how Sebastian fit into all of this. She stood just a few feet from him and Emily, her hand resting on the back of Austin's wheelchair.

"Call me cripple now," Austin taunted as he crossed his arms and aimed a smug look at Sebastian's body.

Jace sighed heavily and knelt down. Sebastian's hands were still cuffed in front of him, his face turned toward the kitchen.

"I'm sorry, Jace," Emily said. "After you and Austin did your thing to save the rest of us, all I had to do was keep an eye on this jerk so we could interrogate him." She shook her head in disgust. "I've gotta tell ya. Police work never was my thing. And I just proved it again."

Jace lifted one of Sebastian's eyelids. The pupils were fixed and dilated. His skin was already beginning to cool and had a slightly pink tinge to it. A small amount of foam was gathered at the corners of his mouth.

"You can quit beating yourself up over this, Emily. None of us would have expected him to have a suicide pill. Looks like cyanide. He must have had a capsule in his pocket. Even if you'd been watching him like a hawk, he'd have figured out how to get to it eventually."

"Yeah, maybe, but still. I should have—"

He squeezed her hand. "We're all alive. I give credit for that to you and Austin for that stunt you two pulled. And I assure you that Devlin is only going to care about the part where you're alive and unhurt. So, again, stop blaming yourself."

She gave him a grateful nod and pulled out her cell phone. "I'll check on the others, see what they've found out and let them know what happened."

"Cell phones don't work in here," Jace and Austin said at the same time.

Austin wheeled around and headed toward the bank of computers. "Come on. I'll show you the landline." He pulled out a chair, and Emily sat down beside him.

Melissa crouched next to Jace. Other than being a little pale, she looked remarkably calm—and gorgeous, as always, in those tight blue jeans and a dark navy-blue blouse. Jace frowned at his lack of focus and went back to the task at hand, searching Sebastian's pockets for anything that might give him a clue about where the man was headed.

"Just so we're clear," Melissa said, as she watched him, "if I ever see you unarmed chasing after an armed man again, I promise I'll figure out some way to make you regret it—if you're lucky enough not to get yourself killed, that is. Got that?"

He smiled. "I'll take that under advisement."

"You'd better. I'll probably have a head full of white hair by the end of the day because of how reckless you are with your life. Tell me what happened."

He finished searching Sebastian's pockets, which were empty. "I knew from Austin's little speech in the hallway that he had a plan to distract Sebastian and that I didn't need to worry about him or Emily if he could get into the living room. I also knew that a bullet wouldn't go through the walls because of what he said about that mesh, which is why I wanted you to stay in the bedroom."

"So Austin, what, grabbed a gun from one of the cases? I heard shots."

"No. I think Austin rattled on about the gun cases to throw Sebastian off the real point, which was that he just wanted to make it into the living room. To the elevator."

She looked past him to the elevator, which sat open as usual. "Why did he want to do that?"

"Come on. I'll show you." At the elevator, he reached in and pressed the button to send it to the basement. As soon as he pulled his hand back, the doors slid shut, revealing three huge dents.

Melissa touched one of the dents. "Bullets. Austin

must have put the speed on and raced in here with Emily after making Sebastian think he couldn't move quickly on the bumpy floor. He pressed the panic button, didn't he?"

"He did. Those doors saved his and Emily's lives when Sebastian fired at them. By the time Sebastian remembered about me, I was already behind him. I'd hoped to interrogate him, but obviously that's not going to happen now."

"How did he get in here in the first place? I thought this was supposed to be a fortress."

He glanced at Emily. Thankfully she was still talking on the landline phone and didn't seem to hear Melissa's question. Beside her, Austin was punching up something on the computer screen.

Jace kept his voice low, so he wouldn't embarrass Emily further. "Emily's theory is that she was followed here. Since Devlin went rogue last year, they've had to maintain a low profile. She was in a hurry and made the mistake of stopping at a busy gas station downtown. She said she believes someone from EXIT must have seen her and called it in. Word must have gotten back to Cyprian. He must have called Sebastian to take over the tail from whoever called in Emily's location. Short version, he pulled a gun on her at the security gate outside this house and got inside her car. Austin didn't know anything was up and buzzed her in. You know the rest."

She nodded. "It sounds like my father really is the one who sent Sebastian here."

"I'm not so sure about that."

"Why not?"

"For one thing, I don't think your father trusted

Sebastian. He certainly didn't seem to like him, either when we saw them together at EXIT or when we were hiding in the basement office at your father's house. And even though last night's conversation with your father was rough, and he sounded pretty brutal, he was obviously incensed that Stefano almost killed you with that tire blowout on the mountain. I'm not convinced your father would risk your life by sending Sebastian, or anyone else, to get you. He'd be too worried you could be hurt."

"A week ago, I'd have agreed with you. I'm not sure what I believe about my father anymore. But if you're right, then who sent Sebastian? You think it was Stefano? Or the Watcher if he isn't Stefano?"

"Hard to know for sure."

She smoothed her hands on her jeans. "If the Watcher sent Sebastian, and wanted me alive, I can only assume the Watcher wanted to use me as leverage against my father. But why would he do that?"

Jace scratched his jaw and considered the possibilities. "Maybe the Watcher believes your father's the one responsible for abducting the rest of the Council, if they're even still alive, and he wants to use you to force your father to let them go. Another possibility is that the Council wasn't kidnapped. They could have gone into hiding because the Watcher told them about Tarek being killed and your father not retaliating by killing us. Maybe they're worried your father will go after them now."

"O . . . kay. Then . . . you're saying the Council might have sent Sebastian after me?"

He shrugged. "I honestly don't know. At this point, anyone could have sent him—your father, Stefano, one or more Council members, the Watcher—

whoever he is. The way everything seems to be imploding makes it look like a power grab to me. Someone, or even a team, may be trying to take over the enforcement arm of EXIT, and they want the rest of the Council, and your father, out of the way. Maybe Sebastian was supposed to kidnap you to make that happen. As soon as you were out of the kill zone, he'd have killed the rest of us. It's a damn good thing that Austin played that stunt. He's the one who saved us today."

She smiled and cupped his face. "You both saved us. Thank you."

Unable to resist a quick taste, he leaned down and kissed her.

"Hey, lovebirds," Austin called out. "If you can quit drooling all over each other for a few minutes, I'm about to start a Skype session with Devlin, Mason, and Ramsey."

Chapter Twenty-one

As Melissa took a seat beside Austin at the computer, Emily got up. Melissa gave her a questioning look.

"I've already spoken to Dev on the phone," she said, turning to Jace. "He wants me to take Sebastian's body to one of our guys at a lab near here. He can look for particulates that might help us figure out where Sebastian has been. It's a long shot, but it could tell us where to look for whoever sent him after Melissa. Can you help me load him into my trunk?"

"No problem."

Melissa pressed her hand to her throat, fighting nausea as Emily matter-of-factly brought in a body bag from her car as if this were a common occurrence in her life.

Maybe it was.

Emily waved good-bye as Jace lifted the now-full body bag over his shoulder and followed her out to the garage.

"Mel, you need some Pepto or something?" Austin asked. "You're looking a little green."

She forced her hand down. "No. I'll be okay. That was just . . . weird."

He shrugged. "You get used to it."

"You're kidding, right?"

"Nope. And I've only been on the team a few weeks."

She shuddered. "Maybe I do need some Pepto."

He grinned and opened a drawer beneath the countertop. "Here you go. I always keep a supply of the chewable pills. Comes in handy when your main sustenance is pizza."

She opened the little packet and popped the pills in her mouth. "If pizza bothers you, then why do you eat it all the time?"

"Because I like it." He blinked at her as if she were crazy.

She laughed, already feeling better.

Jace strode back inside and made a beeline to the kitchen. After washing his hands, he sat down in the chair on the other side of Austin. "All right. Emily is on her way to safety. Devlin doesn't have to worry about her. We can cut the BS."

Austin grinned. "Nothing gets past you does it, genius?" He punched a button and typed in a string of numbers and letters.

"I don't understand," Melissa said. "Taking the . . . bag . . . was a ploy? To get Emily out of here?"

"Of course," Austin interjected. "Dev's overprotective. Or hadn't you noticed? Em is smart and has a heart of gold. And she's a damn fine detective. But when it comes to the hands-on stuff, she scares the hell out of all of us. It's way better for the whole team if she's preoccupied elsewhere while we go after the bad guys."

"And you knew this?" she asked Jace.

"I figured as much. I heard stories from Devlin when we met in Savannah. Like Austin said, Emily's strengths lie elsewhere."

Melissa folded her arms on the desktop in front of her. "I feel like I'm always playing catch-up around you."

Austin punched another button, then pressed ENTER. A Skype session filled the screen, showing Devlin, Mason, and Ramsey sitting together. From what she could see behind them, they were probably sitting in the back of a van, probably the same one they'd used to kidnap her and Jace last night.

"Is Em gone?" Devlin asked.

"She's on her way," Jace assured him. "Austin caught you up on everything here?"

"Yes. And it meshes with what we've found out. Ramsey, tell them what your police contact told you."

Ramsey scooted closer to the screen, the number eighty-eight, his NASCAR idol's racecar number, printed in bold red across his black T-shirt. "One of our contacts at Boulder PD was able to get a copy of the police lab's analysis on dirt from inside the trunk of the Cadillac where the Councilwoman's body was found. It contained a mixture of minerals and soil types that didn't mean anything to the police but raised red flags for us enforcers. We know all about that mix of minerals because it was something they taught us during training, when they explained the merits of the EXIT training facility and how the minerals in the soil there could block most transmissions. That particular mix is rare and only happened as a result of the types of mining going on there for years."

"So you think he was at this training facility?" Jace asked.

"We think there's a high probability. We call it Enforcement Alley, our very own Kobayashi Maru, a pretty good trek outside of town." He grinned. "Kobayashi Maru. Trek. Get it?"

Jace rolled his eyes. "Tell me about this Enforcement Alley."

Mason took Ramsey's place in the middle of the screen. "You've heard of Hogan's Alley?"

"Of course. The tactical training facility in Quantico where the FBI trains its special agents with shoot-out simulations, among other things."

"Right. Well, Cyprian played off that decades ago and made his own version out in the foothills on top of a network of abandoned mines and called it Enforcement Alley. It's where all the enforcers used to be trained. But it proved too dangerous, even for us. The mines beneath the town are unstable, with collapses happening and sinkholes appearing without warning. And there are caches of old TNT explosives buried in some of those mines, too unstable to be removed. After the body count got too high for even Cyprian to stomach, the town was shut down and fenced off. A new facility was built, and this one hasn't been used since. Or at least that's what we thought. Now we're wondering if someone in EXIT is using it as a base of operations."

"Stefano has to be the one who killed those Council members at the hotel," Jace reminded them. When they'd eaten dinner last night, he'd caught them up on everything he and Melissa had found out. "So it makes sense that if he's the one who sent Sebastian here, then he might be there waiting for Sebastian to return with Melissa."

"You said Kobayashi Maru," Melissa reminded him. "What does that mean?"

Jace eyed her as if she'd sprouted horns on the top of her head. "*Star Trek*? Captain James Tiberius Kirk? Any of that ring a bell?"

"Vaguely. Not really a sci-fi fan."

He winced. "That needs to be rectified right away."

Now it was her turn to roll her eyes.

"Kobayashi Maru was the name of a cadet training exercise in the *Star Trek* TV series," Mason explained. "And it was the name some of us trainees started using instead of Enforcement Alley because it seemed impossible to pass the physical endurance tests and survival drills we were put through."

"So we think, what, that the missing Council members are being held at this facility?" Jace asked.

"We do. If they're still alive." He glanced at Devlin and Ramsey before continuing. "We're actually already here at Enforcement Alley. Our van is hidden in the woods on a hill that overlooks the east gate. That's the closest we could get and still be hidden, without losing transmission quality from the limited cell-tower coverage and the minerals in the soil closer into town. Shortly after we got here, we saw an old black Mercedes pull through the gate."

Jace and Melissa looked at each other.

"Wasn't there a car like that on the mountain road?" Melissa asked. "Before our tire blew out?"

He nodded. "It passed the park where we were sitting less than a minute after your father's chef drove by. That must be Stefano's car."

"No," Melissa said. "He drives a red BMW."

"I imagine he drives whatever he needs for a mission," Jace said.

"Good point."

"Bingo," Ramsey said. "Stefano's the one who got out of the Mercedes. Right in front of the old saloon. We're thinking the Council members may be inside if they're alive."

"Cyprian Cardenas arrived a few minutes later," Mason said.

Melissa's heart sank. "That doesn't prove he's involved with the Council's disappearance. Maybe he was lured there by Stefano. Or someone had a gun on him."

"No one had a gun on him." His voice was short, clipped, leaving no doubt that he considered her father an active participant in whatever was happening to the Council. "We're going to hike to the town and round up Cyprian, Stefano, and whoever else might be there and sort all of this out."

Jace rose from his chair. "Send the GPS coordinates to my phone. We'll go in together."

"You got it." The screen went dark.

Melissa jumped up and followed Jace to the wall of weapons. "I want to help. What can I do?"

"Help by staying here, where I know you'll be safe."

"This place wasn't safe an hour ago."

His jaw tightened. "That was different. You and Austin won't let anyone in until I return. And since whatever is going down seems to be focused around Enforcement Alley, this is the safest place for you right now." He rapped on one of the display cases. "How do I open this?"

Austin punched a few buttons on the computer. The glass covers on all of the cases flipped up and out of the way. "Be my guest."

He shed his suit jacket and put one of the bullet-resistant vests over his dress shirt.

"Give me one of those," Melissa said. "I'm coming with you."

"No. You're not." He selected a wicked-looking serrated knife and slid it into a holder inside his right boot.

"Yes. I am. I have to protect you. And I have to protect my father, too."

Jace paused in the process of shoving magazines into his pants pockets. "Protect your father? You do remember that he killed your boyfriend, right?"

She jerked back at his cruel reminder.

His face immediately softened with regret. "Mel, I'm sorry. That was—"

"The truth," she whispered. "I'm not an idiot, Jace. I know that my father has done some horrible things. He should pay for what he's done. But he should pay for his crimes in a court of law. Not at the hands of vigilantes."

He stiffened, then shoved a magazine down into his left boot. After grabbing one last magazine, he faced her, his expression cold. "You act like I'm going out there to kill your father. I'm not a murderer, Mel. If I kill someone, it's in self-defense. Or to save someone else's life." He gave Austin a curt nod and headed toward the garage.

Melissa ran after him. "Wait. We need to discuss this."

He blew out a deep breath and suddenly looked very weary. "I understand your concerns. I really do. But you have to trust that I know what I'm doing." He stepped through the door that led into the garage and pulled it shut with a loud click.

Melissa reached for the knob, then stopped. *Honorable, brave, loyal, trustworthy.* A few days ago, those were simply words on a background report. But Jace had proven them true over and over again. He was right. He knew what he was doing. Jace wouldn't harm her father. She had to believe that and trust him. Dropping her hand, she turned around and joined Austin at the row of computers.

"Don't worry, Mel." His fingers clacked on the keyboard. "I figured this could happen last night when Devlin didn't even try to talk me out of going on the mission. I knew he might sneak out and leave me here. Which is exactly what he did—while I was in the shower, the jerk. And I figured you'd end up left behind, too, because there was no way Jace would want you in danger. So I planned ahead."

He made a flourish out of punching a function key. "Melissa, meet the Equalizer helmet cam. Or rather, the fake-button-on-my-brother's-shirt cam." The screen changed, showing a picture of a chain-link fence at the bottom of a hill. And below that, a dusty street with wooden buildings on either side. A black Mercedes sat out front, beside a black limousine.

"You put a spy camera on Devlin's shirt, and he doesn't know about it?"

"Clever, huh?" He grinned. "It's not the first time either."

"You're brilliant."

"Yeah. It runs in the family." He shrugged as if it was his burden to bear.

Melissa smiled, her worries for Jace, and her father, settling down now that she could at least keep an eye on what was happening.

"Is there any sound?"

"Unfortunately, no. I need to work on that for next time."

The picture they were seeing barely moved, probably because Devlin and the others were waiting on the hillside for Jace before making their approach. A burst of static turned the monitor into white snow for a moment. Then the picture reappeared, although a bit fuzzy and less clear than before.

"That shouldn't have happened," Austin muttered. He punched a few more keys. The picture stabilized.

They sat together for over thirty minutes, their view barely changing. Then it moved to the left, and Jace could be seen shaking Ramsey's and Devlin's hands before nodding to Mason and saying something to him.

"Here we go," Austin said, as the angle shifted again. "They're heading for the fence."

Melissa tensed beside him, wishing they could hear what was going on.

The picture blinked again.

Austin frowned and keyed in a few more codes. But the closer the men got to the town, the fuzzier the picture became, and the more often it blinked.

"Can't you make it clear again?" Melissa asked. She was clutching the countertop so hard, her fingers ached. The men were almost to the gate.

"That's the best I've got. It's the topography and the stupid minerals, I guess. I thought that was a load of crap, to be honest. I've never heard of minerals having that effect on electronics. Learn something new every day I suppose. All we can hope is that it will come through long enough to—" The picture went dark. He swore and typed a long string of commands. But no matter what he did, the picture stayed dark.

He slammed his fist on the table and shoved back in his chair. "We're blind. We've got nothing." The screen flashed again. "Wait, look."

She squinted, trying to make out what was happening between the squiggly lines of interference. "They're inside the fence." Someone ran past Devlin, his pistol out in front of him. "That's Jace! He's firing at someone." He ducked behind the limo and looked over the back of the trunk, aiming down the street.

"There." Austin tapped his finger on the screen, pointing to a dark shape about a block away. Sunlight glinted off the gun in his hands. "They're in a shoot-out."

Melissa clasped her hands together. *Be careful, Jace. Please be careful.*

The camera angle shifted again. Devlin must have turned back to say something to Ramsey and Mason because they were on the screen. The interference was so bad it was difficult to make them out, even though they were just a few feet away. Mason said something. Ramsey nodded and stepped to the left. He suddenly flipped backward onto the ground. Devlin dropped down beside him.

Austin swore and covered the screen with his hands. "Don't look, Mel. Damn it to hell. I can't believe this." He swore again, his voice shaking with anger.

Melissa sat in shock beside him. One moment

Ramsey was talking and full of life. Then in the blink of an eye—or an assassin's bullet—he was . . . *gone*.

"Put your hands down," she choked through her tight throat. "We have to see what's going on with the others."

He blew out a breath and dropped his hands. Devlin appeared to be yelling at Mason who was still crouching beside Ramsey, his hands fisted in his dead friend's blood-spattered shirt. The grief on Mason's face was heart wrenching. Finally, Devlin jerked Mason to his feet and forced him to turn away from Ramsey's body, facing the fake town again.

"Where's Jace?" Melissa asked, bottling her emotions as best she could. Whether Ramsey had a wife, a girlfriend, a family, she didn't know. But thinking about the tragedy that had just happened wouldn't help anyone right now, not when the rest of the team was still in danger. What she had to focus on was what was happening to the others.

Austin shook his head, squinting at the snowy picture. "I don't know where Jace went. I can't see squat."

Devlin ran forward, his pistol extended in front of him, just visible at the edge of the screen. Mason jogged a few feet ahead and slightly to his left. Suddenly, an explosion of dust and dirt flew up, and the picture went dark again.

"What the hell was that?" Austin said.

She shook her head. "I have no idea. It's like they just . . . disappeared."

Austin's face turned pale. His fingers flew over the keyboard, and a few seconds later the picture they'd just seen was on the screen again, replaying in slow motion. Dust flew up. He punched a function key, freezing the frame. "There." He pointed. "See?"

She slowly nodded. "The street collapsed beneath them. Mason and Devlin must have fallen into one of those mineshafts Mason was talking about earlier."

Austin sat back, tapping the table, his mouth in a grim line. "I didn't see Jace. I think he went ahead, down the street. He may not even realize that something happened to them. Or maybe something happened to him, too."

Melissa stared at the screen for a few more seconds, then jumped up. "They need help. I'm going out there." She ran to the wall of weapons and vests and stared at them in frustration. "I thought I knew a lot about guns, but I don't even know what half this stuff is. Help me, Austin. Please."

He wheeled over to her. "You know I can't—"

"You can't what? Let me go? Try to stop me, and I'll dump you on your ass."

He held his hands up in a placating gesture. "Hey. Back up the Humvee, GI Jane. My brother is out there and could be wounded. I'm the last person who would try to stop you. What I was going to say is that I can't help out *there*. Devlin was right not to let me go because my chair would just be a hindrance in that environment. But I *can* help you choose the guns and ammo you'll need after you suit up in Kevlar. Mason's car is in the garage. You can take that. I'll give you the GPS coordinates to punch into the NAV unit. And then I'll do what I do best from here."

She grabbed the bullet-resistant vest he pointed to and pulled it on over her head. "What you do best?"

"Logistics, baby. I've got contacts all over the

country, all over the world. I admit most of them came from Devlin, from the people he met as an enforcer. But I've garnered quite a few sources of my own and am mastering the tricks of the trade. I can put anything you need anywhere, fast." He wheeled around to face the computer again, his fingers flying across the keyboard, topography maps of the land outside of Boulder popping up on the screen. "Hell, I could set an aircraft carrier in the middle of the freaking desert if you need it."

Melissa paused with a large knife in her hand. "I don't need an aircraft carrier. I just need for Jace and the others to be alive."

Chapter Twenty-two

J ace swore and dove back between the two buildings. Bullets whined off the ground ten feet away, in the main street that ran down Enforcement Alley, hemming him in. Every time he tried to make a run for it, the sniper took potshots at him. Once the sniper tired of his game, all he had to do was make his way down the street another fifty yards, parallel to Jace's position, and take him out. It would be like shooting the proverbial fish in a barrel since Jace was surrounded on three sides by smooth, concrete, two-story walls with no windows. He was good and trapped, and beginning to understand why the enforcers called this place Kobayashi Maru—an unwinnable scenario.

He'd lost sight of Mason, Devlin, and Ramsey and had no clue if they were trapped somewhere like him. One minute they were behind him, and the next they were all dodging bullets from the sniper, and he'd lost sight of them.

Something hit his shoulder. He whirled around, his pistol out in front of him. Nothing. He turned in a full circle. Still nothing.

"Jace, up here."

His stomach dropped at the sound of that familiar, feminine voice. He looked up, his mouth hanging open in shock. Lying on her stomach, two floors above him, leaning over the edge of the roof—and holding the rope that must have been what hit him on the shoulder—was the one person in the entire universe that he most wanted to *not* be here.

"What the hell are you doing, Melissa? It's not safe. Get out of here."

She shook the rope, hitting him on the side of the head. "That's not how you thank someone for saving your life. From what I can see, you're trapped. And the only way out without getting shot is this rope. I tied the other end around a pipe, but I don't have the strength to pull you up. Do you think you can climb it?"

He was already shoving his gun in his holster and grabbing the rope. He swore beneath his breath, mumbling all the things he was going to lecture her about when he got his hands on her—like not putting herself in the line of fire, for anyone. Ever.

Pulling himself up hand over hand until he could wrap his legs around the rope, he then shimmied up the rest of the way to the top. He dove over the edge, grateful that the flat, commercial-style roof had raised sides that offered a few feet of protection, so no one from the street level—including his sniper friend—could see either of them. After pulling the rope up and dropping it beside them, he grabbed Melissa and rolled on top of her.

She grinned up at him. "Pretty clever, huh?"

Clever? Clever? How about dangerous, foolish, crazy? The lecture he'd practiced in his mind died on his tongue without being said. Because he cared about her feelings, damn it. And she was looking up at him with such joy in her eyes, so proud of herself for coming to his rescue. If she'd been anyone else, anyone, he'd have been grateful, thankful. But seeing her leaning over the edge of that roof had killed him inside a hundred times over. He would rather have died than have her put herself in danger for him.

He took in the bullet-resistant vest, the guns strapped to her waist, and the . . . knife *duct-taped* to the outside of her pants leg?

"What's with the knife?"

"I didn't have any boots to put it in, or a holder. Austin came up with the idea of using duct tape. Works great."

"Austin, huh? I'll have to remember to thank him for that little gem." Yeah, he'd thank him all right.

"I've got a gun strapped to my ankle, too, in a little holster. Want to see?"

"Not particularly." He dropped his forehead against hers. "There are two things I want to do right now, and I can't decide which one to choose. Either I kiss you senseless, or I shake you until your teeth rattle for putting yourself in danger."

She slid her hands around his neck. "I vote for the kissing."

He groaned and claimed her mouth in a searing kiss that had him instantly hard and aching. Every time he touched her, it was like this, a fever that swept through him, igniting every cell in his body, consuming him with a need to take her, to hold her, to protect her.

To cherish her.

He broke the kiss, drawing in deep breaths as he tried to focus. "You're dangerous, Mel. I can't think straight around you."

Her lips curved. "You say the sweetest things."

"That wasn't a compliment." He rolled off her. "Not thinking straight could get us killed. You should have stayed back at the house where it was safe." He grabbed the rope and began rolling it so he could take it with them in case it came in handy again.

Her eyes flashed with anger, and the sexy siren disappeared, replaced with a ferocious tiger. "Do you have any idea how scared I was that something had happened to you? If I had stayed at the house, you could be like Ramsey and the others."

His head whipped toward her. What did she mean, like Ramsey and the others?

"—so excuse me if I made you lose your focus," she continued. "I lost mine, too. Because I was so scared that I wouldn't find you in time that I lost my head when I *did* find you." She shoved her wild hair out of her face. "This is the part where you say thank you."

"Thank you. Mel?"

"What?"

"What did you mean, like Ramsey and the others? Did something happen to them? Did you see them?"

As fast as her anger had flared, it went out, deflating her like a two-day-old balloon. Bitterness, regret, sorrow reflected in her dark eyes as she stared past him into nothingness. "Ramsey. I saw Ramsey get shot—on the camera Austin rigged to Devlin's shirt. The others, Mason and Devlin, they fell into a hole, one of the old mineshafts we think.

Then the camera stopped working. It seemed like a long fall. I think . . . I think they might have been killed. But I'm not sure."

"Where?"

"Near the saloon."

He tied the rope to his belt loop and took her hand. "Let's get off this roof before the sniper comes looking for me to see why I'm not trying to escape anymore." He squeezed her hand. "And Mel?"

"Yes?"

"You did good."

"You're welcome." She waved toward the back side of the building. "There's a trapdoor at that end. That's how I got up here. I heard shots, so I kept inside the tree line and climbed over the fence behind these buildings."

The reminder of the chances she'd taken had him angry all over again, but he was careful not to let it show. She'd shown incredible courage. And she was such a remarkably good person, risking so much to help not only him but Devlin and Mason, men she barely knew, men who'd drugged and kidnapped her just yesterday. She had to have one of the best, kindest, most generous souls he'd ever met.

A few minutes later, they were inside the ground floor of the building, which was set up like an old general store complete with a long display counter. Jace told Melissa to wait behind the counter while he duckwalked across the room to stay underneath the row of windows out front and tried to locate the sniper.

There, a flash of sunlight reflected on the sniper's pistol as he sprinted between two buildings, then ducked behind a rusted-out air-conditioner unit directly across the street. Since there was no question of the man's skill—he'd managed to pin Jace down for over ten minutes—the fact that he was using a gun with a stainless-steel finish that caught the light instead of a matte black finish like Jace used probably meant he was an arrogant son of a bitch just daring someone to notice him. Was he Stefano? Another enforcer? Some other lackey Cyprian had hired to protect him and help him take out the Council?

Whoever the man was, hopefully Jace could capitalize on his arrogance to defeat him.

He fit his pistol in the hole left by one of the missing windowpanes, hunkered down, and waited. Five minutes later, he still hadn't seen any movement. Had the shooter managed to find a side door without Jace seeing him? Maybe a rotted-out hole in the side of the building behind that A/C unit?

"Jace," Melissa whispered from behind the counter.

"Give me a minute," he said. "I've got the sniper pinned down."

"Jace."

The urgency in her voice had him turning around. Her eyes were wide, her face pale. He hurried over to her, staying low to keep from becoming a target.

"What's wrong?"

She pointed to the other end of the counter. A man lay on his side on the floor, barely visible behind a large bucket, huddled in on himself, facing away from them. Jace grabbed Melissa and shoved her behind him as he aimed his pistol at the other man. But even as he did so, he knew in his gut the man was dead. He was lying more still than a living person could ever manage, and he hadn't drawn a breath since Melissa had pointed to him.

"I didn't see him at first," she whispered. "I was watching you. But suddenly I looked over and . . . I saw him."

"Stay here."

"Don't worry. I will." She kept her face averted.

He pressed a quick kiss against her forehead, then hurried to the body. He pressed his fingers against the man's neck, just to be sure. But his skin was cool. There was no pulse. He turned the man's face toward him. "Son of a . . . it's one of your tour guides, Garcia."

"Ethan? Oh, no."

"Looks like he's been here at least a couple of hours." He bent over, noting the dark stain on his shirt, the slashing cut. "He's been stabbed."

Melissa shivered. "Why would someone kill him?"

He hurried back to her. "Come on. I have no way of knowing if the sniper is still across the street now or whether he snuck out while I was back here. Let's work our way to where you said Mason and Devlin disappeared."

"And where Ramsey was killed."

He swept her long, curly hair back from her face. "You're an incredibly brave woman to have come out here the way you did. We just have to get through a few more minutes. All right?"

Her brows slashed down. "Stop talking to me as if I were a child, or a fragile, delicate flower. I'm not going to fall apart."

"Of course not, sweetheart."

She rolled her eyes.

He grinned and pulled her with him through the back room to the door that led outside. They paused, looked around, then carefully made their way from

building to building: waiting, watching, then sprinting across the few feet that separated each of them.

When they reached the last building, there was
nowhere else to go except over the fence behind
them into the woods, or down the side of the struc-
ture to the street out front. Jace leaned around the
corner, belatedly wishing he'd brought a pair of binoculars.

"The saloon is across the street." He kept his voice
low. "That's where we saw Stefano and your father
go earlier. The limo and Mercedes are still parked
out front."

Melissa remained flattened against the back of
the building beside him. "What about Ramsey?"

"His body is still there. No one has moved him.
I can see a big hole in the street, the sinkhole you
mentioned. I need to check it out, see if Devlin and
Mason are still alive."

She sighed heavily. "Isn't there another way? A
safer way? You'll be in the open, with no cover, vulnerable."

"There's no other way. And we can't wait around,
not if Devlin and Mason are hurt."

"Okay, okay. I know you're right, but I don't like it."

"Me either, but it has to be done. If something
happens to me out there, hop that fence and run like
hell. Is your car close by?"

"About fifty yards past the fence."

He hesitated. "Wait, what car did you drive?"

"I think it was Mason's."

"His restored 1965 Pontiac GTO? The one I saw in
the garage when I left?"

"Yes, why?"

He grinned. "I really hope Mason's still alive. I

want to see the look on his face when he finds out you drove his baby."

She put her hands on her hips. "What is it with you boys and your toys?"

He shrugged. "If I'm not back in two minutes, get out of here." He leaned around the edge of the building again, looking for signs of movement out on the street and in the windows of the saloon.

"Jace?" Melissa whispered.

"Yeah?"

"I'm not leaving you."

He ducked back beside her and gave her a stern look. "Two minutes. And then, yes, you are."

"Well, you can tell yourself that if it makes you feel better. But it's not going to happen. I may not be a badass Navy SEAL, but I'm armed. I'm wearing Kevlar. And I think . . . I think I'm falling in love with you, damn it. So I'm not cutting and running and leaving you here by yourself. We're a team, and I—"

He crushed his mouth to hers and shoved his pistol into his holster. He pulled her against him, cupping her bottom and lifting her so he could get the perfect angle, feeling her heat, her softness against his hardness. It was a mistake. Kissing her right now when he should be keeping watch. But he'd never expected her to say that she was falling in love with him, and hearing that when he was so worried she might get hurt nearly destroyed him.

He finally broke the kiss, gasping for breath, his pulse thudding in his ears. "Damn you, Mel."

"Ouch. Not the response I was going for."

He kissed her again, hard, quick, then cupped her face in his hands. "Say it again."

Her eyes sparkled with humor. "Ouch?"

"Melissa."

"Okay, okay. I love you, Jace. Somehow, impossibly, since I haven't known you very long, and shoot-outs aren't exactly what I call dates, I love you. And I'm miserable about it. Okay? Happy? Now it's your turn."

His hands shook as he feathered them across her cheeks and then stepped back. He pulled his pistol out again. "Not yet. You want to know how I feel? Then you had damn well better do everything I say until we make it out of here. Together. Alive. Understood?"

"That's not fair."

"Life's not fair." He wanted to yank her to him again and cover her mouth with his, but he'd already let her distract him too long. "There's nothing else I can do but run out there and hope no one sees me."

She gripped her pistol in both hands. "I know. Don't worry. I'll cover you."

The first inkling of worry skittered up his spine. "Actually, I'd rather you didn't. I don't want to get shot . . . by *you*."

"Coward. You have no idea how well I can shoot."

"I'd rather not find out if the pistol is pointing at me."

"Just go already."

"I'll be right back." He took off running down the side of the building and didn't stop until he'd reached the sinkhole. He skidded like a baseball player coming in to home plate, stopping a few feet from the edge and aiming his gun down the street, then at the windows of the saloon. Nothing. No one moving in the shadows or peering out through the broken panes of glass. No sunlight glinting off a stainless-steel gun.

He looked back at Melissa. She was leaning around the corner of the building, still holding her pistol with both hands, watching out for him. Nice in theory, but scary as hell in practice, since he'd never seen her in action and had no idea how accurate she was.

He set his pistol on the ground beside him and pulled himself right up to the edge of the hole and looked down. It wasn't as deep as he'd thought, definitely a survivable drop, but it was too deep for someone to get out without a rope or another way out. Since the hole was empty, and there were dark openings that appeared to head under the street, he figured Mason and Devlin had found another way out, maybe an old mineshaft or tunnel, and were hopefully working their way toward an exit.

He grabbed his pistol, checked the saloon windows again and down the street, then took off running toward the building where Melissa was leaning around the corner watching him.

By the time he was close enough to realize how pale she was, it was too late. She was jerked backward, and a man stepped out from the corner of the building, holding a gun to her head.

Stefano.

Chapter Twenty-three

Melissa winced when Stefano pulled her hair, jerking her against him as he aimed his pistol at Jace.

"What do you want?" Jace demanded, holding his hands in the air.

"I want you to toss your weapons. And don't forget that handy lock pick of yours. I saw•that little trick on a camera I installed at Cyprian's house."

Jace hesitated.

Stefano yanked Melissa's hair again, making her gasp at the stinging pain in her scalp.

"Okay, okay," Jace snapped. "Just stop hurting her." He tossed his pistol to the ground, along with his other weapons. Lastly, he pulled the tiny lock pick from over his ear and threw it down, too. "There. You can let her go now."

"I don't think so. The second I do, you'll jump me." Stefano motioned with his gun. "Get moving. That way. And stick to the center of the road. Or maybe I'll use the knife on my belt to cut her and give you some incentive."

Melissa shuddered, and Stefano laughed.

After another long look at Melissa, Jace headed down the main street through Enforcement Alley. "What's the plan, Stefano? Who's giving you orders? Cyprian or one of the Council members?"

Stefano shoved Melissa forward. "Follow him, but don't get too close."

Jace glanced back. "So you're the Watcher, but you've decided, what, to launch a takeover, try to wrench control of EXIT from the Council and from Cyprian? Is that what this is about?"

Stefano laughed. "You're fishing, Atwell. Why don't you just keep your mouth shut? Or you might end up like the guy you found in the general store."

Jace's shoulders seemed to tense, but he didn't say anything. He kept striding forward, with Melissa and Stefano several yards back behind him.

"Why are you doing this, Stefano?" Melissa asked. "We grew up together. We're practically sister and brother."

"Practically?" he sneered. "Ask your father if he considers me to be his son. Then ask him what he considers my mother to be to him. His whore, that's what." He swore, as if he suddenly realized he'd said too much. "Just shut up and keep walking."

Melissa felt sick at what Stefano had just said. Was her father taking advantage of Silvia? Using his role as her boss to force her to do something she didn't want to do? The idea made her want to retch. It couldn't be true. Could it?

"If my father hurt Silvia, I understand your pain and anger, Stefano. And I'm sorry."

"Shut. Up."

A few minutes later, he said, "Take a left, Atwell."

Jace turned, then stopped and looked at the name over the building's door. "You've got to be kidding."

"Keep moving," Stefano ordered.

Jace climbed the steps in front of them and went inside the Enforcement Alley jailhouse.

A foul smell hit Melissa as soon as she stepped inside. She didn't know what that smell meant, but from the way Jace had stiffened, she thought maybe he'd recognized it.

Stefano forced them down a hallway to a row of jail cells, with bars from floor to ceiling. He stopped at the first one, its door hanging open, and waved Jace inside. Stefano kicked the door shut. The lock clicked.

"Let her go," Jace demanded. "If you hurt her, her father will kill you. If I don't kill you first."

Stefano ignored him and shoved Melissa forward. Jace gave her a reassuring nod as she passed him. Seeing that he didn't look worried gave her the strength she needed to face whatever was about to happen. Somehow, they'd figure a way out of this. They had to.

The next cell door was closed. But of course it did nothing to hide what was inside, the reason for the noxious smell that permeated the air. Melissa stumbled to a halt, pressing a hand against her mouth to keep from gagging. Three bodies lay on the floor on one side of the cell, their sightless eyes staring up at the ceiling. A fourth man sat on a cot against the far wall, his back against the concrete, with blood on his shirt near his collar. His eyes widened in surprise when he saw her. Adam Marsh.

"What are you doing, Stefano? Let her go," he ordered.

"You're not the one giving orders. Not this time."

"Stefano," Melissa said, trying to sound friendly, to talk to him as if her heart wasn't breaking for the brother he'd always been to her. "I don't understand. What's going on? Did you . . . did you kill those men?"

He narrowed his eyes. "Get in the cell." He motioned toward the next one over.

She ignored him and tried to buy more time. Because if she got in that cell, she'd be helpless to do anything to help Jace, Marsh, or herself. She looked past him at Marsh. "Stefano brought you here? He killed those Councilmen?"

"The Watcher called me," Marsh said. "He told me to come here for an emergency meeting. But he wasn't here when I arrived." He waved at the others. "They were. And they were already dead. When I ran in to check on them, Stefano snuck up on me. We fought, and he slashed me across the chest with a knife. Before I could recover, he'd locked me up in here."

"How bad?" she asked.

"It's not that deep. I'll be okay."

She nodded with relief. "If Stefano isn't the Watcher, who is?"

Stefano grabbed her hair and yanked her back. "I believe you already met him at the general store. His name was Garcia, and he did whatever I told him to do. Now get inside that cell. I won't ask again."

A thumping noise sounded at the beginning of the row, where Jace was locked up. Stefano turned around.

"Let me out of here, Stefano," Jace demanded. The thumping sounded again. He was kicking the bars. Why? A distraction?

Stefano shoved Melissa toward her cell.

"Don't you ever touch her again," a voice called out. And it wasn't Jace.

Melissa and Stefano both turned to see her father. His suit was dusty and dirt was smudged on his face. He stood at the end of the hallway near Jace's cell. Holding a gun.

Stefano grabbed for Melissa, but she lunged toward the open cell door and rolled away from him.

A shot rang out, deafeningly loud in the small space. Stefano fell to the floor, clutching his stomach. His gun slid across the floor and bounced off the wall. "Damn you, Cyprian," he gritted out. "What the hell are you doing?"

"Shut up. I don't listen to traitors."

Stefano glared at him. "Traitor? Listen to yourself. You sound like a damn zealot, or a dictator, running his own little kingdom. I'm no traitor. I just know when a good opportunity comes my way, and I grab it." He clutched his middle, and sucked in a sharp breath.

Cyprian looked past him to Marsh, saw the bodies inside. "This wasn't supposed to happen, none of it. I told Stefano to meet me here so I could force him to confess." He pulled his phone from his pocket. "I learned how to record on this damn gadget so I could get Stefano to admit that he'd killed those first two Council members. I wanted to use his confession to prove my innocence. But when I got here, I saw him skulking around and realized something else was going on. I've been biding my time until I could surprise him and have the advantage."

His face mirrored his regret as he kicked Stefano's gun under a bench at the far end of the row, too far away for anyone to get it. "I didn't know he'd brought the Council here, or I'd have come more quickly and tried to stop this." He looked at Melissa. "And I didn't know he was bringing you. This is a total mess."

She put her hand on her father's sleeve, relieved that he wasn't responsible for any of these recent deaths. "It's okay, Dad. You were trying to do the right thing. It's over now. Mr. Marsh knows that you didn't kill the Council members. Don't you, Mr. Marsh?"

He nodded, while pressing his shirt against the wound that was still seeping through the cloth.

"Obviously, Stefano is behind everything," Melissa continued. "He must have been using the Watcher as his pawn all along, including forcing him to call the Council to get them here. He already admitted to killing the Watcher."

Stefano cursed viciously at them, reminding her he was still on the floor a few feet away. The fact that he wasn't denying what she'd said only served to prove that she'd come to the right conclusions. It was all starting to make sense in a weird kind of way. Her father wasn't the bad man Jace believed him to be. He was just trying to prove to the Council that he wanted the best for EXIT. And the Council wanted the same thing. Stefano was the one who'd manipulated everyone to try to make her father look bad. His resentments toward her father had twisted him and made him do things Melissa was certain he'd regret later.

"Why?" Cyprian demanded. "Why, Stefano? Why would you turn on me like this?"

Stefano glared at him, his hatred for Cyprian evident in every line of his body. "Turn on you? How could I turn on you when I've hated you my whole life? You treated me like scum while I was growing up. And you treat my mother like a whore."

Melissa watched her father for a reaction. The surprise on his face reassured her that Stefano was wrong, that he'd obviously misinterpreted something.

"You deserve to lose everything and everyone you care about," Stefano sneered. "That's why, when my friend, Garcia, told me about being the Watcher, I couldn't let the opportunity pass me by." He winced and held his stomach, his fingers turning red from the blood seeping from his bullet wound. "All I wanted to do was frame you for those two Council members' deaths and have the Council put you down like the dog you are. But they were stupid and gave you more time." He waved at Marsh. "If you'd done your job, I wouldn't have done all of this." He gasped and clutched his stomach again.

"We need to help him," Melissa said. "We need to get Stefano to a doctor. And we need to let Mr. Marsh and Jace out of these cells."

Her father nodded as he stared down at Stefano. "I think I saw some keys hanging up on the wall where we came in."

She hurried past him and got the keys. She'd just unlocked Jace's cell door and let him out when a gunshot echoed through the room. Jace grabbed her and shoved her behind him, but not before she saw Stefano's crumpled body lying against the wall, a bullet hole dead center in his forehead.

And her father standing over him with his gun.

Jace started forward, but her father turned the gun on him.

"That's far enough, Mr. Atwell."

"What are you doing, Cyprian?" Jace demanded.

"Proving my loyalty to the government, and to EXIT. Mr. Marsh signaled for me to take care of Stefano, and I did. He was a danger to all of us. Now, it's over." He lowered his gun.

Melissa leaned over to see around Jace. The Council leader was nodding his agreement. That her father and that man would calmly act like executing Stefano was the right thing to do had her feeling sick inside.

Jace took the keys from her and leaned down close. "Don't turn your back on either of them," he whispered. "Wait here."

He headed down the row of cells.

"Hold it." Cyprian raised his gun again.

"What now?" Jace demanded.

"Give the keys to Melissa. I don't trust you."

"The feeling is mutual. How about lowering that gun?"

"The keys, Mr. Atwell."

"Not until you point that gun somewhere away from the vicinity of your daughter."

Cyprian frowned but pointed the gun up at the ceiling.

Melissa took the keys and hurriedly unlocked Marsh's cell. "Come on, Mr. Marsh. Let's get you out of here." She started to help him stand but he winced.

"Just a minute," he said. "I need to . . . catch my breath."

She looked at her father, who was standing with

his back to the wall, watching them. Jace had moved past him and was kneeling by Stefano, as if checking his pulse. Why would he do that when it was so horribly obvious that Stefano was dead?

A pained sound came from Marsh again as he pushed himself to his feet.

Melissa turned back to him. "You seem to be in an awful lot of pain. Let me see how bad it is." She hooked her finger in his cotton collar and pulled it down to see the cut.

"No, no, we can check it later," he assured her, yanking her hand off his shirt.

But not before she saw the tattoo. A snake coiled around a dagger.

"Oh my God," she whispered. Her gaze flew to his.

His eyes widened, and he grabbed for her.

She whirled out of his way and charged toward the open cell door.

Her father must have seen what she'd seen. His face turned a mottled red, and he roared a guttural sound of rage, like a wounded animal.

Almost as if in slow motion, Melissa saw everything happening at once.

Jace lunging toward her.

Her father aiming his gun at Marsh.

Marsh dodging to the side.

Bam! Bam! Bam!

Jace falling just short of her.

Her father grabbing her and whirling around to face Jace, the gun pointed at her head.

And Marsh, lying deathly still on the cell floor, a gurgling noise coming from his throat as blood began to pool beneath his head.

Melissa tried to wrap her mind around what had

just happened, around what was now happening, as Jace slowly stood, and her father dragged her backward, using her as a shield.

Marsh, Adam Marsh, leader of EXIT's Council, had the tattoo of the Serpentine terrorist group on his chest, the same group that had killed her mother and brothers. Was he the man the witness had seen in the airport all those years ago? Had he orchestrated the bombing of the plane?

"Let her go, Cyprian," Jace ordered. "She's still your little girl. You love her."

Her father laughed harshly. "Of course I love her. That's why she has to die. Don't you see? EXIT will never be the same. The legacy I fought so hard for no longer matters. It was built on a lie, on the promise of protecting others from terrorists like those who'd taken my family. But all along, Marsh was one of those terrorists. He was probably the man who ordered their deaths. And he probably ordered them for the same reason that I've done much the same thing—to make an enforcer out of a man, to make that man crave justice like he craves his last breath, to want to prevent the same horrors that happened to his own family."

"Oh, Daddy," Melissa whispered brokenly. "Please tell me you didn't do that to anyone."

"I did," he whispered back. "Devlin Buchanan was the first. I ordered the murder of his fiancée to get him to want to become an enforcer. And I never thought a thing about it because it was all for the greater good. But . . . knowing that Marsh probably did the same . . . I know now that it's all a lie. A cruel joke." He kissed her cheek, but he didn't move the gun from her temple or his arm from around her waist. "I love you, Melissa. More than you'll ever know. And it's because I love you that I do this. We'll be with your brothers and my sweet Isabella in Heaven, a family once again."

Melissa shook her head, tears splashing down her cheeks as she pushed against her father's arm. But he was much stronger than she'd ever realized.

"No one else has to die. Please, Father. Don't do this."

She looked at Jace, just a few feet away, and saw the barely perceptible movement of his head toward her right.

"It's just like Tarek, all over again," Jace said.

And then she knew. He wanted her to dodge to the right, like he'd told her to do when Tarek was pointing a gun at them. She moved her head slightly, letting him know she understood. And suddenly she pushed down on her father's arm and leaned to the right.

Jace lunged forward, knocking her father's gun arm up toward the ceiling. A shot sounded, followed by an agonized scream.

The arm around Melissa's waist went slack, and she was falling. Jace caught her and yanked her against his chest, half turning as if to shield her.

There on the floor, her father lay in a puddle of his own blood. The gun he'd been holding had skittered across the floor, out of his reach. And a knife was sticking out of the center of his chest, buried to the hilt.

"Daddy," she screamed. She struggled against Jace's hold. "Let me go. I have to help him!"

Her father gasped for air, arching off the floor.

"I had to do it," Jace said. "He was going to kill you."

"Let. Me. Go." She clawed at his hands.

He swore and released her, but knelt down and yanked the knife out of her father's chest—a knife she now recognized as the one that Stefano had worn on his belt—before she could reach him. Her father screamed, and blood gurgled from his wound.

She glared at Jace. "Why did you do that? You made it worse."

"I couldn't risk his pulling the knife out and using it on you."

She turned her back to him and scooted up beside her father. He lay on the floor, his face a mask of pain, blood soaking his shirt.

"Dad." Her voice broke, and she gathered him onto her lap, clutching him to her breast. "Daddy. I love you."

His eyes fluttered open. "Melissa?"

"I'm here," she said, her tears splashing down onto his face. "I'm here. I won't leave you. I love you so much."

She vaguely registered that Jace had crouched beside her. She ignored him. He didn't matter. Nothing mattered right now but the man who'd raised her, who'd loved her, who—in his own twisted way—had tried to make the world better, for her. And when he gave up on that world, his sick mind thought she would be better off in another world, in Heaven. He'd tried to protect her, by killing her. It made sense in a twisted, macabre kind of way. And she couldn't hate him for loving her.

Her father whispered something, his right hand fluttering toward his breast pocket. "My pills," he whispered. "For my heart."

"Your heart?" She'd never known he'd had a heart

condition. How could a daughter not know that about her father? She shook her head, hating herself in that moment. It was too late, of course. No pills could save him now. But it broke her heart watching him try to pull the bottle out of his pocket.

"Here, I'll help you." She reached for his pocket.

He yanked the bottle out.

Except that it wasn't a bottle.

"No," Jace yelled. He grabbed for the little metal square with a red button in the center.

Her father's hand closed over the button, and he smiled.

A powerful explosion rocked the building. Jace covered Melissa with his body as plaster and pieces of wood rained down on top of them. Another explosion sounded from farther away, rocking the building again.

Jace jumped up and pulled her with him.

"Oh, Daddy," she sobbed, realizing now that the dirt on his suit and his face was probably from him going into the tunnels, setting the explosives. "What have you done?"

His eyes fluttered open.

"Jace, wait, he's still alive!" She pushed at Jace's arm, trying to get him to let her go.

"Leave him. This whole place is going up. We have to get out of here." He grabbed her hand.

"No! Pick him up! Take him with us. We can save him." She desperately tried to tug her hand free.

"Melissa," her father whispered. "Stay with me." He coughed, and blood dotted his lips.

Another explosion sounded from outside. More dust rained down from the ceiling on top of them.

"Come on," Jace ordered. "We have to go."

She shook her head, still twisting and tugging to free her hand from Jace's hold as she stared down into her father's pain-filled eyes.

Jace swore and tossed her on his shoulder, then took off sprinting down the hallway toward the front of the building.

"No, no, no! Go back! We can't leave him!" she yelled as she pummeled his back.

Oblivious to her struggles, he ran with her bouncing on his shoulder, down the front steps, out into a street that had been transformed into a living hell. The whole town seemed to be on fire, with explosions going off all over the place.

He pulled her off his shoulder and tugged her with him back toward the east gate, where the limo and Mercedes were parked just as the ground collapsed, taking both cars with it. He reversed direction, forcing her with him. "Other way, other way," he yelled.

She glanced back at the jail, or what was left of it.

"Now, Melissa. Go, go, go!"

Her heart shattered as she turned away from the jail and ran with him toward the west gate. Pieces of burning wood blew out at them from a building as it collapsed beneath the flames. Jace jerked Melissa away, shielding her once again.

Whumpf. Whumpf. Whumpf. A powerful rhythmic noise sounded in the distance. Jace stumbled to a halt, drawing her with him.

"What is it?" Melissa yelled to be heard above the inferno surrounding them, the heat so intense she could swear her skin was blistering.

"I can't believe it," Jace yelled. "Look!" He pointed up at the sky. An enormous helicopter raced toward them, with two giant rotary blades, one at either end. "It's a Chinook, a military helicopter." He pulled her against his chest, blocking the dust as the chopper touched down in the middle of the street like a lumbering beast.

"Friend or foe?" she yelled.

Jace laughed. "Definitely friend."

"How do you know?"

He pointed at the side door. The number eighty-eight was spray-painted in white. The number Ramsey always wore on his shirts, for his NASCAR idol.

Melissa smiled, tears clogging her throat. Austin must have had the pilot put those numbers there, something quick and easy that they'd all recognize and know was associated with the Equalizers. He'd come through for them.

He'd put an aircraft carrier in the middle of the desert.

"Come on," Jace yelled.

Melissa shaded her eyes against the wind from the rotors and all the dust and let Jace pull her to the ramp that had lowered from the back of the chopper. She ran inside, and the pilot met her near the top of the ramp.

"How many more?" he yelled.

She turned around and realized she was alone. Jace was standing in the middle of the street a short distance away.

"Jace!" she yelled.

But he didn't hear her. His back was turned to her.

"We've got a minute, two tops," the pilot warned. "This whole place is going up."

Melissa nodded and ran halfway down the ramp.

She was about to yell for Jace again when she realized what he was looking at. Two men were running toward them between the burning buildings from the west end of town. They were coated in dust and dirt, but there was no mistaking their silhouettes. Mason and Devlin.

The chopper suddenly pitched forward, throwing her against the wall. Jace ran up into the helicopter and steadied her. "Hold this," he yelled, handing her a tether clipped to the wall. "You okay?"

"I'm good," she yelled over the roar of the fire and the rotary blades.

He nodded and checked on the pilot.

Mason and Devlin were running full tilt toward them now, fifty yards back.

Jace rushed to the ramp. "We have to lift off. The ground is too unstable." He motioned toward Mason and Devlin. "Come on! Hurry!"

"Can't wait any longer," the pilot called back to them. The chopper tilted upright again. The ramp lifted off the ground a few feet.

Jace strapped one of the tethers to his waist, then took the rope still attached to his belt and tied off one end to the side of the chopper. Melissa followed his lead, wrapping her hands in the tethers closest to her.

Mason and Devlin reached the chopper but it was hovering too high now. Jace crawled down the ramp toward them and threw a line out for Mason, then grabbed Devlin's hand with both of his and gave a mighty yank, swinging him up inside. Mason had almost made it inside using the line when both Jace and Devlin reached down and jerked him up into the helicopter. He thumped against the wall, and the ramp started to close. All three men fell onto the floor, laughing as they rolled against the walls.

"What a rush," Devlin shouted. "We should do that again sometime."

It was suddenly all too much for Melissa. How could anyone laugh when so much had happened, when they had nearly died, and Ramsey . . . and her father . . . had paid the ultimate price? She slumped down to the floor, her shoulders shaking as sobs wracked her body.

Jace crawled over to her as the helicopter lurched and took them away from the inferno below. He tried to take her into his arms, but she shoved him away.

"Don't. Don't touch me." The hurt look on his face opened another crack in her heart which was so riddled with cracks that she thought it might shatter at any moment. She didn't want to hurt him, but her grief was too raw, too new. And she didn't know if she'd ever be able to look at him again without seeing those horrible last moments of her father's life flashing in front of her eyes, and knowing that Jace had chosen to leave him there to die.

She covered her face with her hands and wept.

SCARCELY A WEEK after the Enforcement Alley debacle, Jace stood alone on a small rise in the same cemetery that he'd once toured with Melissa. She'd given him her trust that day and placed her life in his hands. And all she'd asked in return was one thing.

"If you ever hold my father's fate in your hands, and you can't show mercy for his sake, please, please, show mercy for mine."

He'd failed her. And for that, he knew she could never forgive him. He'd never even ask her to. Because to ask forgiveness would mean he was sorry for what he'd done.

He wasn't.

If he'd shown Cyprian compassion, if he'd shown him mercy, then Melissa would have died. And a world where Melissa Cardenas didn't exist wasn't a world in which he wanted to exist. So here he stood, like the stalker he'd once likened himself to when he'd tailed her through the Rocky Mountains. But unlike then, he had no intention of "stalking" her again. Today was the last time that he'd ever see her.

He stood far back from the temporary awning sheltering the crowd of mourners at Cyprian Cardenas's memorial service, feeling like the worst sort of hypocrite. But after everything he'd shared with Melissa, after all the pain and joy, the triumph and tragedy, it seemed wrong not to be here, as a show of respect and support on one of the worst days of her life. Even though she didn't even know he was here.

Devlin and Austin had offered to come with him. But he'd let them off the hook, knowing how hard it would be to stand here, even half a football field away, while the priest heaped praises on the man who'd caused so much turmoil in their family. And Mason, well, he hadn't even offered. Why would he? Ramsey was his best friend. He was bitter and grieving, and had taken off for parts unknown with his wife, Sabrina, to try to heal.

Would Mason ever come back? Jace didn't know, any more than he knew what would happen to the Equalizers. Home base had been shut down, at least for now. Devlin had put all of their activities on hold, to wait for things to settle, to see what the future without Cyprian would mean. With no one at the helm of EXIT Inc., and the Council decimated, would the government dismantle the enforcer program, as the Equalizers hoped? Or would they appoint someone new to revamp it, starting the vicious cycle all over again?

The idea that so many people had died under Cyprian's tyranny and that the company could rise from the ashes sickened him. But he couldn't ignore the possibility. Which was why, for now, he was staying in Boulder. Watching. Waiting. And if the phoenix rose again, he'd be right back in the thick of it, doing whatever it took to end EXIT's reign for good.

A cold wind blew across the rows of graves, bringing with it the smell of impending rain—*rain*, not snow. An early taste of the coming spring, as if Nature itself were celebrating that the cold grip of evil, at least for now, had released its hold. The breeze swept down the knoll, shaking the poles that held up the dark green awning. It seemed like half the town had come, which was why the service was held in the field instead of the family mausoleum. All those people, come to mourn a man they'd never have associated with had they known the truth about him.

The service must have ended because people were getting out of their white folding chairs. They broke off in small groups, hurrying toward the parking lot, casting anxious glances at the dark clouds roiling overhead. All too soon, Melissa stood alone, her head bowed over the table that contained an urn and pictures of her father. There was no coffin.

There was no *body* to bury. The explosions had seen
to that.

And so Jace waited, near the stand of trees where
he'd stood for the past hour, where he would continue to stand until she was safely on her way home
in the waiting limo. He glanced up at the sky, which
was looking more and more ominous. They were in
for one hell of a storm.

Workers moved in, packing up the dozens of
folding chairs into the back of a truck. When they
finished, they huddled near one of the poles holding up the awning, restlessly shuffling from foot to
foot, obviously waiting for Melissa to leave. But she
didn't seem to notice them. She didn't move. She
didn't even look their way.

The first big fat drops of rain plopped down onto
Jace's coat. The workers gave up their vigil, leaving
the awning standing as they drove off to wherever
they went when not digging graves. And still, Melissa stood, head bowed.

Jace didn't know how long he waited. But by the
time Melissa raised her head, the rain was blowing in sheets, and he was soaked through. It didn't
matter. *She* mattered.

Thunder crackled overhead. Melissa jumped, as
if surprised to find herself alone, the chairs gone,
the storm raging. And then, suddenly, she turned
. . . and looked directly at him.

He'd chosen this spot, far away, partially obscured
by trees, thinking she wouldn't notice him. But for
some reason, she had. And now she was marching
across the winter-dead grass, oblivious to the rain
drenching her hair, running in rivulets down her

beautiful face, staining the silky material of her black dress visible in the open neck of her coat.

She stopped in front of him, her hands on her hips. But it wasn't anger that he saw in her eyes, in her expression. It was something . . . else.

"Jace." Her voice was hoarse, raw, reminding him of the pain that he'd caused her.

"Melissa." His hungry gaze drank her in, memorized the curve of her cheek, the exact shade of her almond-shaped eyes: walnut, he decided, with delicate flecks of gold and black. Why hadn't he noticed that before?

"Have you been here the whole time?" she asked.

He hesitated, not wanting to hurt her even more. But then he nodded. "I'm sorry if I upset you by being here. I never meant for you to see me. I just . . . I had to know that you were okay."

"Is that the *only* reason you came?" She had to raise her voice to be heard over the rain. "To make sure that I was okay? Don't you have anything else to say to me?"

I miss you. I can barely breathe without you. I would give anything to spend the rest of my life trying to make you feel even one-tenth of the joy that I feel just by looking into your eyes.

The apology she probably expected, wanted, needed, went unsaid. He loved her. God, how he loved her. But he couldn't lie to her again. She deserved better than that. So he settled on a kinder version of the truth. "I wish there had been another way."

Her mouth tightened. "Every day is a struggle for me, Jace." Water dripped off her long lashes, her chin. She wiped her face, leaving a trail of dark mascara across her cheeks.

She'd never looked more beautiful.

As if propelled by an invisible force, he reached for her. But he stopped himself just short of touching her and dropped his arms.

The flash of pain in her eyes nearly brought him to his knees.

"I know that you tried to call, text, after . . ." She shook her head. "I wasn't ready. I needed . . . I wasn't ready. So I turned you away, ignored you. I'm sorry."

"No. Don't apologize to me, Mel. You did nothing wrong. I'm the one who . . . I'm sorry, Mel. I'm so sorry that I hurt you. Losing your father, especially when you've already lost so many loved ones, has to be the worst possible thing you could imagine happening. I just wish that I could have—"

She pressed her hand against his lips, stopping him. "He's at peace now. He's where he always wanted to be: with my mother and my brothers. So, no, Jace. Losing him isn't the worst thing I can imagine ever happening. Losing *you*, if I lost you, *that* would be the worst."

It dawned on him that it wasn't just the rain running down her face. It was tears.

"Have I?" she whispered. "Have I lost you?"

His breath caught in his throat. An emotion he'd thought forever gone for him started leaping through his veins, reawakening the pieces of his soul that had died, the same emotion he now realized he'd seen in her eyes when she'd first walked up the hill.

Hope.

His hands shook. Like a man dying of thirst, afraid to take the cup of water that would save his life for fear that he might spill it, he reached for her. And then she was in his arms, holding him tight as if she never wanted to let him go. And he was crushing her in his embrace, rocking her against his body.

"Thank God," he whispered against her hair. "I love you so much."

She shivered in his arms.

He forced himself to let her go. "You're cold. And here I am selfishly keeping you out in the rain. Come on. We'll—"

"Wait." She grabbed his hands and stared up at him, oblivious to the rain and cold. "Say it again. Tell me you love me. Tell me you forgive me for turning you away when I needed you most. I was . . . broken. I couldn't . . . I was afraid and I . . . I needed space . . . time. Or, at least that's what I thought. But what I really need, what I've always needed, is you. You're the *best* thing that ever happened to me. Please say you forgive me."

He stared at her in shock. "There's nothing to forgive."

She closed her eyes. "And?"

He slowly kissed each of her eyelids, her forehead, the bridge of her nose. "And I love you." He kissed the top of her head. "I love you."

She pointed to her chin.

He smiled and kissed her chin. "I love you."

She tapped her cheek.

His grin widened. He kissed her cheek. "I love you."

She opened her eyes, and very, very slowly, touched her lips.

Just as slowly, and reverently, he cupped her beloved face in his hands. "I love you, Melissa. I will always love you."

"And I'll always love you, Jace. You saved me."

"No, we saved each other." He pressed his lips to hers.

The thrills don't stop here . . .

Keep reading for an excerpt from

Lena Diaz's first heart-stopping

EXIT Inc. novel

EXIT STRATEGY

Available now from Avon Books

Day One—11:00 p.m.

Sabrina crept into her moonlit living room and grabbed the arm of the couch for support. Her right hand, slippery with blood, slid across the cloth and she fell to her knees on the hardwood floor. A gasp of pain escaped between her clenched teeth before she could stop it.

She froze, searching the dark recesses of the room, squinting to try to bring everything into focus. If the intruder was within ten feet of her, no problem, she could make out every little detail. But any farther than that and he might as well be a fuzzy blob on the wallpaper.

Had he heard her? She listened intently for the echo of footsteps in the hall outside, or the squeak of a shoe, the rasp of cloth against cloth. But all she heard was silence. In a fair world, that might mean the stranger had given up and left the house. But in *her* world, especially the nightmarish last six months, it probably meant he was lying in wait around the next corner, ready to attack.

The throbbing burn in her right biceps had her angling her arm toward the moonlight filtering through the plantation shutters to see if the damage was as bad as it felt. Nope. It was *worse*. Blood ran down her arm from a jagged, two-inch gash and dripped to the floor.

She clasped her left hand over the cut, applying pressure and clenching her mouth shut to keep from hissing at the white-hot flash of pain. She had to stop the bleeding. But there wasn't any point in looking for something here in the living room to bind the wound. Only the couch and a wing chair remained of the antiques that she'd brought with her halfway across the country from Boulder, Colorado, to Asheville, North Carolina. She'd sold the other furniture, and even some of her sketches, to pay the exorbitant fees of the private investigators searching for her grandfather and the even more exorbitant fees of the lawyers.

She supposed the Carolina Panthers nightshirt that she was wearing might be useful as a tourniquet. But she didn't relish the possibility of facing an intruder in nothing but her panties. The nightshirt was definitely staying on.

If only she still had a shotgun. Even half blind, she was bound to at least wing her target with the spray of pellets. But convicted felons couldn't own guns. And thanks to her *loving* cousin's schemes, that's exactly what she was—a felon who'd brought shame to the great Hightower legacy. A felon who'd been forced through her plea bargain agreement to sell the gun collection that she and her grandfather had worked years to build.

Sabrina squinted again. She should have grabbed

her glasses before fleeing her bedroom. But she'd been startled from sleep by a sound downstairs and had flailed blindly in the dark, knocking everything off the bedside table: her glasses, her cell phone, and the lamp. It had broken into pieces and one of the shards had ricocheted off the floor, cutting her arm—probably the lamp's way of getting back at her for breaking it.

Still, she'd managed to make it downstairs without being caught, by sneaking down the front staircase while he went up the back stairs. But she hadn't even made it to the foyer before she'd heard him in the dark, and knew he was on the first floor again. So far she'd won the deadly game of cat and mouse. But she was running out of places to hide. It was time to make a run for it.

Easing to the doorway, she peered down the long hall. Was that dark shape against the wall just a decorative table? Or a man, hunched down, waiting? When no one pounced at her, she decided to chance it and took off, running on the balls of her feet to make as little noise as possible. The dark opening to the foyer beckoned on her right. She dashed around the corner and pressed against the wall, her pulse slamming so hard it buzzed in her ears.

Had he seen her? Where was he? In one of the guest rooms? The study? Keeping her left hand clamped over her wound, she hurried down the marble-tiled foyer.

The useless security panel mocked her as she passed it. For what she'd paid for the thing, it should have come with armed guards. But it hadn't gone off tonight, not even when she'd slammed her hand on the panic button in her bedroom.

A dull thump from somewhere around the corner had her stomach clenching with dread. *When had he gotten so close?*

She hurried to the door, flipped the dead bolt, and yanked the doorknob. The door didn't budge! She pulled harder. *Nothing.* She looked over her shoulder before double-checking the lock and trying again. The front door was stuck, jammed, as if nailed shut from the outside. A moan of frustration and fear bubbled up inside her but she ruthlessly tamped it down.

Think, Sabrina. Think.

She could run to the kitchen. It wasn't far, just on the other side of the foyer wall. There was a butcher block of knives on the marble-topped island. But the man she'd glimpsed from the upstairs railing when she ran out of her bedroom was built like one of those bodyguards her alarm system should have come with. What chance did she have against him in hand-to-hand combat? Especially with the cut on her arm? He'd probably end up turning the knife on her. The thought of being stabbed had bile rising in her throat. No thank you. Scratch the kitchen off her list.

The garage. Her Mercedes was inside. But her keys were in her purse. Could she sneak upstairs, get her keys, and make it all the way back to the garage without him hearing or seeing her? Even if she could, the garage door was slow and noisy—one of those irritating things she'd discovered shortly after moving in. Cross the garage off the list too. That was a small list. What other choices did she have?

She ran to the other end of the foyer and stood

looking across the hall to the dining room, with its floor-to-ceiling windows. *Heavy* windows that would be hard to raise even when she wasn't hurt. Her shoulders slumped as she accepted what she hadn't wanted to admit—the only way out was through a door, and the only other door was in the family room, which meant going *toward* that thump she'd heard moments ago.

Before she could think too hard and become frozen by fear, she took off down the long hallway toward the back of the house and didn't slow down until she reached the family room. She felt the rush of warm air a moment before she saw the broken pane in the French door. That must have been the sound that had awakened her. Glass littered the floor in a wide arc like a lethal moat. But if getting cut again was the price of escape, so be it.

Bracing herself against the imminent pain, she raised her foot.

Strong arms clamped around her waist, jerking her into the air. She let out a startled yelp, kicking and flailing her arms. "Put me down! Let me go!"

Ignoring her struggles, the stranger effortlessly tossed her onto his shoulder in a fireman's hold, his forearm clamped over her thighs like a band of steel. Good grief, he was strong.

Clasping her nightshirt with her good hand to keep it from falling down over her head, she tried to beat his back with her other hand. But with it throbbing and weak, her efforts were puny and laughable at best. Using the only other weapon she had, she bit him, right through his shirt. Or tried to. The cloth was thin, but he was wearing a thicker material beneath it. Kevlar. She blinked in surprise. Growing up with a team of armed guards as reluctant baby-sitters had taught her exactly what he was wearing beneath his shirt, even if it was thinner than what her guards had worn. Why was this man wearing a bulletproof vest?

Sabrina twisted sideways to see what he was doing. "What do you want?"

"I want you to be quiet." The slight Southern drawl in his deep voice did nothing to dull its edge of authority, as if he was used to giving orders, and used to having them followed.

He crunched through the broken glass to the door and reached up with his free hand. A wood shim was wedged between it and the frame. Was that why the front door hadn't opened either? Had he wedged both doors shut? What was going on?

The wood shim creaked as he worked it loose.

"Please, *please*, let me go." She was shamelessly considering offering *anything* if he'd just set her down. But the shim popped free and he yanked the door open. Her breath left her with a whoosh as he jogged down the brick steps with her bouncing against his shoulder. He skirted the long, rectangular pool, then sprinted across the lawn toward the woods that bordered her yard and led into the foothills of the Blue Ridge Mountains.

She clutched his shirt during the wild dash to keep her jaw from snapping against his spine. Every jarring step shoved his shoulder against her belly, forcing the air out of her lungs. Just breathing was a challenge. She couldn't have screamed if her life depended on it, and it probably did.

Her shirt slipped down farther to expose her

thong underwear to the humid air. Her face flooded with heat as she realized her nearly naked bottom was bouncing on his shoulder just inches from his face. Tears of humiliation stung her eyes. *No.* She blinked them back, refusing to let them fall. If she acted liked a victim, she would become a victim. No matter how much she was shaking on the inside, she couldn't let him see her as weak.

When they entered the woods, he didn't slow down. She expected the low-hanging pine tree branches to scrape against her exposed skin. But somehow, nothing did. When he finally stopped in a clearing, they were deeper in the woods than she'd ever been. She wasn't even sure whether they were still on her property or if they'd crossed into the nature preserve behind her rental. And now that she could finally draw a deep breath, there was no point in screaming for help. They were too far away for any of her neighbors to hear her.

Suddenly he stood her up and let her go. The blood that had rushed to her head while she'd dangled over his back now rushed to her feet, making everything spin around her. She staggered like a drunk. He grabbed her hips in a firm but surprisingly gentle grip, steadying her.

The feel of this stranger's hands on her bare skin sent a jolt of panic through her. Sabrina shoved him away, wobbling backward. A warm breeze against her belly had her sucking in a startled breath and looking down to see her nightshirt bunched around her waist. She jerked it down to hang mid-thigh and cast an anxious glance up at him. Thankfully he didn't seem interested in her state of undress. He was too busy checking what appeared to be a rather large watch on his wrist.

He towered over her. But then again, most people did. Dressed in black pants and a black T-shirt—like any good burglar or kidnapper should be—he had a solid, muscular frame she'd become intimately familiar with while plastered against him. His dark hair hung like a ragged mane to his shoulders and framed an angular jaw and cheekbones a camera would love. He'd probably look quite handsome in his mug shot. And thanks to the sometimes curse— sometimes gift of a photographic memory, she'd be able to pick him out of a future lineup without any trouble at all. She would even be able to draw his likeness to almost perfectly match the picture in her head. Her artistic skills were rusty, but she'd be happy to polish them up if it meant putting this man in jail.

Tall-Dark-and-Deadly.

That was the moniker that immediately popped into her mind to describe him. It fit perfectly, especially considering the bulky pistol holstered at his waist—a Glock 22, from the looks of it. She was a Sig Sauer girl herself, preferring the solid feel of steel over the "combat Tupperware" of a mostly plastic Glock. Just one more thing to hold against her kidnapper—his lousy taste in firearms.

"You're bleeding," he announced, snapping her attention back to his face.

He reached for her but she quickly stepped back and clamped her hand over her cut again. "Don't touch me," she ordered, trying to sound brave and unafraid in spite of the hysteria bubbling up inside her. If she was going to survive, she had to keep her wits about her.

Impatience etched itself on his forehead but he didn't move toward her. Instead, he checked his watch again, his mouth twisting with displeasure. "We need to get moving. We're behind schedule. If they suspect the mission has been compromised, they'll send someone else to kill you."

The blood drained from her face, leaving her cold. *Mission? Kill her?* Wait, he'd said "they" and "someone else." And he'd seemed concerned, if only for a moment, about her cut. Did that mean that he *wasn't* here to hurt her? Then he was, what, protecting her?

A shaky breath escaped between her clenched teeth as hope flared inside her. If this man wasn't the real threat, then who was? The only person that she knew of who hated her was her cousin, Brian. But kill her? No. That would only delay him from getting what he really wanted—their grandfather's money.

What then? Was Brian planning a worse stunt than his last one? Now *that* she could believe. Had her sister-in-law, Angela, found out that Brian was up to something and sent this man to warn her? Had this stranger misunderstood and thought she was in *physical* danger, and completely over-reacted?

"You said 'they.' Who are *they*?" she asked, trying to fit the puzzle pieces together.

He shrugged. Either he didn't know, or he didn't want to waste his precious time explaining.

"Did Angela send you? To warn me about Brian?"

She gave a nervous laugh. "He'd love for me to stop fighting him in court, but *kill* me?" She shook her head. "You've got this all wrong. He doesn't want me dead. That would just complicate things."

She couldn't help the bitterness and hurt that had crept into her tone. All her life she'd thought Brian loved their grandfather as much as she did. But instead of helping her find Grampy after he went missing, Brian was fighting to have him declared dead so he could cash in on the estate.

"I don't know any Brian or Angela. But someone is definitely after you." Tall-Dark-and-Deadly closed the distance between them and leaned down as if to pick her up again.

She jumped back and clenched her fists in front of her, steeling herself against the throbbing in her right arm. "Touch me and I'll kick your balls all the way up to your throat."

This time it was his turn to blink in surprise. His mouth tightened into a hard line, making her immediately regret her rash words. Angering a man with a gun was never a good idea.

Rushing to fill the tense silence, she said, "You keep saying 'they' and 'someone.' You're here to protect me, right? Someone *other* than my family is after me? *They* want to hurt me? Or maybe you got the wrong house, the wrong person." She latched on to that last thought with the desperation of a skydiver clawing for the secondary chute when the primary failed.

He shook his head as if she were daft. "They don't want to hurt you, *Miss Hightower*. They want you *dead*."

She sucked in a sharp breath, the certainty in his voice and the emphasis on her name telling her there had been no mistake. A renewed stab of fear shot straight to her gut. "Why are you so sure?" she whispered.

"Because I'm the one they hired to kill you."

At Avon Books, we know your passion for romance—once you finish one of our novels, you find yourself wanting more.

May we tempt you with . . .

- **Excerpts** from our upcoming releases.

- Entertaining **extras**, including authors' personal photo albums and book lists.

- Behind-the-scenes **scoop** on your favorite characters and series.

- **Sweepstakes** for the chance to win free books, romantic getaways, and other fun prizes.

- Writing **tips** from our authors and editors.

- **Blog** with our authors and find out why they love to write romance.

- **Exclusive content** that's not contained within the pages of our novels.

Join us at
www.avonbooks.com

AVON

An Imprint of HarperCollins*Publishers*
www.avonromance.com

Available wherever books are sold or please call 1-800-331-3761 to order.

FTH 1013

*G*ive in to your Impulses!

These unforgettable stories only take a second to buy and give you hours of reading pleasure!

Go to *www.AvonImpulse.com* and see what we have to offer.

Available wherever e-books are sold.

AVONIMPULSE